KNOWING WHO YOU LIKE . . .

"What are you thinking about?" he asked, amusement softening the words.

"You."

"And what are you thinking about me?"

"That I like the way you kiss."

"Really? Well, I'm pretty partial to the way you kiss, too."

Champagne bubbles swirled in her belly. She licked her lips. "Are you?"

"Oh yeah," he said with conviction.

Abby felt wonderful. Powerful. Attractive. And the night still held so many possibilities.

She glanced over at Chase. The faint blue light of the dashboard lit his face enough that she could see the straight line of his nose and the shape of his sculpted lips.

She swiveled on the bench seat. "Are you planning to take me home now?"

Chase cast her a quick look. "Do you want to go home now?"

Abby thought for a moment. She shook her head. "No, I think I'd rather go home with you."

"Well, sweetheart, I would love you to come home with me," Chase said, and Abby fell against the back of the seat as the car suddenly accelerated.

GETTING
WHAT YOU
WANT

Kathy Love

ZEBRA BOOKS
KENSINGTON PUBLISHING CORP.
http://www.kensingtonbooks.com

ZEBRA BOOKS are published by

Kensington Publishing Corp.
850 Third Avenue
New York, NY 10022

All Kensington titles, imprints and distributed lines are available at special quantity discounts for bulk purchases for sales promotion, premiums, fund-raising, educational or institutional use.

Special book excerpts or customized printings can also be created to fit specific needs. For details, write or phone the office of the Kensington Special Sales Manager: Kensington Publishing Corp., 850 Third Avenue, New York, NY 10022. Attn. Special Sales Department. Phone: 1-800-221-2647.

First Printing: May 2004
10 9 8 7 6 5 4 3 2 1

Printed in the United States of America

*For my sister—the strongest
and most courageous person I know.
I love you, Cindy.*

Acknowledgments

Many people have helped me to achieve this dream. And yes, I *am* going to thank them all. (Big grin.)

First—my fantastic critique group, The Tarts. Thank you, Chris, Kate, Kathy, Janet and especially Laura, who pitched my book like it was her very own. Ladies, you are the best!

Next—my dear friends, who always believed I would be a writer, even when I didn't. Thank you, Julie, Treena, David, Kristen, Micah and Jen. I love you guys!

And my wonderful and supportive family. Mom and Dad—I couldn't have done it without your help. You saved me! Teresa—thank you for the biochemistry help. (All mistakes are mine alone.)

Bill and Mary Ellen—thank you!

My great editor, Kate Duffy—thank you for believing in me.

And finally—Todd and Emily. I love you!

Prologue

"Hey, where's Cinderella?"

"You ain't gonna find no Cinderella there, Tommy. Nope, nothin' but the ugly Stepp Sisters."

Abigail Stepp looped a protective arm around her sister Ellie's slumped shoulders and narrowed an angry glare at the group of three boys sitting on the stone wall marking the entrance to Millbrook High School.

"Look at their clothes. They look like raggedy old scarecrows. Except Ellie, there. She looks like a raggedy old elephant."

"No, a hippo!"

"Shut your mouths, Billy Norris and Tommy Leavitt!" Abby shouted, but quickened her steps, towing Ellie with her.

"Yeah, you just shut your mouths," Marty, Abby's youngest sister, repeated.

The two boys laughed harder. Tommy Leavitt jumped off the wall and cut the girls off before they could enter the school grounds.

Abby's heart drummed painfully in her chest, but she kept her apprehension hidden behind an irritated scowl.

"How you planning to make me shut my mouth, Abby-normal?" he asked. His cruel grin revealed two overlapping front teeth. "Are you planning to sic the Amazon sister on me? Or the fat one?"

Ellie made a nervous sound in her throat and kept her head down. Marty straightened to her full height, nearly six feet, which would have been tall for any girl but was ridiculously tall for a mere thirteen-year-old.

"You're a real jerk, Tommy," Abby hissed.

"Yeah, and you're ugly."

Billy jumped down and joined Tommy. "You know, you girls should join the circus. You got the fat girl and the world's skinniest giant and," he looked at Abby, "you got the freak."

Tommy doubled over with laughter; the sound was grating.

Abby was amazed their taunts still had the ability to hurt. After all, it was nothing she hadn't heard before. *Freak, geek, dork, ugly, poor.* They were words she'd heard over and over again since grade school.

Maybe what made them hurt was the accuracy of some of the unkind labels. Her family was poor. She wasn't a beautiful blonde like Mandy Blanchard, Millbrook's head cheerleader, so maybe she was ugly. And she was the smartest girl in her class, which did make her a geek, at least to the cool crowd. She never revealed it to anyone, but she wanted to be a part of that crowd. Desperately.

Her gazed strayed up to the third boy still perched on the wall, watching them with pale blue eyes.

Chase Jordan. He was the main reason Abby wished she could fit in. Chase was a bad boy, a rebel, and over half the girls at Millbrook High were madly in love with him. It didn't seem to matter that he was in vocational classes and constantly in trouble. To the female gender, he was damned near perfect. Heck, Abby thought he *was* perfect, and he'd never so much as spoken to her.

He reached into the pocket of his leather jacket and pulled out a pack of cigarettes. Raising one of the white sticks to his lips, he lit the end with a flip-top lighter. A gray stream of smoke escaped his beautiful mouth. All the while, he studied her, his face devoid of any discernible emotion.

"You know, Abby-normal, it's probably a good thing you're such an egghead, cuz with that hideous face you ain't goin' nowhere."

Abby turned her attention back to the other boys. "You aren't going to go anywhere at all, Tommy."

Billy nudged Tommy in the ribs. "She got you there."

Chase hopped down from the wall, took one more drag off his cigarette and then flicked it onto the ground. "Let's go."

"See ya later, ugly Stepp sisters!" Tommy called as they strolled up the asphalt walkway to the school.

Abby hugged Ellie reassuringly with the arm she still had around her and gave an encouraging smile to Marty.

Just one more year. One more year, and I'll never have to set foot in this terrible little town again. With leaden feet, Abby entered the school.

Chapter 1

"I just can't believe you're home!" Ellie exclaimed for the umpteenth time.

Abby laughed. "Geez, you're acting like I haven't seen you in years."

"I haven't see you in *this kitchen* for years. And to be honest, I never thought I would."

"Well, to be honest, I never thought you would either. Funny how things work out." Of course, there was nothing very funny about this situation at all.

The teakettle on the stove began to whistle, and Abby pushed up from the table to tend to it, waving for Ellie to stay put.

No, she hadn't set foot in this old house since the day she left for Boston University. That was nearly fifteen years ago.

She turned the dial on the back of the stove, noting that it still stuck slightly. Automatically, she went to the cupboard to the right of the range and got down two mugs. Both were chipped and stained from age and use. She moved to the avocado-green canisters lined up on the counter, pulled off the lid of the middle one and took out two tea bags.

Pausing, she looked at Ellie with startled amazement. "Absolutely nothing has changed here."

"I've made some changes," Ellie said, a tad defensively,

but then shrugged. "There are things that Grammy always had a certain way, and I saw no reason to change them."

Abby shook her head. "It's like stepping back in time. I'm not sure I like it."

Ellie smiled, accepting the cup and spoon Abby offered her. "Well, I like it." She started to lift a heaping spoonful of sugar toward her cup, then paused and shook most of the white granules back into the bowl. She stirred the small amount left into her tea. "I love this old place."

Abby smiled, but a wave of sadness washed over her. Ellie had stayed in Millbrook to care for their grandmother. After Grammy passed away, she claimed to stay because of her job at the library. Abby knew Ellie wasn't comfortable with change, but she always felt Ellie could be much happier somewhere else. Somewhere far away from the painful memories of their childhood.

Ellie started to reach for one of the cookies she had set out earlier, but stopped, instead taking a sip of her tea.

Abby knew it was the lingering effects of that childhood that caused her sister to skip the cookie. Ellie had always been a bit chubby, but she was by no means fat. In fact, she was very pretty like a sweet-faced cherub, but Ellie couldn't see that. She was forever trying to diet.

"How long are you planning to stay?" Ellie asked, pushing the plate of cookies toward her.

As short a time as possible, Abby thought, but she didn't say it. She knew Ellie would be hurt that her desire to leave Millbrook was stronger than her desire to be with her sister.

"I'll be here for at least four months, depending on how smoothly the grant project goes. Working with Dr. Keene is a great opportunity, and I expect our research to go well. He's quite renowned in my field of study."

"It must be a dream come true for you," Ellie said, a wistful quality to her voice.

Abby didn't respond immediately. Certainly this job opportunity was what she had been working for all her life, but was it a dream come true? Abby didn't really have dreams anymore. She'd long since given up dreams for goals and wishes for reality.

"It is a huge honor for Dr. Keene to choose me out of all the scientists working on this particular research."

"A lot of other scientists are clamoring to study the genes of mice?" Ellie wrinkled her nose.

"Yes, they are." Abby mocked her sister's disgusted look.

Ellie grinned, dimples deepening in her round cheeks. "You should be very proud of yourself. In fact, we should go out and celebrate the occasions."

"Plural? What occasions?"

"Firstly, you getting this prestigious position, and secondly, you actually setting foot back in Millbrook to accept it."

Abby shook her head. "I guess that does warrant a bit of a celebration. Where would you suggest?"

Ellie raised her eyebrows expectantly.

Abby frowned, unsure what Ellie was waiting her to say. Then it dawned on her. "You've got to be kidding. The Afternoon Delight is still in business?"

Ellie laughed. "You forget this is Millbrook, Maine. Nothing changes but the weather. Speaking of which, let me grab a sweater before we go. I'll be right back."

Abby shook her head with a rueful smile. She really couldn't believe she was sitting in her childhood home again. And she was about to go to the snack bar that she'd worked at all through high school.

She had worked so hard to escape this place, and now the very thing she'd pursued to enable her getaway was the same thing that brought her back. She'd almost turned down the research position, but then she realized she was being ridiculous. She'd survived eighteen years here—she certainly could endure another few months.

"Ready?" Ellie asked, reappearing with a sweater over her arm.

Abby forced a bright smile. "Let's go."

The drive to the Afternoon Delight was so familiar, it was as if Abby had just ridden there yesterday. The residential streets were still lined with huge oaks. Main Street still hosted run-down shops, and the local kids still hung out in the parking lot of the Dairy Palace.

"So, how are things with Nelson?" Ellie asked as they passed the high school. Its red brick walls were still faded and worn.

"Fine," Abby said automatically.

"He must be upset you're going to be gone for so long."

Nelson upset? Not likely. Nelson was a focused man. His career was first and foremost. It might take him a couple months to even realize she wasn't around.

"He's very busy with his own research."

Ellie pulled into the parking lot of a white and green A-framed building perched on a hill overlooking the frothy waters of Fiddlehead Bay. Several people waited at the order windows lining the front of the structure.

Ellie put the car into park and twisted in her seat to face Abby. "It doesn't bother you that you two have been together for years, and I've only met him—what? Four times, if that."

"Well, like I said, he's a very busy man."

"Too busy to get to know the family of the woman he loves?"

Love—Abby suspected that emotion was too impractical for Nelson.

"Nelson and I agree that our careers are the most important thing right now. That's why we're together. Our priorities are the same."

Ellie pulled a face. "That's not terribly romantic."

Abby shook her head at Ellie. Her sister was forever the romantic. But Abby's relationship with Nelson went beyond silly starry-eyed idealism. They were together because they had common interests, common goals. He was a natural and sensible choice for a partner.

Ellie sighed. "I don't think we are going to agree on the important points of relationships."

"Probably not."

"Then let's eat," Ellie said, readily dropping the subject. She wasn't the type to start an argument. Normally, that particular trait bothered Abby. She wanted her sister to stand up for her beliefs. But on this occasion, she was quite content with her sister's submissive temperament. Discussing Nelson with Ellie made the relationship seem—cold.

Nelson was quickly forgotten as Abby approached her old place of employment. They placed their order at the screened windows and went to sit at one of the many picnic tables on the grassy hill beside the restaurant.

"It looks exactly the same," Abby marveled.

Ellie smiled. "The food is pretty much the same too. Fried, salty and utterly fattening."

"Well, why mess with perfection."

Abby watched the sun sparkling off the saltwater and had to admit that the view really was a bit of perfection. A perfect scene in an otherwise imperfect place.

Just then a loudspeaker crackled to life. "Number 251, your order's ready."

"That's us. I'll get it," Abby said.

"Ask for extra ketchup," Ellie called after her.

As she approached the pickup window, she noticed a man leaning against the counter, his back to her. Abby wasn't the type of woman to ogle men, but this particular male was fairly hard to ignore. His lean, muscled torso was covered by a tight, white tank leaving his broad, tanned shoulders bare, and faded jeans encased long legs and a firm behind.

Abby could feel her cheeks flush and tore her gaze away from the man. Blatantly staring at strange men, beautiful or otherwise, wasn't her style.

"Number 251," she said, trying to stay focused on the gawky teenager behind the screened window.

The kid slid a tray laden with white Styrofoam containers and two paper cups toward her.

"May I get more ketchup, please?" she asked. As she waited for the teen to get the additional condiments, she felt a prickling sensation creep up the back of her neck. Out of the corner of her eye, she could see the stranger that she had been looking at was now looking at her.

"Here you go." The teen dropped a handful of white packets onto the tray.

"Thanks." Quickly picking up her food, Abby started back toward Ellie, but a rich, chocolaty voice that even fifteen years couldn't erase from her memory stopped her.

"Abby? Abby Stepp, is that you?"

Abby slowly turned back to look up into pale blue eyes that were as mesmerizing as the voice.

"Well, damn. It is you. How are you?"

Abby remained silent for a moment, overwhelmed by the sight before her. The front view was even better than the rear. His icy-blue eyes were still fringed by sinfully long, dark lashes, and a dimple deepened in his left cheek as a slow, sexy smile curved his lips.

"It is Abby Stepp, right?"

Abby nodded, but words still evaded her.

The sultry smile slipped a bit as his dark brows drew together quizzically. "I'm sorry—do you remember me?"

Again, she managed another nod. Remember him? Of course she remembered him. Ellie had said nothing in this town ever changed, and she'd been absolutely right. Chase Jordan was still the most gorgeous man Abby had ever seen.

Chapter 2

Okay, Abby thought, *you need to stop acting like a mindless twit—right now. He's just a man.* And she'd been talking to men—quite coherently—for years. Granted, not such beautiful men, but men nonetheless.

"I'm Chase Jordan," he said after several seconds passed, and she still hadn't managed to get her unco-operative thoughts under control. A full-fledged frown creased his forehead when she still didn't respond. "We graduated together."

Get your act together, gal. He thinks you are a simpleton. Abby straightened and smiled slightly, although both actions felt odd, as if her brain didn't really have control over her body.

"I remember you," she said.

"So what brings you back to these parts?"

"Work."

"Great. What type of work?"

"Research."

"Over at Rand Labs?"

"Yes." How could simple one-word answers require so much concentration?

"Great. Great." His eyes no longer appeared their usual pale blue but rather a mute gray color like brushed steel. His voice was nearly as cool. "Well, they just called my number. Good to see you."

He walked to the pickup window.

Abby remained rooted to the spot, unsure what to do now. She suddenly felt like she was back in the school cafeteria, lunch tray in hand, unsure whom to talk to, unsure where to sit.

You are no longer that pathetic girl, she told herself. *Your school days are long behind you. You are a successful person, a scientist respected by your peers. You aren't here to impress your old classmates. You are here to do a job.*

Who cares if Chase Jordan still finds you so uninteresting that he flees after five seconds' worth of conversation?

She turned without a second glance toward him and headed back to the picnic table.

Abby Stepp. Now there was a blast from the past. Chase hadn't seen her since their high school graduation. He could still recall her standing at the podium, her huge, plastic-framed glasses sliding down her nose as she gave her valedictorian address.

He remembered thinking he should be the one giving that speech—after all, everyone knew Abigail Stepp was going to graduate. It was far more amazing that he had.

He could still see the bright red blotches staining Abby's cheeks as some of the kids mocked her speech. They had been anxious to party, not listen to the class overachiever go on and on. It may have been rude, but he imagined it was a common enough occurrence.

He tossed the grease-stained paper bag containing his dinner, fried clams and coleslaw, onto the seat of his old, rusty pickup truck and climbed in behind it. He started to turn the key in the ignition, then stopped to look across the parking lot to the picnic area where Abby sat with her sister.

Chase didn't recall seeing her at any of those gradua-

tion parties. It wasn't a shock. Abby had never quite fit
in with the other kids at Millbrook High. In fact, she
never really fit in throughout school. She was always
studying, or if she was socializing, it was only with her sisters. She'd had a way of making the other kids think she
considered herself better than them.

He studied her stick-straight posture as she sat at the
picnic table. She looked like she should be in a fancy
five-star restaurant rather than eating greasy fried food
with her fingers.

Apparently she hadn't changed much. She still seemed
cold and unapproachable. She'd been as interested in
talking with him as talking to a rotting stump. Actually a
stump might have been more intriguing to her. Yep, it
seemed that Abby Stepp was still the unfriendly person he
remembered.

A salty breeze blew off the water and caught several
strands of her dark hair, causing it to glint red in the afternoon sun. She reached up to brush the locks from her
cheek, and Chase could see the elegant movement of her
hand and the flawlessness of her profile.

He frowned at his thoughts. He didn't remember
finding Abby an attractive girl in school. In fact, he recalled that she had been rather homely, a bit too tall and
chunky. But she didn't seem either of those things now.
She was actually rather pretty—in a prim way.

It had been her curved body displayed nicely in her
tailored white shirt and dark blue cotton pants that had
initially caught his attention. It had taken a few moments
to realize who she was.

He studied her profile for a moment longer, until he
noticed Ellie, looking in his direction. With a friendly
smile at Ellie—Abby didn't turn to look—he nodded
and started his truck, which sputtered a few times before
it roared to life.

He pulled onto the winding road that led to town, although his mind wasn't on the drive, but back on Abby.

Maybe he had been too quick to decide nothing about her had changed. Her looks definitely had. She really did look awfully good.

Hell, why was he fixating on the looks of a woman who had basically blown him off? Life was too short to waste his time on women who weren't interested. Besides, he had more important things to think about, like where he was going to get his hands on the brass doorknobs for the Martins' renovated upstairs. He'd had a devil of a time getting the bedrooms back to their original condition.

He could always order reproductions if he had to, but he preferred to get the real fixtures if he could. This weekend he'd have to hit a few antique stores outside of Bangor and see what he could find.

He hated to admit it, but Abby's cold reaction did rub him the wrong way. It wasn't the usual response he got from the opposite sex. Not that he considered himself irresistible or anything, but he did seem to get his fair share of appreciative reactions from women.

He turned into the driveway of his house, a huge Victorian he was restoring in his spare time. The stairs of the back stoop creaked in protest as he bounded up them and threw open the heavy storm door. His huge, fluffy golden retriever, Chester, was waiting for him with one of Chase's dirty socks hanging from his mouth.

"Thanks for the gift, Chester," he said, scuffing the dog's large head, then pulling the sock from him. "That's the best greeting I've had all day."

He really needed to let the whole Abby thing go. *So the lady doesn't like you. There are plenty of people who don't care for you, and you don't give them another thought.* But even as he thought it, he knew this particular person wasn't going to be as easy to avoid.

He threw his dinner on the kitchen counter. He knew the clams wouldn't be nearly as tasty cold, but he needed a shower. The hot water would relax his sore muscles and hopefully clear his mind of these strange thoughts about Abby Stepp.

With Chester close at his heels, he headed upstairs, tugging his T-shirt over his head as he went.

He entered a large bathroom done completely in white tile. Turning on the showerhead in an antique-footed bathtub, he sighed.

A long shower was going to feel great.

He took off the remainder of his clothing and stepped into the steaming water. He closed his eyes and groaned appreciatively. The hard pressure of the water did feel wonderful.

Then an image of Abby peeling off her white blouse and cotton trousers and joining him in the hot spray flashed into his mind.

With another groan, this one distinctly frustrated, he reached for the faucet knobs. *So much for a nice hot shower,* he thought as much, much cooler water sluiced over his overheated body.

"I thought I saw you talking to Chase Jordan at the restaurant." Ellie, of course, knew Abby had. She had waited the entire meal for her sister to mention it, but she hadn't. Ellie simply couldn't wait any longer.

Abby turned her head from where she sat looking out the window of the car with a faraway expression that Ellie knew well.

"Yes," she said. "I spoke with him briefly."

Ellie waited for her to elaborate, but it didn't seem that Abby intended to. "He looks great, doesn't he?"

"Does he? I didn't notice."

Ellie held back a smile. She was willing to bet Abby noticed all right. She had been preoccupied throughout their entire dinner, and Ellie didn't think it was the ratio of clams to fries that had been on her mind.

"Does he still live in Millbrook?" Abby asked, the question revealingly casual.

Ellie couldn't contain her smile this time. "Yeah, he still lives here."

Silence passed.

"What does he do for work?" Again the question was posed under the guise of polite disinterest.

"He owns a construction company. He focuses mainly on restoring old houses. He did the Tate place. It looks beautiful," Ellie said.

Abby simply nodded, but Ellie could tell she was intrigued.

"Now he's working on a house up on the Bar Harbor Road. He has restored the outside, and he's doing the interior now. I hear it looks wonderful."

More silence.

"So did he end up marrying Summer-Ann Bouffard?"

Ellie's smile faded. "No, no he didn't. I think things ended rather badly for them."

Abby feigned a look of horror and clapped a hand to her chest. "Cupid's Couple didn't make it? Please tell me it isn't so."

Ellie smiled slightly and shook her head. "Your sympathy is overwhelming."

"Yeah, well, I didn't know either Chase or Summer-Ann very well, so it's a bit hard to get too emotional over it."

Ellie remained silent for a moment. She didn't like to meddle in other people's lives. It wasn't her style, but she knew Abby had had a crush on Chase Jordan all the way through high school. Ellie had known back then, but never mentioned it. She had been nursing her own rather sizable crush on someone unobtainable, and she certainly didn't want anyone to ask her about it.

So she'd never brought up Abby's crush on Chase. But now, she felt like she had to try and discover if her sister was still attracted to him. She couldn't bear to think of Abby spending her life with a passionless, dull man like Nelson.

She knew Abby would think she was being a hopeless romantic, and maybe she was, but she believed everyone deserved nothing less than true love. After all, it was the theme of so many books, plays and poems that it had to be an absolute truth, right?

"Outside of Cupid's Couple, didn't Chase get another senior superlative in your high school yearbook?" she asked.

Abby shrugged. "I don't recall."

"I'm sure he did." Ellie pretended to ponder the subject. "Oh, yes. He got Class Clown too."

Without hesitation, Abby said, "No, he didn't. He got Prettiest Eyes."

"Are you sure you didn't know Chase well?" Ellie asked, gently.

Abby didn't respond. She turned and looked back out the window.

As soon as they got home, Abby excused herself under the pretext of needing to get her clothes unpacked. Truthfully, she needed to get away from Ellie and her leading questions. She needed to be alone.

Why on earth was her sister suddenly so chatty about Chase Jordan? Yes, she did see him at the restaurant. Yes, she did talk with him. Why did Ellie seem to find the encounter so significant?

If anything, Abby would rather have just forgotten the

whole incident. It brought back all the reasons why she didn't want to return to this wretched little town in the first place. The man spoke to her, and she suddenly acted like English wasn't her first language. She acted exactly like she had in high school.

Abby sighed and fell back onto her bed. The springs squeaked like they had every night of her childhood. Why should she be surprised? Things really did not change in Millbrook, Maine.

She curled onto her side, dragging the blankets with her, cocooning herself in familiar scents of lavender and fresh breeze. The homey smells seemed to soothe her frayed nerves, and she let her eyes drift shut. She needed to rest a moment.

Within minutes, she was dozing, caught in a place between reality and dreams.

It was May 30th, 1988. She was standing outside Millbrook High School. Parents hugged their graduating children, smiling proudly and snapping pictures.

She looked down at herself. The gold of her Honor Society sash stood out garishly against the maroon material of her cap and gown.

"Congratulations, sweetie," a voice said. Abby turned to respond, but when she did, she realized the person was talking to another student. Abby immediately looked away.

She continued to watch the scene before her. The happy grins of the graduates and the pleased looks on their parents' faces made her feel envious and out of place. It was times like these when she missed her parents the most. Her grandmother had wanted to attend the ceremony, but her health had prevented it. And even with her sisters there, Abby still felt terribly, terribly alone.

Then she saw him. Chase leaned against the school wall. He was smoking a cigarette and looking bored with the whole event. He took a drag of the cigarette, closed his eyes and leaned his head back against the bricks. The action knocked his cap forward over his eyes. With irritation, he tugged it off and tossed the cap, tassel and all, into the trash can beside him.

His response would have been rather humorous, except Abby felt his behavior went beyond mere annoyance with the cap. He looked upset, hurt even.

Suddenly, Chase Jordan seemed to be just as alone as she was.

"Your speech went great," Ellie said, and Abby stopped watching Chase to glance at her sister.

"Thanks," she said distractedly.

"Yeah, I liked that analogy you made between high school and MTV. It was very hip of you," Marty informed her.

"Thanks," Abby said again, but her attention was already back on Chase.

A group of their classmates now encircled him. His usual easy smile was in place and his posture held its customary negligent grace. Whatever signs of unhappiness that had been there were now gone, if they'd ever been there to begin with.

She'd obviously imagined it. After all, what did Chase Jordan have to be upset about?

"Super speech, Abs" a sickly sweet voice said from beside her.

Abby turned to find Summer-Ann Bouffard and two of her clique, Patty and Candace, grinning at her.

Abby stared for a moment, all logical thought seeming to vanish from her mind. Ellie and Marty stared in the same fashion—as if Summer-Ann were someone famous.

Of course, at Millbrook High, she practically was. She was on the cheerleading squad. She had a huge smile and an even bigger chest, and she was Chase Jordan's girlfriend. That was as close to celebrity as anyone got in this town.

Summer-Ann leaned toward Abby with a look of concern. "Are you all right?"

Abby blinked and then cleared her throat. "Yes, yes. I'm fine. Thank you—for the compliment on my speech, I mean."

Summer-Ann's sugary smile returned. "I was wondering, would you like to come to the graduation party with us?" She gestured to herself and her friends.

Abby's stomach jumped like she had just gone down the first huge drop on a roller coaster. Summer-Ann Bouffard was asking her to go to a party with her. Amazing!

"Yes, I'd like to come," Abby said, trying to sound calmer than she felt.

Summer-Ann's vivid green eyes narrowed as her smile widened. "Great. How about if Chase and I pick you up at your house?"

The ground seemed to shift under Abby's feet. She was going to get to arrive at the graduation party with Chase Jordan. She wasn't going to go as his date—that fantasy was too outlandish to be considered anyway. But arriving with him and Summer-Ann, that was still incredible.

"That would be great."

Summer-Ann smiled again, her eyes glittering. "Good. See you around seven."

"Okay." Abby smiled back. She watched as the three girls walked away in a haze of giggles. She felt like giggling too.

Marty grabbed her arm. "You have to get ready!" she exclaimed, and the three sisters hurried home on their own cloud of laughter and excitement.

* * *

"You can't wear that," Marty stated.

Abby studied herself in the mirror. The bulky cable-knit sweater and baggy jeans did make her look a bit like a fisherman. All she needed were rubber boots and a knit cap.

"Wear your black skirt with the red flowers," Ellie said.

"And my black turtleneck sweater," Marty said as she raced from the room to retrieve it.

Quickly, her sisters helped her change, and she stood in front of the mirror again. Abby scrutinized the outfit, twisting to see as much of her backside as she could.

"It looks nice," Ellie said.

Abby frowned. "I don't know. I think this skirt makes my hips look huge."

Marty shook her head. "It makes you look feminine."

"And the sweater is too tight." Abby tugged at the sides.

"It shows off your . . ." Marty gestured toward her own much flatter chest.

"Great," Abby said with dismay, a blush burning her cheeks.

"Abby, it really looks good," Ellie assured her.

Abby tugged at the sweater one more time, then sighed. "I'll be cold."

"Not once the boys get a load of you." Marty grinned. Ellie elbowed Marty.

"I'm not interested in getting the attention of any of the boys," Abby said a little too forcefully.

Marty looked dubious.

Ellie smiled in her usual supportive way, then said, "I'll get you my shawl. That should be warm enough."

Both her sisters left the room, which gave Abby the chance to look at herself again. She normally wore this skirt with a long oversized sweater, but with Marty's more fitted turtleneck, it did make her look curvier. And there was no denying that the outfit showed off her bust line.

Abby pulled at a lock of her hair that fell from the loose

bun she wore. She should do something different with her hair, but she didn't really know what.

"You better hurry up," Marty called from down the hall. "It's nearly seven."

Sighing, Abby tucked the errant hair behind her ear. This was as good as it was going to get.

She slipped on a pair of worn loafers that she wished were cute sandals and headed down the stairs.

When she stepped into the living room, Marty shouted, "Ta-da!" holding out her hands like she was Vanna White revealing a vowel.

Abby's grandmother looked up from her knitting. "Oh, Abigail," she said, a proud smile deepening the wrinkles around her age-clouded eyes. "You look lovely."

Abby smiled, feeling a bit awkward.

Ellie stepped forward and handed her the shawl she'd promised.

"You have a wonderful time tonight. My smart, hard-working girl deserves to have some fun," Grammy said with conviction.

Abby nodded. "I will."

She left her family in the living room and went to wait for Chase and Summer-Ann on the porch.

The top step creaked as she sat down. The early summer air was cool, and she wrapped the shawl around her shoulders.

A car passed, but it didn't slow down. What type of car did Chase drive? It was an older make and sporty. Abby didn't know much about these sorts of things.

Another car passed. And another. Then there was quiet. The purplish light of dusk became inkier, and Abby pulled the shawl tighter.

Gradually the night became so dark that Abby could see the bright swirl of stars above her.

It must be cold and lonely up there. She leaned her

head against the porch railing, and listened. The night was silent except for the distant bark of a dog.

She stood. It was cold and lonely down here too.

She went to the front door, quietly opened it and stepped inside. Graduation parties weren't her thing anyway.

Abby opened her eyes. The room was now dark. She sat up and squinted at the clock on her nightstand. It read 10:30. She'd slept longer than she thought. And weariness still weighted her limbs. But the night air was downright freezing.

Throwing back the covers, she hopped from bed and scurried over to the open window. She braced both hands on the sash and started to close it, when movement across the street caught her attention.

She paused, peering at the dim circle of light illuminating the porch of the house across the street.

Thanks to her trip to the Afternoon Delight and the dream she just had, she must have had Chase Jordan on her mind, because she could swear she just saw him go inside Old Miss Strout's house.

She shook her head, pushed down the window with a rattling thud, and hurried back to crawl under the covers.

She knew returning to this town wasn't going to be good for her mental health, but she hadn't expected it to make her hallucinate.

Chapter 3

"Is there any particular reason we are attempting to drink ourselves senseless? On a Thursday night, no less." Mason Sweet, Chase's closest friend, looked down at the row of empty beer bottles lined up on the floor between their deck chairs.

"Didn't you once tell me the parties back in college started on Thursdays?" Chase said.

Mason chuckled and then polished off the remainder of his beer. He set the bottle neatly beside the others. "Yes, the weekends did definitely start early. But we're not college students. We're a couple guys rushing headlong toward middle age, running the risk of having nasty headaches when the alarm clock goes off in the morning."

Chase cast him a disbelieving look. "Maybe you're rushing toward middle age. I'm just getting to my prime."

"Well, you haven't been married. That's gotta buy you a few extra years, I'll give you that. It definitely proves you're a wiser man than I am."

Chase shook his head and gestured to the bottles. "I really think you need another."

Mason sighed. "After the mention of marriage, I think you're right."

Chase got up and went into the house. Chester raised his head from where he was sprawled on his dog bed like a giant, furry frog. One of Chase's T-shirts was tucked under his front paws as a pillow.

Chase went over and tugged the shirt out from under him. "Gimme that, you big oaf!"

Chester stared up at him with innocent, watery brown eyes and dropped his head back to his paws. Chase scratched the animal's floppy ears and then headed to the kitchen. Tossing the T-shirt in the general vicinity of the laundry room, he headed to the fridge and got two more beers.

He paused for a moment, and then grabbed two more. Now that the subject of marriage had been mentioned, he knew that Mason was going to need a couple more brewskies to drown his sorrows, or rather his bitterness.

Mason had divorced his wife a little over a year ago, which in Chase's opinion was a good move. Marla had been more interested in Mason's career than her actual husband. Mason was the mayor of Millbrook, but Marla had had far bigger aspirations for Mason.

When she discovered that Mason was perfectly satisfied with small-town politics and small-town life, she had left, but not before she took everything they owned except their house, which was as she put it, "the best house that a lowly mayor could buy, and the worst I would ever live in."

Marla was money conscious, but she had no idea what Mason's house could go for now that Chase had done the renovations. A restored sea captain's home right on the ocean. That was worth a pretty penny.

When he stepped back onto the porch, he could tell by the set of Mason's jaw that his friend was indeed thinking of his ex.

"Here ya go."

Mason accepted the beer, twisted off the top and took a long swallow.

Chase sat back in his chair, twisted the cap of his own bottle and waited for Mason to speak.

But they both remained silent.

Crickets chirped, the cool spring breeze rustled the trees, and Chase could see the cloudy swirl of the Milky Way above. It was beautiful.

Suddenly, Abby Stepp appeared in his mind. What were the chances that the word *beautiful* should immediately remind him of her? But she did sort of have the type of beauty that was comparable to stars. Classic and eternal.

Chase took a long swallow of his beer. Lord, he needed to get laid. He was getting all poetic about a woman he barely knew, and what he *did* know shouldn't inspire such nonsense.

"Did I tell you I ran into Abby today?" The words were out before Chase even realized he was going to say them.

"Who?"

"Abby Stepp."

Mason frowned toward the darkened street. "Ellie Stepp has a sister?"

Chase shifted toward him, giving him a disbelieving look. "Yes. Abby graduated with us."

"Really?"

"Yes."

Mason looked thoughtful. "I remember Ellie, but I don't recall her sister."

Chase looked at him for a moment, in complete amazement, then said, "She was valedictorian."

Mason reflected for a moment, and then his eyes widened. "Oh yeah—yeah. I remember her now."

Chase shook his head. "Damn, I'm starting to think you should have been labeled our class' bad boy. You obviously partied more than I did."

Mason grinned. "Nah, you had the corner on that. I

just took one too many tackles on the football field. So, how is Aggie?"

"Abby."

"Oh yeah, yeah, Abby."

"She's the same—not like that is going to mean anything to you."

Mason took a sip of his beer, then said, "She always sat alone with her nose buried in a book."

Chase nodded, his own beer up to his lip. He swallowed and said, "Yup, that's her."

Mason looked a bit proud of himself. "So, she's still unfriendly?"

"Pretty much. I tried to ask her about what brought her back to Millbrook. She answered, but she acted like she'd rather be talking to a toad."

"A woman giving our class' Prettiest Eyes the cold shoulder? That must have been a first."

Chase grunted. "I'm never going to live that down, am I?"

"Never," Mason agreed.

"She always thought she was above the people of Millbrook, I think. Abby, that is."

"Yeah, well I've had plenty of experience with women like that, and I can tell you they are a waste of time." Mason's voice was heavy with resentment.

Chase nodded.

"Does she still wear those giant, ugly glasses and her hair in a knot on the back of her head?" He gestured toward the back of his own head.

"No."

Apparently something about the way Chase said that single word captured Mason's attention.

"Oh, no, don't tell me you're attracted to her!"

Chase was quiet for a moment, looking out into the darkness. "No, not exactly."

"Well, she has got to be a hell of a lot better looking than she was in high school if she caught your attention."

"You know, for someone you didn't remember a few moments ago, you seem to recall an awful lot about her," Chase pointed out.

"I remember her now. I just hadn't thought of her in years. Has she been back here since graduation?"

Chase shook his head. "I don't think so."

They were both quiet again.

"So what does she look like? Like Ellie?"

"No," Chase said slowly, trying to figure out how to describe her—in a way that wouldn't reveal he was indeed attracted to her. Lord, he was attracted to her. "She doesn't wear her hair in a bun anymore, and she doesn't wear glasses either."

"Ah man, you do want to do her," Mason said with certainty.

How did Mason get that out of what he'd said?

Chase sat silent for a second, then said with resignation, "Yeah, I'd do her. But I don't think it's worth contemplating. Like I said, she seemed as interested in me as a toad."

Mason snorted disbelievingly. "I doubt that."

Chase shrugged. "Well, it doesn't matter, because I don't intend to deal with her again. I've long since lost interest in giving chase."

"Is that what you call it?" Mason chuckled.

Chase smirked, then finished off the remainder of his beer.

"Is she staying with Ellie?"

Chase nodded.

Mason reached over and clapped his shoulder. "Well, buddy, good luck 'cause it looks to me like the lady you're planning to ignore is your neighbor."

Both men stared at the black silhouette of the house across the street.

* * *

The sun was shining when Abby came downstairs the next morning. From the smell of fresh coffee that greeted her, she knew Ellie was already up, but she wasn't in the kitchen.

While in the shower, Abby had made a pact with herself. She was going to be in Millbrook for at least four months, and she was going to make the best of her stay. She would enjoy spending time with Ellie and staying in her childhood home. She would learn from and excel in her work, and she would go back to Boston feeling her time had been well spent. After all, she didn't have to see any of her old classmates if she didn't want to. The truth was, she was far, far beyond her school days, and it was silly of her to even worry about the past.

Abby poured herself a cup of the dark coffee and went to the window. Summer was definitely coming. The brown grass of winter was starting to be peppered with green, and the trees had the beginnings of new leaves budding on their gray limbs.

It would only be a few weeks until Old Miss Strout's lilac bushes would bloom. Miss Strout always had the most gorgeous lilacs. Abby looked over toward her house. The lilac bushes were bigger than ever.

Abby smiled to herself, then the smile slowly faded. But Old Miss Strout's house looked completely different. The chipped and faded gray paint that had always covered the clapboards was now replaced by a fresh, crisp white. And the shutters that had always appeared in danger of falling off were on straight and coated with deep forest green. In fact, the whole house looked beautiful. No longer were Old Miss Strout's lilac bushes the only thing attractive about her property.

Of course, it was silly to be surprised that improvements

had been made to her house. It had been years since Abby had seen it. Although, she was amazed that Miss Strout could afford to fix the old place up. The spinster had been in much the same situation Abby's grandmother had been, elderly with no expendable income.

She must have come into some money. Some serious money. Even the dilapidated front porch had been jacked up and repaired. It looked great.

"Good morning," Ellie said happily as she entered the kitchen. "Did you sleep well?"

"Yes," Abby answered absently and then gestured toward the house across the street. "When did Miss Strout fix up her house?"

"She didn't," Ellie said as she poured herself a cup of coffee. "Don't you remember? Miss Strout died shortly after Grammy. I know I told you."

"You probably did." Abby had been so shaken by the loss of Grammy, and the fact that she hadn't been able to attend the funeral, that nothing else had registered for months afterward.

"A new family moved in then?"

Ellie ducked into the fridge.

"Did a new family move in?" Abby tried again.

Ellie closed the refrigerator with a pint carton of creamer in her hand. She went to the table, sat down and poured some into her cup. She offered the carton to Abby, who shook her head, no. "Just a single person."

Her sister was being far too mysterious about the whole topic, Abby decided. And she couldn't imagine why.

She turned back to the window to look at the house again. "Well, whoever moved in there sure did a fabulous job . . ."

The appearance of the apparent owner leaving the house stopped Abby mid-sentence. The dark hair, distinct jawline and magnificent body made recognition immediate.

"Chase Jordan owns Old Miss Strout's house?" she sputtered.

She *had* seen Chase Jordan last night. It should have made her feel better about her sanity, but alas, it only made her feel worse. Thus far she hadn't acted even remotely sane when Chase was near.

When she realized Ellie hadn't responded, she turned back to her sister. Ellie watched her over the rim of her coffee cup, a decidedly guilty expression on her face. "Yes, Chase Jordan is my neighbor."

"Why didn't you tell me yesterday, when we were talking about him?"

"I didn't think it was such a good idea. He seemed to make you uncomfortable."

Boy, she could say that again. But Abby was going to have to get over it. She wasn't here to moon over Chase Jordan. She had already been there and done that. She was grown woman, for heaven's sake! She could certainly handle living across the street from her high school crush.

"This is silly," Abby declared. "Yes, I did have a crush on Chase Jordan when we were in high school. But why on earth would that matter now? I'm a grown woman, and I already have a significant other . . ." She struggled with the name.

"Nelson," Ellie supplied.

"Yes, of course, Nelson, and I'm perfectly capable of living quite serenely across the street from Chase Jordan."

Ellie looked unconvinced. "Well, he seemed to unsettle you yesterday."

"It wasn't Chase per se. It was just the whole experience of being back here." Abby gripped her coffee cup in both hands. "It was strange. And made me act strange. But I'm fine now."

Ellie nodded with her usual acceptance. "I'm glad. Do

you want something for breakfast? We have bagels and English muffins."

"A bagel would be great." Abby could always count on Ellie to accept her explanations. She may not believe them, but she'd let the subject drop.

Abby snuck another quick look out the window and saw that Chase's driveway was empty. He was gone. And she felt a pang of disappointment, but she quickly scolded herself. Chase Jordan had no interest in a friendship with her, and she had no interest in one with him.

"I think I'll go to the lab today and take a look around."

Ellie popped two bagels in the toaster oven and pushed down the lever. "That's a good idea."

Yes, it was time for Abby to surround herself with the familiarity of her work. It was exactly the thing to make her feel a bit normal again.

Chapter 4

"Dr. Stepp, I can't tell you how pleased I am to have you on our team." Dr. Keene grasped Abby's hand and pumped it vigorously.

Just from the brief moment she had spent in the older man's presence, Abby had the feeling he did everything with enthusiasm. And even though his white hair and the deep wrinkles around his blue eyes showed his age, he gave the impression of being much younger. Abby liked him immediately.

"Please call me Abby, and I'm honored that you accepted me. Your research is very impressive," she said with sincerity.

"As is yours. Did the trip here go well?"

Abby nodded.

"Wonderful. Wonderful. Now let me introduce you to the others on my staff."

Dr. Keene, or Cecil as he insisted Abby call him, showed her around the lab. Rand Labs wasn't a huge establishment, but it did have state-of-the-art equipment and a substantial research team. Abby quickly found herself immersed in the only world in which she felt truly comfortable.

"Abby," Cecil said, after they had toured the lab for nearly an hour, "I'm having a get-together tonight—or rather my wife is. She always throws a May Day party.

After all, it's nice to say good-bye to yet another long
Maine winter. And we would be pleased if you could attend. Most of the people you met today will be there. As
well as a couple other folks."

"I'd love to."

"Wonderful. Wonderful. We'll see you around seven,
then."

Abby left Rand Labs feeling better and more confident than she had since she set foot back in Millbrook.
She *had* made the right decision coming back.

As Abby stepped out of her silver sedan, she straightened her tailored skirt and jacket and ran a hand over
her hair to smooth any wayward locks.

The Keenes' house was an impressive Victorian with
ornate gingerbreading on the eaves and around the roof
of the wraparound porch. The cheerful yellow glow of
lights shone from all the downstairs windows, and as
Abby got closer she could hear the hum of voices and an
occasional burst of laughter.

She stopped at the bottom of the porch stairs and adjusted her skirt again. All her confidence had disappeared,
and despite her best efforts to curb the feeling, she was
nervous. She knew she had no reason to be. Dr. Keene was
a very nice man, as were all the other people she met at
the lab. And she certainly had the common interest of
their research to talk about, but she still felt nervous.

She didn't know how to act at parties. In fact, she rarely
attended any—only scientific banquets and conventions.
In college, she had been too busy with her studies to attend the usual dorm parties, and when she met Nelson,
well, he hated social gatherings. So the opportunity
seldom arose.

She tugged at the lapel of her jacket once more and

mounted the stairs. If she didn't feel comfortable, she would just leave early. No need to worry.

She knocked on the front door, and it was promptly answered by a short woman with silver hair styled in a cute pixie cut.

"You must be Abby Stepp," the woman said with a warm smile and ushered Abby into the house.

"Yes."

"I'm Cecil's wife, Adele. I'm so glad you could make it tonight. You must be tired. Cecil was telling me that you just arrived in town yesterday."

Some of Abby's nervousness faded with Adele's warm reception. "Yes, I did, but the move went smoothly."

"Good. Come meet the others."

Although the May Day party was a much larger gathering than Dr. Keene had led her to believe, Abby was soon caught up in a swirl of conversation, food and drink. And the whole experience was remarkably easy.

Easy until she wandered over to a group of couples that she didn't recognize from people she'd met at Rand Labs. She was suddenly back in school looking at a clique she would never belong to. All the beautiful, all the popular.

She started to turn to go back across the room to the group containing her host and hostess, but the sound of her name stopped her.

"Abby? Abby Stepp, is that you?"

She looked back around to see Mandy Blanchard, beaming at her.

Abby forced a smile. The evening had lost its easy comfort. "Hi, Mandy."

"I can't believe you even recognize me," Mandy said with her signature toothy smile. "I must look much different."

Nope, still as beautiful as ever.

"Three kids tend to make you look old and tired, I think."

Abby nodded.

"You remember Andrea Gates, now Andrea Pepin. And Wendy Thurston, now Wendy Knight. And this is Gary Hoyt and his wife Dawn."

They smiled and greeted Abby as each was reintroduced.

She responded in kind, and then shifted awkwardly, casting a look back at the group of her co-workers standing by the buffet.

"So, are you home for long?"

"A few months."

"Really, that's super. Did you realize that this summer is our fifteenth reunion? You must come."

Abby scanned the faces of her old classmates. They all stared back as if her acceptance to Mandy's invitation was actually important to them.

"I don't think so," she said. She had no desire to go back and spend the evening with the people who wouldn't give her the time of day all those years ago.

"Oh, you really should. You didn't make it to the tenth, and truthfully," Mandy leaned toward her, "you didn't miss much."

Andrea laughed. "Wasn't it Dave Macy's idea to just buy a keg and have the reunion at the Ledges? Celebrating in the woods like we're still underage. Can you imagine?"

Abby shook her head.

"Well, I think Dave Macy's fondest memories of high school happened at the Ledges," Gary said.

Everyone chuckled.

"But this year the reunion is going to be at the Millbrook Inn. Have you seen it?" Mandy asked.

Abby shook her head.

"It's absolutely beautiful. Chase Jordan fixed the place up, and it is amazing. That man has a real gift."

Mandy's last statement was the first thing the group had said that Abby could wrap her mind around.

"Speak of the devil," Gary said and their gazes all followed his to where Chase stood slightly in the shadows watching the group.

Abby had the distinct feeling that he was actually watching her, but she knew she must be imagining things.

"Chase," Mandy said, "do you remember Abby Stepp?"

A strange, mysterious smile curved his lips. "Yeah, I remember Abby." He said the words like they had a hidden meaning that no one but he and Abby would understand.

Abby wasn't in on the secret. She shifted slightly, then looked down at the wineglass she held.

"We were just pestering Abby to come to our class reunion," Mandy told Chase.

"And is she coming?" Again, his question seemed to be filled with innuendo.

Mandy sighed, glancing over to Abby. "We haven't been able to get an answer."

Chase looked directly at Abby and cocked an eyebrow. "Maybe she could be persuaded."

Heat crept up Abby's neck. Why did everything he said seem to have a hidden meaning? The whole situation was making her very uncomfortable.

"Excuse me," she said. "I think I'll get something to eat."

"It was great to see you," Mandy said. The other women said things along the same lines.

Again, Abby nodded and started to walk away, but not before she saw Chase's expression. He appeared annoyed.

Abby Stepp really was a number, Chase thought. She looked at her old classmates as though they were little better than insects. She had always had a standoffish demeanor, but now there was no disguising it. She thought she was better than the lowly residents of Millbrook, Maine.

Chase remained with Mandy and her crowd, but his eyes were on Abby.

No, he amended. She seemed to find the Rand Labs crowd in her league.

He watched as Abby smiled at something one of the scientists said. The slight curve of her mouth transformed her features. It brought a glimmer to her dark eyes and softened the angles of her face. It made her look . . . lovely.

Chase fought back the urge to growl at himself. His plan to stay away from Abby wasn't going to work if he was always finding something attractive about the woman. And how was he finding her so appealing anyway? He should have found her behavior toward Mandy and the others completely unattractive. She had looked like she could barely force herself to stand there and make conversation with them. No, that was too generous. She didn't even make conversation. She had barely been listening to them, much less responding.

Another smile graced her lips, and again Chase found his eyes drawn right to the small gesture. But as he stared, the smile faded. His gaze moved from her lips to her eyes. She was staring back at him, the glimmer gone, replaced by a stoic expression.

With practiced nonchalance, Chase raised his glass to her, and then turned to chat with Gary Hoyt.

Abby was glad the evening was over. She had stayed longer than she really wanted to out of courtesy to Cecil and Adele. But after her run-in with Mandy, Chase and the others, she had kept checking her watch.

As she walked to her car, she thought about Chase. Why did he always seem to be watching her, and why did he make comments that seemed to say more than they actually did?

She must be imagining all of the strange responses she was getting from him. He hadn't paid any attention to her in school, so why would he start now?

As she struggled to fit her car key into the door, she heard the low grinding of an engine. The noise rumbled sickly and then sputtered to a stop. The sound repeated several times and was finally followed by an irritated, "Damned thing!"

Abby immediately recognized the voice and peered through the darkness in the direction of the noise and voice.

A dim light from the vehicle came on as Chase threw open the door of his truck and jumped out. He slammed the door closed and darkness shrouded everything again.

Abby stood there for a moment, listening to Chase fumbling around in the darkness and muttering to himself. Then she moved around her car, using the car's frame to steady herself on the uneven ground. Gradually her eyes adjusted a bit to the lack of light, and she picked her way toward the sound of his low, irritated grumbling.

"Chase," she called tentatively, squinting through the blackness. There was no answer. "Chase?"

Suddenly, a bright white light blinded her. She stumbled and found herself enveloped in a pair of strong, warm arms. She tried to pull herself away, but the arms only tightened.

"Are you okay?" Chase's voice asked, the richly spoken syllables tingling across the skin of her cheek.

"Yes," she managed and pushed away from the solidness of his chest. Chase immediately released her, but the scent of woods and spice and something fundamentally masculine still surrounded her.

"I didn't mean to shine the light right in your face like

that," Chase said, gesturing to the flashlight he held, which now illuminated the ground.

Abby was barely able to register the words, as the shivery feeling of being held by him, even so briefly, reverberated in her very cells. In fact, she had no idea how long she stood trying to control the sensation, but it must have been quite some time, because Chase flashed the blinding light in her face again.

"Abby, are you all right?"

She put up a hand to shield her eyes. "Yes. Yes, I'm fine. I came over to see if you needed help."

Chase turned the flashlight on his truck, which again momentarily caused Abby to be disoriented, as she was whisked back into darkness.

"Ole Helen is not as reliable as she once was."

It took Abby a moment to realize Chase was talking about the truck. She looked toward the spot where Chase's light illuminated, and had no doubts whatsoever that "Helen" wasn't what she used to be. The truck was ancient.

"Is—is there anything I can do?" she asked, fairly certain there wasn't.

"Do you happen to have a starter coil with you?"

"No," she said. "And to be honest, I have no idea what that is."

Chase turned to look back at her, his features sharp and pronounced in the shadows. "Most people don't, unless they need one. It's not a big deal. I'll hitch a ride with Gary, and come back out here tomorrow and fix it. Can I walk you back to your car?" He aimed the light at the ground near her feet so she could see where she was walking.

As they headed the few feet to her vehicle, Abby knew she should offer him a ride. She didn't know where Gary Hoyt lived, but he couldn't possibly live closer to Chase than she did. But the idea of having Chase in a small space like the front seat of her car for even the whole fifteen minutes it would take to get home seemed very dangerous. She wasn't sure she could remember to breathe, much less operate a moving vehicle.

She was being ridiculous. So she had reacted when he'd touched her. Part of it had been the shock of a flashlight being shined in her face, and part of it had been . . . it had been the idea of Chase Jordan, rather than the man himself. She would be fine. Driving a person home when they had car trouble was just something you did, especially when he was your neighbor.

"I—I can give you a ride home," Abby said, coming to a stop.

Chase nearly bumped into her, but managed to stop a few inches away from her. He flashed the light up slightly to illuminate them rather than the ground. He peered at her for a moment, then asked, "Are you sure?"

"Yes, of course. It's certainly on my way."

Chase studied her a moment longer, then slowly nodded. "Okay. I'd appreciate it."

They started to walk again, Chase aiming the light so Abby could see the tree roots and rocks littering their path. As they came to her car, he stepped forward to open the door for her. But the door was locked. It seemed to surprise him.

"Oh, it's locked," Abby said. Like he hadn't figured that out. She fumbled in her jacket pocket and found the keys. She tried to get the key in the lock, but her hands trembled.

Gently, Chase took the keys from her hand, and with one try, opened the door.

Abby slipped past him, making sure she gave his body a wide berth. She started to pull the door shut behind her, but Chase was already pushing it closed. It was a simple action, but it gave her pause. No one had ever opened and closed the car door for her, or any door for that matter. Not even Nelson. She wasn't used to having anyone do things for her. It was unnerving.

Chase startled her out of her comptemplation by knocking on the passenger-side window. She just stared at him, until he aimed his flashlight to the door lock.

"Oh!" Abby said aloud and reached over to pull up the lock.

Much to her dismay, her theory that Chase's presence in her car would be potentially dangerous was absolutely true. He hadn't even gotten in the car yet, and she was losing her mind.

And worse was yet to come. She hadn't been able to get her key in the door lock; how on earth was she supposed to get it in the ignition?

It did take several tries, but Abby finally managed to, and they were on their way.

After several seconds of driving, Chase broke the awkward silence. "I know I had a bad reputation in high school, but I didn't grow up to be a serial killer or anything."

Abby shot him a quick, wide-eyed look. "What—what makes you say that?"

"You're on pins and needles. Even in the dark, I can see how white your knuckles are from clutching the steering wheel. Relax. I promise I won't attack you. I won't even make conversation if you don't want me to."

Again, Abby cast him a glance. "Why would I mind you making conversation?"

Chase shifted, and she swore she could feel his body heat drifting toward her.

"I just get the feeling you don't have much use for the folks in this town."

Abby was startled by both his candidness and his accuracy. "I—" She wasn't sure how to respond. She cleared her throat and started again. "I don't have very fond memories of Millbrook."

She saw Chase nod out of the corner of her eye.

"Growing up can be rough."

"Yes, it can," she agreed.

"But we all grow up, and hopefully, get a little wiser."

Abby frowned. "Do you think you're wiser?"

Chase laughed, the sound a little deriding, but still velvety against the vinyl interior of her car. "Damn, I hope I'm wiser, because I was a total idiot in high school."

"Why do you say that?"

"I did terrible in school. I partied too much. I got into a lot of trouble."

"And you were also good-looking, popular and . . . cool."

He laughed again, the sound still filled with derision. "Yeah, well, those things can take you only so far in life. And certainly not as far as hard work and intelligence."

She was silent for a moment, and then said something she'd never said to anyone. "Intelligence can take you places—or it can isolate you."

Chase seemed to ponder her words, then he said, "I don't think intelligence isolates you, but I think you can use it to isolate yourself."

"Either way, a perfect score on your SATs isn't going to win you prom queen."

Chase shuddered. "Who wants to be prom queen anyway? Besides, high school is far behind us. I bet if you gave the folks of Millbrook a chance you'd see they weren't anything like the twerpy kids you remember."

That wasn't a wager Abby was interested in taking.

They were silent until she parked on the street outside their houses. She started to turn to say good night, but Chase spoke first.

"So you thought I was good-looking, huh?" His disparagement was gone, replaced by a teasing smile.

The effect of that smile on Abby's heart rate was instantaneous. "You know very well you were," she finally answered, a slight smile touching her own lips.

"So what do you think now?"

"You're passably handsome."

He looked wounded. "Well, I guess I'll just have to show you that I'm still at least as cool as I was in high school."

Abby shot him a confused look. "How do you plan to do that?"

"Why don't you go out with me tomorrow, and I'll show you?"

Abby's heart was no longer skipping a beat, speeding up, or jumping in her chest. It had stopped. Had Chase Jordan just asked her on a date?

Suddenly graduation night flashed through her mind. Maybe this was just another setup, another chance to make a fool out of one of the Stepp sisters. He'd said that the people she remembered in Millbrook had changed. But again, it wasn't a chance she was willing to take.

"I'm sorry, I can't. I have a significant other." She could have sworn she saw disappointment in Chase's eyes, but it was quickly masked behind an easy smile.

"Well, if you ever just want to hang out and see some of the old gang, let me know. I appreciate the ride." He got out of the car, and she followed suit.

"Good night," Abby said, feeling awkward and anxious and disappointed with herself that she hadn't accepted his invitation for a date. But it was the right thing to do—she was here to work, and she did have a boyfriend.

"Good night," Chase replied and headed across the street to his house. His strides were loose and relaxed, completely at odds with Abby's measured steps. She literally felt dizzy. How could he make her feel so disoriented?

She made it into the house without her knees giving out and when she turned to close the door, she noticed Chase standing on his porch watching her. He waved, and she waved back. He opened his door and disappeared inside.

Abby closed the door and rested her head on the frame.

Coming back to Millbrook was becoming far stranger than she ever could have imagined.

Chapter 5

"So wait a minute, let me get this right. You asked out the very woman who—just two days ago—you said you weren't going to pursue," Mason said, then took a bite of his sandwich.

Chase nodded, as he swallowed the fry he'd just popped in his mouth. "Yes, and now the pursuit is truly off. She has a boyfriend—or something."

"Or something? What's a something? Is she a lesbian?"

Chase shook his head, but a chuckle escaped him. "No, I don't think Abby's a lesbian."

"The lesbian thing could be good. Maybe you could convince her to get a little three-way thing going," Mason suggested, wiggling his eyebrows.

"You know, you're starting to worry me."

Mason sighed. "Yeah, I'm starting to worry myself. But to be honest, I haven't met anyone who really does much for me. I think Marla got my sex drive in the divorce too."

"Well, she did have you by the balls," Chase said with a smirk, before taking another bite of his burger.

"Ha-ha," Mason said dryly, without any real offense. "So, that's it. No more Abby?"

No more Abby. There hadn't even been *any* Abby, but damn did he want there to be. When he had accidentally shined the flashlight in her eyes and caused her to lose her footing, she had felt so incredible in his arms. Her silky hair had brushed his chin and he'd been able to smell the scent of her shampoo. It was a simple, clean fragrance, but when mixed with Abby's own unique scent, she smelled delectable.

And he'd been barely able to keep his eyes off her as she drove him home last night. She had been so stiff and uneasy, trying to keep him at a distance. Until she had smiled. It had only been a small, fleeting curve of her mouth, but it had showed what lay beyond the walls she had erected around herself.

He then realized she wasn't aloof because she was snooty, but because she didn't trust easily. She had been hurt, and she wanted to protect herself. He could understand that, probably better than anyone.

Damn, he wanted to break down her barriers and see the real Abby. Unfortunately, she had already offered some other guy that opportunity.

"So you planning to answer me or just stare at that fry you're holding?" Mason's voice pulled him out of his thoughts.

"Sorry," Chase muttered, feeling a bit lame to be caught daydreaming. "No, no more Abby. At least, not unless she wants to be friends—which I don't think is very likely."

Mason frowned. "She sounds like too much work anyway."

She would be work, but Chase had the feeling she would be worth every ounce of sweat.

Abby hated to admit it, but she was actually relieved when her first day at Rand Labs was over. She loved the work and the people, but she just couldn't seem to stay on task. It was such an unusual feeling for her that by the time she left the lab, she decided she must be coming down with the flu or a cold. That could be the only explanation for her inability to concentrate.

But oddly, one of the symptoms of this virus was recurring thoughts of Chase. She would be adjusting her microscope, and instead of seeing the cells on the slide, she'd see Chase. Or when she was retrieving a petri dish from the incubator, she would hear the richness of his voice. And over and over, she found herself remembering the way his arms had felt wrapped around her.

Fortunately, she didn't think any of her fellow scientists noticed her lack of concentration. She hadn't made any mistakes on the experiments she had done, but she hadn't lost herself in her research like she usually did.

And not surprisingly, her drive home had been as much of a blur as her day at the lab. But she was determined to get a tight reign on her disruptive thoughts. She was normally a very levelheaded woman and not prone to daydreams. She must be more tired than she realized. A good night's sleep would have her back to normal, and she could commence her research with an uncluttered mind.

Getting out of her car, she grabbed her briefcase and started up the porch steps. She was so involved with *not* thinking about Chase that she nearly stepped on the creature lying in front of her door.

She screamed, and the enormous beast rose to its feet, its bushy tail wagging back and forth as if a piercing shriek was just the greeting he'd been waiting for.

It only took Abby's startled mind a moment to realize the monster lying in wait was actually a dog. And if appearances could be trusted, a very friendly dog.

Abby didn't have much experience with the species, but she liked the ones she had encountered before. So with only slight trepidation, she extended her hand toward the animal.

"Hey, pup, where did you come from?"

The animal immediately lowered its head to retrieve a scrap of cloth from the porch's worn floorboards. Whatever the item was, it was evident the dog was very proud of the scrap, because he nudged it at her opened palm. Apparently, the bit of cloth was a gift for her.

With a pleased laugh, Abby patted the dog's furry head, and then shook out the cloth the dog had brought her.

For a moment she could only stare at the object. Then she laughed again.

The silly mutt had brought her a pair of men's boxers— with chili peppers on them, no less.

"Somehow I don't think you really had me in mind when you chose these," she said to the dog, reaching down again to rub its back.

The dog jerked its back leg in bliss, the movement causing the metal tags on his collar to jingle.

Abby moved her hand to check them. One said that his rabies shot was up to date. That was good.

And the second tag said his name was Chester.

"Well, hello, Chester."

The dog's tail thumped happily against the clapboards of the house in response.

"So, where do you belong, big guy?"

Abby flipped the silver nametag over, and on the back was the answer to her question.

Chase Jordan
117 Fletcher Road
Millbrook, ME

Abby dropped the tag and shook her head as she continued to pet the animal. Even a dog bearing underwear couldn't keep her thoughts from Chase for long.

With that realization, she held up the boxers and looked at them more closely. Hot peppers. She shook her head again and smiled. Somehow they seemed appropriate.

"Come on, Chester. I think I'd better return you and your master's unmentionables. Come on, boy."

Chester happily followed her as they crossed the road and climbed the steps of Chase's porch.

She knocked on the door and waited. There was no sound. She knocked again, and this time she could hear some muffled noise from inside. A few seconds later the door swung open, and Chase stood before her dressed only in a pair of jeans. His hair and chest were damp, and he held a towel loosely in one hand.

His expression appeared a bit irritated, but it quickly dissolved into a look of surprise.

"Abby," he said. Her name sounded absolutely sinful on his lips. "How are you?"

Abby blinked. Fine, except breathing was becoming only a voluntary reaction at the moment. She hadn't expected to find him in such a state of undress. But how he looked in such a state was exactly what she'd expected— he looked wonderful. His skin was a smooth golden cover over the lean muscles of his chest and arms.

It took her a few moments to stop staring and answer his question.

"I'm returning Chester."

The time it took for her to regain her equilibrium had been enough for him to regain his composure too. He leaned against the door frame, a sexy smile on his lips.

Abby could hear the rhythmic thumping of the dog's tail behind her when he heard his name; it matched the beat of her heart.

"He considers himself the welcoming committee on this street," Chase said.

Abby tried to keep her eyes on Chase's face, but they had a will of their own and wandered back down to the ridged flatness of his stomach and the enticing line of fine dark hair that swirled around his shallow bellybutton and disappeared intriguingly under the waistband of his jeans.

When she looked back up, she found him watching her with unconcealed interest. A broad grin deepened the dimple in his left cheek.

Heat burned Abby's already overheated flesh.

"I also wanted to return these," she blurted out, extremely embarrassed to be caught so blatantly admiring his physique.

It took a moment for Chase to realize what she was holding, but when he did, it was his turn to look uncomfortable. But he recovered much more admirably than she had.

He chuckled and took the boxers from her. "That mutt. I'm sorry. Not only does he feel the need to visit, but he also feels the need to bring gifts. You're lucky he didn't bring you one of my dirty socks. They're a favorite of his."

Abby smiled. "I guess chili peppers do beat old tube socks."

She waited for Chase to respond, but his gaze was locked on her mouth. Self-consciously, she touched her fingers to her lips.

Chase watched the action intently and then slid a hand into the pocket of his jeans. "Do you want to come in?"

"I should get home. I just wanted to return your pet and . . . your other thing."

"You know, since you've seen my boxers and all, I really feel it demands that we go out tonight," he said, his charming smile very inviting.

Abby wanted to say yes, though she was still filled with

uncertainty. She didn't ever want to be set up like she had been that May night years before.

"I just finished my first day at the lab, and I need to relax."

"It will be relaxing," Chase assured her. "Just a casual dinner."

She wanted so much to accept, but fear wouldn't let her. "No, I'm sorry."

"No strings attached. I know you have a boyfriend. I just want to go out as friends." He held up the boxers. "This has got to make us friends, right?"

"I'm sorry," Abby said again and started toward the steps, but Chase's hand on her arm stopped her. The touch was light, but it felt like a pure shot of electricity jolting through her skin. She looked back at him.

"Please come out with me tonight." The invitation was so sincere, his pale eyes filled with such earnestness, that Abby found herself nodding.

"Great. I'll be over at seven."

"You said yes?" Ellie said in disbelief.

"It's only dinner," Abby said. She fastened the buttons of her cardigan and tugged at the hem.

"But I thought you said you weren't interested in Chase."

"I'm not. I'm just going to be friendly. It's—it's the neighborly thing to do."

Ellie looked dubious. "I've been his neighbor for almost a year, and we haven't gone out to dinner."

"You want to come?"

"No," Ellie replied quickly. She got up, went to the counter and opened a box of doughnuts. She broke off a piece of a chocolate one and nibbled on it, a thoughtful look on her face. "Does Nelson know about this?"

Abby sighed. "Ellie, you're making more of this than is really necessary."

Ellie stopped eating the doughnut and cocked an eyebrow questioningly.

"No." Abby sighed again. "I didn't think I needed to inform Nelson that I was having dinner with an old friend."

For some reason that answer seemed to please Ellie. She grinned and picked up another piece of doughnut. "So, you and Chase are old friends now?"

Abby let out an exasperated breath. "Ellie, this is nothing."

Ellie nodded, munching happily on her pastry.

"Nothing," Abby repeated and left the kitchen.

She went to her room and stood in front of the mirror. She didn't want to speculate on why she was going to check her outfit for the third time for a dinner date that was nothing. The mirror was clouded with age, just as it had been in her school days. In fact, it was the same mirror she'd stood before that May night of her graduation. But the same girl didn't stare back at her. She was a woman now. So why did she feel so insecure?

She had never been a person to think much about her looks, but for once, she really studied herself. Her height was a bit above average. And her build was, well, maybe a bit below average, but she had nice skin and her hair was a pretty shade of brown and shiny.

The outfit she wore was conservative—a dark blue cardigan over a white cotton shirt and a simple blue and white flowered skirt.

She wasn't likely to raise many blood pressures, but that wasn't her intent anyway. She turned from the mirror, then stopped and unbuttoned her sweater.

Maybe that looked a little better.

Irritated with herself, she headed back downstairs to wait.

Ellie now sat on the living room sofa, reading a book. She looked up as Abby entered the room.

"It looks better unbuttoned," her sister said.

"What?"

"Your sweater," Ellie said. "It looks better unbuttoned." A knowing little smile curved her lips.

"It's not a date," Abby muttered as she pulled the sweater around her and marched into the kitchen. She liked her sister better when she kept her opinions to herself.

Just as she was about to steal a piece of doughnut, there was a knock on the door. Abby shot a quick glance at the clock shaped like a teapot, which hung over the sink. It was 6:55. Chase was five minutes early. She hadn't realized how nervous she was that he wouldn't show up until she heard that sharp knock. As she approached the door, it was replaced by another type of nervousness.

Taking a calming breath, she grabbed the doorknob and pulled the door open.

Chase stood there, looking sinfully handsome in a black button-down shirt and jeans.

"Hi," he said, the single word rich and velvety.

"Hi."

"Hello, Chase," Ellie called from the living room.

Chase stuck his head in the door. "Hey, Ellie. What are you reading tonight?"

"A Regency."

"Enjoy those roguish lords."

Ellie laughed. "You both enjoy yourselves too."

Chase turned a sly look on Abby. "Ready for a night of pure coolness?"

A startled laugh escaped her. "Do I have a choice?"

"Nope." Chase pushed the door open wider so she could step outside.

"Night," Abby called to Ellie.

"Have fun with your *old* friend," Ellie called back.

What happened to my unassuming sister? Abby thought as the door slammed shut, and she followed Chase down the porch stairs.

"So, I see you got Helen up and running again," she said.

Chase followed Abby around to the passenger side of the truck, slipping past her to open the rusted, paint-chipped door. The hinges squeaked noisily.

"Yeah, but she's none too happy about it," he said as he held the door with one hand and turned to help Abby up onto the seat with the other.

Abby looked at the length of his long fingers and the width of his open palm. His hand was as beautiful as the rest of him, she thought. And although she wanted to feel that calloused, work-toughened skin against hers, she opted to brace herself against his arm instead, hoping the barrier of his shirt would be enough to keep her willful pulse under control.

It wasn't.

The hard muscles of his forearm, even through his clothing, caused the sensitive pads of her fingers to tingle. She scooted into the truck and released his arm as quickly as possible.

Why should touching a man's arm make her all edgy? An arm was certainly an innocuous enough body part. She studied Chase as he walked around the front of the truck. His broad shoulders strained against the cotton of his shirt and muscles rippled under his sleeves. Okay, there was nothing innocuous about any part of the man.

"Do you like seafood?" he asked as he hopped into the truck.

The truck's spacious cab suddenly shrunk, just like the front seat of her car had the night she'd driven him home. He really did have a way of consuming space, and it wasn't just his size, but his very presence. It was the same presence that had allowed him, the bad boy from the wrong side of town, to also be one of the most popular kids in school. He made an impression. He had always made an impression on Abby. So why should she be surprised to find things any different now?

"Seafood?" he asked again, and Abby realized she was just staring at him, trying to control her erratic breathing and pounding heart.

"Yes, seafood is great."

Chase started the engine, which sputtered and coughed in Helen's usual cantankerous way.

"I figured it was a fairly safe choice," he said. "Growing up on the coast of Maine makes seafood sort of a staple."

Abby didn't respond. She was, once again, having a hard time concentrating on his words, because now his woodsy scent was surrounding her and wreaking havoc on her breathing again. This man had the potential to cause her severe oxygen deprivation.

"How did you know my sister was reading?" Abby asked, after she had her crazed senses under control.

Chase shot her a quick glance and then returned his gaze to the road. "What?"

"Ellie. You knew she was reading, but you couldn't possibly have seen her from the kitchen door."

Chase looked at her again. A muscle in his jaw twitched, and he tightened, then relaxed his grip on the steering wheel. "Well, she's a librarian. So I just figured she was reading."

Abby supposed Chase's explanation made sense, but his reaction to the question seemed a bit odd.

"Plus," he added, "every time I see her she has a book in her hand."

That was true about Ellie, and they *were* neighbors so he probably did see her with a book every now and then.

"Yes, Ellie is a book junkie. She always has been. But then so am I."

Chase nodded, and although he didn't do anything that Abby could actually put her finger on, she got the impression that he still felt uncomfortable.

"So, where does a cool person go in Millbrook?" Abby asked, hoping she might break the tension in the air.

It did.

"Well, there are several cool places," Chase informed her with one of his easy grins. "You know, the Ledges, the parking lot of the Dairy Palace—but the older set of cool cats go to the Parched Dolphin."

"The Parched Dolphin?" Abby said with a touch of skepticism.

"I know, I know, it sounds a little strange. But they serve a great stuffed haddock." He cast her a teasing look. "All cool folks say so."

Abby laughed, some of the nervousness leaving her. "Well, the Parched Dolphin does sound more appealing than the Poached Dolphin."

"Or the Beached Dolphin," Chase said. "Then you'd have to worry."

Abby settled back against the seat, listened to the loud roar of Helen's engine, and breathed in the wonderful scent of Chase. She felt happy. An emotion she hadn't expected to feel in Millbrook. Maybe it would be a nice thing to have Chase as a friend during her stay here.

She glanced at him from the corner of her eye. She wouldn't deny that she was also attracted to him, but all they could have was friendship. And she planned to enjoy that.

Chase pulled the truck up to the curb in front of a restaurant Abby didn't recognize. The building itself wasn't new, as its grayed, sea-weathered walls revealed, but Abby couldn't recall if the place had been a restaurant while she had lived here. In fact, she couldn't remember the charming little building at all.

"The food's much better than the atmosphere would lead you to believe," Chase said, following her gaze.

But before she could reply that the place looked very nice, he had gotten out of the truck and was heading around to her side of the vehicle.

She felt a bit silly waiting for him to open her door, but she didn't want to appear impolite by not accepting his courteous gesture. And to be honest, she rather liked the attention. It made her feel pampered.

As they walked up the restaurant's steps, Abby noticed the pub-like sign swinging over the door. It bore the name *The Parched Dolphin* in ornate golden lettering with one of the sea animals cheerfully holding a frosty mug of ale in his finned grip.

"I don't know," Abby said slowly. "If people come here to drink like fish, they're in the wrong place."

Chase followed her gaze up to the sign and then cast her a confused look. "Why do you say that?"

"Because," Abby said with a cheesy grin, "dolphins aren't fish, they're mammals."

Chase blinked, then a deep chuckle escaped him. "You know, Abby, that was just bad."

Abby sighed. "Is the hope of being cool futile?"

"I can only do what I can do." Humor twinkled in his eyes, making his icy blue irises shimmer. He opened the pub's door and ushered her inside.

The interior of the restaurant was just as appealing as the outside. The first thing to grab her attention was the buttery aroma of broiled seafood that filled the air. One side of the room was sectioned into booths with antique blown glass buoys hanging over the tables, refracting blue and green light on the walls and ceiling. Several round tables filled the middle section of the floor, and the far wall sported a long, old-fashioned bar made of shiny dark wood and brass.

Even though it was a Monday night, the place was quite busy. Folks, sharing a few drinks and some friendly banter, occupied most of the stools at the bar. Two of the tables were taken as well.

Abby felt the pressure of one of Chase's beautiful hands at the small of her back. The touch caused her to stiffen, not because it was unpleasant—it was far from that—but because it was unexpected. Chase must have misinterpreted her reaction, because he promptly removed it and pointed to a booth in the corner.

"Does that look okay?"

"Great," Abby breathed and followed him. She couldn't help casting a glance down at the hand that had just touched her. Beautiful hands. Had she ever, in all her life, noticed another human's hands? Did Nelson have nice hands? Did Nelson even have hands?

Chase stopped at the table, and it took Abby a moment to realize that he was waiting for her to sit.

"Where did the town bad boy learn such wonderful manners?" she asked as she slid into the booth.

Chase sat across from her. He paused before he answered, and Abby fully expected she had unintentionally offended him again, but instead his laid-back grin appeared.

"That's a good question." He appeared to contemplate the question, then he shrugged. "I guess I must have taught myself."

Abby smiled. "Well, you did a very nice job."

"Thank you, ma'am." His smile deepened, as did his dimple.

Abby's own grin widened in response, and for a few moments they just gazed at each other. Suddenly, Abby didn't feel so nervous and out of sorts. Suddenly, she felt almost comfortable with Chase. If she overlooked the occasional rapid heartbeat and shortness of breath.

"Hey, Chase." A man wearing a bartender's apron over his wide girth appeared beside them, jarring them out of their companionable silence.

"Hey, Paul," Chase said. "How are you?"

"Can't complain, can't complain." Paul placed menus in front of them.

"You remember Abby Stepp, don't you?" Chase asked, casting a smile toward her that sent warm tingles down her spine.

Paul frowned at her for a moment, and then a broad smile split his round face. "Well, I'll be damned!" he said, wiping his hands on his apron, then offering one of the beefy appendages to her. "I'll be damned," he repeated, as his huge hand pumped hers up and down repeatedly. "It's real nice to see you again. You in town long?"

"No," Abby said, overwhelmed by the bartender's enthusiastic greeting. She had no idea who the huge man was. Paul who? "Just a few months."

Paul nodded, his wide grin revealing startlingly white and even teeth. He turned toward the bar. "Hey, Lynn, bring over a round of two of my special brews."

He turned back to Chase and Abby. "On the house."

"Thanks, Paul," Chase said, then watched Abby as though her reaction was important to him.

"Thanks," Abby said too, although she didn't think she did a very good job keeping the bewilderment from her voice.

Chase frowned. Apparently, she had done something offensive again.

"Well, enjoy your meal. And great to see you again, Abby." Paul went back to tend bar.

The woman Paul had called Lynn approached, carrying

two giant mugs filled to the brim with a dark amber liquid. She set down the drinks, somehow managing not to spill any of it on the polished tabletop.

"Hey, Chase." Her two-word greeting held volumes of innuendo.

But Chase didn't seem to notice the waitress's thinly veiled interest. "Hi, Lynn. What's the catch of the day?"

Abby had the distinct impression that Lynn would have liked to offer herself as the catch. But she simply answered the question. "Haddock and lobster."

"Do you need time to look over the menu?" Chase asked Abby.

"Please."

Lynn gave Abby an appraising look, seemed rather unimpressed, smiled at Chase, and then left.

Abby watched her go into a back room behind the bar that must have been the kitchen.

"Did you try the beer? It's pretty good—brewed right here," Chase said.

"Who is Paul?"

Chase set down his beer and studied her for a moment. "Paul Cormier."

Abby cast a look across the bar at the hulking figure filling a pitcher from the tap. "That's Paul Cormier?"

"Ten years can change a person."

Abby continued to stare at Paul. It wasn't so much that he had changed. Sure, he was heavier than he'd been in high school, but he'd always been a big guy. It was the fact that he had genuinely seemed pleased to see her. He'd rarely ever spoken to her throughout their entire childhood, yet now he acted like they had been friends.

"Does he own this place?"

Chase nodded. "Opened it about four years ago, I guess."

Abby was impressed. From what she remembered,

Paul had been fairly intelligent but lazy. He obviously wasn't lazy now. The Parched Dolphin was a booming little business.

Abby flipped open her menu. And the food looked very good.

"You already know what you're ordering?" she asked, when she noticed that Chase hadn't even opened his menu.

He pushed the folded menu toward the edge of the table. "I always get the special."

Abby had the odd sensation that she had somehow offended him again, but she couldn't imagine how. Perhaps she was being oversensitive.

"Have you had this appetizer?" she asked, pointing to the first item on the menu.

Chase hesitated, then pulled his menu back in front of him and opened it. "The scallops?" he finally asked.

"No, the stuffed mushrooms."

"Oh yeah," he said quickly. "Yeah, they're good."

Abby knew it didn't make any sense, but she could swear that Chase was actually bothered by the menu. Maybe locals didn't use the menu. Maybe it was cool to have it memorized.

"Chase, you old coot!"

Abby looked up to see who was calling to Chase. Unlike Paul, she recognized this man instantly. It was Tommy Leavitt.

"Tommy, what are you doing here on a Monday night?" Chase said.

"Getting a bite to eat and a brewski or two." Tommy gave them both a conspiratorial look. "Becky and the girls are over at Bangor for the night with her folks, so I can sneak out and have a little fun. Are you going to introduce me to your lady friend?"

Abby frowned. Maybe everyone else in Millbrook could

appear happy to see the eldest "ugly Stepp sister" again, but there was no way that Tommy Leavitt could. He had been the bane of her school days, and she doubted he could have changed much in his adulthood. If his comment about his wife and kids was any indication, he was still a creep.

"This is Abby Stepp."

Abby waited for the sarcastic remark, the digging barb, but none came. Instead there was a flash of surprise and then a smile that revealed that he still hadn't gotten his overlapping front teeth fixed. "Abby Stepp," he said with a shake of his head. "I haven't seen you in a dog's age. How have you been?"

Abby couldn't answer. How could this man stand in front of her and seem pleased to see her again—after all the hurtful and cruel things he had said?

If Chase thought Abby had been appalled to see Paul, it was mild compared to her reaction to Tommy. She paled. It made her brown eyes appear huge.

Could dislike actually cause a person to become physically ill? Because she honestly looked like she was going to either pass out or vomit.

Tommy frowned. He might not be the most observant guy around, but he obviously noticed Abby's dismay too.

"You remember me, don't ya? Tommy Leavitt."

"I remember you." Abby's steely voice was at odds with her wan expression.

"Well, I wouldn't be surprised if you didn't," Tommy said in his friendly manner, although the wrinkles in his brow showed that he was confused by Abby's behavior. "I wasn't nearly the popular fella that Chase here was. And I certainly wasn't the brain you were."

Chase watched Abby's reaction. She stared at him with

eyes that were aloof and hard. Chase remembered that look. It was the same one she wore every day during high school. A look that said, *I'm better than you, so don't waste my time.*

A nervous chuckle escaped Tommy. "I reckon if I'd had your brains, I'd be doin' something a little more glamorous than fixing cars."

"I suppose you would," Abby said coldly, before taking a sip of her beer.

Chase stared at Abby for a second, shocked she could say something so callous. Maybe, over the years, she had learned to actually say the things her eyes had only hinted at. Maybe she really did consider herself better than the lowly residents of Millbrook.

Tommy stood silent for a moment, then said to them both in a low voice, "Well, good to see you. Chase, see you later."

Chase nodded. "Have a good night. Say hi to Becky for me."

"Will do." Tommy shot Abby another hurt look and then went to sit at the bar.

Chase turned his attention back to Abby, who was now reading her menu as if Tommy had never approached them.

"Is that how folks treat each other in Boston?"

"Excuse me?" Bewilderment crossed Abby's face.

"How you just treated Tommy?"

"I don't know what you mean."

"Tommy doesn't deserve your rudeness. He's a decent, hard-working guy that I happen to respect."

Abby glared at him, her jaw setting with determination. "You respect a guy that runs out to bars as soon as his family is out of town?"

"I don't think it's your place to judge him. But I guess

folks in Millbrook are not quite as refined as the city slickers you're used to."

Abby paled again.

Chase was irritated that he actually felt a twinge of concern for her.

"I . . ." She stared down at her menu. "I think I should go."

Part of Chase agreed with her—she had been unkind, and he didn't think there was much point wasting his time on a person who couldn't be civil to his friends. But he couldn't just let their evening end on such a sour note.

Then Abby lifted her head, and Chase saw the shimmer of unshed tears in her lovely brown eyes.

"Abby?"

"You can so easily say I'm rude, but not once did you step in and tell Tommy that he was being rude to me. Not once did you say to Tommy, 'Hey, the ugly Stepp sisters have feelings too.' You may not have called me names, but not once did you deny them, either."

Abby stood, and with determined, ramrod straight posture, she exited the restaurant.

Chase could have kicked himself. Why hadn't he seen it? Why hadn't he realized that, as before, her cold demeanor was only a defense mechanism to protect herself?

He tossed a couple dollars on the table for Lynn and followed Abby outside. He was relieved to discover that she hadn't made it too far. She stood on the sidewalk a few yards away from the restaurant, looking around like she was trying to decide what to do next.

"Abby." He walked toward her but paused as she held her hand up to stop him.

"I'm sorry," she said, all signs of pain gone from her voice, replaced by aloofness. "I shouldn't have reacted that way in there."

"And I shouldn't have said what I said. I didn't realize the way you felt."

Abby shifted, looking up the street. Chase wondered if she wished she were home or back in Boston with her "significant other." He wished she didn't want to be either place, but for some reason, the second option bothered him more than he cared to dwell on.

She cleared her throat, then said dully, "It doesn't matter. Tommy, Paul and all the others in this town are years and years behind me. It's in the past."

Chase took a step toward her and paused again. "It isn't in the past if it still hurts you. I should have realized why you reacted to Tommy the way you did."

Abby gave him a searching look, and even though her demeanor was stiff and cold, he could still see the hurt in her eyes.

"Why should you have? You don't know what it was like to grow up as one of the ugly Stepp sisters. You don't even remember how we were teased. You were part of the cool crowd, you had other things to concern yourself with."

Man, if she only knew how true that was. He took another step toward her. He was close enough to touch her if he wanted to, but he didn't think she would be receptive to such an overture. But he wanted to touch her, to pull her into his arms, and absorb some of that pain that held her so rigid that she looked like she might snap.

"Listen, I think we should just label this dinner a complete disaster," Abby said with a small smile that didn't lessen the sadness in her eyes. "I wasn't cool in high school, and I think it's safe to say that I'm not cool now. So let's just call it a night."

She started to step past him, and this time he couldn't stop himself from touching her. He caught her wrist, noting how fragile it felt in his hand.

She turned and looked up at him, and he saw that surprise had replaced pain in the depths of her dark brown eyes.

"Do you want to know something else you're not?" he asked, his voice rough.

Before she could reply, he answered, pulling her tight against him. "You are not an *ugly* Stepp sister." He bent to capture her parted lips with his own.

Chapter 6

Whatever Abby had expected Chase to say or do—that wasn't it. At first, she stood stiff in his arms, stunned. Then all she was aware of was the firm demand of his mouth, moving over hers, caressing her, teasing her, coercing her to respond. He nibbled her bottom lip, the hardness of his teeth a thrilling contrast to his supple lips.

She gasped, and he used her reaction to deepen the kiss. His tongue brushed against hers, and she could taste the smoky flavor of the ale he'd drunk and a faint trace of mint. He tasted wonderful.

As if they weren't under her control, her hands traveled up his arms, feeling the lean muscles, warm and powerful, under the soft cotton of his shirt. Her fingers stopped their sensuous journey when they reached the wide, hard expanse of his shoulders. She gripped the solid muscles there, feeling the need to steady herself, even though she was held securely in his strong arms.

All too soon, Chase broke the kiss, stepping back from her, but he kept his hands lightly on her hips.

"I—" His voice sounded uneven and breathless. "I'm sorry. I shouldn't have done that."

Abby stared back for a moment, her fingers still molding the muscles of his shoulders. Slowly, reality washed back over her. She'd kissed Chase Jordan. She felt giddy and confused at the same time.

"Why did you?" Abby asked.

"Because—because I wanted to," Chase said. He ran a hand through his hair. "But I fully intended to respect you, and your relationship with . . ."

He paused, and Abby realized he was waiting for her to respond. She had to think, then answered hurriedly, "Nelson."

Chase nodded. "With Nelson. I'm truly sorry—I promise it won't happen again."

Abby knew he was right. They shouldn't have kissed, and she felt terribly guilty, because it was the most amazing kiss she had ever experienced. And not once had Nelson popped into her mind. Not once had she thought she shouldn't be doing this.

Her gaze strayed back to his mouth. His lips were beautiful. The lower lip was fuller than the upper, but both were sculpted to masculine perfection. She could still feel the pressure of them against hers.

Kissing had always been pleasant enough, but with Chase, she realized that a kiss could be earth shaking.

"Abby." Chase sounded in pain.

She blinked up at him.

"Hell, if you keep looking at me like that, I can't guarantee it won't happen again."

It took her a moment to realize what he meant, then heat burned her cheeks. She looked at the ground. "I'm sorry."

Chase's hand cupped her cheek, his calloused fingers rasping like brushed velvet against her skin. "Don't be. I'm the one who screwed up this whole evening." He dropped his hand back to his side. "Maybe after the trauma has worn off, you'll let me try and make it up to you."

Abby couldn't help but smile at his sheepish expression. "Maybe we're better off just being neighbors."

Chase looked like he wanted to argue, but then he

nodded. He walked to his truck and opened the door. "Well, hop in. After this fiasco, the least I can do is drive you home in my luxury vehicle."

Abby managed a laugh and went to the truck. This time she was careful to avoid any contact with Chase, using the door to lift herself onto the seat.

Neither said anything on the ride home. Chase imagined Abby was kicking herself for agreeing to go out with him. He'd promised nothing more than a friendly dinner. But instead he accused her of being rude and then kissed her. He didn't know what the hell that constituted, but he didn't think the term *friendship* really applied to either behavior.

He snuck a quick glance at her, but was unable to make out her expression in the darkened truck.

She was likely thinking about her boyfriend—what was his name? Nelson. He even sounded intelligent and dignified. The guy *had* to have more decorum than to take Abby to a bar, insult her, and then ram his tongue down her throat.

Chase cringed. He should be ashamed of the whole mess. But he couldn't quite bring himself to feel bad about everything.

He shot Abby another quick sidelong glance.

Nope, there was no way that he could regret their kiss. He did feel bad about not respecting her relationship with Nelson. There were plenty of lousy things he'd done in his life, but messing around with another man's lady wasn't one of them. Yet as soon as he'd pulled Abby into his arms, all thought of right and wrong disappeared.

It didn't make sense, and Chase didn't pretend to understand it, but something about Abby Stepp had him acting like a mindless, horny teenager.

He pulled the truck into the driveway of the Stepp house and shifted into park. The porch light cast enough illumination that Chase could see her features clearly. Her usual stoic expression was back in place, and he fought the urge to kiss her again, to see the flushed, soft look that she wore after their lips parted.

"Well, here we are."

She looked over at him and smiled; the action seemed forced. "Here we are." She turned to reach for the door handle, but Chase put a hand on her arm.

She glanced back.

"I am sorry."

"There is no need for you to be sorry. I'll see you around." She opened the door and slid out of the truck.

He watched her climb the porch stairs. Without looking back, she disappeared into the house.

So much for showing her how cool you are, Jordan. He backed out of her driveway and pulled into his own.

On his front stoop, he paused and stared across the street at the large yellow house. He didn't want to, but he would respect her request. They would be neighbors. How hard would that be?

"What are you doing home so early?" Ellie asked, peering over the top of her book.

Abby had hoped she could avoid her sister, but obviously the fates were conspiring against her. "It's a work night. How late did you think I'd be?"

Ellie looked at her watch. "Longer than fifty-five minutes."

"You know, I think you need more to fill your time."

"You're probably right," Ellie said easily. "But that doesn't explain why you're home."

"Chase and I didn't hit it off quite like we thought we would."

Ellie dropped her book onto her lap. "What happened?"

"Nothing terribly interesting," Abby said. "I'm really tired. I'm going to bed." She moved toward the hallway.

"Are you okay?" her sister asked gently.

Abby turned and offered a strained smile to her. "Just tired."

Ellie nodded but didn't bother to hide her concerned look.

Abby went upstairs and headed directly to the bathroom. She went to the linen closet and pulled out a towel and a washcloth, then moved to the sink.

She turned on the water, and waited. It always seemed to take forever for the water to get hot in this house. She didn't remember having to wait like this at her apartment in Boston.

She tested the water again. It was lukewarm. Wetting the washcloth, she covered her face with it. The coolness felt good against her heated flesh.

It didn't make sense that she could get hot water faster in Boston. Her apartment was in a building easily as old as this house. Maybe the water heater was newer or maybe the pipes were better.

She rewetted the washcloth and put it to her face again. The water was warm this time. She held it there for several seconds, then dropped the cloth in the sink and looked up at her wet reflection in the mirror.

She could ponder the mysteries of plumbing all night, but it wasn't going to keep her mind off what was really bothering her.

What the hell was happening? She had come to Maine to further her career. She didn't come to face her past.

She didn't come to question her future. Do research and go home. That was it.

So how had she found herself kissing Chase Jordan?

She studied her face. Her fingers touched her lips, tracing the shape of them.

Why had he kissed her? *Because I wanted to.* His chocolaty voice echoed in her head.

Why would he want to? Because he felt sorry for her? She felt so stupid that she had cried. Abby wasn't the type of female that got teary-eyed at the drop of a hat.

In fact, the only time she'd cried in the past fifteen years had been when Ellie called to tell her Grammy had died. And she'd known she couldn't leave the symposium she had been speaking at in Austria to make it to the funeral. Ellie told her that Grammy wouldn't want her to leave the prestigious conference. She'd said that Grammy was so proud of her and would want her to do her best. Abby had cried about that.

But why did she cry tonight?

And did Chase kiss her because he felt sorry for the pathetic woman who was still crying about names she was called during her childhood?

She grabbed up the towel and scrubbed her face dry until her skin tingled the way her lips had when Chase had kissed her.

Annoyed that she couldn't get the memory out of her mind, she stuffed the dirty towels into a wicker hamper in the hallway and headed to her bedroom. Without turning the light on, she stripped off her clothes, tugged on her nightshirt, and crawled into bed.

It didn't matter why he'd kissed her. She would forget about it altogether and get back to the reason she was here. Her work. That had always been the focus of her life, and she liked it that way.

And if she did feel the need to think about romance,

she'd think about it with the right person. The person who had been her partner for many very unproblematic years. Nelson.

Chase may be extremely handsome and charming, but he wasn't the companion that Nelson was to her.

She stared up at the ceiling, picturing Nelson. His eyes, his smile, the way he kissed.

She concentrated for several moments, then let out a frustrated groan and rolled over to bury her face in her pillow. No matter how hard she tried, all she could envision were the pale blue eyes, devilish smile and wonderfully sculpted lips of another man.

Chapter 7

Summer was arriving in Millbrook. The days were longer. The weather was warmer. And the mud created by the winter thaw and April showers was everywhere. Not that Abby had given much thought to the mucky substance—until a small person covered from head to toe in the stuff ran smack-dab into her as she stepped out of her car.

Abby squealed, dropped her briefcase and watched in amazement as the muddy being fell to the ground at her feet with a loud "Oof!"

She continued to stare at the individual until she heard the pounding of feet, and another mud-caked creature raced toward her at top speed. Without stopping to retrieve her briefcase, she darted around her car.

But the muddy thing didn't notice her, running straight to the mud-being lying on the ground. Suddenly the two creatures merged into a wiggling, giggling and yipping ball rolling across her front yard.

Abby squinted at the tumbling mass, trying to make out who or what they were. Then the larger of the muddy creatures sat back and let out a deep, joyous bark.

"Chester?" Abby called, and immediately realized her mistake as the dog turned and spotted her. Without further encouragement, the grimy animal hopped up and galloped toward her.

Soon, Abby was flat on her back, covered in mud and dog slobber.

"Chester!" a displeased voice commanded.

Instantly, the dog was off her. She sat up, and used the sleeve of her jacket to wipe the dirt and saliva from her face.

Unsure what to do, she sat there for a moment. She dreaded facing the owner of that irritated voice. For almost a week, she had managed to avoid Chase, but it appeared her luck had run out. And, if she had to see Chase again, this wasn't exactly the way she wanted to meet him—flat on her bottom, covered in goo.

"Here, let me help you up."

Slowly, Abby eyes traveled up him, noting the nice fit of his faded jeans and white T-shirt on the way to his face. A tool belt sat low on his narrow hips, and his lips turned down at the corners as he looked at her. He extended his hand.

Reluctantly, she accepted it, and felt a pang of embarrassment as mud, dried grass and fur squished between their palms.

"Are you okay?" he asked, after she was on her feet.

She looked down at herself. Splotches of dirt marred the cream wool of her trousers and blazer. And her cheeks still felt sticky from the combination of mud and dog drool.

"I'm fine," she managed, then noticed that two faces were peeking around Chase's legs. One was furry, the other freckled, and both looked guilty as sin.

Abby couldn't help but laugh. "Okay, I recognize one of the mud monsters, but who's the other one?"

* * *

Her reaction startled Chase. He had expected Abby to be livid, and who could blame her. From the looks of it, her suit—a very expensive suit if he had to guess—was ruined. The contents of her briefcase were scattered around the driveway, and she was likely going to have a sore bottom from Chester bowling her over.

But instead, she stood there giggling, a delighted expression on her mud-smudged face.

Chase simply stared at her for a moment. She looked absolutely lovely. Laughter danced her eyes, and the curve of her wide mouth seemed to gentle the angles of her face.

After several moments, she must have decided he wasn't going to answer, because she leaned down and grinned at the small boy hugging his left leg.

"And who are you?"

The boy hid his face against Chase's outer thigh and mumbled, "Willy."

Abby squatted down and offered her muddied hand to the child. "Well, I'm Abby. And I must say, I've never had a greeting like that before."

Willy pressed his face harder against Chase's leg and muttered, "Sorry."

Abby reached forward and ruffled Willy's disheveled, matted hair. "I'm sorry that I screamed. I thought you were a big old newt coming out of hibernation."

Willy looked up at her, his blue eyes seeming to swallow up his entire face. "What's a newt?"

"It's an animal sort of like a salamander."

"I like salamanders," Willy told her.

"So do I," Abby agreed wholeheartedly.

Willy looked impressed.

Chase reached down and patted the boy's narrow shoulder. "Okay, Willy, apologize to Ms. Stepp once more, and let's get you cleaned up. Your mother will have my head if I send you home looking like that."

"I'm sorry," Willy said, this time offering Abby a regretful smile.

"No problem, Willy. Mud happens."

"Yes, it does," Willy agreed with a wide smile that showed his missing front teeth.

"Are you really okay?" Chase asked, studying her, trying to see any bumps or bruises.

"I'm fine," she assured him. Some of the softness she showed Willy faded. "Nothing soap and water can't fix."

Chase cast a dubious look at her suit.

She followed his gaze and added with a shrug, "And maybe a really good dry cleaner."

Chase was amazed at her calmness. He'd expected her to be furious. Especially since it had been his dog and his charge that had caused such a disaster. He couldn't help noticing that she had been avoiding him for the past week. This incident wouldn't win her over.

"Should those papers be blowing away?" Willy asked, in the matter-of-fact voice that only a seven-year-old can use.

Both Abby and Chase looked behind them and saw the papers from Abby's briefcase fluttering toward the street.

"Oh no!" she cried, dashing toward the papers.

Chase caught her arm and gestured toward her muddied hands. "I'll get them."

He swiftly gathered the white sheets, relieved to see that not many had been caught by the wind. Once he had collected them all, he straightened them out, careful not to bend the corners. The white pages were covered with words and drawings, none of which Chase could understand.

Abby had picked up her leather case. "Thank you,"

she said with relief. "That's all the information for an article I'm writing."

Chase nodded. "I figured they were important. Let me bring them inside. I don't want you to get mud all over everything."

Abby hesitated and then offered him an appreciative smile. "That would be helpful."

Chase followed her onto the porch and waited while Abby searched for her house key. After a few moments, she let out an irritated groan.

"What?" he asked.

"I left the key in my desk drawer at the lab."

"That's no problem, I'll give you a ride over there to pick it up."

"No, it's too far." She pulled back the sleeve of her now brown suit to check her watch. "And Ellie should be home any minute."

He didn't like the idea of Abby just sitting on the porch in the waning light as she waited for Ellie to arrive.

"Well, at least come to my house and wait. Your clothes are damp, and the air is starting to get nippy."

Hesitation shadowed Abby's eyes.

"I promise I'll be a complete gentleman. And Willy's going to be there too," he assured her.

Abby started to refuse, but Chase shook his head. "I'm not taking no for an answer. My dog assaulted you. The least I can do is offer you a hot cup of coffee and a place to wait."

Abby didn't answer for a second, then gave him an adorably wistful look. "Coffee?"

"Fresh brewed."

"Okay," she agreed.

Chase reached out and took her briefcase. He slipped the papers into it and slid the strap over his shoulder.

"Come on, Willy. I think there's a shower with your name on it."

Willy looked up from petting Chester and groaned. Then a hopeful expression lit his face. "Can Chester take a shower too?"

"Yes," Chase said. "But his will be outside and involve a hose."

Willy groaned again, but fell into step with him and Abby as they crossed the street.

Abby had to admit she was torn. She didn't think it was a good idea to spend any time in the presence of Chase Jordan. But darn it, she really, really wanted to.

She had managed to avoid him over the past week, but that was only in the physical sense. He had been on her mind more often than she cared to admit. And she had relived their kiss so many times that she had it as committed to memory as the basics of meiosis and mitosis.

As she followed him up the steps of the porch, she realized she had plenty of other things about the man memorized, too. The fullness of his lower lip. The shape of the dimple in his left cheek. The rich, enticing sound of his laugh, and the way that laughter filled his voice and made her feel included in his happiness.

That same quality laced his words now as he spoke with Willy. "So how exactly did you manage to get so covered?"

Willy glanced up at him and said with great earnestness, "I think mud spreads. It started on my feet and somehow got all the way to my head."

Chase plucked a large clump of the wet dirt from the little boy's hair. "It certainly did. Good thing I found you, or it would have spread right from you to the whole neighborhood." He looked toward Abby and winked.

Abby wondered who the little boy was and how Chase had come to watch him. Their affectionate demeanor showed that Chase had taken care of Willy before. They seemed to have a bond, a true attachment.

"Are you going to come inside? Or do I really make you that uncomfortable?"

Abby blinked, and she realized she was just standing on the porch, staring at the two of them.

"Coming?" he prompted, pushing the door open with one arm, waving her inside with the other. Willy waited on the other side of the door, throwing confused looks between the two adults.

Abby cleared her throat. "Yes."

She walked past the two of them and into the dimly lit front hallway.

"Why do you make her uncomfortable?" she heard Willy whisper.

She couldn't hear Chase's response, and realized he must not have answered when Willy added, "Chase, I think it's the mud and not you that's making her uncomfortable."

"The mud probably isn't helping," Chase agreed in a low voice, and Abby had to smile.

She turned to look at Chase. He offered her a weak smile. "Let me show you to the kitchen."

Abby knew where the room was from years spent here while her grandmother and Old Miss Strout had played cribbage, but she simply followed Chase down the hallway.

When Chase flipped on the kitchen light, Abby would have sworn she had never seen this room before in her life. The kitchen that Abby remembered had been dim and dingy. This kitchen was bright and tidy.

The walls were now painted a sunny shade of yellow with the molding done in a crisp white. The old, cracked linoleum had been replaced with hardwood planks that looked new, yet still fit the old-fashioned style of the kitchen. The room was lovely.

Abby must have made a surprised noise, because all three males—yes, even Chester—stared at her.

"Did you redo this?"

Chase looked around him and then back to her, pride in his eyes. "Yes. I think it turned out pretty good, even if I do say so myself."

"It's beautiful."

Chase went over to the round maple table that was situated in the center of the room and pulled out a chair. "Have a seat, and let me get that coffee started."

Abby hesitated.

"I swear, I'll be on my very best behavior," Chase said with a reassuring smile.

"It's not that," she said and turned so he could see the muddy mess that saturated the back of her slacks. "I don't think you want me to sit on your furniture."

Chase stopped scooping coffee grounds into the basket of the coffeemaker and brushed his hands on his jeans. "Okay, it looks like both of you need a bath."

"I'm not taking a bath with a girl," Willy said firmly, his jaw set and his eyes flinty.

Chase shot Abby an amused glance before addressing the little boy's ardent declaration. "Okay, why don't we let Abby get her bath first. And you can help me bathe Chester before you get yours."

The suggestion was obviously quite agreeable as Willy let out a whoop and ran to drag a suspicious Chester outside.

"Stay in the backyard," Chase called after them.

"Okay."

As Chase watched the boy and dog leave, a fondness glittered in his eyes. Abby didn't feel quite so cheerful.

"I don't need to take a bath."

Cocking an eyebrow, Chase scanned her from the top of her head to the tips of her toes. His gaze was leisurely and the slight smile on his lips made her feel jittery and . . . warm.

"I'd hate to see how dirty you'd have to get before you did consider yourself in need of a bath."

Abby blushed. Here she was a bundle of nerves under his slow perusal, and he was just seeing a woman in desperate need of water and a bar of soap.

"Listen, there's no need to be so twitchy," he said. "You've got to be cold."

"My sister will be home any minute."

Chase shrugged. "Okay. I'll make you that coffee."

Abby watched him for a moment as he finished filling the coffeemaker and moved to the sink to fill the pot with water.

A chill ran down her spine, and she had to admit her clothing was a little cold and clammy. She wrapped her arms around herself and began wandering around the room.

It really was beautiful, although she wouldn't have imagined it could ever look this way. In fact, she recalled all the rooms in the old house as being rather cramped and dark. Perhaps it was because Old Miss Strout had been a pack rat and not much of a housekeeper.

Chase seemed to be quite a good housekeeper. The kitchen was spotless—with the exception of the mud that Willy and Chester had trailed into the room. She looked down; her loafers were also caked with dirt. She grimaced.

"Don't worry about it," Chase said, leaning against the counter, arms folded across his broad chest, watching her.

Abby stopped, and she could feel a blush heat her damp skin. "I'm making a terrible mess."

"Nothing that won't clean up."

Abby looked down at the dirty floor again and then back up to see that he was still watching her. She shivered.

He frowned and pushed away from the counter. "This is ridiculous. You're freezing." He caught her arm and tugged her out of the kitchen.

The next thing Abby knew she was upstairs standing in the doorway of what appeared to be Chase's bedroom. The shades were drawn and the room was cast in shadows, but she could make out the shape of a four-poster bed and a large bureau. Chase rummaged around in the dimness.

"Here," he finally said, returning to her and holding out what appeared to be a robe. "Let me show you to the bathroom, and you can take a shower."

Abby hesitated again, then accepted the bathrobe.

Chase smiled. A hint of triumph flashed in his eyes like the glint of sunshine off the ocean.

Abby nearly handed the robe back, but decided the reaction would be childish. She *was* cold, and surely taking a quick shower wouldn't lead to anything improper. She was a grown woman, and in charge of all her emotions and desires.

"Lead the way," she said with more poise than she felt.

Chase directed her across the hall, opened a door and flipped on the light.

"The towels are in the cabinet to the left of the sink."

Abby nodded, but remained rooted in place. After a moment, she gathered her wits and stepped into the room. It appeared completely remodeled too. A footed bathtub waited very invitingly on the far side of the room.

"Yell if you need anything."

"Okay." She started to close the door, but Chase's hand stopped it. She looked at him questioningly.

"You'll be glad to note there's a lock on the door." Laughter danced in his eyes.

Abby fought the urge to stick her tongue out at him.

Instead she pushed the door shut and firmly turned the lock. She could hear his footfalls and his deep, enchanting laughter as he went downstairs.

Chase's smile faded as he reached the bottom step. He was finding it damned hard to mask his desire for Abby. But he didn't want to scare her off. She always looked like she was ready to dart as it was. He couldn't imagine how she would react if she realized exactly how much he wanted her.

There was something about her that was so enticing. Far more so than any woman he'd met in years. But he just couldn't place his finger on what it was about her that was so alluring.

Physically, she was definitely striking, but he'd been with women that were prettier. Then he recalled how she'd felt in his arms. She'd been so warm, so responsive. Other women might be prettier, but no woman had ever set him ablaze with a single kiss. A kiss he very much wanted to repeat.

He went to the back door and watched Willy throwing a stick for Chester, although his mind wasn't on the romping dog and laughing boy.

She was forbidden fruit, and he wasn't the kind of guy who found those types of games interesting. In fact, he found her attachment to another man quite a nuisance. Maybe if she wasn't seeing Nelson, he might have a chance with her.

No, he didn't have a chance in hell. She was here for one reason, and one reason only. To work on her research. She'd made it abundantly clear that Millbrook was the last place on earth she wanted to be. And her old classmates were the last people on earth she wanted to interact with. He got the distinct impression he was at the top of that list.

But there were moments—brief, fleeting moments—when he thought she almost liked him. Or she at least liked things that were associated with him. She liked yellow kitchens. And fresh-brewed coffee. And muddy dogs and children.

And she had to like his kiss—she couldn't possibly respond like she had if she thoroughly hated him.

"Damn," he muttered and swiped a hand through his hair. *She's not interested. She's taken. Let it go.*

A small noise behind him caused him to glance over his shoulder. Abby stood at the foot of the stairs, her tall frame engulfed in his thick robe.

Slowly he turned, stunned at how incredible she looked with her wet hair curling slightly around her face and her cheeks pink from the steam of the shower. With all traces of makeup washed away, he could see a dusting of freckles across her nose. It somehow made her wide mouth appear lusher.

"You look amazing." The words were out before he could stop them.

Abby's gaze dropped to the floor, and the pink of her cheeks darkened.

Chase knew he shouldn't, but he found himself walking over to her. Just like his feet, his hand seemed to have a mind of its own. He reached up to touch her damp hair. The dark tendrils curled around his fingers, and he could smell his shampoo in its silkiness.

His shampoo. Possessiveness filled him—as if his scent and his clothing marked her as his.

Abby lifted her head, and as he expected, she looked apprehensive. Then her gaze strayed to his mouth. Yearning mingled with uneasiness in the depths of her dark brown eyes.

His reaction was immediate. Searing hot lightning shot through his body and straight to his groin. Without further thought, he knotted his hand in her hair and pulled her lips to his.

He could tell from the stiffness of her spine that he had shocked her. Then a small moan reverberated from her mouth to his, and suddenly she was returning the kiss just as eagerly. Her lips molded to his, and her fingers dug into his sides, the heat of her palms burning through his T-shirt.

A groan rumbled deep in his chest.

He released her hair and brought both hands to the sides of her face. His thumbs stroked the soft, dewy skin of her cheeks, and his tongue brushed the hot, tender flesh of her mouth.

"Chase?" The faint, uncertain voice was like a bucket of ice water over his head. He released Abby and spun around to find Willy looking at them, a confused frown creasing his small brow.

"Willy." Chase felt like he been caught doing something far more scandalous than kissing Abby.

Of course, he felt far more aroused than a mere kiss should have made him. He cleared his throat. "What's going on, buddy?"

"My mom's here," he said, his eyes straying back and forth between Chase and Abby.

For the first time, Chase noticed that Willy's mother was indeed there, leaning in the kitchen doorway, her eyes also moving from him to Abby and back. But unlike

Willy's puzzled expression, his mother's look stated she understood altogether too well what was going on.

"Summer-Ann, you're early."

Chapter 8

"Not early enough from the looks of it," Summer-Ann said as she pushed away from the door frame and moved to place her hands on her son's shoulders. "Are you going to introduce me to your friend?"

Abby fought the urge to wipe her lips on the sleeve of Chase's robe. Instead she stared at her toes, peeking out from under the puddle of the hem. She'd been discovered kissing Chase by Willy and, of all people, Summer-Ann Bouffard.

Ellie had said Chase was no longer dating Summer-Ann, but Abby couldn't shake the feeling that she'd been caught kissing Summer-Ann's boyfriend.

"Umm, you remember Abby Stepp," Chase said, shifting slightly. He ran a hand through his dark hair and appeared to feel as guilty as she did.

Summer-Ann's cat-like green eyes widened a fraction, but then she smiled. Even though years had passed, Abby still remembered that smile as though she had seen it yesterday.

"Abby Stepp. I can't believe I didn't recognize you." Summer-Ann tilted her head, wisps of honey-blond hair falling across her cheek.

Funny, Abby would have known *her* immediately. She still had a dazzling smile and an even more stunning figure. The only things that had changed were the small creases on either side of her mouth that didn't show her age as much as showcased her flawless lips.

"Wait," Summer-Ann said, "you don't wear those huge glasses anymore. And your hair," she brushed back her own, "are you dying it or something?"

Abby stared at her for a moment. "No, I'm not."

Summer-Ann shrugged. "Well, you *do* look different. Doesn't she, Chase?"

Chase looked distinctly uncomfortable. "You probably want to be heading home."

Summer-Ann started to open her mouth, then looked at Willy and nodded. "Yes. I need to get Willy supper and ready for school tomorrow."

"Let me get his stuff," Chase said, escaping down the hallway.

Abby breathed in deeply and crossed her arms over her chest as if she could hide that fact she was wearing Chase's robe.

"Willy, why don't you go say good-bye to Chester," Summer-Ann suggested, still scrutinizing Abby.

The little boy dashed out of the house, happily calling the dog's name.

Abby wished she could so easily flee. She gripped her elbows tighter and silently prayed for Chase to return.

"So how long have you and Chase been . . . What *are* you and he doing, exactly?"

"We aren't doing anything." Abby realized her answer sounded incredibly lame given the position Summer-Ann had found them in.

"Oh." The one word was rich with disbelief.

"Here's Willy's backpack," Chase said as he came back down the hall. He shoved the bag at Summer-Ann, not concealing his desire for her to leave.

"Well, I guess I'll probably see you around," Summer-Ann said. She didn't sound pleased by the idea.

Abby didn't get a chance to respond before Chase caught Summer-Ann's arm and led her toward the door. "I think you should get Willy home. He got in a mud war with Chester, and I imagine he's starting to get a little chilly."

The door swung closed behind them.

Abby sagged against the banister. What was she doing? She needed to go home and avoid Chase and everyone else in this godforsaken town.

She started to leave, when Summer-Ann's voice stopped her in her tracks.

"Abby Stepp! What are you thinking?" The words were clear even through the closed door.

Abby heard the rumbling of Chase's voice but couldn't make out his words.

"It's bad enough that you're ignoring Willy. He's outside alone, muddy and wet to the bone," Summer-Ann said, her voice rising with her irritation, "and you're inside making out with Abby Stepp. One of the ugly Stepp sisters."

Bile rose in the back of Abby's throat. That awful nickname. Would she ever be free of that title? Free of the pain it evoked?

She blindly began to move down the hall, but was halted once more, this time by Chase's voice.

"Don't say that again." Harshness deepened his words to a low ominous rumble. "We're too damned old to be calling people silly adolescent names."

Abby let out the breath she had been holding. Nausea roiled her stomach again. *They were too old.* Not, she wasn't ugly. Not, she had become a different person from that shy, awkward young girl. No, simply, they were too old, and adults didn't say such things.

"Sugar, all I'm saying is, if you're lonely, I'm here for you. I always will be." The irritation had left Summer-Ann's voice, replaced by a sweet purr.

There was silence. Abby could picture Chase pulling Summer-Ann into his arms, his lips locking with hers, just like she had seen them do a hundred times before in the hallways of Millbrook High.

Unconsciously, her fingers strayed to her own mouth. She could still taste him on her lips, on her tongue.

"Summer, take Willy home. I'll see you tomorrow." He didn't sound like a man who had just finished kissing a beautiful woman. Instead, he sounded weary.

She couldn't make out Summer-Ann's response, but a few seconds later, Abby heard her call to Willy.

Another second passed and the door opened. Chase stepped inside. Abby remained glued to the spot with her arms clasped tightly around herself again.

"Sorry." Chase offered a weak smile.

She held up a hand and shook her head. "Don't apologize. I think we already established that friendship isn't an option we should be pursuing."

He watched her for a second, then walked toward her slowly. His deliberate movements gave Abby the distinct impression of being stalked. Her arms tightened around her waist, but she held her ground.

Stopping only inches from her, he studied her again. His expression was unreadable.

Just when she would have spoken to break the unnerving silence, he lifted his hand to stroke her cheek. The roughened pads of his fingers strummed over her skin, playing the sensitive nerve endings in a deliciously sensual song. She fought the urge to lean into his touch, but couldn't stop her eyes from closing, so she could simply focus on his touch.

"I'm not sorry for kissing you," he murmured, his lips near her ear. His warm breath tickled her neck and sent a wave of desire to her belly. "I'm just extremely sorry that we got interrupted."

The last of his sentence was mumbled against her lips, and again, Abby found herself caught against the solidness of Chase's chest and sweetness of his mouth.

She snaked her hands between their bodies, running her fingers over the flatness of his stomach to rest on the hard muscles of his chest. She clasped the front of his shirt and rose on her toes to return the pressure of his kiss.

He groaned and moved the hand on her cheek to hold the back of her head. His other arm slipped around her back and pulled her tightly against him.

He surrounded her, his mouth, his hands, his strength. The experience was heady and absolutely wonderful.

When she shifted to get her arms around his neck, a thickness prodded against her belly. She gasped and arched harder against him.

Chase let out a sharp grunt and pulled away from her.

Abby swayed and then opened her eyes in bewilderment.

Chase stood with his hands on his sides, bent forward. His breath came in harsh, short bursts.

Abby leaned forward to peer at him and noticed his face was a bit pale.

"Are—are you all right?" she asked concerned, but also afraid that he was overwhelmed with her forwardness. Heaven knows, she was.

He held up his hand, bowed over a little further, and took a deep breath. After a few agonizingly long moments, he straightened.

Abby expected to see disgust in his eyes, but instead he offered her a sheepish grin that deepened his dimple and said, "Let's make a note to remove my tool belt before we get this hot and heavy again. You may get me hard as nails, but a hammer is definitely harder."

Abby's gaze fell to his waist, and she saw his tool belt had indeed shifted into a dangerous position.

"Oh dear," was all she could think to say.

"Don't worry. I don't think there was any permanent damage done," he said as he unbuckled the belt. "But maybe we should double check."

The tools thudded loudly as the belt landed on a mat in front of the back door. The noise caused the reality of the situation to slam down around Abby. She was acting like a sex-crazed teen. She stared at the discarded tool belt, trying to gather her scattered wits. This wasn't who she was. Abby Stepp did not act impulsively. She was not ruled by her emotions. This whole scene was a momentary lapse in reason.

When Chase was about to pull her against him again, she held up a hand to stop him. "Chase." Her voice was low. "What are we doing?"

He offered her a sexy little grin. "Well, we were kissing, and I was enjoying myself very much."

She took a deep breath. "I can't do this."

He looked like he was going to argue, then he sobered. After a moment, he asked, "Nelson?"

Abby nodded and said flatly, "Nelson. Amongst a lot of other things." She focused on his tool belt again. Several nails had fallen out of one of the pouches and were scattered on the floor. She needed to keep her mind centered on the things that were real. Her grant proposal. Work. Nelson. Even that damned tool belt. Unfortunately, other parts of her body seemed to have minds of their own that were far more powerful than her brain.

When she looked back at Chase, he was following her gaze. Then he wiped a hand over his face. When he turned his pale eyes to her again, all signs of flirtation were gone. In fact, he appeared almost angry.

"If there was no Nelson, would you still be saying no?"

The question startled Abby. She didn't know how to reply. She didn't understand why he was asking.

"There is a Nelson."

A muscle in his cheek jumped, and his eyes hardened. "But I have a feeling you would find different excuses—*amongst the other things,* as you mentioned."

Abby frowned. "Why are you acting this way? We both know this isn't real."

"Are you going to try and tell me you didn't feel anything when we kissed?"

"Yes," Abby said as heat crept up her cheeks, "yes, I felt something. But . . ." She couldn't find the right words.

She couldn't tell him that even if there was no Nelson, she could never picture herself with him. Chase was magnificent. In school, he had been the embodiment of beauty and life, and he still was. She could so easily lose herself in him. But he wouldn't ever be satisfied with her. She had intelligence, but she was unremarkable in every other way. In all the ways that would keep a man like Chase interested.

"We're too different."

Chase stared at her, and she felt pinned by piercing shards of crystal blue. Then he nodded. "Maybe. But I swear I felt something between us that could overcome our differences."

"I belong with Nelson."

"Why would I have ever thought otherwise?"

Abby didn't know exactly how he meant his last statement, but she wondered the same thing. Why would he want her?

"I think—I think I'd better leave."

Chase didn't respond.

"I'll return your robe later."

"Don't bother."

* * *

Chase watched as Abby gathered her clothes, shoved her feet in her muddy loafers and headed to the door, looking like a confused, blue terry cloth–covered duck.

He went to the window and watched her cross the street.

Why did the duck cross the road?

"To get the hell away from me," he muttered. He watched her long enough to see that Ellie was home. Letting the curtain fall back into place, he headed to the kitchen.

What the hell had come over him? Why had he acted like such a jackass?

That was simple. He'd acted like a jerk to protect his wounded pride. He'd been so hot and bothered by their kisses, and after both of them, she had seemed unaffected.

No, that wasn't strictly true. She definitely had been affected by his tool belt.

Now, he certainly didn't think the belt was the turn-on for her, and without it, she found him unappealing. No, quite the opposite. If Chase had to guess, she saw that work belt and remembered exactly what he was. A blue-collar stiff.

She was a brilliant scientist, and he pounded things with tools that had been around since the time of cavemen. Hmm, it was hardly a mystery why she'd gone from fiery to frosty in mere seconds.

Chase went to the coffeepot and started to fill a mug with the aromatic dark liquid. Changing his mind, he put the carafe back and went to the fridge to get a beer. He took a deep swallow and then looked at the bottle.

Abby was probably the fine wine type. Maybe even something as posh as martinis, or what were they called? Cosmopolitans. Hell, he didn't even know what that was exactly. Frankly, Chase liked his liquor cold and wet and in something a bit sturdier than a martini glass.

She was right; they were too different. Chase was just a regular Joe. He made good money, but he had to bust his back to earn it. His work didn't require brains, just brawn.

He'd never be a three-piece suit type. He'd never attend cocktail parties and chat about the arts or classical music or the latest novel he'd just read. The last play he'd seen had been Willy's second-grade Christmas pageant. His favorite musicians were the Beatles and the Eagles. And the last novel . . .

He let out a cynical snort. Was *Hop on Pop* considered classic literature?

He started to leave the kitchen, paused, went back to the refrigerator and grabbed another beer. Then he headed to the living room. Sinking into an overstuffed chair, he set the unopened beer on the coffee table and put his feet up beside it.

Truthfully, he didn't understand what he found so attractive about Abby anyway. She certainly wasn't his usual type. He normally went for blondes with naughty smiles and even naughtier bodies.

Naughty was not a word that applied to Abby. She was about as straightlaced as they came.

He took a sip of his beer and rested his head on the back of the chair. She might be straightlaced, but he'd definitely felt passion in their kiss. She had responded, and for at least a moment, she'd enjoyed it. He'd tasted pleasure on her lips and need in the way she'd run her hands over his chest.

Chase released an irritated groan as the memory caused his penis to press rather insistently against the zipper of his jeans.

He finished off the remainder of his beer and reached for the other one.

He needed to get laid. That was the only reasonable explanation for his reaction to Abby. This weekend he'd go find some willing woman, who was more his type, and get his sex drive back under control.

Summer-Ann's earlier offer came back to him. She would be more than willing to help him with his sexual urges. She was definitely a sexy woman. But he promptly dismissed the idea. They had too much past, and frankly her beauty was a bit over the top for him now. Her blond hair seemed too harsh and her mouth was too pouty. Even her figure was too curvy.

He really wanted someone less flashy and more classic. Someone with graceful beauty.

He closed his eyes and tried to conjure an image of his perfect woman. Her body . . . her body still had to have curves, but not quite as generous as he'd looked for in his youth. She needed to be more statuesque. More poised.

He always thought he was partial to blondes, but for some reason dark hair seemed more refined to him now. And dark eyes too. It was a rich, warm combination. And a wide mouth that looked inviting rather than pouty.

He let out another annoyed groan. His image of the ideal woman was the lady who just left here.

Considering that he wasn't her type and he was just a complete ass to her, Chase sort of doubted that she'd want to be the one to hop in the sack with him this weekend.

Chapter 9

If Ellie found it odd that Abby came home wearing only a man's bathrobe and muddy shoes, she didn't remark.

But in truth, she did find it quite strange and a bit unnerving. Unnerving enough that she didn't gather her wits quickly enough to question her sister.

Abby had wandered into the house and straight up to her bedroom with little more than a mumbled, "Hello."

After a few moments, Ellie set down the wooden spoon she was holding and followed, trying to be stealthy on the creaky staircase. Abby's bedroom door was shut, and Ellie raised a hand to knock.

But what if she wanted to be left alone? Abby obviously did want to be by herself, or she would have stopped to give Ellie an explanation.

Ellie moved her hand from the door and instead nibbled on her fingernail, contemplating what she should do next.

Before she could make up her mind, Abby opened the door. Her expression was as tranquil as the powder blue flowers on the flannel pajamas she now wore.

Ellie dropped her hand and offered her a discomfited smile. "Is everything okay?"

"Fine," she said, her voice exceedingly chipper. "Just a muddy run-in with Chester—and Willy."

Ellie nodded, trying not to frown. "Were you hurt?"

"Oh no, no, no." Abby waved the question away. "Just a few dirty clothes. That's all."

This time Ellie did frown. "Was Chase there?"

Abby shifted slightly, but her too-cheery smile didn't change. "Yes, he graciously offered me the use of his shower." She started toward the stairs.

"Are you *really* okay?"

Abby stopped at the question and turned to look at Ellie. This time her smile wasn't quite as fixed, and Ellie thought she saw distress in her eyes, but then she blinked and the emotion was gone.

"I'm fine. I really am."

Ellie studied her.

"I really, really am."

"You'd tell me, right?"

Abby nodded. Then she sniffed the air. "What's burning?"

Ellie squeaked and rushed to the stairs. "Darn it! That's my chowder! And I used real cream too."

Abby watched her sister race down the narrow staircase, greatly relieved that she left. Abby was finding it harder and harder to respond to Ellie's questions without showing her true feelings. But those feelings were there in abundance.

She was upset that Chase was angry with her. Confused about why. She was still aroused by his wonderful kisses, and terribly guilt-ridden that she wanted more. And above all, she was frustrated with herself for feeling any of these emotions.

She should be able to look at this whole situation sensibly. She and Chase were not suited. The kiss had been wrong, but she didn't have to tell Nelson. It was just a minor indiscretion. Nothing to get overwrought about. She should put the whole incident behind her, and be thankful that Chase was incensed, because it would make it much, much easier to avoid him. And if she avoided him, she'd forget the delicious way he tasted and the incredible way he felt against her.

Abby let out an aggravated moan. The goal—the prudent objective—was to stop thinking such things about Chase Jordan.

She started to march down the stairs but stopped again. She clutched the banister and struggled not to sigh forlornly.

Reasonably, how was she going to forget something as amazing as being kissed by Chase? It was unlike anything she'd ever experienced with Nelson. And she highly doubted she ever could share passion like that with Nelson.

No! That was not true. She cared for Nelson. They shared the same interests, the same background. She could talk to Nelson. Surely, two people with such common connections could generate real passion.

So they hadn't produced a lot of sparks in the past. They had always had a lot on their minds, but she intended to rectify that. She would call Nelson and convince him to come up for the weekend. A little time relaxing, enjoying the fresh air, walking along the coast—that was exactly what they needed to get some zest in their relationship.

She went downstairs, sat on the couch and dialed the rotary phone. The ring sounded twice, and Nelson answered with his usual harried manner. "Hello?"

"Hi Nelson. It's Abby."

"Abby? Yes, yes Abby. How are you?"

"I'm fine."

"How is research in the rustic North?"

"The lab is wonderful, fully equipped."

"I find that hard to believe." Nelson snorted, and Abby remembered one of the reasons—perhaps the most important reason—why she'd accepted this position.

"It's one of the nicest labs I've worked in, and my fellow scientists are some of the best."

Again, Nelson snorted. "Well, I'm happy you're satisfied. But I think we both have to agree that the DNA research I'm working on has far more potential. I can't believe you left my team to work on a far less significant study."

Abby gritted her teeth. They'd had this conversation a dozen times before she left, and she was annoyed to see he was still pressing the issue.

"But this study is aimed toward what I worked on at BU."

"Mmmm," Nelson murmured. "Did you call for any particular reason?"

Abby tried to refocus on her plan and let his galling superiority roll off her back. "I actually called to see if you could come up this weekend. You know, maybe we could go to one of the islands, sightsee, spend some time alone."

There was a pause, and then Nelson laughed, the sound dissonant over the telephone line. Abby held the receiver away from her ear.

"You've got to be kidding. You know I'm incredibly busy with my work. I can't take that kind of time away from the lab."

"Nelson, it's only a weekend. It would do you good." She hesitated and then added softly, "It would do us good."

"I think that clean Maine air is getting to you. It's making you giddy. There is just no way. In fact, your timing couldn't be worse. I just lost a research assistant, and that's really slowing the project down."

The line was silent for a moment and then he said with some enthusiasm, "Why don't you come back here?"

Abby wasn't prepared to do that. She knew they would need to get away from everything to kindle something between them. But it did make her feel better to know he wanted to see her, too.

"You can help out until I find another assistant," he said with great practicality. "After all, you do know the research and that would get us back on track much quicker."

Abby fought the urge to slam down the phone. "I'm staying here, Nelson."

"Well, that's your choice. Listen, I really have to go. I need to get some yeasts out of the incubator. Talk with you later."

Before she could say good-bye, the line went dead.

Abby sat there for a moment, waiting for hurt, disappointment, even anger to wash over her. But none of them did.

She only had the dawning realization that Nelson wasn't the love of her life. She'd been much happier when she believed such an entity didn't exist anyway.

"So where are the hot parties this weekend?" Chase asked Mason as he searched his toolbox for a pair of pliers.

Mason looked up from peering into Helen's filthy engine. "What would the mayor know about hot parties?"

"You've got to have some inside info."

Mason smiled. "You'd think, wouldn't you?" He took the pliers from Chase and started loosening a bolt holding the air filter in place. "I think we're too old to go to hot parties anymore. I think we now run the risk of looking either pathetic or pervy. Or both."

Chase rummaged through the toolbox. "So nothing is going on this weekend?"

"Well, there's the CrabFest over in Boone's Harbor."

Chase looked skeptical. "I don't know. I think it's best to stay away from an event with that name. Far, far away."

"Don't knock it. They crown the Crab Queen," Mason said with a knowing look.

"I don't want to contemplate how a lady wins that title." Chase chuckled. "This is Maine, anyway. Why isn't it a lobster festival?"

Mason shrugged. "I guess one crustacean is as good as another. Hey, do you know what they say about the beauty queens?"

Chase started to respond, but a silver sedan pulling into the driveway across the street captured his attention.

Abby got out of the car. She was dressed in a suit similar to the one Chester ruined the other day. Except this one was light blue and accentuated the indentation of her waist and the gentle curve of her bottom to a T.

Chase looked down, and with guilty determination, began rifling through his tools.

Mason let out a low whistle, and Chase jerked his head back up to make sure Abby hadn't heard it. She had disappeared into her house.

"So that's the notorious Abby Stepp. You're right—she doesn't wear her hair in a bun anymore."

Chase grunted and held up an air filter.

Mason took it and turned back to Helen. After a few loud bangs and a couple terse words, he asked, "So I take it things didn't go well after your kiss?"

"What?" Chase's asked, unable to keep the shock out of his voice.

"The kiss?"

Chase stared at his friend. Which one? Wait, how did Mason know about them kissing?

"I hear Abby wasn't wearing anything but your bathrobe and a smile."

"I don't recall the smile," Chase said wryly. "How on earth do you know about that?"

"You don't kiss and tell, do you?" Mason shook his head. "No, you don't. But Summer-Ann sure does. Or at least she tells about other people's kisses."

Chase groaned. "What did she say?"

"Well, I officially heard it from Ginny."

Mason's secretary was a disgrace to any phrase containing the word "secret."

"But the main gist was that you were supposed to be watching Willy, but instead, you were playing kissy-face with one of those awful Stepp sisters. Both Ginny and Summer-Ann thought it was appalling—and very bizarre."

Chase released an irritated sigh. "These are the times when I hate living in a small town."

"Imagine if you had to work with Ginny every day."

"I do have to work with Summer-Ann."

Mason cringed. "You win."

Chase flipped closed the lid of his toolbox and joined Mason to stare into the old truck's engine.

"So was the kiss hot or what?" Mason asked abruptly.

"It was pretty hot."

Mason nodded and looked back at the truck. "Then why are you looking for a party?"

"So I can forget how hot Abby's kiss was."

Mason nodded again and reached in to the motor to check the tightness of the air filter.

"So we're going to the CrabFest?"

Chase blew out a pent-up breath and said with little enthusiasm, "Yeah, we're going to the CrabFest."

* * *

"The entire lab attends each year. There's food and music. It's a wonderful way to enjoy each other's company and talk about things other than mouse genome sequencing or induced mutations or any other aspect of our work."

Abby nodded and smiled, and wondered why she was surprised by Dr. Keene's suggestion. He was different from so many of the scientists she'd worked with. He was brilliant and successful at his work, but he was interested in other aspects of life outside of his own research.

He loved his family and his friends. He enjoyed painting and reading. He collected stamps. And apparently he really liked a good crab festival.

"So can we count you in?" he asked, his eyes filled with anticipation.

"Of course," Abby said, with as much enthusiasm as she could muster. He was so excited, she hated to give the impression she didn't share in his eagerness.

"Wonderful. Wonderful! We'll meet at the Boone's Harbor Park at four on Saturday. The entertainment doesn't really get going until evening."

Abby nodded and watched her boss wander off to merrily invite all the other employees.

Abby returned to adjusting her microscope, but her mind wasn't on the cells magnified in the lens. She was actually finding herself feeling relieved that she had something to do this weekend. With Nelson's curt refusal to visit, she was feeling restless and at loose ends.

And she was also feeling a bit like a stalker. Over the past week, she couldn't count how many times she had gone to the windows of her house, hoping to catch a glimpse of Chase.

She had seen him working on Helen a few days after the shower incident. She'd been coming home from work, but when she looked over to say hi, he'd been searching for something in his toolbox. So she'd gone inside without speaking.

Several days later, she saw him again from her bedroom window. He was in the yard, using a circular saw to cut a large sheet of wood braced on two sawhorses. He had his shirt off, and as he maneuvered the heavy tool through the wood, Abby could see the expansion and contraction of muscles across his back and broad shoulders. The sheen of sweat glistening on his tanned skin made him look like a gilded statue come to life.

Abby had forced herself to leave the window, but the memory haunted her dreams and added to her agitation.

Maybe a crab festival was just the thing to get her mind off both Nelson and Chase. Work certainly wasn't the refuge it usually was, she thought, with no small amount of derision as she realized she had been staring into an unfocused microscope for the last several minutes.

She could only hope that food, music and crabs got her brain back to its usual functioning state.

Abby discovered several things about the CrabFest that she had been reluctant to believe. First, the food was excellent. Second, the music was very good. And third, she was having a great time.

She stood among a crowd at the bandstand. A quartet of middle-aged musicians bopped on the stage, enjoying themselves and the classic rock they were playing.

Abby watched them with a grin on her lips, from time to time taking bites of a crab roll. The sun had started to set. The sinking orb reflected off the harbor and cast the crowd in brilliant reds and oranges. But even with the loss of light, the air was still unseasonably warm.

"Aren't they great?" Leslie, one of Abby's colleagues, yelled to her over the music. The small woman looked like she belonged at Woodstock with her salt-and-pepper hair pulled into a long braid and her blue batik sundress swishing over the top of her brown Birkenstocks.

Abby nodded, her mouth full of sandwich.

"My husband is just so groovy," Leslie crowed, grinning from ear to ear and bouncing up and down to the beat.

Leslie's "groovy" husband was one of the guitarists on the stage. He hopped in a similar fashion to his wife, plucking away at a bass guitar, which sat lopsidedly against his protruding belly. The last remnants of the fading light glowed scarlet off his balding head.

Abby grinned. He *was* pretty groovy.

"Oh," Leslie breathed, once the song finished. "That was wonderful. I feel like I'm seventeen again." She wagged her fingers coyly toward her husband.

Abby wasn't sure if it was the glinting light or not, but she could swear Leslie's husband blushed as he waved back.

"Let's get some beer," Leslie said, grabbing Abby's arm and tugging her toward one of the stands.

"Isn't this fabulous," Leslie stated, rather than asked, as they reached the line at the ale booth.

Abby nodded and surveyed the animated crowd. "It's much better than I imagined."

"You've never been before?"

"No."

Leslie looked stunned. "Really? Gosh, my family came every year, rain or shine."

Abby frowned. "I thought you grew up in New Jersey?"

"I did. But my aunt lived over in West Hill, so we spent a lot of time here." Leslie got a reminiscent look that Abby couldn't miss despite the narrowness of her tortoise-shell glasses. "When I was young, how I wished I lived here. I'd cry every summer when we had to go back to Jersey."

"I've heard New Jersey is pretty bad, but I had no idea," Abby said laughingly.

Leslie returned her chuckle. "No, Jersey isn't bad. It's just that nothing can compare to here. It's utopia."

Abby couldn't hide her disbelieving look. "I guess it's different if you grow up here." She stepped up and placed an order for the CrabFest Special, which was a huge, plastic tumbler of beer with a gummy crab bobbing in the bottom.

"Make that two," Leslie said and then turned back to Abby. "You didn't love living here? All this ocean air and natural beauty and friendly people."

Abby nearly choked on her beer. Millbrook and friendly—those weren't two words she'd ever thought to use together.

"Again, I think it's different when you grow up here."

Leslie's brow creased. She obviously didn't like having her nirvana tainted by Abby's censorious opinion. But she didn't say anything as she picked up her beer, and they headed back to the stage.

They sipped their drinks and waited for the band to start again. Abby glanced at Leslie, noticing that the woman's earlier enthusiasm had waned.

"So, did you meet Herb here?" Abby hoped the change of subject would erase the tension.

It worked. Leslie grinned. "Oh, no, we met in junior high and actually dated for six months or some silly thing like that. We were all of twelve, so dating is a relative term. Then his family moved to New York. And would you believe that when I was registering for my freshman classes at NYU, he was standing behind me in line. We started dating a week later, and here we are today."

Abby smiled deeply. "Destiny."

"Destiny." Leslie nodded.

Abby took a sip of beer, the smile still not leaving her

lips. She gazed over the milling people. But her relaxed perusal stopped when she encountered a pair of eyes watching her. Even in the disappearing light, she knew they were the pale blue of ice-cold aquamarines.

She swallowed her beer and her smile faded.

"You know," Leslie's voice caused Abby to return her attention to the petite woman, "the funny thing about destiny is that you can't predict it, and you can't prevent it."

When Abby looked back, Chase had vanished with the sunlight.

Chapter 10

"No, no, no," Mason said emphatically, steering Chase to the other side of the bandstand. "We didn't come here to moon over the unobtainable neighbor. We're here to find ourselves some easy women who aren't our neighbors."

Chase raised an eyebrow in Mason's direction.

"Well, my neighbor is the Widow Peters." Mason shuddered. "Please let me never be that desperate."

Chase shook his head. "I don't think she'd be interested in you either. She's more concerned with her twenty-eight parakeets."

"Yeah, what is the deal with all those birds? It's creepy."

"She's actually very nice."

"She is," Mason agreed.

"Crab roll and beer?"

"Sounds good."

The two men got their food and drinks and sat at a picnic table set up to the right of the bandstand, near the water. Millbrook's chief rock act, The Wicked Excellent Orchestra, played the beginning licks of *Smoke on the Water*.

Chase scanned the crowd, telling himself he wasn't looking for anyone in particular.

"Stop it."

Chase looked back at Mason. "Stop what?" he asked innocently.

"She's evil. All women are, but we're looking for the least evil ones who will put out."

"How did you get to be mayor, anyway?"

"It's a mystery, isn't it?" Mason smiled with his full campaigning charm, then took a bite of his roll.

Chase chuckled and took a swallow of his beer.

"Hi, boys," a voice purred from the vicinity of Chase's right ear.

Chase had to fight the urge to groan. "Hello, Summer-Ann," he said over his shoulder, without turning to look at her.

"What are two such fine-looking gentlemen doing here without dates?"

Mason masked his snort by taking a drink of beer.

"Where's Willy tonight?"

"Angie's babysitting. He was here earlier today with a friend. I needed a little adult time." She touched Chase's shoulder.

Chase didn't react.

She sat down beside him on the picnic bench, facing out toward the crowd. "I've seen a lot of old classmates here," she said casually. "I even saw Abby Stepp."

Chase didn't respond, except to take another drink of beer.

"I was surprised she wasn't with you."

Chase offered her an indifferent smile. "Well, she isn't."

"You came to your senses?"

Chase shifted to face her and pinned her with a hard look. "Is there any point to this conversation?"

Summer-Ann shrugged with a goading little grin. "I guess not. I just wanted to stop and say hi."

"Hi."

Summer-Ann rose and tugged at the tight-fitting white T she wore. The movement exposed a wide vee of cleavage. "See you on Monday, Chase. Bye, boys."

She sauntered away.

Mason watched her go. "She looks great, but she's definitely evil."

"Definitely."

Abby was feeling a bit peculiar. Leslie and a few of her other co-workers kept buying rounds of the CrabFest Specials, and she'd long since lost track of the amount she had consumed. Four, maybe five. Definitely no more than six.

Leslie's husband's band had been on a break, but now they headed back onstage.

Abby liked them. She liked oldies.

"Yea!" she shouted as they took their places on the platform. She raised her tumbler along with Leslie and the others.

She felt herself blush at her silly behavior, but she looked at her co-workers and figured if they were acting foolish then it was okay for her, too.

Even Dr. and Mrs. Keene had been cheering. No, not Dr. Keene . . . Cecil. Cecil and . . . Adele. They'd been dancing all evening.

"It's too bad Nelson couldn't be here for this." Leslie's remark stopped her cold.

Abby lowered her cup, suddenly feeling very ridiculous and self-conscious. Nelson would never do this. And he would think she was childish for acting this way.

And there was no way on earth that he would drink a beverage with a gelatinous lump of candy stuck to the bottom of it.

Abby took a gulp of her drink. "Nelson wouldn't enjoy this."

Leslie nodded. "Well, then it's *not* too bad that he isn't here."

"No, it's not," Abby said with a huge grin. She didn't want to think about Nelson's reaction to her behavior. She wanted to dance.

Suddenly the band stopped their tuning and started to play. Abby whooped and began to boogie.

Chase was relieved to have lost Mason's company. His friend had won the attention of the leggy redhead who had been runner-up for Crab Queen.

Did that make her the Crab Princess? Chase wondered. Or maybe the Crab in Waiting?

Chase chuckled to himself and ambled through the crowd, half watching the band, half searching the throng of dancers.

You're not looking for her, he told himself even as a dark head caught his attention. It wasn't her, and he continued to look.

A lively, dancing brunette captured his notice, but he nearly dismissed her. Never would conservative, rigid Abby be jigging about with such abandon.

Then the woman turned, and Chase stopped in his tracks. Not only was it Abby, but it was Abby with a huge grin on her face. She danced and sang and laughed.

Chase could literally feel his heartbeat accelerate and his blood burn hot through his veins. She was the sexiest sight he'd ever seen. Like a wild nymph celebrating some pagan ritual.

And like the dance was designed to lure him to her, Chase helplessly went.

* * *

Abby was winded, and her vision was a bit fuzzy, but she could swear Chase Jordan was approaching her.

She blinked and there he stood, his lovely hands tucked in his jean pockets and a charming smile on his lips.

"I don't have your robe," she blurted out and fought the urge to cover her face with her hands. Why on earth had she said something so stupid? Of course she didn't have his robe.

"Shucks, and that's exactly what I was coming to get." His charming smile widened into a completely captivating grin.

"You did?" Stupid, stupid, stupid. Maybe she shouldn't talk. Instead, she stared at his dimple, wondering how something that likely started as a birth defect could be so amazingly sexy.

"Nooo." He stepped closer. "I came to tell you that you look beautiful."

Abby's heart stopped. Her head seemed to float off her shoulders and she could swear she felt her feet follow.

"Thank—thank you."

"Can I get you a drink?"

Abby knew she didn't need another CrabFest Special, but she nodded.

Chase pulled one of those marvelous hands from his pocket and laced his fingers through hers.

"Are you having fun?"

She tried to focus on his question, rather than his thumb rubbing back and forth over the sensitive flesh of her wrist.

Finally she gave up.

"What?"

"Fun? Are you having it?"

She beamed at him. "Oh, yes."

His eyes locked on her mouth for a moment, then he looked away.

Damn, she probably had gummy crab in her teeth.

They were soon standing in a line at the beer stand. People roamed everywhere, some dancing, some just hanging out in clusters, all talking or singing loudly.

Abby imagined it was like being in the center of a beehive, the other bees busily buzzing away.

"Beer?"

Abby turned to Chase. Briefly there were two of him, and she had to clutch one of his four arms to steady herself. One of his other arms caught her from behind, and she found herself anchored against him. Their bodies touched from chest to knee, and Abby let out a small, pleased sigh.

"You feel wonderful," she breathed.

Chase grinned down at her. "Sweetheart," he said gently as he set her away from him, "I think we better get you a soda."

Abby swayed and had to concentrate on his nose to regain her balance. "Yes. That might be a good idea."

Chase turned to order, and Abby tried to watch the crowd again, but the drone and constant motion made her lightheaded.

Without even pausing in his request for a beer and a soda, he reached out and pulled her back to him, tucking her against his side.

Abby was grateful. He was the only thing solid in a sea of movement. She closed her eyes and leaned her head on his shoulder.

"Can you hold this?" he asked, holding up the soda.

She straightened. "Yes. But I think perhaps I should sit for a moment."

"I think you're right." With his arm still around her, he led her to a group of oak trees away from the festivities. People still milled around, but by being out of the main swirl of activity, Abby's head felt much clearer and her equilibrium was at least partially back to normal.

"I'm sorry," she said, as Chase helped her get seated on the grass. "I don't usually drink."

"You'd never know," he said with a wink as he sat beside her.

For a moment, she wasn't sure if he was being sincere or not, then she decided he wasn't and elbowed him.

He let out an exaggerated grunt. With great show, he rubbed his side and offered her a wounded look.

A giggle escaped her.

And he grinned back. "It's okay to cut loose once in a while."

"This is the first time I've ever cut loose."

"Ever?"

"Ever," she admitted. "I was a nerd, remember? No keg parties or bar-hopping. Only study groups and late nights in the library."

"There's nothing wrong with that."

Abby shrugged and watched the crowd dancing in a circle of light around the stage. She and Chase were silent for a moment.

"So, why did you really come over to me?"

He took a drink of his beer before he answered, "I told you, I came over to tell you that you look beautiful."

Abby shook her head. "I can't believe that."

"Why?"

Because I'm an ugly Stepp sister, she nearly stated, but caught herself. That wasn't true. She was no beauty, but she wouldn't think of herself under that label.

"I just never thought you'd be offering me a compliment after how things ended the other day." Abby realized she didn't really want to bring up that subject either, but unfortunately it was already out of her mouth.

Chase picked up a stick and began drawing in the grass.

After a few silent moments, Abby decided she had offended him again.

Then he tossed down the stick and sighed. "I shouldn't have acted that way. Nelson is the man in your life. And you were absolutely right when you said we're too different anyway. Our worlds are completely opposite."

"They are?"

Chase nodded.

Disappointment sat heavy in Abby's chest and she could feel an inexplicable wateriness in her eyes.

"But you're still the prettiest girl here tonight," he said with that devilish charm.

The heaviness she experienced only moments earlier dissolved, and her heart soared with the loss of the weight. He was so enticing. He was everything she had imagined he would be as she had watched him from afar in the lunchroom. In study hall. In the bus lines.

The difference was she didn't have to watch him from afar now. He was right beside her.

Abby leaned against the base of the tree, the bark rough against her back even through her shirt. She tried to concentrate on the scratchiness, but all she could sense was Chase seated so close that she could smell his woodsy scent and feel his warmth.

The evening was magical. It was the best time she could remember ever having outside of acing her final in Biophysics of Macromolecular Assemblies. Although she'd have to say the final was less nerve-wracking than this moment.

She didn't know what to do or to say. But she did know she wanted this man beside her more than she had wanted anything in her life. Even than that "A" in her biochemistry class.

She twisted toward him and placed a hand on his

knee. She felt him tense under her touch, but she didn't move away.

"You said we could overcome our differences. You really don't think that's true?"

Chase looked at her for a moment. His eyes seemed to probe deep inside her, as if he could see all the areas where they differed.

"Abby, it doesn't matter. We *are* different. And you *do* have a boyfriend."

"But Nelson isn't here." Abby couldn't believe she had said something so . . . shameless. She was throwing herself at him. *Note to self: liquor makes you a hussy.*

But at the same time, she felt so free. Abigail Stepp didn't proposition men. Yet here she was hitting on Chase Jordan, the very last man she ever thought she would have the nerve to proposition. She felt wild and crazy.

She watched him closely. His expression remained completely blank. The wildness faded.

He did understand that she was propositioning him, didn't he? Had she done it wrong? Was the invitation too oblique?

"Darling, you've had too much to drink," he finally said, his rich voice so soft, she almost missed it. And part of her wished she had. She'd just offered herself to the man, and he was turning her down.

"I have not," she insisted. "Well, I have. But I'm not doing this because I'm tipsy. I want you."

Chase suppressed a grin at the indignant look on Abby's flushed face. She did look every bit the vixen that she was purporting to be.

And damn, every inch of his aroused body wanted to say, *You're right, honey, Nelson isn't here, and I'm more than willing to scratch any itch you might have.*

But that wouldn't be right. He knew that if Abby was thinking straight, she wouldn't be saying any of this.

"Sweetheart, I'm very flattered. But I don't think either of us would be too happy with ourselves tomorrow morning."

"Oh, I think I'd be very happy." Her dark eyes were so earnest, Chase had to fight back another smile.

"Believe me," he said, picking up her hand, which was burning an imprint onto his knee. "If there was any way we could work it out, I'd already have you home in my bed."

"Really?"

"Oh, yeah." Hell yes. He watched as she bit her lip, her white teeth toying with the soft rosy flesh. He wanted to nibble her there too.

"Listen, I'm going to go get both of us some coffee." He rose, tugging at the legs of his suddenly too snug jeans. "Stay right here," he ordered and pointed at the place where she sat.

She nodded, but she looked as if she'd rather sink into the tree she leaned against.

Chase felt sorry that she was embarrassed by her actions. Impulsively, he bent forward and kissed the top of her head. The fragrance of citrus and Abby surrounded him.

With much reluctance, he straightened. "Stay," he said again.

Again she nodded, and he truly hoped she would.

Summer-Ann watched the couple in the shadows and clenched the straw of her drink between her teeth.

This couldn't be happening. It absolutely couldn't!

She had worked hard to get back into Chase's life. She'd managed to convince him to give her a job as his office manager. She'd become his right arm there. He couldn't run his business without her. After all, she was the major reason why he could keep his biggest secret hidden from everyone. Chase had always trusted her with that secret. That was a bond no one could break.

She really believed it was only a matter of time before they were back together like the good old days. After all, Chase hadn't shown interest in anyone else for a long time.

Until now.

She watched as Abby Stepp turned toward Chase and placed her hand on his leg. And he didn't push it away.

This was a freakin' nightmare. What was he doing? And why on earth was he doing it with her?

Grudgingly, Summer-Ann had to admit that Abby Stepp did look a lot better than she had in high school. She had lost some weight, and she seemed to have a bit more style. Even her wide-set eyes and large mouth looked more proportionate with the rest of her face.

But she wasn't in Chase's league.

Summer-Ann further mutilated her straw as she watched Chase stand and then lean down and kiss Abby on the head. It was an innocent enough kiss, but there was something disturbingly intimate about it.

Chase left Abby sitting against an oak tree and headed toward the food stands.

Summer-Ann tossed the remainder of her watery drink in a nearly overflowing trash barrel and moved in that direction. She wasn't about to give up this fight so easily. Chase Jordan was and always would be hers.

Chapter 11

"There you are."

Chase ground his molars to keep from groaning out loud. He tried to pretend he didn't hear and keep walking, but he couldn't believably ignore the hand grasping the sleeve of his shirt.

"Summer-Ann," he said with little enthusiasm.

"Are you having fun?"

He nodded. "I'm actually off to get a couple drinks."

"Is one for me?" She smiled and hugged his arm with both of hers.

Chase fought the urge to shake her off. He didn't have any interest in listening to Summer's come-ons, but he also didn't want to hurt her feelings.

"Sure," he said in a subdued manner. "What are you drinking?"

"A Curvy Crab with a twist."

Chase made a puzzled face, and Summer-Ann giggled, squeezing his arm tighter. "It's a rum and diet Coke with a lemon."

"Of course," Chase said and started to the closest stand. She still clung to him, easily keeping pace. Chase recalled having Abby tight at his side earlier. He wished it was her body pressed close to him now.

"I saw you with Abby Stepp," Summer-Ann said as if

she had read his thoughts. She kept her voice light and conversational.

Chase knew Summer well enough to know that her casualness was a put-on. She wasn't the type to carelessly accept another woman being with the man she had designs on. And he would have to be damned near dead not to notice that Summer had designs on him—despite his multiple attempts to discourage it.

"Yes, I was talking with Abby."

"And kissing her." Her voice hardened slightly.

Chase nodded. "Yes. Although I don't think that's any of your business."

"It is my business if it affects Willy."

Chase gritted his teeth again; Summer-Ann was hell on his dental work. He hated it when she tried to use Willy to control him. And she did use that little trick quite often.

"Summer, I can't possibly imagine why my friendship with Abby would affect Willy. In fact, I think Willy rather likes Abby." As soon as he made his last comment, he realized his mistake. Not only was Summer-Ann possessive, she was blindly jealous.

"I don't want that woman having anything to do with my son," she said, loud enough that several people turned to look in their direction.

Chase offered a weak smile to the spectators and then leaned in to hush her. "Abby and I are just friends. That's it."

She stared at him for a moment, then blinked her lashes coyly. "That's it?"

He nodded his head once. "So can we drop the subject?"

She smiled broadly. "That, I can do."

Abby's first instinct after Chase left was to slink back to her co-workers. But she still felt a bit dizzy, and she had promised Chase she would wait for him.

So instead, she leaned her head back against the tree and closed her eyes.

She had just made an absolute fool of herself. Hitting on Chase—what had she been thinking? They needed to stop having these odd encounters, or she was never going to survive her stay here.

This last weird incident was solely her fault, but she was making a pact with herself right now. From this moment on, nothing this disastrous was going to happen again. If it killed her, and it very well might, she was going to act like a sane, rational human being in Chase's presence. Starting now.

Be normal. Listen to the music. Enjoy yourself. Don't hit on any more men, she chanted to herself and then opened her eyes.

The band still bounded around the stage, albeit with a bit less energy. But the upbeat music did take her mind off her humiliating behavior. She sat up and swayed slightly to the tune.

Abby clapped her hands with the music, and she turned to see if she could find Chase in the crowd. It seemed like he'd been gone for a long time. She probably scared him away.

Then she spotted him, being cuddled by a curvy blonde. Summer-Ann.

Even after her earlier pep talk, something akin to jealousy gripped her stomach. She watched them, noting the way Summer-Ann smiled up at Chase so prettily. She was stunning, and together they really were the perfect couple.

Abby folded her arms around her bent knees and rested her chin on them. After a night of completely new experiences and sensations, this was a feeling she was familiar with—watching beautiful people from a distance.

She wondered what had happened between them. The

way they stood together, Abby got the feeling they were still close, that there was a connection between them. Something that even a bad breakup couldn't totally destroy.

Willy. Abby straightened. Of course, Willy. She didn't know why she hadn't thought of it earlier. She must have been so unnerved the other day after being discovered by Summer-Ann kissing Chase, and then Chase's abrupt dismissal that it just never occurred to her.

But that had to be Chase and Summer-Ann's lasting connection. Willy must be their child.

Abby rested her head on her knees again and speculated what might have happened between them. Chase didn't seem like the type to not marry the mother of his child. But truthfully, how well did Abby really know the man?

All she knew was that he had a real talent for renovation, he liked seafood and coffee, and he could kiss like a son of a gun. None of those things revealed much about his paternal side.

But that wasn't true. She did know that Chase adored Willy.

Ellie said they had ended badly. Maybe it was Summer-Ann who hadn't wanted to settle down.

She studied the other woman's demeanor with Chase. She certainly seemed interested in him right now. Of course, she was also familiar with him.

Abby sighed and turned to look back at the band. She understood sticking with what you know. After all, she was doing that with Nelson, wasn't she?

When Chase finally got away from Summer, he was relieved to see Abby was still waiting for him. Although from her expression, she was only there physically. Her mind was a million miles away.

"Hey," he said softly so as not to startle her.

She blinked up at him and smiled.

He was astonished that such a simple gesture could affect him so strongly. He sank down beside her and held up two steaming Styrofoam cups. "They're called 'Caffeinated Crabs.' But I'm fairly certain they're just coffee with creamer."

Abby accepted the cup and peered into the slot torn in the plastic lid. "No gummy crab floating in it?"

"I really hope not."

They shared a smile and each took a sip. The music was softer, slower. They both seemed lost in the melody, content with their crab coffee and each other's company.

"I'd like to be friends," Abby said suddenly.

"I'd like that too."

"That means we can't kiss anymore."

"How about just not on the lips?" Chase teased.

"Not anywhere."

"Damn."

Chase could tell that Abby was struggling not to smile as she added sternly, "And we can't talk about kissing or—or any other non-platonic things."

"Okay, but I have one question."

"What?"

"Can we dance?" He grabbed her hand and tugged her to her feet. She squealed and dropped her coffee, which spilled on the ground and disappeared into the new grass. Her surprised yelp turned into peals of wonderful, uninhibited laughter. Chase's chest swelled with satisfaction. Whenever he got her to abandon her habitual seriousness, he felt like he'd just received the keys to the city. Hell, the keys to the world.

Man, he wanted to kiss her. On the lips. And on every other inch of her body. But instead, he dragged her against him and began to sway.

* * *

Abby's laughter faded as her chest encountered the hardness of his. He laced the fingers of one hand through hers, while his other hand found the small of her back. She moved her free hand to rest on his broad shoulder.

Concentrate on the music, she mentally ordered herself. The music. The crowd. The sound of the breeze in the trees. Anything but the heat of Chase's body searing her skin through her clothing. Or his lean muscles flexing under her palm. Or even the warm flutter of his breath stirring the hair at her temple. Especially the last one, because it tempted her to look at his mouth, and she knew if she looked at that yummy full bottom lip she would be tempted to kiss him.

"Relax," he said, his velvety voice tickling her ear.

"I can't."

He suddenly spun her away from him until she was an arm's length away with their hands still laced together. Then, just as quickly, he curled her back into his chest. The movement was so unexpected and executed so easily, it took Abby a second to react. When she did, it was to dissolve into laughter again.

"You shouldn't do that to a novice drinker."

Chase looked horrified. "You're not going to be sick, are you?"

"No. But I am a bit lightheaded."

"It's not lightheadedness," he informed her. "It's because my fancy footwork is like dancing on air."

Abby grinned at him skeptically. "Is that so?"

"Uh-huh." He spun her away from him again, and again, she burst into laughter.

"Having fun?"

Abby settled back into his arms, breathless. Her heart

was racing and her head whirling. "I can't remember a better time."

Chase's smile faded and there seemed to be an almost possessive look in his eyes. "Good." Then they revolved together over the cushiony lawn, their gazes locked.

The song ended, and Abby squeaked as he dipped her.

When he pulled her back to him, the look was gone and his easy smile was back in place.

"You dance like Ginger Rogers."

Abby laughed. "I feel like a giant with two left feet."

Chase shook his head and waltzed her into the next song.

If Abby thought she felt like a giant the night before, it had nothing on how she felt the next morning. Her head seemed like it was at least twice its normal size and weighed about fifteen pounds against her pillow.

She moaned as she flopped over onto her back, flinging her arm over her face to block out the cruel, cruel sunlight.

What had she done? *What had she drunk?*

She groaned again, tossed her legs over the side of the bed, and struggled to sit up.

Whatever it was, she would never, never drink it again. She wasn't even sure she'd be able to look at gummy candy in the same light again.

She shuffled down the hall to the bathroom, when a knock on the front door stopped her. She waited to see if Ellie was going to answer it.

After the third rap, she decided Ellie wasn't, so she headed downstairs, using the banister to support most of her weight.

Why was she even bothering to answer it? Nobody but salespeople came to the front door.

The person knocked for the fourth time, and Abby decided she was going to have to deal with the most persistent salesperson on the face of the planet.

Instead, it turned out to be the most persistent little boy on the planet.

"Willy? How are you? What are you doing here?"

Willy toed a crack on the porch floorboard with his canvas sneaker and peeked up at her shyly. "I just wanted to come say hi."

Abby stuck her head out the door and looked around. "Are you staying with Chase?"

He nodded.

"Does he know where you are?"

Willy shook his head. "He told me I couldn't come over 'cause you need to rest. But it's a real nice day, and we're getting ready to go fly kites. And I really wanted to ask you to come too."

Abby's melting heart far overshadowed the pounding in her head. "Oh, honey, I'd love to fly a kite with you."

Willy's head shot up. "You would? You don't need to rest?"

"No. But I do think you'd better make sure it's all right with your d—"

"Willy!"

"He's over here, Chase." Abby waved to him.

Chase strolled across the street. The fit of his jeans emphasized the length of his legs and the muscles of his thighs. And his plain white T-shirt showed the perfect masculine vee of his torso. He looked delicious.

And Abby looked . . . She glanced down at herself. The worn flannel pajamas did nothing to display her figure. She looked like a frump. A frump with an enormous throbbing head.

"How are you feeling?" Chase asked in a quiet voice as

he came up onto the porch. He'd obviously experienced this post-drinking, large pounding head phenomenon.

Abby made a face. "I think if I see a Crab Special any time in the next decade, it will be too soon."

Chase smiled. "I have coffee and Alka Seltzer at my house."

"I think I need a shower first."

"Then she's going to fly kites with us," Willy said with a huge grin that revealed he'd lost a bottom tooth since she last saw him.

"Only if I'm invited," Abby quickly added.

"Of course you're invited. Why don't you come over after you get showered and dressed. By the way, I like the jammies."

Abby crossed her arms around herself and made an uncomfortable noise at his compliment, then said, "Give me ten minutes."

"We'll be waiting."

Chapter 12

Chase had never met a woman who was actually ready in ten minutes.

But Abby, it turned out, was the exception to the rule. Not only was she at his back door in ten minutes, but she also managed the feat with a hangover, and she looked fabulous.

She entered his kitchen wearing a white T-shirt with a big red cotton shirt unbuttoned over the top, black capris and white canvas sneakers. The ensemble wasn't put together to look even remotely sexy, but Chase found the outfit incredibly hot. The style was relaxed and carefree, both of which looked very, very good on Abby.

He held out a mug of coffee, which she accepted. She took a deep drink. After she swallowed, a content moan escaped her. Chase promptly thought of several other things he'd like to do to her to produce that same sound, but he squelched the images. He needed to keep platonic thoughts.

Abby sat at the kitchen table, crossing her legs and taking another sip of her coffee. Chase watched her, his eyes drawn to her ankles, and the delicate bones and milky skin revealed by the cut of her capris.

When had a woman's ankles ever turned him on? Platonic? Yeah, he was doomed.

When he stopped leering at her ankles, he realized

that Abby must have spoken to him. She sat, watching him, amusement dancing in her eyes.

"Did you say something?"

"Yes. I said you make a mean cup of joe."

"It's one of my many talents."

Abby had no doubt about that. Just the look on his face as he watched her drink her coffee made her feel warm all over. But she had to assume his stare wasn't really directed at her, but rather some personal musing. Heaven knew that nothing about her would inspire such a heated look. Unless he was driven to distraction by Keds.

"Can I get you the Alka Seltzer?"

Abby held up the coffee. "This is helping a lot. So where do you fly kites?"

Chase straightened up from where he leaned on the kitchen counter and brought the coffeepot over to refill her mug.

"We're going to Hobb's Field. That's where you get the best breeze off the water," he informed her with authority and a quick grin.

"So you have kite-flying to a science, do you?"

"Not me. This is Willy's judgment, not mine. And yes, he takes his kite-flying very, very seriously."

"I'll make sure to follow his lead then."

Chase grinned. "He won't have it any other way."

"That's the way," Chase shouted to Abby, when, after a half dozen attempts, she got her kite airborne.

"Yeah, that's the way," Willy cheered too, hopping up and down while still keeping his own kite aloft.

Abby reeled out more twine and returned the two males' happy grins. She looked up at her kite, a bright blue triangle with a yellow creature on it that Willy informed her was called a Pikachu. He also advised her that it was his old, "little kid" kite, but it would probably be good for her.

Given the many attempts it took to launch the small plastic thing, she decided he was right. There was no way she would have ever gotten the large nylon stunt kites that both Willy and Chase flew off the ground.

But her modest little kite still looked pretty flying high against the bright blue sky.

She laughed as Willy successfully made his kite do a large spiral. He whooped and grinned proudly at Chase.

"That's too cool, Willy," Chase shouted and gave him a wink.

Abby stopped watching the kites and studied her two companions. Chase constantly encouraged Willy, cheering for him, teasing him, laughing with him. Abby tried to imagine Nelson here, playing with a little boy.

Try as she might, she couldn't. Nelson was too serious. He wouldn't see the importance of child's play. He would find it frivolous and a waste of time.

She focused on Chase. He was laughing, his eyes sparkling like the waves behind him. The sea breeze tousled his hair.

Abby liked his hair. It wasn't as long as he wore it in high school, but it reached the collar of his chambray shirt and always looked like he'd just run his hands through the dark locks.

"Watch out!"

The warning took a moment to register. When she looked up it was too late—her little kite had dive-bombed Chase's large, multi-colored, multi-stringed one. And both kites were crashing to earth, or rather, crashing toward her.

She squealed, dropped the spool of twine, and ducked

for cover. A second later, the kites hit the ground several inches from her feet.

"Crash and burn!" Willy hollered with unrestrained glee.

Chase jogged over. "Did you see your life flash before your eyes or what?"

Abby feigned a look of horror. "I definitely thought I was a goner."

They turned to look at the fallen kites. There was nothing but a mass of string and nylon with only the left ear of her Pikachu visible among the wreckage.

"I think I'll get our lunch," Chase said.

"Good idea," Abby agreed. "We're going to need sustenance to get this mess untangled."

"We?" Chase cocked a dark brow. "Who hit who here?"

"Well, if you weren't so darned distracting." Abby nearly groaned after the words were out of her mouth. Her big ole mouth.

Chase's eyebrow raised again, but this time with surprise.

She was thankful that he didn't comment, instead going to the truck to get the basket containing their lunch.

Abby sat down on the grass and dragged the kites toward her. Better to keep busy than fixate on what she'd just said. And maybe if she concentrated on the kites, she wouldn't say anything else so stupid.

By the time Chase returned, she had managed to make matters worse. Now the strings were not only twisted with each other, but also around her.

"You didn't really have to do that."

"I don't mind." Abby tugged at one of the strings, which had somehow gotten tangled with the lace of her right sneaker.

Chase set down the picnic basket and then knelt to unknot the twine from around her.

"I'm used to cataloging genomes all day. What do I know about kites?" she said with a self-disparaging chuckle.

"Kites, I know. So you relax and eat." He flipped open the lid of the basket in invitation, then sat on the other side of her.

She watched for a moment as Chase's nimble fingers worked at the knots, but decided she'd better look away. It was too easy to fantasize about how those hands would feel on her body.

No good could come of such musings.

She turned to poke through the lunch Chase had packed. For some reason, she assumed it would be prepackaged "kiddie" fare that she'd seen advertised on television. Things that came in abnormal shapes and strange colors and didn't seem to resemble food at all.

Instead, she discovered turkey and swiss on thick wheat bread, potato chips, carrot and cucumber sticks, granny smith apples, bottles of water and a couple sodas.

"Wow, this looks good."

Chase cast her a curious look. "You sound surprised."

"I just didn't expect real home-cooking."

He leaned over her and peered into the basket. "What in there is home-cooking?"

Abby playfully pushed him and grabbed a sandwich. "In my book, this is cooking. I can barely prepare a bowl of cereal."

Chase returned to the stringy mess. "You'll have to come over for dinner then. I make a mean beef stroganoff—even meaner than my coffee."

"Mmm," Abby closed her eyes and moaned, half at the sandwich, half at the idea of his stroganoff. When she opened her eyelids, she discovered he was studying her, his pale gaze locked on her lips.

Self-consciously, she reached up to brush the corner of her mouth. His eyes followed the motion, and she fought the urge to moan again. His gaze alone had the ability to make her want to do things she had never even considered before. Like make love in an open field, in broad daylight . . .

"Did you bring pretzels?"

With Willy nearby. Willy! Abby stopped staring at Chase and turned to look at the little boy who stood there oblivious to the tension between the two adults.

"Pretzels? Yes, he did. They're right here. There you go." Abby knew she was talking ridiculously fast, but she couldn't seem to control it. She was embarrassed. Embarrassed that she could feel so out of control. Embarrassed that she was very much learning to like the sensation.

Chase tried not to laugh at Abby's nervous babble. It was cute, and he liked it. A lot. Of course, he couldn't think of much he didn't like about the lady. There were a couple things, like when she put up her guard and got all starchy. And there was Nelson. He definitely didn't like that about her.

But he didn't have to worry about either of those dislikes, because she was just a friend, so neither was going to affect that relationship. He wouldn't let it.

He looked over at Abby, who now talked at a normal speed with Willy. The breeze played with the tips of her hair that stuck out from the bun on the back of her head.

She was wearing the infamous bun, but the style was different from the one she'd worn in high school. It was looser, with tendrils escaping the knot to caress her cheek and the back of her neck.

She had an amazing neck, long and elegant, like a portrait on a cameo.

Chase returned his attention to the kites, concentrating intently. He was going to stop thinking things like that about her. She was a friend. A friend. And he didn't notice the curve of a friend's neck. Or the shape of a friend's mouth. Hell, he'd never noticed whether Mason had kissable lips or not. Of course, if he had, attraction to Abby wouldn't be an issue.

"Did you see that last spin I did?" Willy asked, moving to plunk down beside him.

"I sure did, buddy."

"It's too bad Abby had problems with her kite. It's probably because it's old," Willy stated.

Abby smiled over at the little boy. "Or I'm just not a good kite flyer."

"Nah, I had problems when I first started, too," Willy reassured her. He squinted toward a group of boys down by the water. "Hey, that's Charlie. Can I go say hi?"

"Sure, but don't get wet."

"I won't!"

"Famous last words," Abby said as she watched him dash across the field toward the other boys.

"Yep." He continued to fiddle with the strings, although his fingers itched to toy with the stray strand of hair blowing across Abby's cheek.

"Want me to try?"

Chase looked at the kites for a minute, then shoved the jumble away. "Nah. When I get home, I'll just cut the strings and start anew."

"You can do that?"

"Of course you can. You aren't going to tell me you studied so much in grade school that you never flew a kite before?" Chase said the words teasingly, but Abby didn't seem to appreciate the jest.

She brushed the stray lock of hair from her face and looked back to where Willy was playing.

"Did I offend you?"

"No."

Uh-oh, here comes the wall, clattering down around her like a steel cage designed to keep him and everyone else out.

"Listen, Abby, I didn't mean that in a negative way."

"I know you didn't."

Chase frowned. She still didn't look in his direction. The tendril of hair returned to her cheek, and he couldn't stop himself from reaching out to smooth it back.

She turned wide smoky brown eyes to him.

"I'm sorry," he said. "I didn't mean to hurt your feelings. You should never be ashamed of your education and your success. Hell, I would have done anything to have your brains."

She stared at him for a moment, and then he wasn't sure whether it was his apology or the shock of his touch, but the wall lifted.

"I'd have done anything to have fit in like you did. To have a normal childhood like you did."

His life, normal? He bit back a humorless laugh, afraid she would misunderstand his bitterness. "Believe me, no one would want my childhood."

Her gaze roamed his face. "I just wish I had been normal."

"You were normal. What wasn't normal?"

"I've never flown a kite. I grew up on a bay, and I don't know how to swim. I never went to school dances or parties. I never even went on a real date."

Chase frowned. "How could you be with Nelson and never have been on a real date?"

Abby toyed with a blade of grass. "We met in microbiology. We were lab partners. He'd come to my dorm room to study or we'd go to study groups. From there, we just sort of became a couple. He never officially asked me out."

"But you went out together, right?"

"Yes, but it was never really a date, it was just sort of an assumed arrangement. I don't think I'm a hopeless romantic, but I would have liked at least one real date where he actually asked me, then arrived at my door with flowers or chocolates. I know, I know it sounds hokey."

Chase thought about her words. "It doesn't sound hokey. Although Nelson does kind of sound like a prick."

He expected her to get defensive at his insult, but instead a burst of laughter rushed from her. "I bet Nelson has never been called that before."

"But overall, you're happy with him, aren't you?"

Chase found her delay telling.

"We're content. We have common goals. We're both very dedicated to our work."

"If that's the best you can say about the relationship, I can see why there aren't any hot dates."

Abby fiddled with the grass again, and he worried that he'd overstepped his bounds.

"Maybe I don't inspire him to get—hot," she murmured.

Chase captured her chin and turned her face until their eyes met. "Then he must be blind, because everything about you gets me hot."

Abby tried to look away, but he held her fast, brushing the soft skin of her cheek with his thumb.

"I'm not saying this to make you uncomfortable. I'm saying it because it's true. Your lips, your eyes, hell, those adorable little freckles across your nose. The way you look in those pants. Everything about you makes me want to drag you into bed."

Abby looked at him, her expression unreadable. "Yet you turned me down last night."

"Are you offering again—right now? Because I couldn't take advantage of a lady who was drunk. But I could easily take advantage of a lady with a mere hangover."

Abby watched him for a moment longer, and then she broke into a smile. "You're a nice guy."

"You don't have to be so surprised about it."

"I thought bad boys were notoriously not nice."

Chase sighed. "Yeah, this is one of those moments when I really, really regret my decision to reform."

Abby reached up and touched his face, her fingertips brushing over his skin like whispers of silk. "I have to admit, at times, I regret it, too. But we're doing the right thing."

Her fingers left his jaw and moved to hold his hand that still caressed her cheek. They sat looking at each other for a second longer, then she simply turned and got him a sandwich. Chase couldn't recall an afternoon that had been nicer, or more maddening.

Chapter 13

Abby spoke to Chase every day for the next week. Many evenings, he would be outside working when she pulled into her driveway after work.

She liked to think he was waiting to see her, but she knew that realistically he was just getting some remodeling done on his place. Still, she looked forward to seeing him at the end of the day.

So when she drove into her driveway on Friday evening and didn't see him outside, she felt more than a little disappointed.

She walked up on her porch and paused, searching his yard again. No, he definitely wasn't there.

She went in the front door and dropped her briefcase in the foyer. What did she expect? She couldn't expect she was going to see him every day. That was a bit impractical. Who saw their friends every single day?

She went to the kitchen and straight to the fridge. She stared at the well-stocked shelves for a few moments. Finally, she just grabbed a diet soda, popped the tab and went to sit at the table.

Where was Ellie? She could count on her sister for companionship on a Friday night—when the rest of the world was on dates or out with friends. Was Chase out on a date?

Not any of your concern, she told herself.

With a sigh, she reached across the table and pulled one of the sections of the unfolded *Millbrook Telegram* toward her. She straightened the paper and began to read with only halfhearted interest. Then a noise caught her attention.

She looked up and listened more intently. It was the sound of laughter. She pushed up from the table and went to the window that overlooked the front yard. The street was quiet.

She heard the laughter again. The sound was two deep chuckles mixed with a higher, more nervous giggle. She crossed over to the sink and looked out the window into the backyard.

At the wrought-iron table, nestled in among her grandmother's peonies, a blond man sat across from Ellie. Ellie sat forward on her seat. Even from a distance, Abby could see that her cheeks were flushed. Chester lay under the table by Ellie's feet. Chase stood at a gas grill, a pair of tongs in his hands.

Abby quickly headed to the back door.

"Hey, there you are. We thought you were going to miss this here fine cooking," Chase said.

"Hi. I didn't know we were having a barbeque tonight."

Chase inclined his head toward Ellie. "Neither did your poor sister," he said with a contrite smile.

"Yes, we sort of invited ourselves," said the blonde.

Abby really looked at him for the first time. Even in his seated position, she could tell he was tall. His blond hair was worn longish, not quite as long as Chase's, but shaggier than the current style. He was a very handsome man, but what struck Abby most about him was the hard look in his gray eyes. A bitterness that his winning smile couldn't erase.

He stood and extended his hand. "Hi. I'm Mason Sweet. We actually attended high school together."

Abby frowned and then her eyes widened with recognition. "Of course, Mason. Yes, you were the quarterback."

Mason nodded with a reticent smile. "Yes, that was I."

Abby wouldn't have recognized him if he hadn't said his name. In high school, he had been the type of kid who seemed to have a golden aura around him. A constant smile. Always laughing.

While Mason still had his tremendous good looks, the radiance that had surrounded him was doused. She couldn't help wondering what had happened in his life to kill that vivacity.

"Mason is the mayor of Millbrook," Chase told Abby, as he flipped what appeared to be a piece of chicken on the grill.

"Really?"

Mason shrugged and sank back into his chair. "I try not to let the glamour of the position jade me."

"He's a very good mayor," Ellie said softly but with a conviction that caused Mason to study her over his drink.

Ellie didn't return Mason's look, instead making a great show of idly reaching out to snap a dead blossom off one of the peonies.

She likes him, Abby realized, and immediately felt sorry for her little sister, who lived in a world of dreams and fairy tales. She didn't have the type of personality that could deal with a hardened man like Mason. It was as hopeless and dangerous as her own attraction to Chase.

Leave it to the Stepp sisters to long for the unattainable. Wasn't that what the stepsisters in *Cinderella* did, too? Shoot for the prince when, realistically, they should have aimed for the frog.

Don't do this to yourself, Abby scolded. She wasn't aiming for anything other than a nice platonic relationship with Chase—at which she was succeeding. Okay, there were still the occasional bouts of racing pulses and sweating palms, but otherwise she was achieving the goal she'd set for herself the night of the CrabFest. She was acting normal around the man.

She wandered over to Chase and peered at the grill. "So is this one of your specialties?"

Chase shook his head and picked up the bottle in the sideboard of the grill. "Not if you consider Heinz Barbeque sauce a specialty."

"It smells good."

"I'm not sure that's my doing either."

"It looks good. You know, not burnt or anything."

"Now that I can take credit for." He winked at her, and one of those odd spells of heart palpitations occurred. But Abby was sure it was about the chicken, rather than how charming Chase was. She did like chicken a lot.

"How was work?"

Abby's heart fluttered again. He asked her that every evening, and although she spared him the details of her research, it still made her feel good that he asked.

"It went well. And your day?"

Chase nodded. "Not too bad. Had a bit of a struggle with a crumbling chimney, but otherwise pretty good. But I'm glad today is over. I need to relax." He lifted his arms over his head, bending to one side to stretch the muscles in his back. Abby couldn't help staring at the way his T-shirt hiked up, giving her a glimpse of washboard belly.

She tried to focus on his shoulders, but she suddenly had an image of kneading the muscles there, her hands then moving to the leanness of his torso, then to the hardness of his stomach. And then down . . .

A sudden, shrill ring erupted in the tranquil evening air. Abby jumped.

"That's me," Mason said and stood to retrieve a small black phone from his belt. "Sorry."

He flipped the phone open and moved across the lawn to speak, whether to not interrupt their conversation or to keep his own private, Abby wasn't sure.

"Okay, I brought the chicken. What did you make?"

Abby gave him a bewildered look. "Me? I . . . I provided the backyard."

"Well, hell, I had one of those already."

"I don't cook. I told you that."

"You did, didn't you?" He offered her a warm smile that she could feel to the tips of her toes. "It's a good thing you're so cute. And you got your sister."

He went to Ellie and threw an arm around her. She'd been absorbed in watching Mason and was confused by her sudden inclusion in their conversation.

"Huh?" She cast a muddled glance up at him and then to Abby.

"I was just telling Abby that she's lucky to have you, because I happen to know you are one helluva cook."

Ellie frowned up at him. "Are you sweet-talking me for some of my chocolate-chip cookies?"

"And maybe some of your pasta salad."

"You think that face will get you anything, don't you?"

He smiled, and Abby suspected that dimple did go a long way to getting most things.

Ellie chuckled. "Lucky for you, I made cookies earlier. But the salad's going to take a while."

"It's worth the wait." He gave Ellie a quick hug. "Thanks."

"Yeah, yeah, yeah." Ellie got up and headed into the house.

Abby was a bit perplexed by the scene that had just played out. Chase and Ellie appeared to be quite comfortable with each other. Chase's behavior didn't surprise her. He had a natural ease with just about everybody. But Ellie's relaxation with him was unexpected. She could be painfully shy, especially with men.

"You've had Ellie's pasta salad—often?"

Chase, who was walking back to the grill, paused for half a second, then continued his approach. "A few times."

Abby fiddled with a long-handled spatula resting on the edge of the grill. "When?"

"So do you think being a scientist made you nosy, or you were nosy so you became a scientist?" He asked the question teasingly, but she got the feeling he was avoiding her question.

She debated querying him further but decided it wasn't necessary. Being a scientist did teach her that frequently the most obvious answer was the correct one. They were neighbors. Ellie loved to cook. Chase seemed to love to cook, too. They must have done this sort of thing before. It also would explain Ellie's comfort with him.

"Hey, guys, I'm sorry to duck out like this, but there's a crisis at the town council meeting. I thought this would be a safe one to miss. The topic on the agenda was supposed to be a simple vote on the new hours of operation for the landfill site. But apparently Milton Howe and Cliff Newcomb are practically coming to blows over the subject. I should have known nothing is simple when it involves the dump."

"The folks of Millbrook take trash very seriously," Chase stated.

"Indeed they do." Mason held up a hand as he headed toward the driveway. "Nice to see you, Abby. And say good night to Ellie."

After he left, Abby realized that she was alone with Chase in the waning evening light. She watched him use the tongs to flip the chicken.

"Finally, I have you all to myself."

Abby's head shot up. Had he read her mind?

He stood only inches away. She could feel waves of heat caressing the skin of her bare arms and face.

Don't be so overdramatic, she scolded herself. The warmth was from the flames of the grill.

Then Chase's gaze strayed from her eyes to her mouth and back to her eyes again, and Abby wasn't certain. The man did have the ability to make her sizzle.

He reached out and brushed a wave of hair from her cheek. The touch was fleeting, but it gave Abby no doubt that the heat she was feeling had solely to do with him.

"Did I mention that you look beautiful tonight?"

Abby shook her head.

"Well, you do." He gave her a quick smile and then turned his attention back to the grill.

Abby fought the urge to groan with frustration. How could he say things like that and then just flip chicken?

She watched him turn a piece of the meat. Juice dripped through the rack, causing flames to rise up and briefly engulf the cuts of chicken.

Chase was like that fire. Whenever she was with him, he surrounded her and heated her to the core. How could such torment be so scary and so wonderful, all at once?

"So, let me ask you something." Chase's frank tone jarred Abby out of her thoughts.

"Okay."

"Is this platonic thing really working for you?"

"What?"

He put down the utensil and crossed his arms. "This idea to keep things between us strictly platonic? Are you finding that easy?"

Abby hesitated. "No."

Chase let out a sigh. "Good, because I don't want to be the only one suffering this torture."

"But we're going to stick to it."

"Right. Right." He looked back to the grill, then after a few seconds turned back to her. "Why are we going to stick to it, again?"

Abby couldn't help smiling. "Because of Nelson. And because we make better friends than romantic partners."

He seemed to consider her explanation, nodded and went back to tending their dinner. Seconds later, he said, "Should we really make that judgment without testing it out first?"

Abby laughed.

"What did I miss?" Ellie's innocent question caused them both to jump like guilty teenagers.

But Chase quickly recovered, and said with his usual aplomb, "I was hitting on your sister, but she turned me down."

"Well, that was dumb," Ellie replied.

"Then you'll have to work on her for me."

"I will."

Abby nearly groaned. It was hard enough to resist Chase without having her sister pushing her toward him, too.

Who was she kidding? She didn't need a push. A tap would work just fine.

Ellie observed Abby and Chase throughout the meal, and she was struck by how similar the two really were. They liked the same music. They liked the mountains. They liked history and old houses and antiques. But most of all, they liked each other.

Ellie rested her cheek on her hand and watched them in the flickering light from the candles arranged in the middle of the table. They were crazy about each other. It was obvious in their gazes, their smiles, in the way they teased each other.

"It's late," Chase suddenly noted. "I have to go out to the Martins' in the morning and finish their chimney."

"On a Saturday?" Abby asked.

He got up and stretched. "No rest for the wicked."

Ellie noticed the way Abby's eyes ate up the sight of the muscles straining under his shirt.

He began to gather dishes, but Ellie stopped him. "You cooked. No cleaning."

"But you cooked too."

Both of them looked at Abby. She rolled her eyes and said grudgingly. "I know, I know. I've got clean-up duty."

"I'll help," Chase said.

"No, you go home," Ellie insisted, taking the plates from him. "I can help her."

"Yes," Abby agreed, although not quite as adamantly. "You should get some rest."

Chase hesitated and then nodded. "Okay, well, I'll see you both later." His look lingered on Abby, but then he nodded again and headed toward the driveway. With one final wave, he disappeared into the darkness, Chester trailing along behind him.

In silence, Ellie and Abby cleared the table and headed into the kitchen. Abby put the drain stopper in the sink and began to fill it with hot water. She then moved to scrape the remnants of food off the plates into the trashcan.

Ellie leaned against the counter and waited for her sister to speak.

Finally, she did. "What?"

Ellie widened her eyes innocently. "Nothing. Just watching you."

"No, you're thinking something."

Ellie couldn't contain herself any longer. "You're right. I think you two would be wonderful together."

Abby slid the plates into the foamy water and began to

scrub them with more force than necessary. "I don't know what you're talking about."

"You and Chase. Anyone could see you're crazy about each other."

Abby rinsed the plate and placed it in the dish rack.

After a full second of silence, Ellie thought she wasn't going to discuss it, when Abby said, "It's just physical attraction. Nothing more."

"What I saw was a lot more than physical attraction," Ellie said softly.

"It's not. But even if it was, I have Nelson. Why would I end a relationship with a man that I've been with for years? To be with my high school crush, who is attractive and amusing. Is that really a suitable reason?"

"Are you happy when you're with Chase?"

Abby stopped washing the cup she held and frowned. "What?"

"Does Chase make you happy?"

Abby shrugged. "I don't know. I guess."

"Then I can't think of a better reason to take a chance on him."

"Take a chance? You make it sound like I'm scared to be with Chase." Her voice grew defensive. "Rather than the fact that I'm with another guy, and I happen to treasure that relationship. It has absolutely nothing to do with taking chances."

Ellie nodded, but she must not have looked convinced, because Abby threw down the sponge she held and put her wet hands on her hips. "What, do you think if I have some fling with Chase, you can live vicariously through me?"

"What?"

"I saw the way you watched Mason Sweet earlier. Just because you're pining for our old high school's golden boy, doesn't mean I'm longing for the class's bad boy."

Ellie could feel the blood drain from her face. Without another word, she left the room.

"Ellie . . ." She heard the remorse in Abby's voice, but she didn't care.

Chapter 14

Abby was still feeling like a huge jerk on Monday morning. Ellie had accepted Abby's apology, but she was quieter and more reserved than usual. Abby knew it would take a while for her sister to truly forgive her.

She also knew that a lot of what Ellie had said was true, and that was why Abby had gotten so riled. She did want to be with Chase. The fact that he could make her laugh and joke and even feel beautiful held a tremendous magnetism.

But Chase could make anyone feel that way. Charm was second nature to him, and there was no proof that he really had true feelings for her—because she was someone special.

Abby took a sip of her coffee, set it on her desk and started to read the report Harold, the resident expert on molecular phenotyping, had wanted her to check out.

She shared an office with Leslie and another co-worker, Darren. They were both in the lab and that left her alone to think about the argument with Ellie. She put down the paper and picked up her coffee again.

If she didn't have doubts about the extent of Chase's feelings for her, would she call things off with Nelson? She didn't want to think she was fickle.

No, she wasn't fickle. She'd been with Nelson nearly twelve years. There was nothing capricious about that.

Twelve years. That was a long time. They had matured, started careers, and created their lives. And yet, on the whole, their relationship had changed very little. They just stayed in this odd frozen state of being "a couple." Not married, not a family. They didn't even live together.

Abby took another sip of coffee. She shouldn't be worried about a relationship with Chase. She should be worried about her relationship with Nelson. Nothing stagnant could survive. She had to make Nelson see their relationship needed to change.

Maybe she should go to Boston this weekend and see him. After twelve years, there had to be something there worth saving.

"Hey, Dancing Queen." Her officemate, Darren, wandered in. With his perpetually mussed hair and wire-rimmed glasses low on his nose, he looked like the stereotypical absentminded scientist.

Despite his scruffy appearance, he was brilliant in his field of research, Large-scale Mutagenesis Informatics.

He had taken to calling Abby "Dancing Queen" after the CrabFest, which she didn't mind. It was certainly nicer than the nicknames from her youth.

"Hi, Darren. Did you get the centrifuge working?"

"Yeah, just needed a couple whacks on the side."

"Very technical of you."

He nodded with a pleased grin. "So, you ready for the shindig this weekend?"

Abby paused with her coffee halfway to her lips. "What shindig?"

"It's the big Rand Laboratories fund-raiser."

"What?" This was news to her.

"Yeah, it's when we get all gussied up and try to convince the community and, of course, investors that we aren't creating monsters from spare body parts. Or cloning sheep." He gave her a serious look. "As we know, no good can come from cloning farm animals."

Abby smiled, but then grew serious again. "Cecil didn't mention it."

"He will. And he'll likely want us to prepare a little dissertation on our work."

"Really? Well, that should be easy enough. Especially given the cool stuff we've just discovered about Functional Genomics via Mutagenesis."

David poured himself a cup of coffee and added a ridiculous amount of non-dairy creamer to it. "We could give a speech made up entirely of nonsense words. They don't care about the nitty-gritty of what we do here. Investors just want to be able to take some credit when one of us finds the cure for cancer or discovers the gene that causes crooked teeth. They'd be all over that. Zap the gene, and voilà! A perfect smile."

Abby shook her head. "Jaded, jaded."

"Nope, realistic. So, make sure you wear something stunning. It's black tie. I even get my hair cut for the occasion."

Abby looked duly impressed.

"Okay," he saluted her with his SCIENTISTS DO IT HYPOTHETICALLY mug. "I'm off to spin some stuff."

Abby absently watched him leave, her mind already on the fundraiser. This was the perfect opportunity to get Nelson to visit and for them to work on their relationship. He might not be willing to take a vacation, but he was always willing to network. And while she had him here, she could get their relationship back on track.

"Nelson. This is Abby."

"Oh, Abby. How's the great white North?"

"It's decidedly green. You do realize you are only in Boston?"

He sniffed. "Did you just call to chat or did you have something in particular to discuss?"

"Actually, I do have something specific to ask. Rand Laboratories is having its annual fund-raising gala this weekend." Okay, Abby realized "gala" might be extreme, but she was trying to get his attention. "And I would love for you to come up and attend with me."

"Rand Labs has a gala?"

Okay, maybe that had been a bit too much. "Yes."

There was silence on the other end of the line. Then he said, "I don't know, Abigail, let me check into a few things and get back to you."

"Great. I hope you can make it. I really want to see you."

He grunted in acknowledgment and then said his good-byes.

Abby hung up the phone, feeling good. Nelson would come. He couldn't resist the idea of investors forced to listen to him.

By Thursday night, Abby was beginning to think even the lure of free money wasn't enough to get Nelson to come to Maine.

But when the phone rang at twenty past ten, she was there to snatch up the receiver.

"Abigail?"

"Hello, Nelson. I was starting to think you forgot."

"No. I didn't forget. However, I can't attend. I'm far too busy here to get away."

Abby bit the inside of her lip to keep from screaming at him. He was an intelligent man. Couldn't he see that their relationship was in a terrible state?

"Do you think you could make it up another time?"

A pause. "Possibly."

"Maybe I'll come to see you soon."

Another pause. "Why don't you see how your schedule works out? I'm sure you are busy too."

"Yes. Well, I should go."

"Abby?"

"Yes?"

"I am sorry I can't make it."

Abby hung up the phone and clamped the tender flesh of her lower lip. Nelson had never been the attentive type, but this was absurd. Was he really that obsessed with his research that nothing else mattered? And why hadn't she seen it before?

To be honest, she had seen it—all the time. So why hadn't it bothered her until now?

She went into the kitchen. She got a glass of water and sat at the table. The house was quiet. Ellie was in her room, reading and more than likely avoiding her.

Abby sipped her drink and then set it down a bit too forcefully. The sound seemed to reverberate off the silence. She sighed, got up and wandered to the window.

Lights were on in Chase's living room. Without giving it further thought, she was out the back door.

A knock thudded on his front door, and Chase squinted at the clock on his VCR. It was almost eleven. Who was stopping by at this hour?

He looked around for his T-shirt and after a few seconds, gave up. Wearing only a pair of jeans, he padded barefoot to the door and pulled it open.

Abby stood there, her arms wrapped around her waist and a sheepish smile on her lips. "Hi. I know it's late."

"No, no. Come in." He stepped back to let her pass.

She hesitated for just a second, and then stepped inside.

"Can I get you a drink? I have coffee, orange juice, beer."

"I'm fine."

He pointed to the living room. "Want to sit down?"

She nodded. Perching on the edge of the couch, she looked up at him, waiting for him to sit. He sat on the couch too, at the opposite end.

She continued to sit forward on the seat cushion, her posture rigid, her hands resting on her knees. Her gaze seemed to be focused on a point in the corner of the room.

Chase frowned, perplexed. Not only did her demeanor and the mere fact she was here confuse him, but he was also puzzled by her behavior the whole week. She had been avoiding him.

He'd seen her on Tuesday night when she'd gotten home from work. They'd spoken, but she'd been distant. He thought maybe he'd made her uncomfortable with his comments at the barbeque. He never should have mentioned that he was having problems with the platonic arrangement. But he hadn't gotten an opportunity to apologize. He hadn't seen her again, until now.

"Abby, is everything okay?"

She looked at him and smiled brightly. "Yes, I just noticed that your light was on and thought I'd come say hi."

"I'm glad."

"Are you? Really?"

"Yes," he said, and then reached forward to touch one of the hands still pressed to her knee. "Abby, what's going on?"

"I have a big fund-raiser this weekend for Rand Labs." Her eyes now locked on his hand holding hers.

He waited.

"And I invited Nelson to come up to attend with me,

but he can't make it. He's always very busy with his work, you know."

"You've said that he's dedicated to his work."

"Yes. Yes, he is." She continued to stare at their joined hands, and Chase started to get uneasy. Something was really wrong.

"Do you know how long I've been in Maine?"

"A little over a month?"

She nodded, but still didn't look at him. "Yes, I've been here almost five weeks. And in five weeks, Nelson has only called me once—to tell me that he can't come to see me." She laughed humorlessly. "What does that say about me?"

"I don't know what it says about you, but it certainly says that Nelson is an idiot."

Abby's head shot up and she looked at him, her eyes crystalline in the lamplight. Then she laughed; this time the sound was tinged with wounded amusement. "You're good for my ego."

Chase watched as she again looked down at their hands.

They sat in silence for several seconds, until Chase slid closer to her. "Abby, why are you here?"

She hesitated. "I wanted to see you."

"But you avoided me all week."

"No—I . . ." she faltered.

"Abby, I won't deny that I'm very attracted to you. I think you already know that." He pulled his hand away from hers and tucked a strand of her hair behind her ear. "But I don't plan to be the guy you jump in bed with because your boyfriend just ticked you off."

Abby's eyes widened. "I'm not here—to—for . . . That isn't what I'm here for."

Chase was immediately sorry for his words. He didn't want to embarrass her. He realized her guarded nature had probably made it very hard to seek out his companionship. And what he'd said hadn't been strictly true either. He'd love to be her rebound boy. He actually couldn't imagine anything more appealing than rebounding with her all night long.

She stood, and he caught her arm.

"I shouldn't have said that." He slid his hand down her arm to capture her fingers. They were delicate and smooth against his calloused skin. "Please sit back down."

She cast a look at the front door, but then did sit, her posture even more stiff, if that were possible.

Again, a heavy silence filled the room.

"You were right." She said the words so abruptly, so quietly that they were almost lost in the thick stillness.

He squeezed her fingers. "Right about what, baby?"

"I did come here hoping—hoping you could make me feel attractive. Make me feel like there was a man out there who wanted me. I shouldn't have denied it."

He ran his thumb over the backs of her fingers, noticing the tidy shortness of her nails.

"Well, we're even then. Because I shouldn't have denied that I want to be the man you come running to." He brought those neat little fingertips to his lips and kissed them. "Because I do. I want to be the only man you ever come to."

He leaned forward and pressed his lips to hers. A small moan escaped her, and she twisted to wrap her arms around his neck.

Her position arced her against him, and he could feel the hardened peaks of her breasts against his bare chest. The cotton of her shirt added to the sensation, abrading his skin deliciously.

Her fingers twined into his hair and her tongue tentatively mingled with his. Her kiss was artlessly sensual, and she gave the impression of being chaste despite her long-term relationship with Nelson. Rather than hinder his arousal, Chase found her innocent reactions powerfully alluring.

He moved his hand to cup the back of her neck as he peppered her mouth with gentle, probing kisses. She clutched his shoulders as if she was afraid he would pull away.

Even though he knew he should, he had no intention of moving away. Instead he leaned into her until she was lying back against the cushions of the couch. His hand left her neck, sliding down her shoulder to her side. He toyed with the hem of her shirt, desperate to touch her bare skin.

His fingers slipped under her shirt, brushing the smoothness of her belly.

She gasped, her breath hot in his mouth.

He smiled against her mouth and nipped her bottom lip.

She gasped again.

His hand slowly moved upward, savoring the heat of her silky flesh. She felt as warm and wonderful as he had imagined she would. And he had given that particular subject a lot of thought lately.

At the underside of her right breast, his fingers stopped, and he lifted his head to watch her.

He swirled his thumb around the pebbled nipple.

She arched into his touch. Her eyes closed and her kiss-swollen mouth opened slightly, and Chase felt himself losing control of his desire.

He pushed up her shirt and found the nipple, drawing the tightened bud into his mouth through the white nylon of her bra. Her hands clutched his sides and he felt the bite of her tidy little nails in his flesh.

Her instant reaction spurred his desire on. His erection, which was already rock hard, strained like an iron spike against the denim of his jeans. He shifted, so he was positioned with his knees between her spread legs.

He sat up and looked at her sprawled against the cushions, her eyes half-closed and her hands still gripping his sides.

She looked amazingly beautiful. Her breasts were full and creamy, swelling above the restraint of her bra. A light smattering of freckles dusted the skin of her chest. He bent forward to taste the tempting little specks.

Abby wiggled under him, and he couldn't resist moving to press himself against her.

Her eyes widened at the feel of him against her belly, and he had to chuckle, the sound raspy with his desire.

"See what you do to me?"

Abby looked down to where he was thrust so intimately against her. She squirmed again, and he groaned as white-hot need shot through him. But her movement had positioned her on the couch so that she could pull back to make a little space between their bodies.

Tentatively, she reached down and touched the bulge that strained against his zipper. This time his groan came out more like a growl, and he dropped his forehead to hers.

"You feel wonderful," she whispered, cupping his arousal.

"Abby, baby?"

"Mmm," she murmured as her mouth found the skin of his shoulder, and her hand still caressed his erection.

He captured the wrist of the hand at his groin and moved it up over her head. He caught the other wrist and moved it above her, too.

She stared up at him, wide-eyed.

"Damn, you're gorgeous."

Her cheeks flushed to a deep pink, but her eyelids dropped and she writhed against him.

"Abby?" If she continued that, there was no way he could stay focused, let alone keep her focused. "Abby?"

"Mmmm?"

"I don't want to do this now."

She opened her eyes, and the passion was gone, replaced by a wounded look that darkened their brown depths. She struggled to sit up, but he kept her pinned under him.

"Don't look at me like that. I'm not saying that I don't want to make love to you." He pressed slightly against her. "I think it's fairly obvious that I do. But I really want you to think about what *you* want before we take this step. When we make love, I don't want there to be any regrets."

Abby stared up at him for a moment and then nodded.

Chase released her wrists, pressed a quick kiss to her lips and then pushed away from her. Holding out his hand, he helped her sit up.

Again, the room was quiet, but this time, the silence was laced with irregular breathing and the rustle of clothing being straightened.

"I didn't think things would get that out of hand that fast," Chase said.

Abby nodded.

"You aren't angry, are you?"

She shook her head.

"Can I see you tomorrow?"

She looked at him, an expression akin to relief in her eyes. "Yes."

He smiled, and she offered a timid smile back.

"Damn, I wish I wasn't reformed," he muttered, and then kissed her mouth quickly.

When they parted, Abby still had an uncertain tilt to her lips, but she managed another smile. "I should go."

Chase stood and held out his hand. She accepted it and they walked to the door, their fingers linked.

"Good night," she said softly, as she moved out on to the porch.

He didn't release her hand, and she turned to look at him.

He leaned out and stole another swift kiss, wishing he could just scoop her into his arms and take her up to his bed. But if he ever did make love to her, he didn't want there to be any doubts between them.

When he pulled away, she seemed dazed. But then she squeezed his fingers and tugged them out of his grasp. She rushed down the steps and across the lawn.

At the edge of the street, she paused and turned back to him. "Chase?"

"Yes?" His voice sounded rusty.

"Would you go to the fund-raiser with me?"

"I'd love to."

She offered him a tiny smile and dashed across the street.

Even after Chase heard Abby's back door bang shut, he leaned against his door frame, letting the fresh night air cool his overheated body and clear his jumbled thoughts.

What was he getting involved in? He wasn't happy with the idea of being anyone's second choice, but damn, he wanted Abby. Could he be satisfied to be with her whatever way she wanted him?

He took a deep breath and then went inside. What did he expect from her anyway? She was a brilliant scientist. He was a carpenter. She had her doctorate. By the grace of a few sympathetic teachers, he was lucky to have his high school diploma. She lived in the city. He lived in a town that was about as small as a place could get.

But when he looked at her, none of that seemed to matter. He wanted her. More than any woman he'd ever met.

Chapter 15

The grating buzz of the alarm clock jarred Abby out of her fitful sleep. She whacked the irritating device several times until the horrible noise stopped, then she buried her head under the covers.

She wanted to stay in bed forever.

Last night, *ugh*, last night. It was too humiliating to even think about. But unfortunately, she couldn't seem to concentrate on anything else.

She had done it again. And, worst of all, this time she was sober. She threw herself at Chase. He had to be thinking she was the world's flakiest tramp. Both times, he had handled it with great composure. Of course, he was probably used to crazy women propositioning him.

The worst part of the scenario was that he thought she was just using him to make herself feel better about Nelson's rejection. That wasn't the case at all. She wanted to be with Chase.

During the endless hours of the night, she had come to the realization that she just didn't have the feelings for Nelson that she should have. She was trying to resuscitate a relationship that had been dead for a long, long time.

She planned to phone Nelson and tell him they should end things. She didn't think he would be either surprised or upset. In fact, she suspected Nelson felt the same way.

But there was only one way to find out.

She rose and headed downstairs. In the living room, she paused and listened. She didn't want Ellie to hear this conversation. The house was quiet.

Abby sat on the couch and dialed Nelson's number. To her surprise, he answered on the first ring.

"Abby, you just caught me on the way out the door."

"Sorry, but we need to talk."

He sighed. "Abigail, if this is about me not coming up there, well, it's simply impossible."

"No, it's not. Well, it is, but . . ." How did she say this? "Think it's time for us to call it quits."

There was a pause.

"It isn't working, is it?"

Abby was shocked by his candidness. "No, Nelson, it isn't."

There was another pause.

"Are you okay?" Abby asked.

"Yes," he said. "It's not a total shock. I suspected when you decided to go to Maine that we were headed in this direction."

"I didn't."

"Listen, Abigail, I have to go."

"Are you okay?"

Dead air.

"I will be. I always have my work."

For the first time, Abby realized that Nelson was hiding from the world just as she had been. "Keep in touch, okay?"

"Okay," he agreed, but she knew he probably wouldn't. "Bye, Abby."

"Good-bye." Abby hung up the phone.

She had done it. She and Nelson were no more. She

felt sad, but not as sad as she would have suspected. If anything, most of her sadness was related to the fact that she didn't feel worse. But Nelson was right; they had started their breakup when she came back to Millbrook. She hadn't seen it, but it was true.

She looked at the phone and took a deep breath. She really hoped that one day Nelson would find something beyond his research. She did wish him happiness.

She wandered into the kitchen and rummaged around for some breakfast. After making a piece of toast and some tea, she sat at the table and reflected on her decision.

She knew she'd done the right thing with Nelson, but it didn't solve her other dilemma. Her overwhelming attraction to Chase.

When they had kissed last night, her mind had gone to mush. For the first time in her life, she wasn't thinking. She was only feeling. The touch of his hands, the brush of his tongue with hers, the wicked sensation of his mouth on her breast. She had never experienced anything so arousing. And she wanted more.

Abby did believe Chase was aroused by her. But she suspected he was more interested in a good time, rather than a real relationship.

Part of Abby found that idea very intriguing. She'd never had a fling. She'd only been with Nelson. But going from Nelson to Chase was like going from a high school biology class straight into a graduate seminar on single molecule detection of DNA hybridization and protein-DNA binding.

She got up and put her plate and cup in the sink. Even if Nelson had been the most amazing lover on earth—and she hated to be unkind, but he hadn't been—he couldn't have prepared her for her reaction to Chase. Just a single look, a single touch, and she was on fire.

Lord, she wanted Chase.

She was in Millbrook for three, maybe four more months. Then she would go back to Boston. It was the perfect timing for an affair with Chase. She believed he would agree to it.

Her only real concern was . . . could she spend the summer with a man like Chase and just leave with her heart intact?

Even knowing the answer to that question, there was no way she was going to miss this chance of a lifetime.

When Abby entered the small building on the corner of West Street and Oak, the last person she expected to see was Summer-Ann. But the woman sat behind a paper-cluttered dark wood desk and appeared to be quite at home there. Her feet were up on the corner of the desk, and she was chatting animatedly on the phone. At least, until Abby entered the office.

"Candy, I'll have to call you back." Summer-Ann sat up straight in the padded desk chair and dropped the receiver into the cradle. She regarded Abby with narrowed eyes like a sleek Siamese cat sizing up a scruffy stray. "May I help you?"

"Hi," Abby greeted, trying to keep the discomfort from her voice. "I'm supposed to be meeting Chase here."

"Did he tell you to meet him here?"

"Yes."

"Are you sure?" she asked in a condescending way that stated she thought Abby had just dreamed the invitation.

"Yes. I spoke with him earlier this afternoon."

Summer-Ann shrugged. "Well, he isn't here yet. You'll have to wait."

Abby nodded. Like that wasn't what she intended to

Zebra Contemporary

To start your membership, simply complete and return the Free Book Certificate. You'll receive your Introductory Shipment of 3 FREE Zebra Contemporary Romances, you only pay $1.99 for shipping and handling. Then, each month you will receive the 3 newest Zebra Contemporary Romances. Each shipment will be yours to examine FREE for 10 days. If you decide to keep the books, you'll pay the preferred subscriber price (a savings of up to 20% off the cover price), plus shipping and handling. If you want us to stop sending books, just say the word… it's that simple.

FREE BOOK CERTIFICATE

Yes!

Please send me 3 FREE Zebra Contemporary romance novels. I only pay $1.99 for shipping and handling. I understand that each month thereafter I will be able to preview 3 brand-new Contemporary Romances FREE for 10 days. Then, if I should decide to keep them, I will pay the money-saving preferred subscriber's price (that's a savings of up to 20% off the retail price), plus shipping and handling. I understand I am under no obligation to purchase any books, as explained on this card.

Name _____

Address _____ Apt. _____

City _____ State _____ Zip _____

Telephone ( ) _____

Signature _____

(If under 18, parent or guardian must sign)

Thank You!

Offer limited to one per household and not to current subscribers. Terms, offer and prices subject to change. Orders subject to acceptance by Zebra Contemporary Book Club. Offer Valid in the U.S. only.

CN054A

THE BENEFITS OF BOOK CLUB MEMBERSHIP

- You'll get your books hot off the press, usually before they appear in bookstores.

- You'll ALWAYS save up to 20% off the cover price.

- You'll get our FREE monthly newsletter filled with author interviews, book previews, special offers and MORE!

- There's no obligation —you can cancel at any time and you have no minimum number of books to buy.

- And—if you decide you don't like the books you receive, you can return them. (You always have ten days to decide.)

lll..d...lll....ll.l.l..l.l..l.l..lll.l.l..lld.l.lll..l

Zebra Contemporary Romance Book Club
Zebra Home Subscription Service, Inc.
P.O. Box 5214
Clifton , NJ 07015-5214

do. Summer-Ann did have the ability to make her feel uncomfortable, but she didn't have the ability to drive her away.

Still, seeing Chase again after their little make-out session on his sofa was going to be awkward enough without Summer-Ann practically hissing in the background.

Abby moved to sit down on the rust-colored tweed loveseat that was against the far wall. There was an end table beside the sofa, layered with magazines. She picked up one, but didn't look at it, instead examining Chase's small office. The desk where Summer-Ann sat took up a good portion of the room. A drafting table sat in the corner behind Summer-Ann, and there was a door behind her sporting a poster of Chase's construction logo. She wandered over to the frames on the wall, near the front door. They were awards of recognition from Millbrook Elementary School, and a nursing home and even Millbrook Town Hall.

The door opened, and Chase hurried in. Abby got the distinct impression that he had hoped to beat her there. Perhaps he was worried that Summer-Ann wouldn't keep her claws sheathed. She had, but Abby suspected it was only a matter of time before the blonde lost her cool.

"Hi." His slight breathlessness conjured images of last night's kiss.

"Hi."

"Have you been here long?"

"No, just a few minutes."

"I almost sent her away," Summer-Ann said. "You rarely come here at this time of day."

"That is true. Listen," he looked to Abby, "do you want to walk over to Eddie's Diner and get a cup of coffee or something?"

Abby nodded. "Sure." She got the feeling he wasn't

any more eager to have a conversation in front of Summer-Ann than she was.

As they crossed the street toward the old diner, Abby noticed Summer-Ann stood in the office's bay window watching them.

"I didn't realize Summer-Ann works for you."

Chase let out a dry laugh. "Yes, she does. I hope she was well behaved. Summer can be a bit difficult at times."

"She was fine. As long as I didn't make direct eye contact or any sudden movements."

Chase laughed again, this time the sound rich and full of amusement. "It seems you understand her very well."

They reached the restaurant, and Chase held the door for her as she entered. Eddie's Diner was straight out of the fifties with marbled linoleum floors and Formica-topped tables. Each of the booths even had its own personal jukebox.

Abby slid into the booth closest to the door, the red vinyl creaking under her weight. Chase slipped into the other side. And then they simply sat there, both uncertain what to say.

A woman approached the table, her gray hair piled high on her head like a beehive made of old wool.

"Chase, honey-sweetie, what can I get you, dear?"

"Hi, Sandy. I'll just have a coffee." He looked toward Abby.

"A coffee would be great."

The waitress nodded, and wandered off, the cloying scent of hairspray and the loud smacking of gum following in her wake.

"Is that Sandy Arsenault?"

"Yep."

Abby cast another quick glance at the woman. "I thought she was old when we were in high school. And yet, she looks exactly the same now."

"She's got to be in her late sixties."

Abby shook her head and took in the diner. It looked exactly the same too, not that she had come here often.

"Is this still the place all the 'in' kids go to after school?"

Chase shrugged. "I don't think so. I think the Denny's out on Route One is more the 'in' thing now. But you didn't call me to discuss where the local teens hang out, did you?"

Abby breathed in deep. "No. I didn't."

"Is it something with Nelson?"

Abby picked up one of the sets of silverware wrapped in a white paper napkin on the tabletop. She fiddled with the paper band that held the utensils together. Finally, she gathered her courage. "Yes, I've talked with Nelson. And we've decided to call it quits."

Chase reached out and stilled her fingers that continued to pluck nervously at the paper ring. "Are you okay?"

Abby nodded. "Yes, it was definitely the right thing to do."

"Good."

She looked down at their touching hands and took another deep breath. "But that is only one reason I asked you to meet me."

"Okay." Chase seemed confused by her nervousness, but he waited patiently while she attempted to screw up her bravery again.

Finally, seeing no other way than to just state her purpose, she blurted out, "I asked you to meet me, because I'm interested in being your lover."

It took a moment for Abby's words to sink into Chase's shocked brain. Fortunately, Sandy returned with their coffees, which bought him a few additional seconds.

By the time the older woman left, Chase managed to form some coherent thoughts.

"Abby, are you sure you're ready for another . . ." He hesitated to use the word "relationship," because he wasn't sure that was actually what she had in mind. "Are you sure you want to be with another man so soon?"

Her cheeks flushed to a deep red that matched the crimson of the flowers on her blouse. But she looked him straight in the eyes and nodded. "Yes. That is, if you are interested."

He nearly snorted at her polite reply. If he was interested? He felt like grabbing her hand and placing it on the erection straining against the fly of jeans. Oh yeah, he was definitely interested.

"I realize that we can't hope to have anything permanent," she said, "but while I'm here, I thought, if we are both agreeable to the idea, we could—see each other."

Chase blinked at her words. It was like she was setting up a professional agreement. Of course, in some ways, that was probably exactly what she was doing. A good time for a short time. Nothing long term, no emotions. Nothing beyond gratifying sexual urges.

Chase knew he should be happy with such a situation. Hell, most men would consider that a *Penthouse Forum* story come to life, but the offer made the hair on the back of his neck bristle.

Did he really want just a fling with Abby?

Ah, hell, it wasn't worth debating, because he knew he wouldn't say no to her anyway. He wanted her with an intensity that he found more than a little unsettling.

All day, he'd felt frustrated and on edge. Twice, he'd yelled at Dave Macy, one of his workmen, and Chase wasn't the type to lose his patience so easily. And he knew it all stemmed from his unfulfilled encounters with Abby. He wanted to make love to her so badly it was literally making him crazy.

So there was no point in meditating over her offer. He was going to accept anything she proposed, so why worry about it?

He reached across the table and captured her hand. Her fingers were cold. And she had such a frightened expression on her face as she stared into the depths of her coffee that he thought for a moment she was regretting her suggestion.

Then her gaze rose from the coffee to him, and he saw it was anxiety that darkened her eyes to the color of the liquid in her cup. She wasn't feeling remorse over her invitation, but concern that he would reject her—the silly, silly woman!

But he decided to approach her request in the same business-like manner she had. She would probably be more relaxed if he also kept his attitude professional.

"I should tell you up front that I'm clean as a whistle. I've been tested, and I give blood, but condoms are still a must."

Abby's eyes widened and she didn't seem to know how to respond. After a full ten seconds, she said, "I've only been with Nelson, and I give blood too. And I'm on the pill."

He nodded. "That's good, but I have a rule. If there's no cover—there's no lover."

Abby blinked. "Catchy." She blinked again, still looking a bit dazed. "Okay."

"Then," he said softly and squeezed her slender fingers. "I can't imagine anything I would want more than to be your lover."

* * *

Summer-Ann stood in the window even after Chase and Abby entered the diner. She knotted her hands in anger, until the sharp pain of her nails digging into her palms forced her to relax them.

This could not be happening. It couldn't!

She returned to her desk and sat down in her chair. Her desk. Her chair. Her office. *Her Chase.* That was how this was all supposed to play out.

She had spent the last three years making herself indispensable to Chase at work. And it was only a matter of time before he realized that she was indispensable to him in his personal life too. That was the plan, and it was a damned fine one. Until that wretched Abby Stepp returned to town.

Abby Stepp. Into what alternate universe had Summer stumbled where Abby Stepp was a threat to her? There had to be some reasonable explanation for Chase's interest in the dowdy woman.

She leaned back in her chair, again mentally making herself slough off the rage that tensed her spine and set her jaw.

Maybe he was helping her with some construction project. There was no denying that Abby's childhood home could use work. It was little more than a hovel. That could very well be the situation.

She smiled to herself. Yes, that must be it.

But her comforting conclusion was quickly dispelled by the memory of the way Chase had looked at the mousy woman when he came into the office. He'd appeared quite anxious to see her. And there was the kiss at the CrabFest. And in Chase's house.

He'd told her there was nothing going on between them, but Summer-Ann highly doubted his denial.

She had to go on the assumption that there was something between him and frumpy Abby Stepp. After working so many years to get him back, she wasn't going to lose Chase by being naive. The best defense was a strong offense.

The answer was quite simple really. No matter what the association between Chase and Abby Stepp, she needed to put a stop to it.

The question was, how?

Chapter 16

Abby was a bundle of nerves. She wanted to be calm and collected. She wanted to be relaxed and nonchalant. Instead, her hands shook so badly that she couldn't put on her mascara. Which didn't matter anyway, since her eye was twitching.

Taking a deep breath, then another, she left the bathroom in search of Ellie. Her little sister was still being a bit standoffish, but even if Abby had to grovel, she was going to get Ellie to forgive her. And hopefully, talk her through this little panic attack.

Ellie sat on the sofa, her feet curled under her and her face buried in a book. Abby seriously doubted that she would be pleased to turn her attention from the scantily clad hero on the front cover of her novel, to her twitching, hyperventilating older sister. But Abby didn't have any choice but to try.

"Ellie, can I get your help?"

Ellie dropped her book to her lap and frowned at Abby. But her frown was quickly replaced by a wide-eyed look of concern.

"What's wrong with your eye?"

"It's twitching."

"I can see that. And your voice sounds strange."

"I think I'm having trouble breathing."

Ellie stood and grabbed Abby's arm, directing her to sit on the sofa. "What on earth is wrong?"

"I—" Abby struggled with her breathing. "I have a date with Chase tonight."

"A date?"

"Yes, you were right. I'm crazy about him. I broke up with Nelson today, and told Chase I wanted a relationship with him." That was roughly what she told him. Her romance-minded sister would certainly rather hear that version than the truth. She offered the man a fling. A fling with ground rules, like condoms. A fling she was so, so ill prepared for.

Ellie captured Abby against her chest. "Oh, Abby, that is wonderful!"

"No, it's a disaster. I'm a wreck. I can't do this."

Ellie grabbed both of Abby's hands into her smaller, softer, warmer ones and squeezed them reassuringly. "Of course you can do this. I saw you and Chase together at the barbeque, and you are crazy about each other. Nothing has changed with that."

"We were just friends then."

"So, you're friends now. Let me help you get ready."

Abby knew she could count on her sister. Ellie had a huge heart, and she always forgave so easily. In Abby's opinion, it was a strength and a weakness. Ellie had the ability to set herself up for terrible pain.

But at this moment, Abby was extremely glad to have her sister's compassionate assistance. She needed that steady warmth to soothe her frayed nerves.

Ellie led Abby back to the bathroom and pushed her down on the toilet lid. Then she picked up the discarded mascara, and began to brush it onto Abby's lashes, timing the sweeps between the twitches. Next, she moved to the other cosmetics, adding blush to Abby's cheeks and a rosy red gloss to her lips.

"There, you look beautiful."

Abby checked her reflection in the hand mirror Ellie gave her and had to admit that, other than the occasional jerk of her left eyelid, she did look nice.

Ellie ushered her to her bedroom and helped her slip on her evening gown of black satin with a black chiffon overlay.

"I'll put your hair up," Ellie said, already gathering the locks up onto her head.

Abby sat patiently as Ellie pulled and pinned and twirled and tucked. When Abby thought her sister might never stop, Ellie released a pent-up breath and said, "Done."

Abby hesitated for a second and then went to the full-length mirror. The reflection that peered back at her caught her off guard. The woman in the mirror was elegant and poised and almost pretty.

Ellie had pulled her hair into a classy twist at the back of her head. The simple A-line cut of her gown emphasized the narrowness of her waist and the gentle fullness of her hips. The thin strap of the top accentuated the curve of her shoulders and the delicate cut of her collarbone. She felt feminine.

"You look beautiful," Ellie sighed, gazing at her like she was a fairy-tale princess. And she almost felt like one.

Her eye twitched. Almost.

"You get your shoes on, and I'll go get Grandma's pearls."

Ellie left the room.

Abby perched on the edge of the bed. Picking up one of the strappy black high heels, she stared at her reflection again.

She could do this. She had wanted to be with Chase since high school, and she was getting her chance. She could do this.

By the time Ellie returned, Abby had her shoes on, the filmy chiffon shawl that matched the gown draped over her shoulders, and the twitch in her eye relatively under control.

Ellie crawled onto the bed behind her and placed their grandmother's pearls around Abby's throat. The creamy white beads felt cool against her overheated skin.

"There, that looks perfect," Ellie pronounced, leaning over to see the necklace in the mirror.

Abby followed her gaze. The pearls did look lovely with the simple black gown. She was as ready as she was ever going to be.

"You look fabulous," Ellie said in a silly accent, a goofy grin deepening the dimples in her rosy cheeks.

"Why, thank you." Abby curtsied, her face split in a foolish grin of her own.

A loud rap sounded on the front door, and both women's smiles faded as they spun to look out at the hallway as if the person knocking would somehow magically appear outside Abby's bedroom.

"Well, don't just stand there," Ellie said, her grin returning. "Go down there and show Chase how wonderful you look."

Abby hesitated, then nodded and headed downstairs.

By the time she reached the front door, she was fairly certain the twitch in her eye had now moved to the whole side of her face.

She placed her hand on the doorknob and took a deep, calming breath. There wasn't any reason to get so worked up. She was attending the Rand Fundraiser with Chase, a friend. Okay, a friend who could very well see her naked before the night was over.

She should have told Chase that she was interested in an affair after the fundraiser. That way she could have at least remained composed throughout the evening.

With this situation, all she was going to be able to concentrate on was the possibilities that lay ahead. It was
daunt—

Another loud knock caused her to jump. With one
more cleansing breath, she twisted the doorknob and
pulled the door open. The sight in front of her not only
stopped the tic in her eye, but brought her pounding
heart to a standstill as well.

Chase stood before her, wearing a single-breasted
black tuxedo jacket. The cut of the tux enhanced the
broadness of his shoulders, and the white wing-collared
shirt underneath sharpened the cut of his jawline. His
bow tie was slightly crooked, but the lopsided accessory
only seemed to highlight the perfection on his features.

He hadn't cut his hair, Abby thought with relief. She
loved the tousled look of his unruly mane. Somehow the
disheveled hair also added to his flawlessness.

Her fingers itched to touch the dark, shiny locks. Instead, she whispered, "Hi."

He took a moment to answer, his own gaze devouring
her. "Hi," he finally said, his voice warm, melted chocolate, but it was the sweet scent of lilacs that surrounded
him.

They stared at each other for another moment, and
then Chase moved the hands that he was holding behind his back out to offer her a giant bouquet of
fresh-cut lilacs.

Abby's breath hitched and she took the flowers from
him. "Chase, they're beautiful."

"You are beautiful."

His adamant pronouncement caused heat to burn her
cheeks, but thankfully, her eye remained steady. That
is, until a glaring flash blinded her, leaving only white
spots in her field of vision.

"Sorry," Ellie said from the vicinity of Abby's right

shoulder. "I think there's something wrong with my flash."

"I think you may be right," Chase chuckled, and when Abby could finally focus her eyes again, she saw that he was blinking in a similar fashion.

"But I need to get pictures. You both look so stunning."

Abby frowned, still widening her eyes now and then, trying to get them readjusted to normal light.

"I'm not sure I can drive if you take another one," Chase said, making a similar face to the one Abby had just made.

"Well, wait here. I think I have a disposable one in my bedroom. Hold on." Ellie hurried up the stairs.

Abby turned and gave Chase an apologetic wince. "My sister gets excited about things like this. I'm sorry."

"Your sister is a romantic. That's one of the most endearing things about her. You know, she actually cried at the end of a very silly, very unrealistic medieval romance. But it was sweet. I like that about her," Chase said. He blinked hard again, then rubbed his eyes with the pads of his fingers.

Abby studied him as he tried to save his eyesight. How did he know what a romantic Ellie was? And when had he been around as she was crying over the end of a romance novel? Abby hadn't seen them visit much since she arrived, but it was obvious that they must have. Why did Ellie never mention it?

Ellie's rushed steps pounded down the staircase. "I found it! Okay, stand together. Abby, hold the flowers in front of you. Chase, what a beautiful bouquet. Okay, smile."

The flash popped, and then Ellie was herding them to the door. "Okay, have a fantastic time. Dance and drink and, oh, just have a great time."

Once Chase was out the door, Ellie caught Abby's

wrist, tugging her back in a tight embrace. "Have a magical night."

Abby half-frowned, half-smiled at her little sister. "It's the Rand Fundraiser, not a ball."

Ellie rose on her tiptoes and tilted her head toward Chase waiting by a red sports car, the orangey light of sunset reflecting off the glossy paint job, making the vehicle glow. "I don't think Prince Charming gets much better than that," Ellie whispered.

The evening air ruffled his hair and an amazingly sexy smile curved his mouth as he held the door open for her.

A shiver shimmied down Abby's spine, coiling low in her belly. Ellie was definitely right there. Prince Charming was a drooling oaf with pockmarks and an overbite compared to Chase.

Ellie tugged the lilacs from her numb fingers and then nudged her lightly in the back. "Well, what are you waiting for? Go have a great time."

A great time—if Ellie only knew. But Abby was hardly going to explain that her great time was very likely going to involve nakedness and lots of heavy breathing. Actually she would be lucky if she was breathing at all. She'd forgotten how to perform the function at the sight of Chase in his tux—what would happen when she saw him without it?

Her eye twitched. What were the chances that Chase would actually want to have intimate relations with a mindless, irregularly breathing, sexually-stunted scientist with a tic?

"We better get going," Chase called to her. "I don't want Rand's premier scientist to be late."

Abby smiled weakly and started down the stairs, clutching the thin shawl like it was a life jacket saving her from drowning. And there was no doubt; she was in over her head.

Once settled in the car, and after many, many deep breaths, she managed to ask, "Where did you get this car?"

Chase cast her a quick look, then his eyes went back to the road. "I was starting to wonder if you noticed I wasn't driving Helen. I've always had this, parked out back. But I don't use it too often. I have discovered that GTOs aren't really designed for hauling lumber and the like."

He shot her a quick smile, then sobered. "Abby, relax. We'll just have fun, and take things slow. I don't have any expectations on the evening other than enjoying your company. Let's just take it as it comes."

Abby lessened her death grip on her shawl and offered him a grateful smile. "So this is a date?"

"I don't don a tuxedo for a mere friend."

Abby's smile deepened. This time the action was easier. "So how many folks are going to be at this get-together?"

She shrugged. "I have no idea. I just found out on Monday that Rand did a fundraiser."

"That sounds like Cecil. The man is too busy to keep anything straight. Between his work and his family, he is forever on the go."

"Are you and Cecil good friends?"

Chase nodded. "Fairly good. I've done a lot of the renovations on his house. And Adele seems to feel the need to feed poor, lonely bachelors. So, I've had more than a few meals with them. They're nice people."

"Yes. I really like working with him."

Chase pulled his car into the crowded lot in front of the Millbrook Inn. The sun had set during their drive, and now the evening sky was a vivid indigo dotted with millions of tiny stars.

"What a gorgeous night." She sighed, accepting Chase's hand and stepping out of the car.

Chase kept his hold on her fingers, pulling her to him. "To be honest, I haven't been able to notice anything but you." He looked into her eyes for a moment and then placed a kiss on her mouth.

Abby's free hand moved up to find the silkiness of his hair, as she had wanted to since he first arrived at her door.

The kiss intensified, their tongues touching briefly, then retreating only to repeat the action. Abby sank her fingers into his unruly locks, smelling the fresh scent of his shampoo mingling with the spiciness of his cologne.

His hand slid around her waist, his long fingers splaying across the small of her back. His heat surrounded her.

Chase let out a low groan and pulled back. Resting his forehead against hers, a lopsided smile curved his lips. "If we keep doing this, I don't think you're going to make it into the party."

"So much for taking it slow," she said with her own sheepish grin.

"Yep, so much for slow." He straightened. Still holding her hand, Chase led her toward the inn's French doors. He paused with his hand on the handle. "Ready?"

She nodded.

Chase seemed to take a deep breath. He pulled open the door and ushered her inside.

At the entrance hall of the old inn, Abby was struck by the magnificence of the building. The foyer was huge and open, with a curved staircase that swept up to the second floor. An enormous, glittering chandelier hung high in the center of a domed ceiling cast with intricate patterns of leaves and flowers and fruit.

"Did you do this?" Abby asked, releasing his hand and turning to take in the view of the whole grand hall.

Chase looked around with her, a pleased turn to his lips. "Yeah, let's see. Two winters ago now, I guess. It took the entire winter. This place was really rundown."

"I remember." Abby couldn't stop gazing around her. The molding on the ceiling, the glossy parquet flooring. Every detail was perfect. It was like stepping into the past. A past of opulence and money.

"This inn was built in 1873, and was initially a social club—men only. The rich and famous would come here for vacation. The Vanderbilts, the Morgans, the Pulitzers, all the wealthy mucky-mucks stayed here. The inn touted itself as a literary and social society. Sort of ironic that I would be the one to restore it to its former glory."

Abby frowned. "Why?"

Chase came to an abrupt stop, and she bumped into his side. "I just meant—" He seemed to search for the right words. "I mean, that it took a lowly carpenter to get it back to the way it once was."

Abby shook her head and gazed around the room. "You are not a lowly carpenter. You're an artist."

Chase didn't respond, but his posture seemed less rigid than moments earlier. "Do you want to hear more about the inn's history?"

"Oh, yes."

"Well, let's see. In 1899, President McKinley came to the inn for a four-night stay, which was, of course, a huge coup for all of Millbrook."

"I never knew a president stayed here."

Chase led Abby down a long hallway that was lined on one side with large multi-paned windows that over-looked Fiddlehead Bay. The sky was now too dark to see clearly, although Abby could make out the silhouettes of several schooners bobbing serenely in the waves and moonlight.

"In 1922, women were finally allowed entrance into the inn, but only by special invitation. The ladies didn't have the benefit of equal status with the men that belonged to the club. In fact, they wouldn't have been allowed in the meeting room where the Rand Fundraiser is being held tonight."

Abby raised an eyebrow. "Well, I imagine a few Vanderbilts and Morgans are rolling in their graves at not only women, but educated women, being in their hallowed halls."

"Nah, I imagine the tourists that stay here wearing T-shirts that say things like LOBSTAHS ARE WICKED GOOD and MOSQUITO: THE MAINE STATE BIRD have already gotten most of those guys facedown."

Abby laughed. "So, when did this place fall into such disrepair?"

"It happened gradually. The financial cost to maintain the inn was very high, so by the time the Depression hit, it quickly fell into ruin. Or relative ruin. It was always used as some sort of lodging. In fact, the Navy used it as an observation post in World War II."

"I never knew any of this. It's strange they never taught us that in school."

"They may have taught it in school." Chase shrugged. "I never paid attention, so I wouldn't know."

"Well, I would have, since I did little else but study. And they didn't. And you do know it now."

Chase paused just outside a double doorway. Abby could hear the low drone of voices just beyond the dark oak panels.

"Are we here?" she asked.

Chase nodded. "Ready to make a first appearance as a couple?"

Abby's heart stopped, and all the calmness that she'd felt listening to Chase's story of the inn, vanished. First appearance as a couple? Was that really what they were?

"Here we go."

Abby had no memory of stepping into the meeting room. Her mind was too busy trying to decide if being a couple was different from being lovers.

But soon her colleagues were greeting them, and she was swept into a flurry of polite small talk.

When Chase left Abby's side to go to the bar, Leslie leaned toward her. "I didn't know you were dating Chase Jordan," she whispered.

"We just started—seeing each other."

"He's absolutely gorgeous." Leslie sighed, watching him as he stood among the crowd at the bar. She then reached over and patted her husband's arm affectionately.

Abby, however, didn't stop staring at her date. There was no denying it; Chase Jordan was the best-looking man in the room. And he was here with her. That fact was unbelievable.

Chase had started to talk with James, one of Abby's colleagues, his posture relaxed, his smile easy. And when the bartender came over to take his order, Chase offered him the same comfortable grin. He looked as at ease in his tuxedo as he did in his tool belt and work boots.

Abby wondered what it would be like to just naturally fit in anywhere. She certainly didn't know. A pang of envy snaked through her chest, but the sensation was replaced by admiration. Chase was amazing.

"Abby." A voice startled her out of her reverie.

"Cecil. This is wonderful." She gestured to the tables. Candlelight flickered off glassware and silver that circled flowing centerpieces of spring flowers.

Cecil cast an admiring look at his wife, standing in a group on the other side of the room. "You can compliment my lovely Adele. She arranges this event every year. And it is always splendid. Why last year . . ." Cecil's thought trailed off as Chase joined them, handing Abby a glass of wine.

"Chase." The older man grasped Chase's hand and pumped it enthusiastically. "It's great to see you. You're here with our Abby?"

Chase's dimple appeared, as he cast a look toward her that she could feel to the balls of her feet. "Yes, I am. How are you?"

Cecil gave his standard reply. "Wonderful, wonderful."

"This is a great spread," Chase said, nodding in the same direction that Abby had.

"I was just telling Abby that none of it was my doing. Adele always arranges the catering and such. And of course, you restored this place to its full grandeur."

Chase shrugged and took a sip from his beer glass. "All in a day's work. Hardly in the same class as what you and Abby do."

Cecil grunted. "Don't be too sure. It takes a similar mind to visualize the structure of something. We picture the structure of DNA. You picture the structure of a building. Both require understanding a specific configuration and the purpose of that configuration."

Chase inclined his head in polite agreement, but Abby got the impression that he didn't have the same opinion.

Cecil thumped Chase on the back with a warm, almost fatherly affection. "You two enjoy yourselves."

"We will," Chase said.

Abby simply nodded.

"He really likes you," she said after Cecil walked away. "He's a nice guy."

"And he's right, you know. The work you do is truly astounding."

Again, although he didn't make any particular expression or movement that said he disagreed, she got the feeling he wasn't comfortable with the subject. "So which people are you supposed to be schmoozing out of their money?" The change of topic was much clearer than his body language that he didn't want to discuss his career any longer.

Abby couldn't help wondering why, but she followed his lead. She scanned the crowd. The room was a sea of black mingled with flashes of color and the twinkle of jewelry. "I guess anyone I don't recognize. But I'm terrible with that sort of thing, so I think I'll just leave that task to the others."

She tried not to stare as a woman passed, gobs of glittering gems at her throat and ears. "I didn't realize people had so much money around here," she whispered.

"Most of the town doesn't, but Millbrook does have its wealthy areas."

Abby nodded, realizing that she did know that Millbrook had plenty of upper-class people. Their children had teased her about her tattered hand-me-downs. And she had watched as they barely got passing grades but went to expensive colleges. She'd had to work hard to get where she was. No one had given her a free ride. Now the same people wanted to invest in her knowledge. It was a little ironic.

"You look like you're about to go over there and gnaw on that lady's ankle."

Abby blinked, and gave Chase an apologetic smile. "Just thinking about the duplicity of money."

Chase nodded sympathetically. "Unfortunately, it's a necessary evil."

"Abby! Chase!" Mandy Blanchard, or rather Mandy

now married to so-and-so, approached them, her bright, cheery smile taking up half her face.

"Hi, Mandy," Chase said, and Abby realized she couldn't tell if he was really pleased to see her or not.

Her own forced smile definitely leaned to the latter.

"Now, I know why Abby is here. But why are you escorting her, Chase?" She cocked an inquisitive eyebrow. "Is there romance in the air?"

"How is Glenn? I heard he had a little accident. Did he make it tonight?" Chase asked, sidestepping the question.

Abby wasn't sure if she was relieved or not.

Mandy rolled her eyes, then waved a hand. "He's fine." She turned slightly to include Abby in the conversation. "He slipped on wet grass on the fairway. It was his own darn fault, I'd say. Playing golf in the rain. He's obsessed."

"Well, I'm glad he's okay," Chase said.

"He is," Mandy assured him. "Oh." This time her full attention was centered on Abby. "Wendy sent out the invitations for the class reunion just yesterday. I do hope you will come."

Abby nodded slowly. "I'll try."

Mandy's blinding smile returned. "Good. Well, I'll leave you two now. I'm supposed to be getting Glenn another drink. Talk to you soon. And let me know if you want to be on any of the reunion committees."

"Talk about obsessed," Abby said after Mandy crossed the room. "She is fixated on this class reunion thing."

"And you find this surprising? Don't you remember her at pep rallies? Go, Millbrook Millers!" He raised his beer glass.

Abby laughed. "She did have school spirit."

"And she just happened to find the two people that had the least school spirit. She feels the need to save us."

"Who needs to save you from what?" Darren approached them, although it took a moment for Abby to recognize him. He had indeed cut his hair for the event and not a single strand stuck out in its usual disorderly fashion.

"Darren. Do you know Chase Jordan?"

"Of course, I know Chase." Darren held out his hand, and Chase shook it, but then Darren's attention turned back to Abby.

"So did you finish up your part of the speech?"

"Yes," Abby said. "Although I'm afraid it's a little dry."

"I'm sure it's fine. There's only so many ways you can dumb down our research and still keep it interesting."

Abby frowned. "Our work is fascinating."

"To us. To the average Joe, it's a bunch of gobblety-gook."

"Now, gobblety-gook, is that a layman's term?" Chase asked with an amused look that didn't quite reach his eyes.

Darren chuckled. "I suppose I could throw it in my speech and see if our investors think it's a real scientific term."

"Did you need more wine?" Chase asked Abby.

"No, I'm fine."

"Okay, I'll be right back."

Abby frowned as she watched Chase head to the bar. Had something offended him?

"So when did you start seeing the town hottie?" Darren asked.

"What?"

"Chase Jordan. He's a bit beefcakey, isn't he?" When Abby simply stared, he tapped his neatly groomed head. "You know, nice to look at but not a lot going on upstairs."

Fury congealed in Abby's belly. She glared at her co-worker. "Chase is a very intelligent guy."

Darren held up his hands. "Sorry, I didn't mean to be insulting." He started to back away. "Listen, I'll talk to you later."

After he left, Abby stood there for a moment, shocked. Darren had never struck her as a snob before, but obviously he was. What he'd said about Chase was terrible. To assume because Chase was handsome that he was stupid.

She clenched the stem of her wineglass. It is seemed that plain or pretty, smart or average, no one could avoid labels. Ooh, that made her angry.

Chapter 17

Chase picked up the beer that Neil, the bartender, had just brought him. He downed half of it in one gulp.

Man, people like that Darren guy really ticked him off. Like his intelligence gave him the right to ridicule others. Like Chase wouldn't understand what Abby did for a living. Of course, the thing that irritated Chase the most was that Darren was probably right.

Chase turned to look at Abby. She now stood alone, staring in front of her, her spine rigid, her jaw set. It was obvious she was upset.

"Are you okay?" Chase asked, once he had returned to her side.

"I don't even want to be here."

Chase looped his arm around her back and started her through the crowd.

"Where are we going?" she asked, bewildered, but she continued to follow him.

He wiggled his eyebrows. "It's a mystery."

On the other side of the room, he opened an oak-paneled door and they stepped into darkness.

"Should we be in here?"

"Does it look like there's anyone to stop us?"

"I don't know." Abby's hand clutched his sleeve. "I can't see a thing."

He chuckled. "Just follow me."

He moved through the shadows until he reached drawn curtains that hid another set of doors. Unlocking them, he pushed the doors open. The sea air rushed through the open portal, brushing against their skin and ruffling their hair.

Chase could hear and feel Abby's sharp intake of breath.

She released his hand and went to the railing of the small terrace and looked out over the bay. The night was perfectly clear. Moonlight danced across the black water and stars twinkled in the inky sky. "Oh, this is lovely."

Chase moved to stand beside her, but he didn't look at the view, instead gazing at Abby.

Her skin appeared silver in the moon's soft glow. The silky black material of her gown fluttered around her. She was flawless. Like a goddess—a goddess of night serenely overseeing her realm.

He reached out and twirled one of the curls at the nape of her neck around his finger.

"You are so beautiful."

She turned to gaze at him, her eyes as black as her dress, the fullness of her mouth a celestial invitation.

He bent forward and accepted it.

She immediately leaned against him. Her hands moved over the sleeves of his jacket.

He longed to feel those slender fingers touching his bare flesh. Instead, he touched her skin, the warm smoothness of her bare arms, the gentle curve of her shoulders.

She moaned as he nipped her plump lower lip and moved to press kisses along her jawline to her neck. She gave a quavering gasp, and her head fell back, offering him better access to the sensitive skin of her throat.

He tasted her there. A heady combination of Abby and the salty night air mingled on his tongue. Then he returned to her lips, reveling in their softness, their hunger.

With a reluctant groan, Abby broke the kiss, only to rest her forehead against his chest, her hands holding his sides. "I want to stay right here." She sighed.

"Okay," he agreed, lifting her chin and kissing her again.

She returned his kiss, then pulled away slightly to smile against his lips. "I *can't* stay here, though. I have a speech to give, remember?"

This time Chase sighed. "I remember." He linked his fingers through hers and started toward the doors. "I guess I'd better get you back before we turn into pumpkins."

Abby stopped, jerking him to a halt.

"What's wrong?" he asked.

She shook her head. "It's—it's nothing."

"Something upset you."

"No, it's just me being silly."

Chase pulled her against him, leaning his head so he could whisper against her ear. "So tell me then."

She remained very still in his arms, then pulled back and looked directly in his eyes. "Okay—that's the first time someone has made a Cinderella reference to me, and I wasn't the ugly stepsister."

Chase stared at her for a moment and then pulled her tight against him. "When are you ever going to realize you never were the ugly stepsister?"

They stood in each other's embrace for a moment.

"We'd better get back."

Abby nodded and followed him through the shadows.

They made it back in time for Abby's speech, and despite his concern about Darren's prediction, Chase didn't find it to be gobblety-gook.

Abby stood at the podium, looking elegant and poised. She spoke about her research with such excitement and conviction that Chase couldn't help being interested in her words.

He glanced around the room and found that everyone else appeared as fascinated with her speech as he was. She finished her portion of the discourse and stepped back to let Darren give his part of the speech.

As she stood, listening to her colleague, Chase studied her, and his thoughts went to graduation day and her valedictorian address.

She hadn't been as sophisticated, but had that been the only difference? Had she spoken with the same conviction? Had she been as excited about her success and her future as she was her research now?

Had she been absolutely beautiful, and he missed it?

Abby Stepp, one of the ugly Stepp sisters.

He had listened to and accepted that awful description. He'd been stupid and shallow. Abby Stepp was an amazing person, and he had the feeling she always had been. But he hadn't given her a chance back then.

He came out of his musings and discovered her gaze was on him. When they made eye contact, she rewarded him with a huge, happy smile. Her lips were rosy from his kisses.

Damn, he was lucky to be with her.

But would she be smiling at him like that if she knew the truth about him? Chase wondered.

"So was that the most horribly boring thing you've ever had to sit through?" Abby asked as Chase pulled out of the Millbrook Inn's parking lot.

"Okay, you do recall Mason mentioning the town meeting where they were voting over the hours of operation for the dump?"

Abby nodded, fighting back the urge to giggle.

"Well, I've been to hundreds of meeting just like that one."

"I don't know, that meeting sounded pretty exciting. Old men were going to come to blows."

"Yeah, well, that doesn't happen too often. Usually they're dead dull," Chase said, then he sobered. "Seriously, your work is very interesting, and it's obvious from how you explained the research that you love it."

"I do." She closed her eyes, enjoying the giddiness that coursed through her, making her limbs light. Her speech had gone great. Cecil had been thrilled with the investors' interest in the lab's research. She'd drunk several glasses of champagne in celebration and she just felt . . . bubbly.

But what had her feeling the most bubbly was the memory of Chase's kiss in the moonlight. Even now, she could taste him on her lips. And the social part of their evening was over and they were finally alone.

She opened her eyes and watched him drive, a broad-shouldered silhouette beside her.

"What are you thinking about?" he asked, amusement softening the words.

"You."

"And what are you thinking about me?"

"That I like the way you kiss."

"Really? Well, I'm pretty partial to the way you kiss, too."

The bubbles swirled in her belly. She licked her lips. "Are you?"

"Oh yeah," he said with conviction.

Abby felt wonderful. Powerful. Attractive. And the night still held so many possibilities.

She glanced over at Chase. The faint blue light of the dashboard lit his face enough that she could see the straight line of his nose and the shape of his sculpted lips.

She swiveled on the bench seat. "Are you planning to take me home now?"

Chase cast her a quick look. "Do you want to go home now?"

Abby thought for a moment. She shook her head. "No, I think I'd rather go home with you."

"Well, sweetheart, I would love you to come home with me," Chase said, and Abby fell against the back of the seat as the car accelerated.

By the time they stepped into Chase's house, the champagne and Abby's boldness had worn off. She stood in the middle of his bright kitchen and wondered why on earth she thought she could ever be daring enough to actually have a fling with Chase Jordan.

"Come on, you lazy oaf," Chase coaxed, holding open the back door. "Get up, and go do your business."

Chester, who had been regarding Chase from his doggy bed, thumped his tail twice and struggled to his feet. Ambling first to Abby for a pat on the head, he finally followed Chase's order and went outside.

"My dog likes his sleep."

Abby smiled.

Chase paused from loosening his bow tie and considered her.

"Are you okay?"

She nodded, trying to keep her expression calm.

"No," he said as he shrugged out of his jacket, the thin white material of his dress shirt straining against the muscles of his shoulders. "You're not okay."

"Why do you say that?"

"I can tell when you're uncomfortable by your posture. You get stick straight. You're stick straight right now."

Abby crossed her arms over her chest and tried to relax the taut muscles in her back. "I may be a little nervous," she admitted, moving her arms back to her sides, although the movement didn't help her feel more relaxed. "I've never done anything like this before."

She crossed her arms again.

"You've stood in this kitchen several times before."

"Please don't be obtuse. You know what I mean." She almost cringed at her abruptness, but she felt like a violin that had been strung too tight. She had no idea what to do now that she had Chase alone.

Her eye twitched. Great.

Instead of being offended by her terseness, Chase chuckled. "I'm not being obtuse. I'm being serious. We're just hanging out in my kitchen after a very nice evening together. There shouldn't be anything nerve-wracking about that."

"Easy for you to say," she muttered.

He laughed again. "Sit down. Would you like a drink?"

Abby was so nervous she felt like she'd just eaten a heaping spoonful of flour. "That would be great." She sat down.

Chase opened the refrigerator door and peered inside.

"Let's see—I have soda, OJ—" He braced his hand on the fridge door and leaned forward to look at the lower shelf. The movement pulled the fabric of his trousers tighter against his firm backside.

Abby stared. Her eyes moved from his bottom to the defined muscles of his back and then to his butt again.

After several seconds, she realized Chase had stopped talking and was looking at her, an amused smile turning up the corners of his mouth.

"So what will it be?" he asked, the grin widening. He knew full well she had no idea what he'd been saying.

"The last one," Abby said, cursing the blush that burned her skin.

"Iced tea, it is."

Thank goodness. For all she knew, she'd agreed to do shots of tequila.

Chase bent into the fridge to retrieve the pitcher of tea, his firm bottom tempting her again.

On second thought, she'd been feeling much braver when the champagne had been bubbling merrily through her system. She could only imagine what tequila would do to her courage.

Chase fixed a glass of tea and then joined her at the table.

"So what's got you so nervous?"

The directness of Chase's question caused her hand to falter as she took the drink. Amber liquid sloshed onto the tabletop. She stared at him with wide eyes, uncertain what to say.

"Come on, tell me what's bothering you." He gave her an encouraging smile.

Abby paused. She'd already told him plenty of things that were embarrassing—the hurts of her past, the monotony of her relationship with Nelson. Heck, he could probably guess what she was uptight about.

"I don't think I'm very good in bed."

Chase nearly laughed but thankfully, caught himself when he realized she was being serious. "And how did you come to this conclusion?"

Abby ran her neatly trimmed finger around the rim of the glass. "I've never been overly—" she struggled with the right words. "I've never been overly successful with sex."

Chase watched her. Gee, could have something to do

with her ex-partner being a clueless automaton. But he didn't reveal his irritation, afraid that she would either stop telling him about her concerns or think he was angry with her.

"So neither you nor Nelson enjoyed sex?" he asked.

Abby shook her head, staring at the table. "Nelson had this theory that intellectuals didn't have primal urges, such as sexual desire, to the same extent that—average people did."

Chase stared at her, until she finally raised her head and made eye contact with him.

"You didn't buy that, did you?" he asked, keeping his voice level.

"No," she said, her gaze back on her glass, her finger moving again. "But it was a nicer explanation than the truth. I didn't—turn him on."

"You know the more I hear about this guy, the more I dislike him and the more I doubt his intelligence."

Abby peeked at him from under her lashes. "But the fact remains that I'm not altogether sure that I wasn't the problem. And I'm definitely not proficient enough in the act to satisfy someone like you."

Chase blinked, then frowned. "Someone like me? What am I, the town horndog?"

Abby cringed, then adamantly shook her head. "I didn't mean it that way." She fell silent, running her index finger up and down the condensation beaded on the outside of the tumbler.

"I just don't want to disappoint you—or myself for that matter," she said faintly.

Chase studied her, his eyes straying from her downcast face to the repetitive movement of her finger. Up. Down. Up. Down. Water glistened on the tip of her finger, on the smoothness of her short nail.

Chase could imagine that same long finger running

the length of his hardened penis. Up. Down. Up. Down. His moisture dampening her finger, glistening on her nail.

He shifted, the scratchy material of the tuxedo pants growing more uncomfortable by the moment, with each stroke. Damn, what was this woman thinking? She drove him wild by merely fidgeting with a drink glass. There was *no* way he'd be disappointed. And he sure as hell planned to make sure she wasn't disappointed.

"Come here," he said, his voice low, the command undeniable.

Abby hesitated, but after a few hushed moments, the chair scraped against the floor. Abby moved to stand in front of him, her hands loose at her sides, her coffee brown eyes wide and uncertain.

"You were amazing during your speech," he told her. "You had everyone in the room captivated. I was captivated. I wanted to understand your research. I wanted to understand you."

The pink that had stained her cheeks since they entered the kitchen deepened. Her eyes searched his.

He placed his hands on her hips, caressing his thumbs back and forth over the smooth fabric of her gown and the slight jut of her hipbones. "And after your speech, I simply watched you. The brilliance in your dark eyes. The curve of your beautiful mouth. The way excitement colored your cheeks."

His hands slid slowly from her hips down the outside of her thighs, until he reached her knees. Then he slowly brushed his palms back up, following the same path to her hips.

"And I want to create that same response in you. With my hands, and my mouth, and my body. Until you're under me, eyes glittering, cheeks flushed, a satisfied smile on those gorgeous, lush lips."

A shaky breath escaped her parted lips, and he felt her tremble.

In one quick motion, he stood, gripped her waist and twisted to place her onto the table directly in front of him.

A squeak escaped her, and she looked up at him, uncertainty replaced by surprise.

He grinned, cupped the back of her head and pulled her mouth to his. She tasted like champagne and strawberries and timidity, but her lips clung to his, searching for his reassurance. He continued to kiss her slowly, telling her with small, teasing sweeps of his tongue that everything would be fine. Wonderful, in fact.

Her hands came up from gripping the edge of the table to caress his cheeks, the pads of her fingertips like the softest silk against his skin. Then she sank her hands into his hair, and kissed him with all the desire he was keeping a tight rein on. Her tongue tasted his, brushing temptingly over his lips. Her teeth nipped at his bottom lip.

A small moan of satisfaction sounded between them.

He wasn't sure which of them had made the noise, but it summed up his feelings with total accuracy. Her full, supple lips were stealing all of his softness, leaving him hard and vibrating.

He let her continue her incredible assault, loving the textures of her mouth, until he felt his tight hold slipping. Tonight wasn't about him. It was about Abby and about making her understand how truly beautiful and sexy she was.

He sat back in his chair, slowly running his hands from her waist back down the outside of her legs. He stopped at her knees and left his hand there. Gently, he began to hitch up the material of her dress, each handful exposing another inch of long, shapely legs. "Did I tell you how sexy you look in this dress?" he asked.

She didn't respond, mesmerized by the slow rise of her dress.

Once the hem reached the tops of her tightly closed knees, he paused.

"I want to touch you, Abby."

Her eyes were heavy. The deep brown of her irises appeared nearly black under the sweep of dark lashes. She nodded, the movement so small, he wasn't absolutely certain he hadn't just wished her consent. But then her squeezed thighs parted, just slightly.

He smiled and placed a kiss on her knee. His hands slipped under the gathered gown. He expected to discover the mesh of pantyhose covering her smooth skin. Instead, he was delighted to find his fingers sliding over warm, naked flesh.

He grinned up at her. "I would have pegged you for a staunch nylons-wearer."

Abby licked the width of her bottom lip, her eyes flashing from his hands disappearing under the puddle of black material to his face and back to his wandering fingers. "I am. I just happened to get a snag in my last pair, and I didn't have time to go buy more."

His grin widened. "My lucky day."

His fingers spanned the firm top of her thighs, the pads of his thumbs brushing leisurely over the edges of her panties at the apex of her thighs.

A small sound that was a combination between a gasp and a hiss escaped her lips. Her eyes closed, and she bit her bottom lip, the pink flesh pillowing around her white teeth.

He leaned forward and kissed the fragile, pale skin of her inner thigh. His butterfly kisses advanced forward, relentless in their fluttering assault.

Her legs fell farther apart, and he could see lacy red panties that stood out like a beacon against her milky skin. The underwear surprised him too; he would have suspected she was a true blue white cotton girl, which would have been fantastic. Red lace was just a bonus.

"I like the panties," he whispered against her thigh.

She wiggled, and said breathily, "I *did* have time to get those."

He looked up at her. "I think you made all the right decisions about your clothing tonight."

She smiled.

Then his thumb found the sensitive center of her through the silky panties.

Her eyes closed and her mouth parted. This time a true gasp escaped her.

He increased the pressure, feeling the slide of silk over springy curls. The sensation was thrilling, but it made him hungry to touch her with no barriers. To feel those curls with his fingers, to feel them tickle his lips and to taste the hot, moist flesh that lay beyond their springy limits.

He ran both hands up to hook his thumbs under the waistband of her panties. "Lean back, baby, and lift your bottom," he murmured against the skin near her belly button.

"What?" Abby asked.

He looked up to find her peering at him, confusion creasing her brow.

"I want to take your panties off," he told her, pressing another kiss to her belly.

"Oh." Her voice was still vaguely dazed. She leaned back and started to raise off the table when she lost her balance and slipped, kneeing him in the chin.

He grunted.

She caught herself and straightened back up, her hands clapped over her mouth, her eyes wide. "Are—are you all right?"

Chase nodded, rubbing his jaw. "Are *you* okay?"

She glanced at the table. "I think I slipped in the condensation from my glass of iced tea."

He chuckled. "And to think, only moments earlier, I was finding that condensation very sexy."

Abby gave him a puzzled look, but he didn't take time to explain, instead standing to kiss her. She responded immediately, and he lost himself in the heat of those soft lips.

He braced an arm behind her and leaned her back. The other hand brushed down her body, tracing her curves until he reached her panties. He bent his index finger over the edge and tugged. She shifted and the scrap of material glided down. He gently pulled off her high heels and the panties followed.

He straightened and studied her. Her hips were rounded; her legs long and the dark curls at her thighs were . . .

He looked up at her.

She watched him with wary eyes as if he would be disappointed. Disappointed? God, she was . . .

"Abby, you're breathtaking."

The guarded expression lessened but didn't completely disappear.

"Do you want to know what I'd like to do to you?" he asked, running a fingertip from her knee to her hip and back again.

She nodded, her cheeks burning red.

"I want to taste you." He leaned forward and nipped the sensitive skin of her inner thigh.

She gasped.

"I want to feel you come against my tongue." He ran his tongue dangerously close to those dark corkscrew curls.

She shivered.

"And then I want to sink inside you until I fill you, and we can feel nothing but each other." He brushed a finger against her, parting her.

She groaned and raised her hips.

He obeyed her silent command and placed his mouth over her, finding the tight bud with his tongue. Her taste and scent surrounded him like misty salt air. It was intoxicating. It was heaven. And Chase couldn't remember wanting anything more than he wanted to make Abby scream with pleasure.

She collapsed back against the table as if his tongue had stolen her strength and pinned her to the polished wood.

He swirled the tip of his tongue around her, and she arched her back, her hands knotting in his hair. He flicked his tongue faster, and she began to squirm.

"Chase." She whimpered, the sound distressed, the sound euphoric.

He caught her writhing hips, holding her steady, and increased the pressure. Her legs fell over his shoulders, and she ground her heels into his back, straining, striving.

"Chase!"

With each of pulse of her against his lips, he hardened. With each gasp, his penis leapt. He wanted to be clasped by the hot, throbbing flesh that surrounded his tongue. But not until he tasted her fulfillment, not until she experienced something that he was certain she had never had—with a partner, anyway.

He increased his speed, and he could feel her tense. Her pebbled clitoris quivered under his lips and he could taste the sweetness of her response.

She groaned, throwing out her arms to clutch the edges of the table. One of her hands hit the forgotten iced tea glass.

He heard the tumbler skitter across the tabletop.

In the same instant, Abby cried out and bucked against him. Simultaneously, she and the glass shattered into a million pieces.

Chapter 18

Abby tried to focus on the round ceiling light, but the hammering of pleasure and pounding of her heart were too overwhelming, so she closed her eyes and focused on them.

She had orgasmed! Holy cow, had she ever orgasmed!

She knew she should feel embarrassed or ashamed to be spread half naked across Chase's kitchen table, but she didn't. She felt wonderful. She felt amazing. And she couldn't believe she had so easily achieved something that had always seemed elusive to her.

She felt Chase stir and opened her eyes. He leaned over her, his hair ruffled from her fingers, his lips still damp from her. His pale eyes shone and the curve of his lips was extremely sexy.

"So do you still think you aren't any good at sex?"

Abby smiled, the action languorous. "I think you're good. I don't think we've actually put me to the test."

"Well, I guess we'd better do that."

He pulled her toward him, and she slid easily across the table.

"I don't think this is going to be a fair test of my ability, as I'm already done," she warned.

Chase nodded sympathetically, but his eyes twinkled. "Well, if you fail, I'll just test you later after you do some more boning up on the subject." He grinned at his bad joke.

"That was terrible."

"Mmm-hmm," he agreed and kissed her.

Abby loved his mouth. His lips were soft and smooth, yet he kissed her with such hunger and strength. She could feel his possession to the tips of her toes.

He tugged at her bottom lip. Her toes curled.

Very quickly, she realized that her theory that she was done because he'd brought her to orgasm was a silly one. Just kissing him was creating another wave of longing deep inside her. Electricity zipped through her nerve endings and sparks zoomed through her veins, all centering in at that little point between her legs.

She wanted more of Chase. She wanted her turn to touch him, to feel his hard muscles and taste the faint saltiness of his skin. To see every inch of him naked.

And when he had told her earlier that he wanted to fill her, well, she wanted that more than she thought possible. She wanted to be his.

Her hands snaked up between their bodies and found the buttons of his shirt. She fumbled with the tiny plastic circles that seemed impossibly large to fit through the buttonholes.

Chase lifted his head. "Do you want me to help?"

The sight of that gorgeous dimple caused her fingers to trip up further. "Yes. Please."

Chase straightened and began to work the buttons free.

Abby leaned on her elbows and watched as each unfastened button revealed a bit more golden skin. Finally, he shrugged off the shirt and tossed it onto the chair with the discarded tuxedo jacket. The ceiling light directly above him highlighted his broad shoulders and the lean muscles of his arms, and created intriguing shadows under the taut muscles of his chest and his stomach.

He started to move back toward her, but she shook her head.

One dark eyebrow rose. "No?"

"I want to look at you."

A slow, sexy grin spread over his face. "You're getting awful cocksure all of a sudden."

"You're developing a corny sense of humor all of a sudden."

"Yeah," he agreed guiltily. "Well, stressful situations do that to me."

Abby rose up slightly, frowning. "How is this situation stressful for you? I'm the one sprawled on the kitchen table half-naked."

"Mmm," he nodded. "I do like that." He grazed a fingertip down her belly to brush over the small triangle of curls above her closed legs.

Her lips parted, and she struggled to control the uneven breath his fleeting touch caused. Closing her eyes briefly, she managed to gather her wits and her rampant desire. "Well, there should be no stress. You succeeded at your end of the job quite impressively. I'm the one that has no idea if what I'm doing is right or not."

Chase studied her for a moment, his expression unreadable. "Baby, you can't do anything wrong. Do whatever feels right to you. I'm pretty damned sure I'm going to enjoy it."

She breathed in deeply. "Okay, then lose the pants."

He immediately unbuttoned and unzipped them. "See, I'm enjoying this already." The black material slid down, leaving him in his hot chili pepper boxers. He looked down at them and then at her, smiling lopsidedly.

"I figured they would be a nice touch, if we did make it this far."

"Very nice," she agreed with a small laugh. "Off."

He promptly pushed them down. They disappeared out of view beneath the table with his pants. He straightened.

And Abby simply stared. His erection jutted up against his belly, the tip nearly touching his shallow navel.

"You're so . . . magnificent," she murmured, and then, as if the thick, hard shaft was a lodestone, she sat up and reverently ran her fingers down its length.

He made a noise in the back of his throat, and his penis jerked under her tentative touch. Abby pulled her hand away, but he caught it and brought her fingers back to him, curling them around his width.

"No, touch me."

She did, moving back and forth over him, testing the different textures. The granite hardness sheathed in velvety skin. The spongy softness of the head dampened with his arousal.

"Amazing," she breathed.

Chase caught her chin and kissed her. His mouth devoured hers, demanding and full of need. He continued to imprison her mouth with his, while his hands hooked behind her legs and pulled her to the edge of the table.

As his tongue brushed and swirled with hers, his fingers slipped between her legs and mimicked his tongue's motions. The tiny bud, still sensitive from his earlier attention, convulsed under his touch. Her legs fell helplessly open.

She fondled him in return, running her palm over him.

Both of them groaned into each other's mouth so their reaction seemed to be one, their arousal unified.

He continued to circle the calloused pad of his thumb around her, while a finger slipped inside her, then another, stretching her, filling her.

Vaguely, she wondered how the width of his erection would ever fit, if his fingers could make her feel so full.

"Baby, you are so warm," he murmured against her mouth.

She felt more than warm. She felt on fire.

He seemed to be burning up too, his erection searing hot in her hand. She ran her fingertips over the tip to spread his moisture over the heated flesh, but the wetness only seemed to ignite him further.

"Abby, you're killing me. I have to be inside you," he muttered roughly against her ear, the huskiness of his voice tickling her skin.

"Yes." She released him to grab his narrow hips and move him between her splayed legs.

"Wait," he said and pulled away from her.

Abby suppressed a frustrated groan.

Or maybe she didn't, because Chase smiled and said indulgently, "Just one second."

He leaned over and fumbled with his tuxedo pants, and promptly returned with a couple silver packets.

Condoms, she realized. Then another realization hit her. "You had those at the fundraiser?"

He smiled sheepishly. "It was like my choice in boxers— be prepared, just in case."

He tore one of the packages open with his teeth, and slid the condom on with practiced ease that Abby didn't really want to think about. And she didn't have much time to, because he returned to the vee of her thighs and all rational thought was lost.

She felt the head of his penis against her, and she shifted, anxious to have him fill her.

He was eager too, reaching down to guide himself into her. She gasped as he pressed slowly forward, spreading her, stretching her.

"Are you okay?" he asked, studying her with his icy blue eyes that seemed to penetrate her as deeply as his erection.

She nodded.

"Good," he groaned and held her hips and began to move within her.

Clutching him around the neck, she buried her face into his shoulder and concentrated on the sensation of him inside her. She could feel each pulse of his erection, each tiny ripple. And he felt so right inside her, like a piece of herself that had been missing.

"God, baby, you're driving me crazy," he groaned, nipping the bare skin of her shoulder. "I don't know if I can be gentle."

She bit his shoulder in response. "Then don't," she breathed against his neck. And whether it was the bite or her words, Abby didn't know, but Chase lost his tightly reined control.

Holding her hips, Chase began to thrust into her, each entry more insistent than the last. She anchored her legs around his waist and arced against him, accepting his powerful thrusts, loving his wild strength.

She fell back against the table, the angle allowing him to penetrate her deeper, fuller. And with each fierce stroke, she felt the tightness low in her belly

She clutched him and shouted. Distantly, she heard Chase's own roar and then they collapsed onto the tabletop.

Abby panted up at the ceiling, concentrating on the

tingles of bliss flowing through her limbs and his wonderful weight on her body.

She felt giddy—far, far more so than the previous effects of the champagne. She wanted to sing, to shout, to
laugh joyously. She'd made love with Chase and it was
amazing, stupendous, perfect.

He looked up at her, resting his chin on her chest.
"How are you?"

Abby grinned stupidly. "I've never been better."

Chase shared her smile, but then sobered. "Despite
the fact that an unintelligent oaf with primal urges just
took you on his kitchen table?"

She stroked his cheek. "I don't recall there being any
unintelligent oafs involved, but when it comes to your
primal urges, you can take those out on me anywhere."

To her dismay, his easy smile faded. "I'd be careful. I
might very well hold you to that."

Her heart fluttered. "I certainly hope so." She moved
her hand to trace the shape of his lower lip with her
index finger.

"Abby—"

A sharp scratch on the back door caused both of them
to jump. The scratch was followed by a high, pitiful
whine.

"Chester," Chase said with a measure of relief.

"Oh no, we forgot about him," Abby said.

Chase gently withdrew from her and offered her an
apologetic smile. "I guess we couldn't lie on the table all
night anyway." He leaned down and kissed her tenderly,
lingeringly. Her hands twined into the silkiness of his
hair.

Chester whined again.

"Go let him in," Abby murmured against his lips. She
hated to give up his kiss, but she couldn't enjoy herself
knowing poor Chester was stuck outside in the dark.

He placed another quick kiss on her lips, then padded to the door, dropping the condom in the wastebasket as he passed.

Abby leaned up on her elbows and watched him. He swung open the door, let Chester in, and scruffed the dog's ears. He herded the dog into the living room, so he wouldn't cut his paws on the broken glass still shattered on the floor.

Then he came back to her, all the while acting like he wasn't bare-naked. He had no reason to be self-conscious. His body was absolutely gorgeous, long and lean, covered in muscles and golden skin.

"Do you wander around the kitchen naked often?"

He considered her question. "Not too often. And never with a lovely woman lounging on the table, watching me."

Abby laughed, although she could feel the heat in her cheeks. Despite her wanton appearance, she wasn't nearly as comfortable with her own nakedness. Sitting up, she straightened her dress.

Chase stopped her hands with his, holding them in their large, calloused warmth. "What are you doing?"

"Trying to make myself presentable."

"To who? Me?" He cast a look down at himself. "I think you were better suited to me before."

"Yes, well . . . I can't very well walk across the street with my dress up around my waist."

"Who said you were walking across the street? You're spending the night with me."

"I—" She was? Did their affair include sleeping over? In some ways, that seemed more intimate to Abby than what they had just done. Maybe because she hadn't often slept in a bed with a man. Nelson was always very defensive of his own space. And given the awkwardness of their sex life, she hadn't been too disappointed when he left afterward.

Chase captured her hand and tugged her off the table. "Come on, you're sleeping over."

This was a night of firsts. And so far she was really, really enjoying them. She had no doubt spending the night in Chase's arms was going to be the best of them. Well, okay, at least a close second to his incredible lovemaking.

On rubbery legs and with her heart thumping violently in her chest, Abby followed.

In the dark hallway, it was *almost* possible to overlook Chase's nudity. But once he turned on his bedside lamp and the soft light filled the room, his bronzed skin seemed to glow.

She tried to cast a look around her, but over and over again her eyes were drawn to that warm, golden skin.

Despite what they'd just done, staring seemed rude. Although she did long to examine every detail of his magnificent body.

"This is nice," she managed, although she'd given up looking around and studied the carpet.

"What got you uncomfortable?"

She shot him a quick glance. "I'm not really uncomfortable, but I am finding it hard not to stare."

Against the carpet, she saw his shadow shrug. "So stare. I don't mind. I fully intend to strip you naked and spend the whole night learning every inch of your body."

Abby's head snapped up. "We're not going to sleep?"

"Are you tired?"

Her limbs were weighted and heavy, but it was a wonderful, sated feeling that actually had little to do with fatigue and all to do with satisfaction. "No, I'm not tired."

He walked over to her. Each step caused the lean muscles under his skin to roll with the sleek grace of a tiger. Even his eyes held a feral spark.

He ran his hands over her sides to catch her around

the waist. The slide of the silky material between her skin and his hands was pleasant, but it wasn't nearly as exciting as Chase's calloused hands rasping against her bare flesh.

He kissed her shoulder with gentle, sucking kisses that caused shivers to dance along her spine.

"I know what would make you more comfortable," he murmured against her skin.

"What?" Her breath hitched as his tongue flicked out to taste the indentation of her collarbone.

"If we even the playing ground." He tugged the skirt of her dress up. "Raise your arms."

Abby did, with less reservation than she thought possible.

He peeled the dress up over her head, leaving her in only a lacy, red strapless bra that matched the panties. Wherever those were now.

She slowly lowered her arms and watched Chase's expression.

He consumed her with his eyes, the blueness of them shifting to a liquid silver like pools of mercury under a clear blue sky.

"Abby," he said with awe, before capturing her lips with all the greedy hunger reflected in his gaze.

She melted against him, for the first time really feeling all of his hard steely body against hers.

She touched him with all the sureness she hadn't had downstairs, tracing each groove of his muscled back, each bulge of his shoulders and arms.

His hands also touched her, shaping the dip of her spine and the roundness of her bottom.

After much exploration, they broke their kiss. They stared at each other, both breathing hard, both a bit dazed.

"I," Chase controlled his breathing, "realized I was remiss downstairs."

"You were?" Abby couldn't imagine how so.

He nodded and ran his hands up her back to the clasps of her bra.

Abby stiffened, as the tightness of the elastic, holding the garment in place, loosened and slid away.

Even though she was aroused beyond reasonable thought, she fought the urge to cover herself. She'd always been self-conscious about her breasts. They were too large and not perky like the women in fashion magazines that her sister, Marty, modeled for.

Her areolas were large and her nipples, when distended, looked like rose-colored bullets. In her opinion, they were definitely designed to be utilitarian rather than sexy.

But instead of covering herself, she closed her eyes. She waited to hear Chase's sound of disgust or worse, the obligatory sort of praise Nelson used to offer.

Instead the room was silent, except for the nervous drumming of her heart in her ears. Finally, the quietness was too much. She opened her eyes.

Chase stood slightly away from her, his lips parted, his chest rising and falling in quick, shallow breaths. His eyes, like swirls of molten silver and sapphire, were locked on her.

Gently, reverently, he cupped a hand under one of her breasts, the roundness and weight of it filling his palm.

"Perfect," he whispered, leaning forward to catch her puckered nipple between his lips.

Abby jerked and closed her eyes again, as a riot of sensation shot through her.

His fingers found the nipple of her other breast and she braced her hands on his shoulders, afraid her knees might give out. She had no idea that attention to her breasts could create such forceful need in her. It was overwhelming and thrilling and driving her stark raving mad.

"Chase," she said, her voice serrated with longing.

He continued his assault, rolling both nipples, one between his teeth and tongue, the other between his thumb and forefinger.

Her head fell back and she fought the urge to rub herself against his solid body.

"Chase," she tried again, more desperate than before.

But he continued his onslaught, tweaking, squeezing, sucking.

Shivers rolled down her spine and moisture collected between her thighs. She teetered on the precipice, but she didn't want to go over alone. She wanted Chase with her, plummeting through ecstasy with her.

"Chase," she cried, this time gathering enough sense to sink her fingers into his hair and tug him away from her.

He looked up, those pale silver blue eyes half shielded by thick, black lashes. "I can make you come this way."

Abby's heart pounded. "Yes, you can," she agreed. "But I want you to come too."

He grinned, the action slow and sexy. "Mmmm, that does sound nice." He caught her hand and led her to the bed. At the edge, he kissed her and pressed her down, following her.

Once they were spread out across his quilt, his hot, hard body touching every inch of hers, he said, "This is my plan. First, I'm—" He flicked his tongue over her pebbled nipple, and she arched against him. "I'm going to make you come and then after a lot of kissing and touching and exploring, we will both come. That's the plan." His lips found her nipple, drawing on the distended peak.

Abby arched again as electricity exploded through her.

"That," she gasped, helpless to argue with such a talented and determined man, "sounds like a good plan." She felt Chase's pleased smile against her breast.

Abby would just have to make a plan of her own, when and if her brain ever floated back down from paradise.

Chapter 19

Rays of sunlight dappled the quilt and Abby's creamy skin. Chase lay beside her, his head on his elbow, watching her sleep.

Most of her hair, which had been pulled back in an elegant twist for the fundraiser, was now free. Locks clung to her sleep-flushed cheeks.

He picked up a piece and rubbed its silkiness between his fingers. The dark strand was intermingled with rich, dark red that glinted like spun threads of garnet in the sunlight. He lifted the hair to his nose, smelling traces of citrus blended with the warm scent of her skin and their lovemaking.

He'd made love to her three times during the night, and even now his penis was stirring against her thigh. At this rate, the woman was going to kill him. He couldn't recall ever being so insatiable. Not even in high school, when all he'd ever thought about was partying and getting lucky, and not necessarily in that order.

The last time they'd made love, they'd kept eye contact throughout the whole encounter. Her dark eyes had smoldered with desire and an emotion that Chase didn't dare to name. And never had he felt more complete. He'd found perfection in a life that had been so far from perfect it was often scary.

There was something about making love with Abby

that went far beyond just gratifying his sexual needs. He couldn't label it exactly. Maybe the difference was that she was so responsive, or maybe it was because she made him feel like he was the only man she'd ever really wanted. But he did know that when he was buried in her hot, tight body, it simply felt right.

Of course, he wasn't totally kidding himself. He knew that whatever he thought she was feeling could very well be a figment of his own imagination. He was basically stud service for her. She had made the arrangement very clear at the diner. And if he was going to be honest to himself, in bed was the only place he *could* gratify her. He certainly couldn't satisfy her intellectually.

He focused back on her face now. Her features were relaxed with sleep. She looked so lovely, her long lashes against her cheeks, her pink lips parted slightly.

Tightness tugged in the vicinity of his heart, but he didn't allow himself even a second to contemplate what was causing the sensation. There was no point, so instead, he pressed a kiss to the tip of Abby's nose.

She stirred, but didn't open her eyes.

He kissed her nose again, and again she shifted. This time a tiny smile curved her lips, but her eyelids remained firmly closed. Chase could tell from her smile that she was struggling to stay asleep.

Given how little he'd let her sleep during the night, he knew he should take pity on her now and let her rest, but he couldn't. Lying here, watching her, gave him too much time to think about what he wanted from her, and the reality of what he was going to get.

He rose over her and kissed her again. This time on the mouth, molding his lips to hers.

Her arms came up to wrap around his neck, and she responded to him with sweet need. Her hands found his hair, twining into the sleep-and-sex-mussed waves.

After several unhurried moments, he pulled away and grinned down at her. "Good morning."

"Good morning." She touched her fingertips to his jaw. For a few moments, she caressed the planes of his face. Her fingertips traced the bristly line of his unshaven cheek, the indentation of his dimple and the shape of his lips as if she were trying to commit their shape and texture to memory.

He allowed the exploration, even though the tender look in her dark eyes made his chest tighten even more.

God, he wanted the emotion he saw in her eyes to be real. But he knew her feelings had to do with lust, nothing else.

When her fingers moved to the waves of unruly hair across his forehead, he had to stop her gentle admiration before the constriction around his heart became too much.

"I think you have a hair fixation," he said.

Her fingers paused, and she frowned at him. "Why do you say that?"

"You forever have your fingers in my hair."

She cast a glance at her hand buried in his tousled mane, then promptly removed it, dropping her hand to his shoulder. Deep pink colored her cheeks.

"I didn't say I didn't like it," he said, returning her hand to his head.

She immediately stroked him. "I do like your hair," she admitted. "I like that it's long."

"This isn't long. It's downright short compared to how I wore it in high school."

She absently brushed her fingers through the strands, her gaze faraway. "I loved your hair in high school." As soon as the words were out of her mouth, she seemed to snap back to the present. "I mean, I recall it suiting you very well."

"So wait—you thought I was good-looking *and* you loved my hair?" he teased, but the realization pleased him.

The pink in her cheeks darkened to scarlet. She dropped both her hands to the bed and struggled to get up, but he shifted and pinned her with his weight.

"Oh no, you're not getting away," he declared.

"Chase," she said, wiggling under him. The friction of skin against skin created a flash of heat and the flare of arousal.

Abby stilled, staring up at him.

"I wish things had been different in high school," Chase said. "I wish I'd gotten to know you."

Her eyes widened. "Why?"

"Because I missed knowing a smart, fun, amazing girl." He placed a gentle kiss on her lips. "Plus," he added with a lascivious grin, "if I'd known how hot you were in the sack, I'd have had you parking at the Ledges every night."

Abby sputtered, then whacked Chase's shoulder, although she wasn't upset. In fact, she was thrilled with both of his statements. He thought she was amazing, and he thought she was hot in the sack. No man had ever thought either of those things about her. And this wasn't just any man. This was Chase Jordan, perfection incarnate. The way she could feel the rumble of his laughter to the tips of her toes. The rub of his chest against her peaked nipples. The tickle of his leg hair against her thighs. All of it, perfect.

The whole night had been beyond anything she could have possibly imagined. She truly didn't believe that she was a sexual being, but, boy, had Chase proven her wrong.

The memories of his method of proof made her toes curl. He'd brought her to ecstasy again and again. It had been extraordinary and, lying under him now, she realized she wanted more. It seemed impossible.

Then he grinned down at her with that sexy tilt of his lips and that sinfully deep dimple, and she realized that she would never, ever get enough of this man. The realization hit her like a brick to the forehead. Did she really think she was going to have a fling with him and just go on afterward as though nothing had happened?

She touched his beautiful face again, committing every facet of it to her memory. Not that she would ever forget.

"You look altogether too serious," Chase said.

She forced a smile. "Just thinking about how wonderful last night was."

"Mmm, it was pretty amazing." He kissed her.

Abby felt the weight of his thick erection on her stomach and started to reach down to touch him, but he caught her wrist.

"You've got to be sore, baby," he said, placing a kiss in her palm before pinning it above her head.

Abby stretched. Her muscles did feel a bit achy and there was an unfamiliar tenderness between her thighs. But none of that could offset the temptation of feeling him inside her again. To be one with him.

"I feel fine," she murmured, smiling at him sweetly. She stretched again, this time slowly and with purpose, rubbing her breasts against his chest and her belly against his rigid shaft.

She felt his muscles tense and his breath catch.

"Witch." He groaned, then caught her mouth in a ravenous, openmouthed kiss.

The sun was high in the sky when Abby and Chase awoke again. Chase lifted his head and peered over her to the digital alarm clock on the nightstand. "Lord, it's almost twelve-thirty."

Abby followed his look. "I have never slept this late before," she said, astounded.

"Well, as you barely slept, I think your record is safe," Chase replied. He pressed a quick kiss on her forehead, then rolled out of bed. "I'm starving. Are you?" With his usual lack of modesty, he padded to the dresser.

Abby watched as he tugged on a faded pair of jeans and a gray T-shirt, feeling a sense of loss that their night together was officially over.

"What would you like to eat?" he asked, turning back to the dresser and fishing around in one of the drawers.

Abby continued to watch him, trying to decide if she could eat or not. "I don't think I'm hungry."

He threw her a disbelieving look. "Of course you are. We haven't eaten since, what, seven or so last night? How about an Italian from DeMato's?"

The image of a vinegar- and oil-soaked sub layered with cold cuts, cheese, thick slices of tomato, green peppers, onion and black olives flashed in her mind. A loud rumble reverberated from her belly.

Abby blushed, and Chase chuckled.

"DeMato's, it is," he said. Turning, he tossed a pair of plain white boxers and a white T-shirt onto the bed. "Why don't you get showered or sleep or whatever, and I'll go get the food."

She picked up the boxers. "I can just run across the street, get dressed and come back."

"You can do that, but you'd better be quick because it's only going to take me a few minutes to run and pick up the food. And I can't guarantee there will be any left for you, if you take too long."

Abby laughed. "I'll be very quick."

He gave her a brief kiss. "Okay, I'll be back."

She waved.

As soon as Chase left the room, Abby fell back against the pillows and listened to him bound down the stairs. She heard him talking to Chester and the door slammed. Then there was the inevitable sputter and loud roar of Helen's engine.

She lay there for a few moments, taking in the heady scent of Chase among the rumpled bedding. Then she sat up and looked at his room. It was pleasant with dark wood furniture, but the cream and light blue wallpaper kept the eaved room from being too dark. Chase's large bed was situated between two windows, and she watched the sunlight play along the patchwork of his quilt.

After a several minutes, she heard the door open and close again, and someone rustling around in the kitchen.

Reluctant to leave his room, as if doing so would truly bring to an end the glorious time they had shared, Abby waited for a second for Chase to come back upstairs. After a few minutes, when he didn't appear, she slipped out of bed and pulled on the clothes he'd provided.

"What, no breakfast in bed?" she called as she came down the back staircase and into the kitchen.

But she didn't find Chase. Instead Summer-Ann knelt on the floor, where she was cleaning up the glass Abby had broken last night.

Abby wasn't sure if Chase or Summer-Ann had picked up their scattered clothing, but it was now heaped in a chair—her panties in a ball on top like a bright, red cherry.

Surprise widened the blonde's eyes, but she recovered quickly. "Well, considering it's afternoon, I think you're demanding the wrong meal in bed." Her voice was calm and laced with sarcasm.

Abby stiffened and crossed her arms in front of her. "I didn't realize you were here."

"Obviously," Summer-Ann said, giving her outfit a pointed look.

Abby fought the urge to tug at the loose-fitting boxers that rode low on her hips.

Summer-Ann finished sweeping the shards of glass into a blue plastic dustpan with a small hand brush. She stood, threw the glass in the waste can and then put away the brush and dustpan in the cabinet under the sink.

Abby couldn't help noticing that Summer-Ann knew her way around Chase's kitchen very well. A pang of jealousy knotted in her chest.

Summer-Ann leaned on the kitchen table, her expression disdainful like a cat that had just stepped out into wet grass. "It seems you and Chase have been having a wild little time—breaking glasses and whatnot."

Abby remained in the doorway, uncertain what to say. She couldn't deny it. She'd had the wildest, most exciting moment of her life right on the table that Summer-Ann rested against.

Fortunately, or rather unfortunately, Summer-Ann didn't seem to need a response. "I'm sure you think that whatever is going on between you two is real and will last," she said, with a sharp edge to her voice.

Abby's pride would never allow her to admit to Summer-Ann that the woman was right. She and Chase weren't going to have anything that would last. But the blonde was wrong about one thing—to Abby at least, what she had experienced with Chase was very, very real. Maybe too real.

"But nothing will ever break the connection that I share with him," Summer-Ann stated, her voice resolute, with a stoniness to her eyes making them glint like emeralds.

Abby studied her, noticing the harsh draw of her mouth and the deep creases in her brow. She looked hard. She looked tired. And Abby suddenly understood the other woman's adversarial stance. She was a mother protecting her family.

"I would never come between Chase and Willy," Abby said softly.

Summer-Ann frowned. "What?"

"What Chase and I are—doing, it will never come between Chase and his son. I would never do that."

Summer-Ann blinked. The woman seemed confused by Abby's promise. Did she really think Abby was going to try and create a wedge between a little boy and his father?

Summer-Ann still looked taken aback. "Willy isn't . . ." She blinked again and fell silent.

"I want to you feel confident about that, Summer-Ann. I would never hurt Willy."

The blonde nodded. "I do."

"You do what, Summer?" Chase asked, entering the kitchen, a paper bag in his arm and a frown on his face.

Abby looked at Summer-Ann, and she could clearly see the pleading in her green eyes. Abby didn't understand exactly what she wanted, but she tried to follow the woman's lead.

"I just asked her if she knew where you kept the coffee filters. I couldn't find them," Abby said.

Summer-Ann nodded.

"I'm assuming you didn't invite Summer over to ask her that," he said, setting the bag down on the counter. When he turned back to them, his brow was still creased and even though his last comment was aimed at Abby, he narrowed a suspicious glare at the other woman.

Summer-Ann laughed, the sound brittle. "No, I actually stopped by to see if I could come in late on Monday. I have a dentist appointment."

"That's fine, but you could have just called me."

"Well, I was driving by, so I figured I'd just stop."

Chase nodded, but Abby could tell by the angle of his

eyebrows and the set of his lips that he didn't believe her.

"I should go," Summer-Ann said abruptly and headed for the door. "Thanks, Chase. Abby."

Abby watched her leave, confused by the woman's sudden departure. No, forget that. She was confused by the whole exchange.

"Did Summer give you a hard time?"

She shook her head. "Not really."

"Well, that would be a first. She can be disagreeable when the mood strikes her."

"She was fine," Abby assured him.

She'd told Summer-Ann that she wouldn't become involved with his relationship with Willy, and she didn't intend to. It wasn't her place. If she and Chase were going to develop a long-term relationship, then maybe she would feel the need to discuss the situation with him, but they weren't headed toward anything permanent. So she would simply stay out of the whole thing. But she would make sure her relationship with Chase never, never hurt Willy. She wanted this affair, but not at the cost of others.

And what about the cost to you? She was a big girl. She knew the price, and she was willing to pay it. At least she hoped she was.

"So did you get the Italians?"

Chase seemed willing to let the visit from Summer-Ann go. He nodded. "Why don't we go back to bed and eat them there," he suggested with a wiggle of his eyebrows.

"You read my mind."

Summer-Ann stood on the porch, listening to Chase and Abby through the screen door. When she heard them decide to go back to bed, she snuck down the

steps. Jealousy pooled in her stomach, but the resentment was diluted by an incongruent wave of satisfaction.

She couldn't believe it! Abby Stepp thought that Willy
was Chase's child. It was just the tool she needed to put
an end to their relationship.

As much as she disliked admitting it, Abby was a decent person who wouldn't break up a family. Hell, the
mousy woman had even hidden their conversation from
Chase just out of some misplaced sense of loyalty.

So, all Summer had to do was convince the nice, and
thus easily manipulated, Abby that if she backed out of
the picture then she, Chase and Willy could become a
happy family again. Abby didn't need to know it wasn't
actually "again," but rather, finally.

But she had to work fast; Abby could find out at any
time that Chase wasn't Willy's father. Not that half the
town didn't believe he was, but if Abby said anything to
Chase, he'd tell her the truth.

No, speed was the key to making this plan succeed. She
needed to find a way to get Abby alone.

Chapter 20

"Where are we going?" Abby asked, unable to keep the excitement out of her voice.

"We're going on a date," Chase said with an evasive smile.

That was the same frustrating answer he'd given her since they'd gotten in his sports car.

"Are dates always such a mystery?"

"Sometimes. Now, sit back and enjoy yourself."

Abby sank back against the leather upholstery. She was enjoying herself immensely. The past week with Chase had been like a dream. And every day got better.

So far, this was their fourth official date. Monday night, he had prepared them dinner at his house. He was an excellent cook, making a delicious beef stroganoff. But her favorite part of the meal had been dessert, which had involved strawberries and whipped cream and christening the dining room table in much the same way they had the one in the kitchen.

On Tuesday, they went to the movies, although neither of them could have told anyone a thing about the motion picture as they'd spent the whole time making out like oversexed teens.

Wednesday, they went to dinner in Bar Harbor and then walked around the different shops, holding hands and talking.

Thursday, they had spent the night together, but it wasn't a "date." Instead, they lay on his couch and watched television—well, sort of—in between talking and kissing and finally making love on the floor, while Jay Leno chattered away in the background.

And now tonight, well, she had no idea where they were headed, but in truth, she was perfectly happy to ride in the car beside him.

Although, when he pulled off the main road onto a winding dirt lane, Abby's curiosity got the better of her again. She leaned forward and peered at the road. It was a narrow road with grass growing in the middle where tires hadn't worn away the growth to gravel. The headlights reflected off nothing but the trees lining both sides of the road.

"Okay, where the heck are we going?"

He smiled, but didn't take his eyes off the snaking road. "You don't recognize it?"

"Not at all."

Finally, the trees parted, and he parked the car. He gave her a mysterious grin and got out of the car. When he opened her door, Abby heard the crash of waves and smelled the briny scent in the breeze.

"Do you know where you are now?"

Abby stepped out of the car, holding his arm. "I have no idea. I can't see a thing. We're obviously near the ocean."

Chase looped his arm through hers and led her to a rock wall. Gradually, her eyes adjusted and she could see millions of stars blanketing the dark sky above them and the black waves crashing below them. A full moon hung bright and full over their heads.

"We're at the Ledges," she realized.

"Mmm-hmm. You said you wished you'd had a normal childhood, and the normal place that a guy took his girl to was . . ."

"The Ledges," they said in unison.

Abby laughed and fell against him. "I think we're too old to be here now."

"Nah. Come with me."

She followed him and watched as he got a blanket and a picnic basket out of the back of the GTO. She helped him spread the blanket on a cushy patch of grass, and they sank onto it.

Chase pulled out a bottle of wine and two glasses from the basket.

She accepted the glass he poured. "So what did normal kids do at the Ledges?"

"Got drunk and screwed," he said without hesitation.

"Did you do that?"

This time Chase hesitated. "Did you ever hear any of the rumors about me during our school days?"

Abby nodded. She'd heard plenty and had wished she'd been the one he'd been doing those wild things with. "I heard some."

"Well, anything you heard probably wasn't true. It was probably worse. I was out of control, and I'm lucky I didn't end up in prison or dead. Actually, I'm even luckier that I didn't hurt someone else. That's just a miracle, in fact." He reached forward and caught a piece of her hair, twirling it around his finger as he talked. "I used to drink—and, of course, drive. I did drugs. I stole stuff, mostly shoplifting, although I did once break into a summer home out at Birch Hill Pond. I had unprotected sex. I smoked. Name anything self-destructive, and I did it."

"Where were your parents?" she asked gently.

The crash of waves and the rustle of the trees were deafening against his silence. Finally, when she thought he wouldn't answer, he said in a low voice, "My mother died when I was four, and my dad . . ." A bitter snort escaped him. "My dad is a sadistic bastard who occasionally does a little fishing, but mostly just gets falling-down drunk. He couldn't care less about me. He thinks I'm a waste, an idiot, and to be honest, I did seem to prove him right."

Abby sat still for a moment, her heart breaking at the pain she heard in his voice. Chase always put on an easy-going, happy-go-lucky front. She never would have guessed his family life was anything other than normal.

Then she remembered graduation day and how she thought she saw hurt in his eyes as he leaned against the high school wall. She'd always assumed she'd just imagined it, but now she wasn't sure.

She caught the hand that still played with her hair. She pulled it to her lips and placed a kiss in his palm.

"I lost my parents when I was six. I don't think anyone ever really recovers from that," she said softly. "You just made it through childhood however you could. We all did."

She pressed another kiss in his open hand. The sensitive skin of her lips touched the calloused skin of his palm. Callouses created by hard work and determination.

She slid her hand up his arm feeling the strength under his shirtsleeves, until she reached the broadness of his shoulder. Bracing herself against him, she leaned forward and pressed a gentle kiss to his mouth, then another and another.

He remained still under her tender ministrations until her compassion seemed too much for him. He pulled her against him and kissed her back with fierce, uncontrolled need.

They fell back against the blanket, and as the waves pounded and the wind blew, they tore at each other's clothes, desperate to touch bare skin, frantic to be one.

* * *

Chase tugged the edge of the blanket over himself and Abby as best he could and curled back around her. She wiggled so her smooth back was nestled against his chest and her soft, round bottom was pressed snugly against his groin. Then she was quiet.

Chase suspected she was asleep. His own limbs were heavy and weak from their lovemaking, and he'd been even more relentless with her, taking her again and again to the summit before letting her find release.

He'd been rough, desperate for her. Initially, he was afraid his forcefulness might scare her. But his sweet, tender Abby had responded in kind, biting his shoulders and digging his back with those short little nails. Her reaction was all he'd needed to lose control.

Hell, when it came to Abby he had lost control in every aspect of their relationship. He'd told her things about himself that he never discussed. He never mentioned his family. He rarely talked about the illegal things he'd done in the past. But for some reason, he wanted Abby to know him. The real Chase. The kid with the abusive dad. The teen that did anything to draw people's attention from his weaknesses. The little boy that couldn't . . .

He pulled Abby tighter against him, rubbing his nose in her hair, breathing deep her scent. She had accepted everything he'd told her tonight, but he didn't think she could accept all his secrets. Some of them would just make it too startlingly clear that they weren't in the same league. That Abby was infinitely above him.

She roused, turning to face him. "Sorry, I fell asleep."

"That's okay. I'm feeling pretty spent, too." He caressed her cheek. "Are you okay?"

She nuzzled her face against his neck. "I've never been better. I think the Ledges brings out a bit of your bad boy side," she murmured, pressing her lips against his throat.

"Mmm," he smiled, placing a kiss on her tousled head. "It brought out your wild side too. My back's going to have the scratches to prove it."

Abby rose up. "Oh no, are you okay?"

Chase fell back on the blanket, his arms crossed behind his head. "I'm fantastic."

Abby lay her head on his chest and brushed her hand idly over his stomach. They were quiet, listening to the rhythmic crash of the ocean.

"Is this how it was when you were a teen?"

Abby's carefully asked question caught him off guard. "No, nothing like this," he stated, before he had time to think about it.

"How was it different?"

Chase paused, trying to find the right words without admitting too much. Without admitting that Abby was different from everyone else. That when he was with her, he finally felt complete.

"Well, when I was young it was—less about the build-up and more about getting to the final outcome."

"So the only difference is you've gotten more patient?"

He caught her chin and turned her to face him. "Did you sense any patience awhile ago? I was out of my head to be inside you, to feel every inch of your hot skin around me. I can't even compare what I feel with you to the way it felt with others. You're different in every way possible." He dipped his head and kissed her soundly.

She rested her head on his chest again, and he could practically feel the satisfaction radiating from her. And although he might have said more than he wanted to, he was glad he had. He didn't want her thinking that he'd shared this kind of overwhelming passion with any other woman.

"And what about me? How do I compare to your other

lovers?" He couldn't believe he'd been so insecure as to ask.

Abby laughed, the sound light and incredulous. "Nelson, you mean? Well, let's put it this way. He was a single strand of DNA, while you are a double helix."

Chase grinned up at her. "I take it that means I'm better."

"Oh yeah, that means you are much, much better." She inched up until her body was completely on top of his and their faces were level.

"Good. Otherwise I'd have to try harder to prove myself." He smiled up at her.

"Oh, you can still do that," she encouraged.

He twisted, so she was pinned underneath him. "Okay, I'll give it my best effort." He grinned down at her, but he quickly sobered.

She looked gorgeous. Her hair spread over the blanket in dark waves like the water below them. Her eyes glittered like the star above. And he realized that if he allowed it, this woman could become both sea and sky. She could so easily become his whole world.

"You two are the perfect couple," Ellie said dreamily. "Like Scarlett and Rhett."

Abby cringed at the analogy. "I hope I'm a little less bratty." And she really wanted her relationship with Chase to come to a better end. Although it wasn't likely.

"She wasn't bratty," Ellie stated. "She was determined. But that isn't the point. I'm trying to say that you have found your true love."

Abby didn't have the heart to tell her sister that love didn't play any part in her relationship with Chase. At least not on his side. "I think we're just enjoying ourselves."

"Well, you spent practically the whole week with him. That's some pretty serious enjoyment."

Oh yes, it was. Very serious. Much enjoyment. But Ellie was far too romantic to understand that it was just sex. Really, really good sex.

Sure, they'd been having an amazing time together. They had the same sense of humor, even the corny stuff. They could talk about anything. He even understood the small details of her research. But she knew she wasn't the type to keep him interested forever. Even though he seemed to be having as much fun as she was, she knew he was better suited to a different type of woman. One that was beautiful and as outgoing as he was. Someone exciting. Despite the wild side he'd brought out in her, she was still fundamentally a nerd, more comfortable in her lab than with people.

But she hoped she would keep his interest a while longer. She wasn't ready to give him up. If anything, he was like a drug. The more she had of him, the more she wanted. Heck, she'd only been out of his company for less than ten hours, and she wondered what he was doing. She longed to be with him.

She sighed. At this rate, it was going to take a lot more than a twelve-step program to get her over her addiction to the man.

But she wouldn't think about that now. A small smile crept over her lips. Maybe she was more like Scarlett O'Hara than she realized.

"What are you grinning about?" Ellie asked, taking their empty cups and getting up from the table to pour more. She filled them, then paused to look longingly at an Entenmann's danish on the counter. Sighing, she returned to the table with nothing else but the refills of tea.

"So what has you smiling?" she asked again.

Abby looked down at the tea Ellie slid toward her, then back to her sister. "I'm smiling about Chase," she admitted.

"I'd be smiling too. He's so handsome, and so nice."

"It seems like you two have spent a lot of time together."

But before Ellie could respond, there was a knock at the back door.

Abby jumped up, her heart skipping a beat at the sound. Maybe it was Chase. She hadn't seen him all day. Maybe he was done helping Mason Sweet with his leaky roof. Maybe he was missing her as much as she was missing him.

So when she opened the door she couldn't keep the surprise tinged with disappointment from her voice. "Summer-Ann. Hello."

Chapter 21

"I'm sorry to just show up here, but I need to talk with you." The blonde glanced over Abby's shoulder at Ellie. "Alone, please."

Abby nodded and followed the other woman out onto the back stoop. She threw a puzzled glance at Ellie before closing the door.

The evening air was cool; Abby wrapped her arms around herself. "If this is about Chase and Willy, I told you the other day that I wouldn't become involved."

Summer-Ann stood there silent for a second, her shoulders hunched, her head hung. When she lifted her eyes to Abby's, they glistened with tears.

"Did you know that Chase and I dated from the time we were fourteen years old?" she said softly, the quiet words heavy with anguish.

She seemed to be waiting for a response, so Abby nodded.

"We had so many firsts together, first date, first kiss. We lost our virginity to each other." Again, Summer-Ann paused.

Abby shifted, trapped between the sympathy and the envy she felt for this woman.

"We have shared more experiences than you could even imagine," Summer-Ann continued, her voice quavering with pain. "We had wonderful times, and I won't lie, we had bad times too. We were going through a rough time when I found out I was pregnant with Willy. And when I told Chase . . . Well, he wasn't ready to be a father."

Abby listened, but she couldn't correlate Summer-Ann's words to the man she knew.

"At the time, Chase was still so wild, still living life in the fast lane. So when I decided to keep the baby, I told Chase that I would never tell Willy that he was his father. Not unless Chase decided that he wanted Willy to know. And not too long ago, Chase did decide he wanted to tell Willy. Right before you came back to town, we resolved to try and make a go of it again, for the sake of Willy." A tear rolled down over her high cheekbone.

Even when she cried, she was beautiful, Abby noted. Her tears seemed to make her eyes greener, like fresh grass wet with dew.

"But after you arrived," Summer-Ann sniffed, "he became obsessed with you."

Obsessed with her? Abby found that hard to believe. Plus, Chase wasn't a flighty guy who would abandon a relationship he'd decided to save, even if he thought he might be interested in another woman. "Maybe you misunderstood his intentions."

Summer-Ann's tormented features hardened. "Maybe you lured him away."

"I didn't."

"Well, obviously you did, because he was in bed all last Saturday morning fooling around with you, rather than being at his son's Little League game."

Her accusation caused nausea to roil in Abby's belly. Was that true? Had Chase ignored his son to pursue his own pleasure?

She could visualize Willy in his uniform, wearing a baseball glove that was a little too big for him, searching the stands for Chase. "I'm sure he forgot. I know he wouldn't miss Willy's game for anything."

"Chase is a good man," Summer-Ann agreed. "But he is a man, and he's ruled by a body part other than his head or his heart. Please, Abby, don't ruin our chance to build a happy family. Please."

Abby stared at the gorgeous woman. She never thought she'd see Summer-Ann Bouffard begging her to break things off with Chase Jordan. It was unbelievable. Like an elaborate fantasy she would have constructed while watching them in study hall.

But this was real, and it involved the emotions of a very real little boy.

"I would never discourage Chase from claiming his son, and I certainly would never come between them," she promised again.

"That's not enough," Summer-Ann insisted, again her green eyes appearing hard like emeralds. "I need that chance to save my relationship with him. Willy needs him. He longs for a father, and every time I see tears in his blue eyes, I ache to tell him that he has a daddy. That Chase is his daddy. Please. We need to be a family."

"I . . ." She didn't know what to say. As selfish as it was, Abby wasn't ready to walk away from Chase. She would never want to hurt Willy, or Summer-Ann for that matter, but she couldn't lose the person that was making her happier than she'd ever been before.

Summer-Ann's shoulders began to shake. She dropped her face into her hands and sobbed.

Abby didn't know what to do, how to comfort the distraught woman. Hesitantly, she reached out and touched her shoulder.

Summer-Ann wept harder.

"Shh, it will be okay," Abby finally whispered.

The blonde raised her head, brushing her honey-colored hair out of her face. "You will help us?"

Abby felt her heart break, but the pain was for herself, not for the distressed woman in front of her. She nodded.

Summer-Ann's crying stopped, and she peered at Abby. "You promise you will help us? That you'll stop seeing him?"

Abby nodded once more.

"Good," Summer-Ann smiled warmly. Her tears were dry.

Abby was reminded of the warmth the beautiful girl had bestowed on her nearly fifteen years ago, on graduation day. Her instincts told her she was making a mistake to help this woman.

Then Willy's freckled nose and gap-toothed smile flashed in her mind. What if she wasn't? What if Willy's happiness depended on her? Whatever she decided to do, Willy would come first.

"So you're her boy-toy, eh?" Mason grinned as he passed a two-by-four to Chase.

Chase didn't like the title, only because he feared it was a little too close to home. "We're just going to have a good time this summer and then see what happens."

Mason shook his head. "Man, I would love an arrangement like that. I swear you have all the luck."

Chase nailed the new board to the exposed studs. He didn't feel lucky. He felt frustrated, because even after a full week of mind-blowing sex, he wanted more. He wanted more of Abby. More than a fling.

It was crazy. One week with the woman, and he wanted her to give him forever.

"Oh, no," Mason groaned. "You're falling for her."

Chase's hammer missed the nail, nearly hitting his thumb. How did his friend have this uncanny ability to recognize his emotions before he even understood them? He found it highly eerie, and even more irksome.

"I'm—hell, I don't know how I feel about her."

"If you're feeling that confused, then you're already too far gone."

Chase didn't respond, pounding in the final nail with more force than necessary.

"So, are you planning to try and convince her you want more than just this summer?"

Chase shrugged. "It's complicated. She has a job and an apartment in Boston. Her project at Rand was never a long-term thing. And there are other obstacles."

"Like what?"

Chase held out his hand for another piece of lumber. "Just—things."

Mason nodded and let the topic drop, for which Chase was infinitely thankful. Mason didn't know the extent of Chase's problems, and he wanted to keep it that way.

Chase had considered the idea of suggesting to Abby that they make their affair something more, but he couldn't figure out how to have a real relationship with her and still keep his secret hidden. And he knew she wouldn't want him if she discovered the truth. It would just make their differences glaringly obvious.

So, he was going to continue on, status quo. And hopefully the sex was fantastic enough that she wouldn't lose interest too soon. Personally, he couldn't imagine losing interest ever. If anything, each time he was with Abby he wanted her more.

He had the sensation of being in the desert dying of thirst, and Abby was water. No matter how much he drank of her, he couldn't get enough. He'd never experienced this kind of need.

Before Abby, sex was all about having fun. He'd dated several ladies, and while he liked them, he didn't feel this consuming drive to be with them.

Even his years with Summer-Ann had been more about amusement than commitment. He had believed himself in love her, but by the time the whole incident with Willy happened, he had been more than ready to call it quits.

"So at least answer this, for a poor deprived guy, who isn't getting used for his body," Mason said.

Chase looked up from lining up the next board.

"Does she have a sister?"

Chase shook his head with a sympathetic smile. "I don't think Ellie would touch you with a ten-foot pole."

Mason chuckled self-deridingly. "I think you are right."

It had gone well, Summer-Ann decided as she drove back to her house. And fate had been on her side, because it was apparent from Abby's reaction that she hadn't questioned Chase about Willy's parentage.

Everything might work out after all.

She turned up her radio and hummed along with the song.

Okay, sure, she did feel a little bad about double-dealing, but there was some truth to the lies she told Abby. Chase would be a wonderful father for Willy. She couldn't count the times that she'd wished he was really Willy's father.

And she did believe they would be a very happy family. She and Chase had been good together, before she'd gotten stupid and thought she could find something better.

Part of her felt like she got what she deserved for not believing in Chase, for comparing him to other men who
had perfect families and expensive educations.

Expensive educations like Abby Stepp's. See, she was
doing Chase a favor getting him away from a know-it-all
like Abby Stepp. He needed a woman who understood
him. A woman who he could really relate to.

She began to hum louder. Yes, she was doing what was
best for everyone.

"She's in bed, Chase." Ellie's voice was uneasy.

"It's only eight o'clock. Is she feeling all right?" Chase
sounded confused.

"I don't know. I don't think so."

"Should I check on her?"

"She said she was really tired."

"Will you tell her that I'd really like to see her?"

"I will, Chase."

Abby pulled the blankets over her head and buried
her face in the pillow. She knew she was being a cow-
ard, but it was still easier than actually having to tell
Chase that she didn't want to see him again. Especially
since she wanted to see him with every beat of her heart.

She heard her bedroom door creak open. Reluctantly
she pulled the covers off her head and peeked at her sister with one eye.

"I don't know why you're doing this, but I'm not send-
ing Chase away again. You have to talk to him." Ellie's voice
was the sternest Abby had ever heard it. Without waiting
for a reply, Ellie pulled the door shut with a resounding
click.

Abby moaned and hid her face again. Ellie had sent
Chase away last night and this morning, too. Abby knew

it wasn't fair of her to make her sister deal with her problems.

She sat up and looked at the clock. Only quarter past eight. Chase would be up for hours yet. She couldn't use the time as an excuse to put this off.

She just wished she knew what to say. She didn't want to destroy a family, but part of her didn't believe that Chase would ever be with her if he'd intended to reunite with Summer-Ann. Yet, another part of her couldn't live with possibly being a home wrecker, if Summer-Ann was telling the truth. And there was even a tiny part of her that wondered if Willy was really Chase's son.

Ellie was right to show her disapproval. Abby did need to handle this herself even if the outcome wasn't what she wanted. She knew that ultimately she did have to talk to him. She couldn't continue, even just a brief affair, without finding out a few truths.

"Chase? Are you there?"

Chase turned from the baseball game he was only half watching to see Abby standing on the other side of the screen door.

"Yeah," he said, rising from the overstuffed chair. "Come on in."

She stepped into the living room. Everything about her looked . . . tight. All her hair was yanked back in a ponytail, her lush mouth was thinned to a narrow line, even her skin looked taut.

"Are you okay?" he asked, concerned by her drawn features and confused by her unwillingness to see him over the past two days.

"I'm . . . all right." She looked anything but okay. Her posture was straighter than he could recall ever seeing it, even when she'd admitted the pain of her childhood outside the Parched Dolphin.

The axe was about to fall. He knew she intended to end their fling.

"Want to sit down?" he offered.

She shook her head, clasping her arms across her stomach as if she was in physical pain.

"What's going on, Abby?"

Her eyes strayed to the flickering television and after a few moments came back to him. "I think maybe we should stop seeing each other."

Chase nodded. Exactly what he'd expected. "Why?"

"I just think that you should give more of your time to Willy."

Now that, he hadn't seen coming. "To Willy?" He shook his head, perplexed. "I don't see what Willy has to do with us."

Abby frowned. "He's your son, and he needs you. I don't want to take time away from him."

Chase stared at her, at first shocked, but then rage rose in his chest until he felt almost strangled by it. "You think Willy is my son?" he said, his voice stiff, but otherwise deceptively calm.

Abby nodded, although the look in her wide eyes wasn't as certain.

"Have you ever heard the boy call me 'Daddy'?"

Abby shook her head. "I thought—I thought maybe he didn't know."

Chase swallowed the bile that burned the back of his throat. He swallowed again. "You think I'm the type of guy that would deny my own child?"

"No," she said, her features grew ashen. "I . . ."

"Leave." The single word was quiet and dangerous.

"Chase." She took a step toward him.

"Leave now."

She stared at him for a moment, and then nodded. "Good-bye, Chase," she whispered.

He couldn't speak. His anger succeeded in choking him.

Chapter 22

The door banged behind her, and Chase fought the urge to pick the beer bottle up off the coffee table and hurl it across the room. Abby thought he was such a bastard that he wouldn't even claim his own child.

He'd expected her to realize that he was too small town for her. Or that he wasn't her intellectual equal. Or, hell, even that he was just plain boring. But never—not once—had he ever believed she would think he was so dishonorable, such a lowlife.

He cursed and picked up the beer, downing half the contents in one swallow. Then he stared at the bottle, not really seeing the jumble of letters on the label or the glint of the television in the green glass.

He felt like his chest was being squeezed tight, like a boa constrictor was wrapped around his torso, crushing him.

Abby believed that he wouldn't claim his own son.

He sank into the chair. Why did it matter? Hell, half the town thought Willy might be his kid, and that never bothered him. Well, not much anyway.

But Abby, oh Abby. He thought she understood him, at least understood that he'd worked hard to become a better man than his upbringing had slated him to be. That despite his other flaws, he would never be the callous, hateful man his father was.

Abby's distrust in him hurt far worse than anything that his father had ever said or done to him. He didn't want to speculate on why that was so. But her disbelief in him was much harder to bear than his own father's condemnation.

Because you were falling in love with her, you stupid fool. Because despite all the obstacles and all the rational warning he'd given himself, he had begun to believe he had a chance to win Abby's heart. Like some lowly, but gallant knight in one of Ellie's romance novels, that against all odds, won the hand of the fair princess.

He'd been deluding himself. Something he never did. He prided himself on being realistic, and reasonable and astute, all the things he hadn't been in his youth.

But maybe he wasn't any of those things. Maybe he'd been deluding himself about the type of man he'd become.

Abby obviously thought he was still an unfeeling, self-centered reprobate.

He dropped his head against the back of his chair. He had gotten the sense from Abby before that she didn't believe that people really changed. And maybe she was right, but not in the way she thought. It seemed more likely to Chase that people wanted to change, but their past wouldn't let them.

Nausea still churned in Abby's stomach as she walked into her office the next day. She'd spent the entire night pacing her house, wondering how she could convince Chase to speak to her again. So she could beg his forgiveness. But she didn't think he'd agree to speak with her ever again, and she couldn't blame him.

She'd been so wrong. As soon as the words were out of her mouth, she knew that none of Summer-Ann's story could be true. And when she saw the anger and hurt in Chase's eyes, she knew she'd done irreparable damage.

She had taken Chase's trust and pride and shoved it back in his face.

Her stomach lurched again, and she collapsed onto her office chair. Propping her elbows on her desk, she dropped her head in her hands and closed her eyes.

He'd told her about his own father, his own child-hood. And she knew, if he were a father, he would never, never be anything but doting and supportive and active in every part of the child's life.

She was such a fool to believe a word of Summer-Ann's lies. A stupid, gullible fool. Exactly like she had been in high school.

"Abby, are you all right?"

Leslie's concerned voice startled her. She raised her head and gaped at the woman.

Leslie's eyes widened, and she immediately came to Abby's side. "Lord, girl, you look terrible. What's wrong?"

Abby touched a hand to her face, then dropped it to her lap and attempted a smile. The gesture seemed to stretch her face and made her feel like she was grimacing. "I'm fine."

"If you're fine, then I'm about to win the Nobel Peace Prize. What's going on?"

Before she knew it, Abby was telling Leslie the whole story, unable to keep her pain and shame inside a moment longer. And in the vain hope that Leslie would have an answer to this awful dilemma.

Leslie sat there a moment after the whole tale was told, contemplating it. Then with the true practicality of a Mainer, even a transplanted one, she stated, "Well, I don't know if you will ever get Chase to forgive you. But I sure as hell would give that Summer-Ann a piece of my mind."

* * *

"Damn it, Jed, do think you could actually get the mantelpiece level before you start pounding away at it!" Chase shouted at his workman.

Jed stopped hammering and gave him a bewildered look. "It was level."

"I think *was* is the key word," Chase stated angrily, placing the level up to show him. The yellow bubble in the level's cylinder floated slightly above the red center mark. Both Jed and Chase's other workman, Dave, leaned in to study the tool.

"It's pretty close," Dave said.

"Not close enough," Chase sneered. "What, do you think I run some half-assed construction company where we don't care if the mantelpiece is crooked and the floors are slanted and the roof leaks?" He tossed the level back into his toolbox and slammed down the lid. "Shit, I could get better help from a couple of baboons."

Chase remained crouched by his toolbox, his hands hanging between his knees, his head down. After few seconds, he rose and sighed. "Listen, I'm sorry. I'm not myself today."

The two workmen remained still, only their eyes moving to exchange confused glances.

"Keep doing what you're doing. It's fine, Jed. I'm going to get out of your hair and head back to the office. I've got some things I need to get done there."

Jed nodded, but still looked unsure.

Chase started to apologize again, but instead nodded, left the old Victorian and climbed into Helen.

For once, Helen took pity on him and started on the first attempt. He shifted the truck into drive and headed toward his office. In truth, he didn't really have anything he needed to get done there, but he knew he wasn't going to be any help on the worksite today.

He was agitated. He was angry. And he had an ache in

his chest that infuriated him, because during the wee hours of last night, he decided that Abby Stepp wasn't worth the hurt he was feeling. But somehow he couldn't shake the feeling. But he would. He would.

Abby wasn't one to leave work early for any reason, but Leslie had convinced her to, insisting that Abby wouldn't get any work done anyway.

"Plus," she'd said, "you need to strike while the iron's hot. If you wait to confront Summer-Ann until later, you'll cool down. And this woman needs to be told what for."

So Abby found herself in her car charging, albeit about five miles under the speed limit, to tell Summer-Ann exactly what she thought about her lies.

She was irritated with herself that she didn't feel more confident about the impending confrontation. She felt like the old Abby Stepp who could still be intimidated by beauty and popularity.

Suddenly, the emotions of graduation night mixed with the pain of losing Chase, and she knew she had to face Summer-Ann once and for all. Until she did, she'd always be that pathetic, naïve girl sitting on her front porch waiting for a dream to come to her, rather than making the dream come true.

She pressed the gas pedal and the speedometer rose five miles over the speed limit. Now, she was taking control.

When she arrived at Chase's office, she didn't give herself time to reconsider. She stomped up the office steps and threw open the door.

Summer-Ann looked up, her eyes wide with surprise. She sat in much the same position she had the other time Abby had been there, her feet on the desk, the phone to her ear. But rather than greet her coldly, she masked her surprise behind an affable smile.

"Candy, I'll have to call you back." She hung up the phone and gave Abby an innocent look, her sweet smile still in place. "Abby, what brings you here?"

Abby mustered up all the ire roiling through her. "You lied."

Chase pulled Helen into the small dirt lot behind his office. He was surprised to see Summer's car still parked near the building. She usually made it a habit of closing down the office for at least an hour to meet Candy Moore for lunch. Actually, he'd been counting on that fact. He wanted to be alone for a few moments, somewhere that didn't remind him of Abby.

He considered leaving, but decided against it. He did have a few supply orders that he needed to go over with Summer. Then maybe he'd go to Birch Hill Pond and do a little fishing. Or maybe he'd go to the Parched Dolphin and get drunk.

Just as he reached the top step and had his hand on the doorknob, a raised familiar voice stopped him.

"You lied." It was Abby, and even from the brief sentence, he could tell she was furious.

"What?" Summer-Ann asked, her voice puzzled.

"Don't play innocent with me. Not this time. You know exactly what you did."

"Abby, I don't know what you're talking about."

Abby laughed, the sound brittle and humorless. "Why are you still pleading ignorance? You know what you did. You planned it all out. And the plan was perfect, wasn't it? You knew I wouldn't risk hurting Willy."

Chase frowned. What had Summer done?

There was momentary silence, then Summer-Ann snickered, all innocence gone. "You were pretty predictable."

"Yes, I was," Abby said with a measure of self-derision. "And given your past trick, I should have known I couldn't trust you."

Summer snorted. "Oh please, don't tell me you're still whining about something that happened nearly fifteen years ago. I think it's time you grow up and move on."

"Me! I'm not the one who has to resort to lies to get a man. It's time for you to move on. Chase doesn't want you."

"He does!"

"You told me that Willy was Chase's son. You guilted me into believing that I was hindering your little boy's chance of finding happiness."

"You are," Summer shouted. "If you weren't around, Chase would be with me. And Willy would have the father he's always wanted. I didn't lie about that."

"The worst part of this whole deceit is you convinced me to hurt a man who I knew was innocent, who I knew would never reject his own child. But I was stupid and gullible and I believed you over what I know about him. I can't blame him for never forgiving me. He shouldn't. But I just want you to know that I'm not going to sit back and let him believe it was solely my idea."

"What are you going to do?" Summer sounded agitated.

"I'm going to tell him the truth. And somehow I don't think you're going to get the perfect family you were planning on. At least not with him."

Again, there was silence.

Chase started to turn the doorknob, but before he could get the door open, he heard an enraged screech and a loud crash. His heart pounding, he shoved the door open, terrified at what he would find.

The two women stood on either side of the desk.

Summer-Ann's face was scarlet with anger. A stapler was clutched in her fist, poised to be thrown.

Abby held her ground, although her eyes were large with alarm. The telephone and one of Chase's framed awards lay on the floor near the wall behind her. Broken glass and the frayed phone cord were proof of Summer's wrath.

"Summer, put down the stapler," Chase ordered. Under different circumstances, the order would have been rather funny.

"Chase," Summer said, with relief. "Thank God you're here. This crazy woman came in here making all kinds of threats. Saying that I told her crazy things about you and Willy. She's nuts." She dropped the stapler and started around the desk to him.

Chase shook his head. "Summer, I heard the whole thing."

Summer's eyes widened, then narrowed again with anger. "She's lying."

"Summer," he said again slowly. "I heard *everything*."

"I did it for you. For us." She came to him, clasping his arm. "You know we're meant to be together."

He shook his head again. "Summer, go home."

"But Chase—"

"Summer, go home," he said more firmly. "I'll talk to you tomorrow."

"But it's only noon," she said inanely.

Chase cast a pointed look at the telephone lying amid the shards of glass. "I don't think there will be many calls this afternoon."

"Chase—"

"Go home. I will talk with you tomorrow."

Summer-Ann hesitated, then nodded. She walked

shakily back to the desk and retrieved her purse. With one final glare at Abby, she left.

Chase turned to Abby, who stood with her arms wrapped securely around herself. Her face was so pasty white that Chase feared she was going to pass out.

He put an arm around her back, steadying her as he led her to the sofa. She crumpled onto the cushion, staring straight ahead, dazed.

"Are you okay?" he asked, sitting beside her.

She nodded.

"The phone didn't hit you, did it?"

She shook her head.

"Are you going to talk to me?" he asked, his lips quirking slightly.

She turned to him, blinking. Then suddenly her dark eyes welled with tears, and she began to weep. "I'm sorry. I'm so sorry."

Chase didn't hesitate. He pulled her against him and hugged her, desperate to touch her.

She sobbed harder, shudders quaking her body.

"Don't cry, baby. Shh, it's all right," he soothed, brushing her hair from her face, pressing comforting kisses to her damp cheek.

"Why—why are you being so kind?" she stammered. "It was unforgivable—what I said last night."

He held her tighter, rocking her like a distraught child. "Summer-Ann can be quite persuasive. She had me convinced of the same thing at one time."

Abby gaped up at him, tears still brimming in her eyes, making them gleam like smoky quartz. "She did?"

Chase nodded and relaxed his hold, although he couldn't quite bring himself to stop holding her completely. He rubbed her back. "When we broke up, it was Summer-Ann who ended things," he started carefully, needing Abby to understand the whole truth.

"Why?" Abby asked. The indignation in her voice caused him to smile.

He shrugged. "I was still wild, working part-time on a construction crew in Bar Harbor, going nowhere. Summer-Ann wanted more. She started seeing a guy from Massachusetts. He was a rich college kid spending the summer at his folks' place outside of Bar Harbor. They were pretty hot and heavy, I guess. I know she really thought they were serious. So when his break was over and he headed back to his Ivy League school, she truly believed he'd call and ask her to join him."

"But he didn't," Abby said, sympathy creasing her brow.

Chase brushed a strand of hair from her cheek, overwhelmed with tenderness and amazed she could still find compassion for someone who had just hurt her.

"After the guy left," he continued, "we started seeing each other again, every now and then. I think we both knew our relationship was over, but sometimes it's just easier to fall back on the familiar. So when she told me she was pregnant, I didn't question that I was the father. She said she was about two months along, which made the timing right. I never considered that Summer would lie about something like that."

"But she did," Abby said with sad certainty.

Chase nodded. "But to be fair to her, she did it out of fear. She didn't have anywhere else to turn."

"And she knew you'd never turn your back on your child," she murmured, guilt lacing every word and darkening her eyes.

Chase kneaded the tense muscles of her back. "Then at Thanksgiving time who should reappear but Mr. Ivy League. He showed up, seeming to be interested in picking up where they'd left off."

"And she chose him over you," she said, again indignation heavy in her voice.

Chase nodded, a broad smile curving his lips. God, he loved this woman.

She frowned, not understanding his reaction. "But you had to be devastated, thinking she was going to take your baby away from you."

Chase smile faded. "It was Thanksgiving Day, when she finally told me the truth. That she was nearly five months along and the other guy was the father."

"You must have been so upset," she said, touching her fingertips to his cheek.

He captured her fingers, pressing them firmer against him. "I was so angry and so hurt. I thought I was going to be a daddy, that I was going to get the chance to be the type of father that mine wasn't. And with her admission she took that all away."

"How did you ever forgive her?" she asked softly.

Chase shrugged. "She more than paid for her lies. As you've probably guessed, Mr. Ivy League hit the road again as soon as Summer told him that he was soon going to be a father. As far as I know, he has never even seen Willy. His family paid for Summer's hospital bills and gave her a little more to help raise Willy the first year. But I don't think she's ever received any more help."

"That's not true," Abby said adamantly. "She's gotten help from you, hasn't she?"

Chase didn't answer, instead catching a piece of her hair and concentrating on its silky texture.

"You gave her this job despite the pain she caused you. And you watch Willy for her. And I bet you do a lot of other things to make sure Willy is okay," Abby said.

He didn't openly agree, instead looking away from her. "In a strange way, Summer-Ann helped me too. She made me take a look at myself and realize I didn't want to be a thug my whole life."

Abby shook her head. "You would have realized that anyway."

"You have an awful lot of faith in me."

"The past two days to the contrary. I'm so sorry."

"Like I said, Summer can be persuasive."

"Is she going to persuade you to forgive her again?"

Chase snorted with a bit of self-mocking. "Yeah, probably."

"You're too good," Abby said, although she didn't seem surprised by his answer.

"You really think so?"

Abby nodded. "Definitely."

"Good enough to have a relationship with? Not just a fling?"

Chapter 23

Abby blinked up at Chase, unable to answer, barely able to think. "What—what do you mean?"

He moved a hand to hold the back of her neck. She fought the urge to nuzzle against his palm like a greedy cat.

"Baby, I'm crazy about you."

She blinked again. "You are?"

"You can't tell?" he said, his thumb rasping the fragile skin on the side of her neck.

She shook her head, not because it was her answer, but because it was what her misfiring synapses told her to do.

"Well, I am. And I want more with you than an affair."

"You do?"

Chase smiled broadly. "I get the feeling I'm not communicating something right here."

Wonderingly, Abby touched his face, her index finger resting in the indentation of his dimple. "Why? I don't understand why you would want a relationship with me."

"You were there this past week, weren't you?"

Abby managed a smile. "Yes."

"It was pretty damned amazing."

"Yes."

"Abby, I want to see where this thing can take us."

Abby's heart felt like it was floating, like the organ was defying all laws of gravity. "Even after yesterday?"

He kissed her, his lips moving over hers in sweet, light caresses. "Yesterday is forgotten."

She pulled back, giving him a stern look. "You shouldn't forgive so easily. It lets people walk all over you."

Chase grinned. "Okay, I'll only forgive you if you come home with me and spend the entire afternoon, evening and night in my bed."

"Okay," Abby agreed slowly, trying to control the smile that struggled to break free. "But you'd better hold me to it."

"Oh, I will."

True to his word, Chase kept Abby in bed all day. During which time, she didn't allow herself to do anything, but taste, touch and feel Chase.

It wasn't until the wee hours of the early morning, when Chase was sleeping, and her limbs were weak with fulfilled exhaustion that Abby began to think.

Her head rested on Chase's chest. The steady thump of his heart created a lulling rhythm, but she couldn't sleep.

She lifted her head, then placed her chin back on his chest, regarding him. His dark hair fell across his brow in messy waves, and his sinfully long, black lashes curled against his cheek. A faint hollow hinted at the deep dimple in his left cheek, and his beautifully sculpted lips were parted slightly. In sleep, his features looked almost feminine, except for the sharp angle of his jaw and the slight flare of his straight nose.

No, not feminine, she decided, but rather stunningly perfect—like an archangel fallen to earth.

She lay her head back down and again listened to the steady beat of his heart.

Why did he want a future with her? She was as dowdy as he was beautiful. She was as reserved as he was approachable, and she was as ill at ease as he was easygoing.

There was another hindrance that neither of them seemed willing to address. Her life was in Boston and his was here. They both loved their work. It was as much a part of their identities as their name or their age.

She rubbed her cheek against his skin, loving the contradiction of textures, like silk over warm steel.

He stirred, his hand moving to the curve of her hip. Still deep in slumber, he lazily caressed her. His work-roughened hand rasped over her skin, the sensation arousing and comforting all at the same time.

Suddenly, her doubts didn't seem quite so important. They would sort out their problems. They would make this relationship work.

"What do you mean?" Summer-Ann shouted, jumping up. The chair rolled back and hit the wall behind her.

"Just what I said," Chase said coolly. "I'm letting you go."

"You can't do that."

"Yes, I can."

"But you need me," she said, her eyes narrowing to angry slits. "You know you need me."

"I have someone who will help out until I can find another full-time person." He had already spoken to Ellie this morning after Abby left for work. Ellie had readily agreed to help Chase with the ordering and billing for a while. As for his customers, they could reach him on his cell phone until he could get a new office manager.

This information seemed to shake Summer. Chase knew she considered herself indispensable.

"You're doing this for her, aren't you?" she hissed.

Chase didn't bother to act confused by who "her" was. "Abby didn't ask me to do this. But I decided if things are going to work out with her, I can't have you around meddling."

"I won't meddle," she vowed.

"You already have. What you did is unforgivable, and I won't have you ruin my chance at happiness."

Summer snorted. "Happiness with her? With a frumpy, mousy woman like that?"

Chase gritted his teeth, anger coursing through his veins, but he managed to keep his voice even. "Keep Abby out of this. This is really about you and me. And the truth is, I should have stopped protecting you years ago."

"Protecting me!" Her eyes widened with disbelief. Then she laughed coldly. "I've been the one protecting your little secret since junior high. You're the one who needs me."

Chase's anger faded, and he suddenly felt weary. "I'm not doing this to be cruel. It's best for both of us. It's time we both stand on our own two feet."

The tiredness of his voice seemed to calm her. She stared down at the office desk for what seemed like hours. Finally she raised her head, and tears clouded her eyes. "What about Willy?"

Chase sighed. "I'll be there for Willy if he needs me. But you can't keep filling his head with the notion that I'm going to be his father."

"I haven't."

"Good," he said and started to leave the office.

"I didn't mean to hurt you, Chase," she called after him.

He stopped, turning to look at her. "Just like you didn't mean to hurt me when you told me Willy was mine?"

"I was young," she said, her voice beseeching. "I was scared."

Chase nodded. "I know."

She seemed to relax a bit, offering him a wobbly smile.

"But what are you now?" he asked coolly. "Please have all your stuff out today and leave your key in the desk." He shut the door firmly behind him.

Summer-Ann watched Chase leave, then collapsed into her office chair. She gripped the arms, her nails digging into the tweed upholstery. Tears formed in her eyes, but she fought them away.

She didn't cry, not really. Not unless it would help her get what she wanted. Real tears only showed that a person was weak and ineffectual.

But Chase's dismissal hurt more than she would have imagined. They hadn't been involved for years, but Summer-Ann never really let go of the idea that Chase was hers.

It was true that Chase hadn't shown any romantic interest in her since the day she'd told him the truth about Willy. But even when Chase had dated other women, he'd remained close to her.

A couple of years earlier, he'd been quite serious about Lisa Harris. Yet he would still come to Summer-Ann whenever she called, which she did often. Often enough that Lisa had finally ended things, saying she couldn't compete with Summer.

Summer smiled smugly. And that's why she had been so demanding. Just to show other women that she'd always be first in Chase's life.

And other women did seem to recognize her control.

Chase did date now and then, but his relationships never developed into anything noteworthy. Yet, Abby Stepp—insignificant, frumpy Abigail Stepp—had waltzed into town and messed up everything.

And how? What on earth could Chase see in a woman like that? She was attractive in a plain sort of way, but she wasn't a beauty by any stretch of the imagination. And Chase had always been drawn to a certain style.

Summer-Ann wasn't blind. She noticed that all the women he'd dated in the past had similar qualities. Blond hair, high cheekbones, petite curvy bodies. Just like her. Chase kept looking for someone to replace her. And Summer-Ann knew eventually he'd realize that he would never be able to do that, and come back to her.

But he wasn't going to now . . . not unless Abby Stepp left for good. And what would make a freakishly intelligent woman turn tail and run?

Summer-Ann leaned back in the chair, steepling her fingers together in front of her. She had just the ammunition to get that exact reaction.

She frowned. But if she did use her secret weapon, would Chase be able to forgive her this time? He had forgiven her before, many times, and when he realized there was no one else who really understood, he would again. And she would have a family—the family her son deserved.

"Oh Chase," Abby said, her fingers pausing in his hair. "You didn't."

Chase lifted his head from her lap. "I don't want Summer-Ann around where she can cause more trouble. And you did say I was too forgiving."

"You are," she said resolutely, stroking his head again.

He lowered his head. Closing his eyes, a contented smile curved his lips.

Abby tried not to think about the worry that tugged at her, instead concentrating on the silkiness of Chase's hair and the warm breeze grazing her skin. But after a few moments, the worry won out. "But what is she going to do?"

Chase opened one eye. "She's getting a large severance check, and she was a hairdresser before she began to work for me. I know Marnie Gagnon will take her back at Shear Pleasures."

"Will she make enough?"

Chase smiled indulgently. "She'll be fine. And so will Willy."

He reached up and pulled her down to him, kissing the troubled little frown from her face.

When they parted, it was Chase's turn to look pensive.

"What?" Abby asked, confused by his concerned look.

"In my office, you mentioned that Summer-Ann had pulled another trick on you—back in high school. What was that?"

Abby shifted. She didn't want to tell him. She didn't want him to feel pity for her. But she knew she was going to have to tell him. If there was one thing she'd quickly learned about Chase, it was that he was as tenacious as he was forgiving.

"On graduation day, she asked me if I wanted to attend the graduation party at the Ledges with you guys," she said, keeping her voice light and indifferent. "I was thrilled that Summer-Ann asked. I said yes, rushed home to get ready and waited. And no one ever showed up. It wasn't a big deal."

Chase sat up. "I had no idea she did that."

Abby smiled. "I know. I mean, back then I thought you were probably a part of it. But now I know you, and I know that wasn't your style."

"Well, you give me too much credit. I could be a real jerk, but I honestly didn't know Summer did that."

"It's really no big deal," she assured him and realized it truly wasn't. It was just a stupid thing that occurred a long time ago.

"I'm sorry," he said, pulling her against him.

"I'm not." She nuzzled his neck. "In fact, I'm rather glad it happened."

Chase moved away to give her a dubious look.

"I really am. If I had gone, I probably would have been uncomfortable and had a terrible time. But now, I'll always remember the Ledges very fondly." She wiggled her eyebrows.

He chuckled.

The sound was so warm and rich that Abby could practically feel it trickle over her.

"But who's to say you wouldn't have discovered that same fondness fifteen years earlier," he said, cocking his eyebrow.

Abby shook her head with great certainty. "Nah, I would have passed out if you had even talked to me."

Chase laughed incredulously. "Why?"

"Because I was hot for your body," she admitted as she placed her hands on his chest.

"You were?" This time it was surprise that raised his brows.

"Mmm-hmm." She placed a kiss against his neck.

He pulled her tight. "Damn, I wish I'd gotten to know you back then."

"Well, I never believed in things like destiny and fate, but now I have my doubts."

"Me too," he agreed, capturing her mouth.

* * *

"Wake up, lazybones!" Chase called to the pile of twisted blankets in the middle of his bed.

The blankets rustled and eventually, Abby poked her head out, squinting at him.

"What are you doing up?" she mumbled, her voice low and drowsy.

Chase loved her voice, especially in the morning. It was husky and a bit deeper.

"I didn't even hear you get out of bed," she said, modestly holding the blanket to her chest as she sat up. "What time is it?"

"Around eleven, and time for you to get up."

She looked unconvinced. "Why don't you come back to bed?"

With her tousled hair and sleep-flushed skin, Chase found the temptation strong, but he managed to shake his head. "Nope, we've got something to do today."

"We do? What?"

A flat brown paper bag materialized from behind Chase's back. The green logo of a local clothing shop was imprinted on the parcel.

"What's that?" Abby asked, as some of the sleepiness left her eyes.

Chase sat on the edge of the bed and held it out to her. "Look."

Taking the bag with hesitant interest, she cast a look at him.

When he nodded encouragingly, she unfolded the end of it and peeked inside. Slowly, she reached in and pulled out a twisted scrap of red material. Holding it up, she studied the item, confusion evident on her face.

"What is it?" she finally asked.

Rolling his eyes, he tugged the cloth out of her hands, and spread it out on top of the rumpled quilt.

"It's a bathing suit," Abby said with dawning recognition, but puzzlement still creased her face.

"That's right. It's a bathing suit. We're going to learn to swim today."

A look somewhere between doubt and fear crossed her face. "I don't know, Chase. I think I'm too old."

"You're never too old." He grabbed the suit and jumped off the bed. "Come on. Put it on."

When Abby remained in the nest of bedding, he caught her hand and yanked her from the bed. She came, still clutching a sheet to hide her nakedness.

"You said you wanted to learn to swim," he said.

She shook her head. "I believe I said I wished I had learned to swim."

"No difference," Chase informed her as he dragged her to the bathroom. "Now put this on and I'll get my trunks on."

"Do I gotta?" she asked as she accepted the red suit.

Chase laughed. "Yeah, you gotta." He pushed her in the bathroom and closed the door behind her.

He returned to the bedroom and got into his swimsuit, which was actually just a pair of old cut-off jeans. Then, deciding he'd given Abby more than enough time, he headed back to the bathroom.

The door was still shut and not a single noise came from inside.

"Abby," he called through the panel, "does it fit?"

There was a pause. "I guess. Sort of."

"Well, let me see."

Another pause. "Maybe you should bring me a T-shirt to wear over it."

Chase smiled, but kept any signs of humor from his voice. "Okay, but let me see it."

Yet another pause, and finally the doorknob slowly

n Abby stepped out she was still draped head to toe in the sheet she'd dragged from the bed.

"That's not going to be easy to swim in," Chase observed with a grin.

"The suit is sort of skimpy," Abby said, her cheeks growing pink even with the sheet shrouding her.

"It's not a bikini or anything. I was tempted by one particularly tiny little suit with pink flamingos all over it, but it wasn't your style."

Abby looked exceedingly thankful. "No, that isn't. Although I don't think any bathing suit is really my style."

"Well, let me be the judge of that."

Abby started to loosen her hold on her sheet, but stopped.

"Abby, I've seen you naked—a lot."

Her color deepened. "But I didn't have to go out in public naked, too."

He caught her around the waist and planted a comforting kiss on her forehead. "I'm sure it looks fine. You're being too hard on yourself." His hands moved to her sides, and he gently peeled the white cotton away.

At first, she continued to clutch the cloth, but after a few insistent tugs, she released it.

Chase stepped back and he tried to keep his eyes from popping wide open.

"Fine" was not the word to describe Abby in the suit. She looked fantastic.

The simple style of the tank hugged her trim waist and accentuated the womanly flare of her hips. The bottom of the suit rose slightly on her hips and made her gorgeous legs look like they went on forever. And the small plunge of the neckline showed a delectable hint of cleavage. All of that would have been impossible to ignore. But given that all those lovely curves were encased in bright, poppy red, it was damned near impossible to look away.

"You look—" He gave up and let his eyes pop. "You look gorgeous."

Abby cast an unconvinced glance down at herself. "I'm not sure."

"I'm sure," Chase said adamantly. "Every man on the beach is going to be crazy as a loon. They won't be able to take their eyes off you."

Her expression conveyed that she didn't find that particularly reassuring. And suddenly Chase didn't either. He had no desire to share his lady with others, even if it was just a poppy red–covered hint of her amazing attributes.

"Maybe you do need a T-shirt," he decided.

Chapter 24

Birch Hill Pond was really a lake by most people's standards, but as Abby stood on the pebbled beach, looking at the wide expanse of water, it might as well have been the ocean.

Dread gripped her stomach, and she struggled to swallow.

"How deep is this lake?"

Chase thought for a moment. "Maybe sixty feet. Not terribly deep."

It sounded terribly deep to her.

"I don't want to learn how to swim," she concluded.

Chase chuckled, which wasn't the reaction she was looking for. "I'll be right with you the whole time. You'll love it."

She stared at the ripples of the greenish blue surface and concentrated on the gentle lap of the water against the beach. She had always wished she could swim. She loved the water from the distance, but now that she had the opportunity to go into it, she felt frightened.

"It's really going to be fine," Chase assured her. "You've faced bigger challenges than this. You survived thirteen years of school in Millbrook."

He had a point there.

"And you got your doctorate with the highest grades." She glanced at him. "How do you know that?"

"Did you?"

"Yes," she admitted begrudgingly.

"There you go. And you dated a guy for how long?"

She was confused, but answered, "About twelve years."

Chase winced, horrified, then said, "And you dated a guy for twelve years without having an orgasm."

"Chase!" she hissed and looked around to make sure no one had overheard. Fortunately, the only people around were a couple all the way on the other side of the beach.

"If you survived that, believe me, you can survive a little water." He appeared very sincere about that fact.

Abby glanced back out at the water. He did have a point. She'd handled difficult situations before.

"Okay," she agreed, taking a step toward the water.

Chase caught her wrist. "Take off the T-shirt."

"I thought you agreed the shirt was a good idea."

"I did when I thought there might be guys here to ogle you, but the beach is deserted. And I want to ogle you," he said with a devilish little grin.

"What about the people over there?"

They looked over at the distant couple. It was immediately apparent they weren't going to help her cause, as they were intertwined on their towel, too busy making out to notice her bathing suit, bright red or not.

"Lose the shirt, babe," he repeated with a smug grin.

"I'm going to buy you a Speedo and see how you feel."

He shrugged and reached for the button of his cut-offs. "I'll skinny dip if that makes you feel better."

"No," she said quickly, then added, "at least not now."

His grin broadened, and he moved his hands to the hem of his T-shirt. He peeled it off, and Abby stared.

There was no way she would ever get tired of looking at him. His jean shorts rode low on his hips, and she could count each ridge of muscles down his stomach.

His small belly button showed above the waistband, and whorls of dark hair surrounded the little indentation and disappeared into his shorts. His upper body was deep gold from working in the sun without a shirt.

He looked perfect. Beyond perfect, if there was such a thing.

"Okay, if you get to ogle me, then I definitely get to ogle you," he stated.

Abby stuck out her tongue, but found the bottom of her T-shirt and pulled it off.

Even though she still felt self-conscious, Chase's expression went a long way toward calming her. Or exciting her. Either way, she did feel better about the suit.

After a few seconds and shared appreciation for one another's scanty attire, he caught her hand and started toward the lake.

At the first touch of the cold water, Abby stopped again, digging her heels into the pebbles.

"That's cold," she declared.

Chase, who had released her hand, now stood in the water up to his knees. "It's invigorating."

"That's what people say when it's cold."

Chase waded back. "It will feel good once you get in, I promise. Just come in a bit."

Abby took a few steps, then halted, shivering.

"Doesn't that feel nice?"

"No, it feels cold."

"It'll get better."

"I don't know," she said with a doubtful shake of her head.

"It will," he said again.

Before she realized his intent, Chase scooped her into his arms and began to charge deeper into the lake. She squealed, clinging to him as cold water splashed up onto her bottom and back.

The next thing she knew, she was completely submerged in the icy fluid, and she imagined the feeling was similar to being encased in liquid nitrogen.

Maybe worse; she'd likely survive this.

Then she was pulled to the surface, her numbed fingers still grasping Chase's shoulders.

"See, isn't that great?"

Abby used one hand to sweep the tangle of sopping hair from her face and clutched him with the other. After letting out a sound halfway between a yell and a groan, she finally managed to mutter, "You're evil."

Chase chuckled, not one iota remorseful. "You won't think so when you're diving through the water like a dolphin."

She grunted and clung to him like a barnacle, her arms around his neck, her legs around his waist.

He walked out farther into the lake, the water rising gradually up their bodies. When it was up to their chests, Chase stopped.

"Are you still cold?"

Abby had been so concerned with how deep he was going to go, she had forgotten about the temperature. And in fact, the water didn't feel nearly as cold as it had initially.

But she wouldn't give him the satisfaction. "It's a bit better."

"Okay," he said, releasing his hold from around her back. "Put your feet down."

She still remained attached to him like a starfish stuck to a rock. "Is it slimy?"

Chase laughed. "No, it's pretty sandy."

Gingerly, she unwrapped one leg and tested the bottom. It was sandy, no weeds or muck. She unwrapped the other.

"Who knew you were so girly," he said.

"That's not girly," she said, reasonably. "Who likes to stand in mucky stuff?"

Chase nodded, but Abby got the feeling he still thought she was girly.

After years of being treated like one of the guys by her fellow students and co-workers, it actually seemed sort of nice to be seen as a little girly.

"Okay, ready to swim?"

She nodded.

"All right," he said, "lean forward, and I'm going to place my hands under your belly."

She looked skeptical, but she did as he said.

He placed his hands flat and palm up in the water. Abby leaned onto them.

"Good. Now lift your feet."

She did, floundering a bit before she allowed herself to float, balanced by Chase's hands.

"Excellent," he cheered. "Now paddle with your hands and kick with your feet. I'll stay right with you."

She did and began to move clumsily through the water.

And so the swimming lesson went, Abby paddling and kicking, and Chase staying right with her to make sure she didn't sink.

By mid-afternoon, Abby wasn't diving through the waves like a dolphin, but she was moving right along with the grace of a dog.

"You look great," Chase said, standing back and letting her go on her own.

She swam by, hands splashing, head high out of the water, feet fluttering behind her, looking as proud as the proverbial peacock. If a peacock could swim like a dog.

She turned and passed by him again.

"I'm telling you, baby, Chester is going to be downright jealous of your form," he called.

She paddled back and rose in front of him, an offended look on her damp face. "You're making fun of me."

Chase blinked innocently. "I meant that any dolphin would be jealous."

"Well, I don't care if I look like a dog," she declared loftily. "Because I can swim." She paddled off again.

Chase laughed. She was so damned adorable. Way cuter than a dog, or dolphin—or a peacock for that matter.

He watched her for a moment longer, happiness and a funny feeling of pride welling in his chest. Then on her third pass by him, he snagged her ankle and pulled her back.

She yelped but allowed him to catch her. "What are you doing? I was practicing."

"I think our swimming lesson is over for the day," he said.

Disappointment curled her lips downward.

"And now it's time to pay your instructor." He jerked her against him, running his hands over the slick material of her suit.

Abby raised an eyebrow. "And how much do I owe?"

"Oh, quite a bit. How much money do you have?" He nibbled the wet skin of her shoulder.

She wriggled against him, her legs fluttering around his.

"None," she murmured, mimicking his action on his shoulder.

"Well, I'm not letting you go without payment," he said firmly and licked the curve of her collarbone.

"But how can I possibly pay?" Her tongue traced the line of his collarbone in return.

His lips moved up her neck until he reached her ear.

"You'll have to think of something," he whispered, then tugged her earlobe with his teeth. "Can you think of anything?"

She released a shaky breath, then drifted a few inches away from him. "All I have is myself."

Her voice was low and coy and so incredibly sexy that Chase's heart hammered in his chest and his penis seemed ready to pry its way out of his cut-offs.

She floated just out of his reach. The sunlight lit the water so he could see her creamy limbs and all her poppy red curves moving in sinuous flutters under the rippling surface.

"And what would I do with you?" he asked, trying to keep his voice impassive.

"Whatever you want." Her lips parted, and her wet lashes fanned low over her eyes.

Damn, he'd died and gone to heaven. But he wasn't quite ready to let the game end. "Anything?"

She nodded.

"I can strip off that sexy red suit?"

She glanced at the beach. It was deserted. She nodded.

"I can touch you all over?"

She nodded—quite eagerly.

"I can sink myself deep inside you?"

She whimpered, and nodded.

He pretended to think it over. "Okay," he agreed, reaching forward to catch her.

She glided toward him, until her arms were wrapped around his neck. She pressed her lips to his.

But Chase took control of the embrace, his mouth moving over hers in needy, eager caresses, his tongue brushing against her lips, her teeth, her tongue.

As they kissed, their bodies touched in much the same fashion. Long, wet strokes of skin over skin.

His mouth left hers, and he trailed hungry, openmouthed kisses across her shoulder, tasting the crispness of the water on her sweet flesh.

Abby slipped away enough so she could skim his hands over his chest.

"I love how you feel, all hard and wet," she murmured, nibbling on his neck, her hands still slipping over his torso.

"I think there are places that are harder."

She lifted her head and grinned naughtily. "I think there are places that are wetter as well."

"You're becoming a regular strumpet, you know that?" He grinned back and ran a hand over the sleekness of her bathing suit to cup her bottom.

"I can't imagine where I learned such behavior," she said innocently. "I think it must be the influence of the local bad boy."

Chase rolled his eyes toward the sky. "Thank heavens for the local bad boy."

"Mmm-hmm." Abby captured his nipple, suckling him.

He hissed, feeling his penis jerk as pleasure exploded through him.

He tugged at the straps of her suit. "We need this off now."

Abby released his hardened nipple and smiled like the Cheshire cat. "You have the most sensitive nipples," she informed him.

This was an ongoing battle between them, whose nipples were the most responsive. And Chase decided that once and for all, he needed to prove the truth.

He pushed both straps off her shoulders and down her arms, peeling the stretchy material down to her waist. Her beautiful, full breasts bobbed in the water, the rosy crests appearing just above the surface.

He cupped one mound, loving the softness and the

weight of it. Her nipples were already gathered to hard points, from the coolness of the water or from his touch, he didn't know. And he didn't care. Either way, they begged to be tasted.

He trapped the beaded flesh between his lips, sucking on it.

She gasped and dug her fingers into his shoulders.

Abby had the most incredibly responsive nipples. He could bring her to orgasm by just stimulating her there. And although he knew it was just how Abby was designed, it still made him feel powerful. Like he had some magical touch.

She gasped again, pressing herself harder against him.

He nipped her, and she let out a sharp moan, grasping his head to keep him still.

"You win," she panted.

Chase raised his head. "You're finally admitting it?"

"Yes," she said, her eyes glazed with unfulfilled desire, "yes, I'm more sensitive."

He grinned arrogantly. "Told you."

"Conceit isn't attractive," she said, attempting to be stern, but the effect was lost with her bedroom eyes and her pink parted lips. "Now get back to what you were doing."

He cocked an eyebrow. "I'm the one who should call the shots here, since you're the one who owes me."

She nodded. "You're right."

"And I want to see you naked."

"Okay."

Within seconds, she was naked. Chase flung her suit over his shoulder so it wouldn't float away and then he concentrated on the gorgeous woman in front of him.

He could see all of her. The refraction of the sun and water rippled over her body, making her look like a watercolor painting come to life. A masterpiece, alive and his.

He moved his hands to her waist and lifted her to him. The buoyancy of the water made her feel weightless. The impression added to the surrealism of the situation. She was a figment of his imagination, created by water and sun and his own desire.

Then she wrapped her arms around his neck and her legs around his waist, and the touch of her skin became very real. The chafe of her taut nipples against his chest. The tickle of the dark curls between her legs against his stomach. Suddenly she was excruciatingly real, and so was his need to have her.

His mouth found hers, hard and demanding.

She responded in kind, squeezing him with her arms, with her thighs.

"I don't think I can just stop at kissing," he muttered against her lips.

"Then don't," she said simply.

He groaned at her invitation. "Baby, we don't have a condom."

"I am on the pill."

He debated her comment. He didn't take foolhardy risks, not anymore. But they were a couple now, not just two people sharing a fling.

"Are you sure?"

Abby smiled at him, her lids heavy. "We both know we're safe. We've been truthful with each other, right?"

Chase froze. About his sex life? Yes, he'd been truthful. About other things . . . "Yes, I'm safe."

"Then make me pay."

He groaned again. Grabbing her hip, he positioned her away enough so he could get to the fly of his jeans. The button and the zipper unfastened easily in the enveloping water, but the denim shorts clung to him, stiff and immovable.

He yanked at them, but they only budged a millimeter. He let out a frustrated growl.

"Are they stuck?"

"Yes," he said. "This has to be what a chastity belt feels like."

Abby smiled sympathetically, then uncurled her legs to stand. "Let me try."

She snaked her fingers under the waistband and wriggled the sides up and down quickly. Gradually, the unyielding material shimmied down his hips and slipped off.

"There," she said with great satisfaction.

Chase released a sigh of relief. "Thank God."

Abby smiled. "Where were we?"

Chase snared her to him, placing her arms around his neck and pulling her legs up around his hips. "Here." And he kissed her.

Quickly, the aggravation of his shorts disappeared, and he felt nothing but the slick brush of Abby's smooth body over his.

She moaned as his hand slid over the sleek roundness of her bottom, gliding between her legs to the tight passage spread wide against his stomach.

Abby gasped as he slid a finger inside her, her own moisture like oil to the water around them.

He pulled out and entered her again.

She cried out, this time biting his shoulder and squeezing him with her arms, her legs, and those tiny muscles deep inside her.

He wanted those muscles to clench more than his finger.

"Lie back," he said roughly, unwinding her arms from around his neck.

She complied, laying back in the water with her legs still anchoring her to him.

He watched her for a moment, floating in front of him, only her perfect face and the rosy peaks of her breasts rising above the water's surface. Dark hair billowed around her, and she looked like how he imagined the Lady of the Lake must have looked, rising magnificently out of the dark depths to bestow Excalibur to the worthy King Arthur.

If only he were as worthy. A moment of guilt and shame washed over him. But the sight before him was too enticing, and he wanted Abby too much.

His remorse drifted away, and he was touching her, her lovely breasts rising out of the water like inviting islands in an endless sea. The curls between her thighs swayed around his fingers like exotic sea life.

Again, he was struck by how otherworldly she seemed, and he had to make her magic his. Like the sailor following the song of the mermaid, he had to go, to surge forward, to make this gorgeous creature his. And damn the consequences.

He positioned his penis and entered her slowly, feeling her hot textures encircle him, amazed at how slippery her wetness was in comparison to the water. He began to move, lost between the contrast of her heat and the lake's coolness.

He held her hips as she bobbed in front of him, water and sun lapping her bare skin.

Small sounds of pleasure escaped her parted lips. Her eyes were closed and her arms out to her sides as she accepted him fully. The vision was as thrilling as the feel of her silken warmth gripping him.

When the sensations became too much, Abby reached for his arms, and he pulled her tight against him, still thrusting in and out of her. The motion grew more frenzied, more desperate. And when he heard her cry out with her release, he followed headlong into the dark, wet abyss.

Chapter 25

"I'm starving," Abby said as they waded out of the lake arm in arm, their swimsuits a little twisted and their skin a bit waterlogged. "Are you hungry?"

"Are you kidding? After that, I could eat an entire peck of clams myself," Chase said, bending to retrieve their beach towels. He handed her one and began to dry himself off with the other.

"Ooh, fried clams," Abby said longingly.

"Mmm, that does sound good. Afternoon Delight?"

"I think we already had that," she pointed out, with a happy little grin.

"Your sense of humor is getting as corny as mine."

She smiled wider, quite pleased with herself and very pleased with the whole wonderful afternoon.

She'd learned to swim! And she'd compensated her handsome instructor with incredible sex. Although, she sort of thought that she made out better with that particular method of payment. She felt fabulous. Her belly rumbled. Fabulous and ravenous. "I would love Afternoon Delight," she said, grabbing her T-shirt and starting in the direction of the small dirt parking area.

Chase caught her wrist, and she turned back. He touched her face and pressed a kiss against her mouth, his lips gentle and caressing.

When they parted, his pale eyes searched her face.

Her skin tingled under his icy blue gaze.

"Abby, I love you," he murmured. His voice was rich, chocolaty and so sweet.

Abby's heart raced, then stopped. She felt elated and scared and . . . speechless. Chase Jordan said he loved her. Her!

She continued to stare at him. And all she finally managed was a nod.

Chase glanced away from her, and when his eyes returned, they were a shade grayer, but his easy smile was in place.

"You ready to get something to eat?"

Abby nodded again, all connection between her brain and her tongue severed.

Chase Jordan loved her!

When they reached the truck, her jumbled, useless brain kicked back into working order and she said, over the back of the flatbed as if she said it every day of her life, "I love you, too."

Chase drove Helen to the Afternoon Delight on autopilot. Thankfully, he knew the route well, because if he didn't, they would have ended up in a ditch. There was no way he could concentrate on the road. He was too riddled with conflicting emotions—happiness and uncertainty and guilt.

What was he doing?

He glanced at Abby. She leaned back against the vinyl seat, her eyes closed, a contented smile on her lips. The air from the opened windows stirred pieces of her damp hair.

She looked lovely, and he was the world's biggest heel. How could he be so selfish to make her think this relationship could last?

Even if they sorted out their residences and their careers, which were big enough obstacles, they still had one major difference that was insurmountable.

He looked at her again. But it was as if he were powerless when it came to this woman. He wanted to be with her so much, he could convince himself of anything to achieve that goal.

Even now, he could feel his qualms fading. He'd always been a realist, and suddenly, he found himself in a fantasy world. The worst part was he liked it there.

He was overjoyed that she'd told him she loved him. His heart swelled every time he replayed those four words in his head. "I love you too," said in Abby's practical manner. As though it was a given.

He sighed. He might as well resign himself to the fact that he was lost, hopelessly lost. When it came to Abby, his emotions for her were like a freight train that he was trying to stop with a twig.

As they got out of the truck and approached the snack bar, Abby had to control the glee rioting through her. She felt like doing pirouettes and leaps. This was how love was supposed to feel. And it was better than anything she could have imagined.

She would make a note to tell Ellie that everything she believed about romance and true love was one hundred percent real. Ellie had always been the quietly wise sister.

Well, she read a lot, didn't she? Abby told herself and felt like giggling.

Instead, she linked her arm through Chase's and rested her head on his shoulder.

"I'm going to get a chocolate malt," she declared merrily as they waited in one of the four long lines.

"Mmm, I think I'll get a vanilla one."

"And I'm getting the clam dinner."

Chase nodded his agreement. "The lunch size just isn't going to cut it."

"Nope, I want lotsa clams. And onion rings."

"With extra ketchup."

They grinned at each other.

"Chase?"

Both of them turned to see Tommy Leavitt coming toward them, sporting a broad grin and a toddler on his narrow shoulders. Three other children of varying ages darted around him. At his side was a short woman with a scarf arranged on her head.

When Tommy realized Abby was with Chase, his warm smile faltered, but he nodded in her direction. "Abby."

She smiled, but she felt embarrassed at her behavior toward him at the Parched Dolphin.

"How are you?" Chase addressed the question to the woman.

She smiled, her teeth nearly as crooked as Tommy's, but they were overshadowed by the warmth in her soft gray eyes. "I'm right as rain. The doctors over to Bangor said that everything looks just fine."

Chase stepped forward and hugged the petite woman. "I'm so glad to hear that."

"No one is gladder than me," Tommy vowed, pulling the woman to his side. They beamed at each other, their crooked teeth suddenly looking kind of nice.

"Becky, do you remember Abby Stepp? She was a couple years ahead of you in high school," Chase said.

Becky looked at her, her gray eyes thoughtful.

Abby noticed that Becky didn't have any eyebrows, which made her pretty eyes look bigger.

"Yes." She nodded. "Although I recall your sister,

Martha, a little better; we graduated together. And of course I see her sometimes in the fashion magazines."

Abby smiled again. "Yes, she's actually in France right now, doing a fashion show."

Becky looked impressed. "Imagine that."

"And Abby's a scientist. She's working at Rand Labs," Chase said with pride.

"She was the smartest girl in our class," Tommy told his wife. "Gave that graduation speech and all."

"Really? That's something. I did okay in school. But Tommy's the one that got a trade. He works two jobs to keep this clan in food and clothes." Becky patted Tommy's arm, her affection for him written all over her face.

The little girl on Tommy's shoulders held her arms out to her mother and squealed.

The other children, two more girls and a boy, ran around on the grass. They were all pretty little children and obviously happy.

"Chase," Tommy said, "we're having a party next weekend to celebrate Becky's recovery. And we'd love you to come." He looked at her. "You too, Abby."

He'd invited her! One of her biggest tormentors from high school, the man she had been rude to, was inviting her to a party that was obviously an important and meaningful celebration to them. Suddenly, her resentment toward him seemed so silly.

Summer-Ann's words came back to her. *You should grow up*. Despite Summer-Ann's other lies, that had been the honest truth. Abby did need to grow up. She had changed since high school. Why on earth wouldn't everyone else have changed, too? That fact was so obvious, so apparent, and yet she had missed it. Some scientist she was.

"I don't know," Chase was saying, "I need to check what's going on."

302 KathyKathy Love

"We'll be there," Abby said firmly. "Thank you for the invitation."

She could feel Chase's eyes on her, but she continued to smile at the couple in front of them.

"Great." Tommy seemed genuinely pleased. "Around three o'clock."

Chase caught Abby's hand and squeezed it.

"What can we bring?" Abby asked.

"Yourselves is just fine," Becky assured her.

"Would you all like to join us now?" Chase offered.

Tommy shook his head. "We're just getting the kids some ice cream. But maybe next time."

They corralled their herd and headed to the last and longest line, which was the "ice cream only" line.

"You don't have to go if you don't want to," Chase said quietly.

"I want to."

He simply nodded, but she got the feeling that he was very pleased.

By the time they got their food, a heaping pile of clams, fries, onion rings and giant shakes, the Leavitts had piled back into their beat-up station wagon, with dripping ice-cream cones and lots of smiles.

"What was wrong with Becky?" Abby asked, after they drove away. She sat on the bench of one of the Afternoon Delight's picnic tables. She reached for a straw, plunging it into her thick malt.

"Hodgkin's Disease," Chase said, then popped a clam in his mouth.

Abby paused, her malt halfway to her lips. "Has she been fighting it long?"

"A little under a year, I guess. That family has had a rough time of it."

"How?"

"Well, their oldest girl had some problems when she

was born that required surgery and quite a long hospital stay. Tommy got pretty in debt getting her the help she needed. Then Becky got sick. Tommy took on two jobs, one at Sargent's Garage and the other at the Millbrook Seafood Company. Between the two, he got pretty comprehensive insurance, but that meant that Becky was alone with the kids a lot."

"It must have been hard for her when she was sick and worn down from the chemo." Abby felt terrible for the kind-eyed woman, and for Tommy.

"Well, she went over to her folks' place in Bangor every now and then to get some rest."

Abby took a sip of her malt, but she couldn't taste it. Her mind was on that night at the Parched Dolphin. Tommy had said Becky was in Bangor then.

"That's why Tommy was at the Parched Dolphin that night. When we first went out."

Chase swallowed the fry he was eating. "Yeah, I guess."

"He was just trying to relax, maybe find some people to talk to so he wasn't just alone, worrying about his wife."

He nodded. "He told me once that he had a hard time sitting around an empty house. Said he got to thinking about things he'd rather not."

Poor Tommy. And she had been so rude to the man. A guy who was already depressed.

"I feel terrible that I was so abrupt with him," she said, pushing away her container of clams. She'd suddenly lost her appetite.

"You went a long way today toward making him feel better," Chase said. He nudged the foam container back toward her. "These are some great clams. Shame to waste them."

Abby looked at the golden brown, battered clams and

begrudgingly picked up one. She made a face at him before she popped it in her mouth.

She had to admit it did taste pretty darn good.

Chapter 26

Friday afternoon, Abby was in her office working on an article for *Science Weekly* when Dr. Keene came in.

"Abby, I've been wanting a moment with you."

She pushed away from her computer. "Of course."

He pulled up a chair, which Abby found unusual. Dr. Keene, or rather, Cecil, always stuck his head in the door when he had something to say. He was too busy and too energetic to sit. This must be something important, or something that was going to take a while. Even though she thought everything was going fine, a modicum of apprehension crept down her spine.

"I think you know how important this genome research is to Rand Labs," he said, after he'd settled in the seat.

She nodded. "Yes."

"And I think you also know that your help over the past several months has been invaluable."

"I hope so."

"It has," he assured her.

The lurking anxiety dissipated.

"But," he continued. "I think you also realize that your time here is almost over."

A smidgen of the fear returned. Was he going to ask her to leave sooner than planned?

"I thought the amount of time I spent here was

dependent upon how far we got in the study. There's still quite a bit to do."

Cecil nodded. "Yes, that was the arrangement. And you're right, there is still plenty to do. As with all research, each discovery leads to new questions. And I see this project going on longer than anticipated. So I called Dr. Peters to discuss extending your stay."

Abby's heart leapt.

"Dr. Peters said she was willing to spare you. That is if you are willing to stay."

Abby had started nodding before he even finished his sentence. "Yes, Dr. Keene, I mean Cecil, I would love to continue working here."

"Wonderful. Wonderful," he said, a pleased twinkle in his eyes. "There is more, and this doesn't need to be decided until you've had a chance to consider it. But Dr. Peters and I also talked about keeping you here permanently. That is, you would work here a majority of the year and then go to the lab at Boston University and do a month to six weeks there. So we can work more fully in conjunction with each other."

Abby fought the urge to jump up and kiss this wonderful, wonderful man. He was giving her the perfect solution to the biggest impediment to a long-term relationship with Chase.

They could be together. They could both do the work they loved. It was perfect.

"Now, don't feel the need to answer now. Think about it," he said.

"I will," she assured him.

He stood and returned Darren's chair back to his desk. At the door, he paused. "Are you still seeing Chase Jordan?"

"Yes."

"Nice to hear. He's a good guy. You two are well-suited."

Cecil waved and disappeared down the hall.

Abby knew she was sitting all alone, grinning from ear to ear like a fool, but Cecil's words made her feel jubilant.

Who would believe that Abby Stepp and Chase Jordan were well-suited? But Cecil Keene was a genius, and if he thought so, then it must be true.

Feeling very cheerful, she returned to her article. But it took her twenty minutes to even type a single word.

After finishing up at the lab, Abby drove through town looking at the place she would now call home—again.

Main Street was lined with the same ancient oaks that she'd seen all her childhood, but she realized the shops weren't the rundown buildings she thought they were.

They had been restored. The carpenters had maintained the buildings' old-fashioned charm. They looked quaint and welcoming, rather than the dilapidated places she remembered. She wondered if Chase had worked on them.

The waterfront had undergone a makeover too. Lobster boats and trawlers still filled the harbor, and lobster traps and fishing nets still littered the wharfs, but the docks had been rebuilt, the wood not even weathered yet. And there was a working fish market now. Even that looked charming.

It really was a pretty town, Abby realized.

She passed the Dairy Palace. Kids still sat on the wooden fence surrounding the ice-cream parlor, but they didn't look like the high school kids she remembered. They looked very young, and she realized that for the most part she could barely recall ever being that young.

Just like Tommy Leavitt, the town had changed. It still had elements of the Millbrook she remembered, but so much was different.

And there was so much different about her, too. She wasn't Abby Stepp, one of the ugly Stepp sisters. She was Abby Stepp, the doctor. Abby Stepp, the scientist. The kite flyer. The fan of music and dancing. The swimmer. The girlfriend of Chase Jordan. So many things she never thought she would ever be. And she was now going to be Abby Stepp, a resident of Millbrook, Maine.

Chase wasn't home when she pulled into her driveway, but Ellie was. Abby was so excited about Cecil's offer and her decision to accept that she had to tell someone.

"You're staying?" Ellie said.

Abby nodded.

Ellie clapped her hands and began to jump around the large kitchen. She paused and looked back at Abby. "Really?"

"Yes," Abby said with a huge smile.

Ellie squealed and began hopping again.

The reaction was so silly and so happy that Abby couldn't contain her peals of laughter.

Ellie bounced over to her, grabbed her hands, and they began bouncing together.

Suddenly they were young again, laughing and spinning, acting very foolish.

The loud cranky rumble of Helen announced Chase's arrival home. Abby and Ellie stopped twirling.

Ellie squeezed Abby tight. "I'm so glad you're home for good."

"Me, too." And she really was.

"Now go tell that hunk of yours that you are officially here to stay."

Abby didn't need to be told twice. She dashed out onto the front porch.

Chase was unloading tools from the back of his truck. He stopped when he saw her.

"Hey, you," he called to her, putting a hand up to shield the sun from his eyes.

"Hey, you," she shouted back, her voice joyous. "I've got some news for you."

He started to walk down his drive. "Oh yeah, what's that?"

"I got a full-time position at Rand Labs."

Chase froze at the edge of the street. "What did you say?" he asked slowly.

"I got a permanent job at Rand Labs," she repeated and rushed down the stairs.

Chase whooped and moved toward her. They met in the middle of the street. He scooped her up and spun her around and around, both of them laughing.

Finally he slowed and set her back on her feet.

"That," he declared, "is the best news I have ever heard." And he kissed her senseless.

"I've never seen anything so romantic," Millie Lime-burner said as Summer-Ann shoved the highlighting cap over the older woman's huge perm. "They were in the middle of the street, spinning and laughing, and then they kissed. It was just like the end of any old movie."

Summer-Ann began threading Millie's hair through the tiny holes in the rubber bonnet with a hook that looked just like a plastic crochet hook. Although any self-respecting hairdresser would say it absolutely wasn't. It was a highlighting tool.

Summer-Ann had started at the salon the day after Chase let her go. Marnie had been thrilled to have her back, and to be honest, she didn't really mind the work either. A lot of her old clientele were glad to see she'd returned, and she liked working with the girls again.

Wendy, Marnie and Patty had always been fun to spend time around.

"Just like an old movie," Millie said again, her voice dreamy. "One with Cary Grant and Katharine Hepburn."

Summer-Ann shot a look at Patty, who rolled her eyes in response. Patty was actually stationed behind her, but with the mirrors lining the walls, they could see each other's reflections. Millie couldn't see anything without her bifocals.

"Abby Stepp looks a bit like Katharine Hepburn," Millie said.

That received another eye roll from Patty.

"I have always liked those Stepp girls. Of course, Lillian Stepp was such a nice lady—we were neighbors for nearly forty years. It only stands to reason her granddaughters would be nice girls, too."

Summer-Ann yanked a piece of hair through one of the holes.

Millie gasped and reached up to her head.

"Sorry," Summer-Ann said.

Millie nodded, accepting her apology. "Now, I wouldn't have ever pictured Abby with Chase Jordan," she continued.

"No, neither would I," Summer-Ann agreed whole-heartedly.

"He used to be such a wild young man. You worked for him, didn't you, dear?" Millie didn't wait for her answer. "He does have quite a successful business, I hear. I've considered asking him to fix a door in my house. It swells every summer. But he must have changed his wild ways, if he's gained Abby's interest. She's a smart girl. Valedictorian of her class, you know."

"Yes, I went to school with her," Summer-Ann said coolly.

"That boy is handsome though. No Cary Grant now,"

Millie added. "But very nice looking. Although he should trim up that hair."

Millie was silent, and Summer-Ann plucked at her head in peace. But only for a few brief moments.

"Ellie came over to my house this morning to pick up a few library books that were due. She does that for me—brings me books and takes them back for me. You know, since she's going to the library anyway. She picks up groceries for me, too. Usually just milk and bread, things like that." Even Millie seemed to notice her story wasn't going anyplace. "Anyway, I got the chance to ask her what those two were celebrating in the street. And she told me that Abby is staying permanently in Millbrook."

Summer-Ann dropped the crochet hook. "For good?"

Millie nodded. "With a kiss like that, right in the middle of the street, I imagine we'll soon be hearing wedding bells on Fletcher Road."

Summer-Ann felt nauseous.

"Just like the end of a movie, I tell you," Millie said again.

Summer-Ann felt like she was in a movie, too. A horror movie.

Fortunately Millie was Summer-Ann's last client of the day, although it was the longest two hours she'd ever had to live through. By the time she left the salon and got into her car, the nausea had worn off and had been replaced by pure anger.

After Chase had fired her, Summer-Ann had gone over to talk to her best friend, Candy Moore. Her friend calmed her down and convinced her not to do anything stupid.

So she let her plan go. After all, she'd heard from

Mason Sweet's secretary, Ginny Tibbetts, that the oldest ugly Stepp sister was only in Millbrook temporarily. Then she would go back to her job in Boston.

Summer-Ann just assumed that would bring a natural end to the bizarre romance, and she could make her move without causing Chase any upset. But now it didn't look that way.

And after hearing at least fifteen recounts from old Millie Limeburner of their mid-street kiss, it seemed she needed to take drastic measures.

Willie was waiting on a bench outside Millbrook Elementary when she pulled into the schoolyard. He jumped up and ran to the car, dragging a beat-up Harry Potter backpack behind him.

"How was your day?" she asked, leaning over to kiss his tousled head. Her son always had the most adorable case of bedhead, even after she washed and combed the unruly locks.

"Good," he said, dropping the bag on the car floor. "We're learning about the Solar System."

"Really? That's cool."

"Yeah," Willy agreed. "I want to make rockets when I grow up."

Summer-Ann smiled, but a bittersweet feeling swept through her. She'd had big dreams too at Willy's age, but things didn't go quite the way she had imagined. She desperately wanted things to be different for Willy.

She worried all the time. Worried that he'd make the same mistakes she had. Worried that when he got older, he'd need more than her. He needed a male influence. Someone who was levelheaded and consistent and would encourage him to succeed.

"I'm going to ask Chase if he'll help me make a model rocket. We saw them down at Shore Market, and he said we could build them, then take them to Hobb's Field and shoot them off."

Chase was the perfect dad for Willy. And Summer-Ann knew she could be happy with him too. Their teenage affair had been wild and passionate. She honestly believed that Chase had never really gotten over her, and in truth, she'd never really gotten over him either.

It would work. They would be happy. It might take a little unpleasantness, but she was willing to do what she had to do.

She looked over at Willy. He was pretending that a round hairbrush that he'd found in the car's cup holder was a rocket.

She would do anything for her little boy with big dreams.

Chapter 27

"You look beautiful," Chase said, looking at Abby in the mirror.

She had to admit she felt beautiful. She'd bought a new sundress to wear to the Leavitts' today. It was a simple cut, fitted at the bodice with a flowing skirt, in pale blue cotton. The color had reminded her of Chase's eyes, but the real selling points had been that it looked nice with her skin tone and made her feel almost delicate.

He came up behind her, slid his arms around her waist, and placed a kiss on her bare shoulder.

Abby studied their reflections. Chase made her feel delicate, too. She was tall, but he still had a good four or five inches on her. And their dark hair mingled nicely together, his very dark and hers, a couple of shades lighter.

Her gaze moved to his bronzed, muscular arms. They looked pleasing against her paler skin.

"What are you thinking?" he asked after a few moments of watching her scrutinize their images.

"I was thinking that we actually look like a couple." She nuzzled her cheek to his.

"As opposed to what?"

She smiled and shrugged, feeling the muscles of his chest against her back. "I don't know. I guess I'm being silly."

He straightened and inspected them in the mirror. "We do look good together."

"You're just humoring me."

Chase shook his head and narrowed his eyes to really study them. Finally he pronounced, "It's the noses. We have the noses of a couple."

She elbowed him and tried to pull out of his embrace. "You're funny," she said without any real affront.

He held her tight. "You know why we look like a couple?" he asked, his voice serious.

Abby stopped squirming and looked at him; their eyes locked in the mirror. She couldn't reply. His gaze was so intense, she felt trapped between strong arms and a pale blue stare.

"We look like a couple because we are crazy, mad in love."

He turned her in his arms and kissed her. Her toes curled in her sandals. Yep, that was it exactly.

"Maybe we should just stay home," Chase suggested, nibbling her ear.

"You're insatiable."

"Only for you," he said, a roguish twinkle in his eyes.

"Is that true?" She hated to be needy and insecure, but the words just seemed to burst out.

The twinkle vanished, and his expression became solemn. "I've never felt like this about anyone else. Never."

Abby's heart soared; it twirled like one of Willy's kites. "I'm glad. I wouldn't want to be the only one feeling this way."

"Believe me, you're not." He kissed her.

It was only the obligation to Tommy and Becky that kept them from tumbling into bed for the afternoon. Although, it didn't seem to stop them from tumbling to the floor for a while.

Chase glanced at his watch. It was only half past three. Not too bad, although he didn't feel nearly as satisfied as he'd like to. Abby was in for a night of very little sleep.

She was bent over, getting a basket of goodies out of the GTO. The skirt of her sundress was draped over the curve of her bottom and swirled around her trim ankles.

When she straightened and turned around, she caught his admiring expression. "What?"

He couldn't quite contain the devilish smile that tugged at his lips. "Just admiring that dress."

She raised an eyebrow, suppressing her own smile. "Well, stop and carry these brownies." She held out a pan of the bars, topped with chocolate frosting and chopped nuts.

"When did you make these?" he asked, taking them.

"I didn't; Ellie did. I told you, I can't cook." She brushed past him, with her basket of cheese and crackers and a couple bottles of wine balanced in the crook of her arm, his own Little Blue Riding Hood.

Chase shook his head and followed. He actually found her insistence that she couldn't cook very funny. He had no doubt that she could learn to cook if she had the desire. Hell, she could be a gourmet chef, if she wanted to.

He had the sneaking suspicion she could cook just fine, but she didn't like to. It didn't matter to him; he liked cooking.

"Holy cow," Becky said as she opened the door. "Looks like you brought enough for an army." She took the brownies from him. "You were supposed to just bring yourselves. But I do appreciate the goodies."

Abby followed Becky into the kitchen, and Chase wandered through the small house to the sliding glass door that led to the back deck. Several people Chase knew sat in resin lawn chairs, drinking beer. Tommy was down on the lawn, getting a grill started. Kids ran around everywhere.

"Hey, Chase," Paul Cormier greeted, saluting him with his beer.

"Hi, Paul, it's good to see you," he said as he stepped outside.

The greetings kept coming until he reached Tommy.

"Glad you could make it." He thumped Chase on the back. "Did you get a beer?"

"No, where are they?"

Tommy gestured with a spatula to a cooler on the lawn near the deck steps. "Help yourself. I think I'm about to have a weenie bonfire here." He started scooping some rather charred-looking hot dogs onto a plate.

Chase went over to get a beer and chatted for a moment with Chad Moore, before returning to talk with Tommy.

"So, is the weenie roast under control?"

Tommy cast an uncertain look at the pile of blackened wieners sitting in the middle of the picnic table.

One of the kids dashing around the yard actually stopped and stared at the pile quizzically.

Chase chuckled. "I hope you've got more."

Tommy nodded. "Where's Abby? Did she come?"

"Becky whisked her away to the kitchen." Chase glanced at the sliding glass door.

"She's fine. Beck will take good care of her."

Chase didn't doubt that, but he was still worried. He knew Abby felt a little awkward coming here.

"You're really interested in her, huh?"

Chase looked back at Tommy. "Yeah, I'm crazy about her."

"I can tell. She turned out to be real pretty."

Chase nodded.

"I kinda forgot how we picked on her." Remorse filled Tommy's voice. "I didn't actually remember until I happened to tell Billy Norris about the incident at the Parched Dolphin."

Chase looked surprised. "You talked with Billy?"

"Ayuh, down at the docks. He's still fishing out of Portland, but he drove his boat up here to visit his folks."

"Well, I think Abby had a hard time with the teasing she took. But I do think she's starting to realize that we were all just stupid kids."

"That we were," Tommy agreed, taking a swig from his beer.

They fell silent. Tommy wrestled with his new batch of hot dogs, and Chase thought about being a stupid kid.

He had been the stupidest of them all. Hell, even Tommy, who had barely passed general courses, could—

"Why is it men love to grill things?" Becky's voice hauled him back from his thoughts.

Becky and Abby approached them.

Chase could tell from Abby's relaxed posture and her smile that she was having a nice time with Becky.

"Try burn," Tommy said sheepishly, jerking his head toward the picnic table.

"Tommy," Becky said sternly, then giggled.

"I like burnt hot dogs," Abby said politely.

The four of them exchanged looks and began to laugh.

Chase put an arm around Abby and pulled her close. He really believed she would eat those scorched dogs just to convince Tommy she was sorry for her behavior.

"Well," Becky said, going to the table to pick the platter up. "I don't think anyone needs to eat these. We've got plenty more hot dogs and a ton of hamburger. These are going to the trash."

"Do you need help?" Abby asked.

"No, you stay here." Becky headed inside.

There was lots of good-natured ribbing as Becky passed. The guests seemed to be having a great time.

In fact, Chase thought the party was going very well, and Abby was getting more and more comfortable with all the guests, many of whom she had gone to school with. That is until Summer-Ann arrived.

She sashayed out back and waved to the crowd of people gathered around several picnic tables. "Hi, Tommy and Becky. Hi, everyone."

Chase could tell by Tommy's confused expression and Becky's anxious one that they hadn't invited her.

He looked beside him at Abby. Her face was calm, but her spine was as straight as a beanpole. He placed a hand on her back.

She offered him a reassuring smile.

"Candy told me you were having this little shindig," Summer-Ann said as she advanced toward Becky, which meant she was also advancing toward them. Becky and Tommy sat directly across the table.

"And I had to come help you celebrate your great news," Summer-Ann said, a huge smile curling her lips.

Becky smiled uneasily. "Thank you, Summer."

Summer-Ann continued to smile until she noticed Chase and Abby on the other side of the table.

Her smile curled into a sneer.

"Hello, Chase."

He nodded.

"Well, this could be awkward," she declared.

Chase couldn't agree more, but instead he caught Abby's hand and stood. "That's okay. We should probably be leaving."

Abby didn't move.

Chase frowned down at her.

"This is a small town, We're going to run into each other. I'm not uncomfortable," she said softly.

Chase wanted to argue, but thought Summer would enjoy that, so he nodded and sat down.

"She's right," Summer-Ann agreed. "We can't avoid each other forever."

Instead of walking away and joining the table where Candy sat as Chase thought she would, Summer-Ann sat down at the end of their table. She began talking with Nancy White.

"Are you sure?" Chase asked Abby.

Abby nodded and took a sip of her wine. "She'd love us to run and hide."

Tommy leaned forward and said quietly, "I'm sorry. We didn't invite her."

"I know," Chase said.

"So you've probably heard that Chase fired me." Summer-Ann's voice carried down the table, throughout the whole yard in fact.

A hush fell over the crowd.

"After nearly three years."

A few people at the other tables made forced conversation.

"And all because that ugly Stepp sister asked him to."

Chase jumped up. "I think you'd better watch yourself, Summer."

"It's the truth," she stated.

"That isn't the truth. Abby didn't ask me to fire you, that was solely my decision. And I should have done it sooner. Let's go." Chase grabbed Abby's arm, and this time she followed.

"Thank you," Abby murmured to Tommy and Becky.

As they stepped over the bench of the picnic table, Summer-Ann spoke again, this time to Abby. "How does it feel, Abby?"

Abby frowned at her. "What?"

"How does it feel to be so incredibly intelligent and be dating a guy who can't even write his own name?"

The air was crushed out of Chase's lungs. He tried to pull in a deep breath, but couldn't.

"What?"

He could hear Abby's voice, but it sounded like it was far, far away.

"That's right." Summer-Ann's voice filtered into his brain. "Chase can't write. He can't read. So tell me, what is a woman with a doctorate in biochemistry to do with some illiterate guy? I mean, after the great sex has lost its appeal."

He dropped Abby's arm.

Tommy stood. "That's enough, Summer-Ann."

"That is just the truth, too," she said, looking innocently around at the stunned crowd. Looking as though she truly didn't realize she had just destroyed his world.

Chase turned and began to leave, but Abby ran after him. She caught his arm, halting him.

"Chase—" she started.

But he couldn't let her finish. When he looked into her dark eyes all he could see was pity. Pity for the idiot who couldn't even read.

He pulled his arm away.

She tried to stop him again, but he shook her off. "Don't," he shouted, then lowered his voice. "I have to go."

Abby watched him, her heart breaking. She heard his car door slam and the engine start. Then she saw a flash of red as he tore down the wooded road.

Tears filled her eyes, but she controlled them. She wasn't going to cry in front of Summer-Ann. She would enjoy it too much.

Instead she walked back to the table and glared at the blonde. "You should be ashamed."

Summer-Ann looked unimpressed.

"Chase helped you with Willy. He gave you a job so you could take better care of him. He forgave you when you lied and told him Willy was his child. And you repay him like this? Humiliating him in front of his friends."

Summer-Ann cast a look around at the others. No one, even not Candy Moore, made eye contact with the blonde.

"You know," Abby said, anger churning through her. "I actually felt sorry for you. I was concerned when Chase told me he'd let you go. I was concerned for your little boy. I worried that you wouldn't make enough money to care for him and yourself. But now I realize my concern was misplaced. I should have been worrying about how someone so spiteful, so cruel could possibly raise a child."

Abby turned toward Tommy. "May I please have a ride home?"

He nodded. "Summer, I think you'd better go, too." But he didn't wait to see if she left.

When she and Tommy reached her house, she saw that Chase wasn't home. He had been shaken to the core. He needed time alone to calm down. She just prayed that he was all right.

"I think Chase will need a while to cool off," Tommy said, as if he'd been reading her mind.

"Yes. That was the most hurtful thing Summer-Ann could have done to him."

Tommy nodded. "As far as I know, he hid it from everyone. I certainly never knew. That must have been hard."

Abby knew it must have been. Much harder than anyone could probably ever know.

"Thanks for the ride."

"Anytime, Abby."

Ellie was in the kitchen when Abby entered.

One look at Abby, and she stopped wiping down the counter. "What's wrong?"

Abby didn't know where to start. How to explain the situation without letting another person know Chase's closely guarded secret?

"Did things go bad with Tommy Leavitt?"

Abby immediately shook her head. "No. Tommy and Becky were wonderful."

"Then why do you look so upset? Something didn't happen with Chase, did it?"

"Sort of." Abby sank onto one of the wooden chairs at the table.

Ellie joined her, worry creasing her brow as she waited for her sister to continue.

"Summer-Ann showed up at the party, and she told everyone a secret that Chase has obviously worked very hard to hide."

"Oh no," Ellie whispered, visibly distressed, much more upset than Abby's vague description warranted.

Abby frowned, but then the reason dawned on her. "You know that Chase can't read."

"He can read," Ellie said defensively, her dark blue eyes brimming with tears. Then she amended her statement. "He can read some and write a little too. He's severely dyslexic."

"And you taught him to read." Suddenly everything made sense. Ellie's relaxed demeanor with Chase. His knowledge of her cooking skills and, of course, what she read.

"A little," Ellie said. "It's difficult and frustrating for him. He can do it, but it's very slow. He tries so hard." She started to cry.

Abby hugged her sister, and she felt like crying too.

For the boy who had looked so alone at graduation. For the guy who wore a relaxed smile when he must have always been on guard. And for the man who had been so wounded today, his pride horribly injured.

"Where is he?" Ellie sniffed.

"I don't know."

By the following Thursday, Abby still didn't know where he was. Sometime, she guessed while she was at work, Chase had returned home to get Chester and to pick up his truck. But other than that, Chase Jordan had disappeared off the face of the earth.

"Well, he does have to come home eventually," Ellie said practically.

Abby knew he did, but after checking his driveway for the umpteenth time that evening alone, she was starting to doubt the fact.

Sitting down at the kitchen table, she sighed and lay her head onto the table.

Ellie came up behind her, rubbed her back and placed a cup of tea near her nose. "What are you going to do?"

She lifted her head, staring at the steam curling out of the cup. Ellie always boiled the water when she made tea. Abby was too lazy; she just got it warm enough to get the tea bag to steep. And everyone thought Abby was the perfectionist.

"I'm going to go to Boston."

Ellie nodded. "So you've made up your mind?"

"Yes." Although the decision might be the worst mistake of her life. "I'm going to pack up my apartment, find someone to sublet it, and move here." The surety she heard in her own voice impressed her.

"How long will you be gone?"

"Hopefully only two weeks at the most."

"He'll have to be home by then," Ellie said reassuringly.

"Yeah." And if he wasn't, Abby would continue to wait.

Chapter 28

Chase sat on the dock, drinking a beer and half-heartedly dangling a fishing line in the water. Chester lay on the dock beside him.

When the dog's tail started thumping against the weathered boards of the dock, Chase turned to look at the long path that led from his cabin to the water.

"I knew you'd be here," Mason said, his wing-tipped shoes making a staccato clack on the boards.

"Beer?" Chase hauled up a rope that was dangling in the water. A six-pack of beer was tied to the end. Three cans were already gone from the plastic rings.

Mason sat down beside him and pulled one off. Chase grabbed another and dropped the single can back in the water. It bobbed for a second, then sank.

The crack of their cans being opened seemed to echo over the silent lake.

Chase imagined what people would think if they happened upon the odd couple. Chase looked like a crazy hermit. His hair was a mess, and he hadn't shaved in a week. He was wearing a pair of cut-offs and a sleeveless sweatshirt that even he noticed smelled a little funky. Mason wore polished shoes, tailored slacks, a long-sleeved dress shirt and a tie with little things on it that looked like . . .

"Are those bananas on your tie?"

Mason picked up the tie, studied it for a moment, then dropped it. "Yeah, I thought they were just random half-moon shapes when I bought it."

Chase nodded as if the same thing had happened to him many times.

"I've seen Abby. She came to me looking for you. And I know what Summer-Ann did. Ginny," he added as though that were explanation enough.

It was.

"So when do you plan to stop this little self-pity fest?"

Mason's question caught him up short. "What?"

"Chase, you can't just hide. No one thinks any less of you."

"I can't read," Chase said flatly. "I'm sure they don't think I'm a genius."

"Actually I think quite a few people do. They sure think it's pretty darn amazing you kept it a secret all through school. How did you do that?"

"Got kicked out of class a lot," Chase said dully.

"Tricky."

"Mmm."

"It is," Mason said more emphatically.

Chase didn't respond again.

"So this is the plan—hide at your old fishing cabin, drink beer and feel sorry for yourself?"

Chase took a sip of his beer.

"Abby is really worried about you."

"Well, you can tell her I'm fine," Chase said.

"It would be better if you stopped wallowing in self-pity and told her yourself," Mason stated.

"You seem to have a theme going here."

"I'm trying to get a point across."

"I thought you were no longer an advocate of relationships."

"I'm not. Not for myself, anyway. But I've seen how

happy you were lately. And I also saw how worried and upset Abby is."

"Don't forget pity," Chase added bitterly. "Don't forget the pity she's feeling for me."

Mason snorted. "Like I already said, the only pity I've seen is the pity you're wallowing in." He got to his feet, took a drink of his beer and set the can down on the deck. "I'm going. But I thought you should know that there are a lot of people out there worrying about you."

Chase didn't turn to watch Mason leave, instead listening to the click of his shiny dress shoes grow more distant.

He took another drink of beer and shook the fishing rod. He wasn't feeling sorry for himself. He was taking a much-needed vacation.

Hell, when was the last time he'd taken any real time off, other than a day here or there? Over a year anyway. That was all he was doing. Taking a break.

He reached over and patted Chester's huge, yellow head. The dog's tail thumped lazily.

He knew Abby would be looking for him. And he also knew, if she found him, she'd tell him that his learning disability didn't bother her. But it would have to. Someone so exceptionally intelligent couldn't help but feel embarrassed.

Okay, so he had technically run off, rather than take a planned vacation. But he'd been doing Abby a favor; giving her the out she would be too nice to make for herself. She didn't deserve a guy who couldn't read her articles in the science magazines or read to their children at night. Hell, he couldn't even read the menu at a restaurant.

Well, that wasn't exactly true. He could read some. Ellie had taught him more than any teacher had throughout school. But the process was slow and tedious. And it frustrated him that he couldn't seem to get any faster. No

matter how many books he and Ellie sat and read. And
they had read—probably a hundred together, ranging
from children's books to romance novels. It just never
seemed to get easier.

He sighed. Ellie hadn't told Abby his secret. Of course,
he knew she wouldn't. Ellie didn't think it was anyone's
business but Chase's. Still, he wondered if Ellie disap-
proved of him being with Abby. If she thought Abby was
too good for him.

Nah, not Ellie. She was a kind soul, a romantic. She
would have seen his relationship with Abby as a real-life romance. God knows, her romance novels were riddled with
strife. He guessed he should be thankful this was the only
problem he and Abby had. No uncles trying to kill them
for an inheritance. No secret babies. No amnesia. All and
all, his reading disorder was small potatoes.

But it wasn't. Not to him.

He should have known Summer-Ann wasn't going to
take being fired without a fight. But he'd never believed
she would go this far. She'd known about his dyslexia for
years and years. It was one of the reasons she had
dumped him for the college boy. She wanted someone
who was going to be able to make a good living. She
wanted someone she could be proud of.

At the time, her rejection had hurt like hell. But now,
he could understand it. Chase had been a very poor
prospect indeed. And ultimately, he had forgiven Summer for all her lies, because he understood her desire to
be someone else, to live somewhere else, to have more.
He wanted all of that too.

And to some extent, he had been able to get more, to
make over Chase Jordan into a different person. He'd
changed his wild ways. He'd built a successful business.
But he'd gotten greedy, like Summer-Ann had been. He
wanted something that was too far out of his reach. Abby.

She appeared in his mind. So lovely, so classy, so intelligent. So out of his league.

What had he been thinking? Had he really believed that he could hide his dyslexia from her forever? The answer was easy—he hadn't been thinking. He'd been a lovesick fool, believing everything would simply work out.

He took another swallow of his beer, draining it. He looked down at the rope binding the beer to the dock and considered pulling up the last one. Then he decided against it.

He was livid with Summer-Ann, but she had made him see the truth and come out of his fantasy world. Abby was *so* far above him. He was a stupid schmuck, stuck on earth reaching for a star.

He eased back against the warm boards of the dock. Chester lifted his head to look at him, then dropped it back down onto his paws with a loud sigh.

The sky was a deep blue scattered with puffy clouds. A dragonfly buzzed over Chase's head, and the lap of the water against the dock's pilings created a peaceful cadence.

Abby materialized in his mind, how she'd looked the day he'd taught her to swim. She had paddled back and forth in front of him, her head high out of the water, water splashing everywhere as she pumped her arms and kicked her feet. She'd looked so silly and so beautiful.

She'd told him a secret that she was ashamed of, that she couldn't swim. She'd trusted him not to laugh or feel bad for her. And then she had trusted him to teach her how.

Another image of her standing outside the Parched Dolphin, tears dried on her cheeks, her spine ramrod straight, admitting how much the jeers of her past still hurt. Again, she trusted him with the truth.

Suddenly, he realized that he hadn't trusted Abby at all. He hadn't even given her a chance.

He sat up.

He did owe her that chance. And he owed himself a chance too. He *was* wallowing in self-pity.

"What do you think, Chester? Wanna go find Abby?"

The dog was on his feet and halfway up the path to the cabin, before Chase could gather the beer cans and the fishing rod. It seemed Chester was a tad smarter than his owner.

Chase went directly to his house. It was almost seven, and he figured that Abby would be home from work by now. But her car wasn't in the driveway. Neither was Ellie's.

He wandered into his house, tossed down a pile of mail and checked his messages. Five messages were from Abby, but they were all from almost a week ago. She sounded increasingly upset with each message. Chase punched the END MESSAGES button halfway through the fifth one. He was a shit.

Going to the window in the living room, he looked at her house. Still no one home.

Maybe she had to work late. He paced a bit and decided he couldn't wait around. He'd go check the lab.

He noted every car he passed to make sure it wasn't Abby heading in the opposite direction.

When he pulled into the lab parking lot, he didn't see her car, but he figured he'd go inside and see if any of her co-workers knew where she might be.

As he stepped into the entrance hall, a woman seated in a tiny, square office, only her head visible through a small window, greeted him.

"May I help you?"

"Yes, I'm looking for Dr. Abby Stepp."

"Oh, I'm so sorry," she said, with a wide smile that be-lied her words. "Dr. Stepp has gone back to Boston."

Chase stood there for a second. "She has?"

The woman nodded, again her smile incongruent with his perplexed reaction.

"When did she leave?"

"I'm not sure. Yesterday or the day before."

"Okay. Um, thanks." He headed back out the door, al-though he wasn't paying any attention to where he was going. He was too confused as to why he had just thanked the woman for giving him the worst news of his life.

During the next week, Chase kept as busy as possible with work, which wasn't too hard given how behind he was from his vacation/pity party. At night, he often went over to Mason's to have a few drinks and, mainly, to avoid his house. It was too hard to be there. To keep looking across the street in hopes that he'd see Abby's car.

Tonight, he'd arrived at Mason's as usual and his friend already sat on the porch, two beers waiting.

"You aren't getting sick of me showing up here?" Chase asked as he walked up the steps.

"Nah. Saves me from drinking alone."

Chase smiled, but he suspected Mason was telling the truth. His friend was as depressed as Chase. Love really did stink.

"I got a call from Mandy Blanchard today. I haven't replied to the reunion invitation, and it is this Saturday, you know. She mentioned you haven't responded either."

Chase shook his head. "She's relentless."

"Yep. You going?"

"No."

"If I have to go, you have to go."

Chase frowned. "Why do you have to go?"

"I'm mayor," Mason stated.

"That isn't mentioned in the job requirements, is it?"

"No, but I think it's kind of assumed. You'll go?"

Chase twisted the top of one of the beers, took a drink, then nodded. "Yeah, I guess I have to deal with everyone sooner or later."

"He's still not home?" Abby said as she entered the kitchen, carrying one of the many boxes stuffed into her car.

Ellie rushed forward to help her. "I didn't even hear you pull in. Yes, he's been home, but I haven't seen him around. I only hear Helen. He gets home late at night and leaves early in the morning."

"Well, at least he's okay," Abby said as they placed the box on the floor.

Ellie gave her a dubious look. "I guess if working yourself to death is 'okay.'"

Abby shrugged. "Better than the other scenarios I've had in my head." She didn't think Chase would do anything stupid, but she was still concerned. His ego was pretty battered.

She went out to get more of her stuff.

Chase's house looked lonely, the yard empty, the house still.

With the help of Ellie, they had her car empty and the kitchen full within a half an hour.

"Your apartment wasn't that big," Ellie said, shaking her head at the towering pile of stuff in the corner.

"I know, and this is with all the furniture in storage. I guess I'm a packrat."

"Oh," Ellie said suddenly and went to the counter, rummaging through a pile of mail. "Here."

She handed Abby a piece of cardstock, a bit larger than a postcard. It was addressed to Abigail Stepp, and the other side was decorated with a border of graduation caps, diplomas, ribbons and confetti.

It was her invitation to the class reunion.

"This is tonight?" she said after reading the date and time. "At seven o'clock."

"Yes. But you have almost two hours. You can still go."

Abby shook her head. "No, I'm going to stay here and get all this junk put away."

"You have to go. What if Chase is there?"

Abby thought for a minute. She planned to find Chase and make him talk to her, but the reunion wasn't the place. "I don't think so. He didn't seem all that interested, and after what Summer-Ann did, I don't think he will go."

"You're probably right."

"So, want to help me with this stuff?"

Ellie eyed the pile reluctantly. "If you buy me dinner afterward."

"Deal."

Abby was surprised how quickly the two of them got the huge mountain of things put away. At 6:30, the kitchen was nearly empty.

"So where should we go for dinner?" Abby asked, collapsing into a chair with a weary sigh.

Ellie was considering the question, and Abby suspected she was trying to think of the most expensive place around, when there was knock at the door.

Ellie answered it, then just stood there looking at the person on the back stoop.

"May I please speak with Abby?"

Abby recognized the voice immediately. Ellie looked at her, and she nodded.

Her sister stood aside, and Summer-Ann stepped into

the kitchen. She was wearing a long, emerald green gown that clung to her lovely figure. But her features were drawn and her eyes looked puffy. "Will you please accept my apology?" she blurted out. "And will you please come to the reunion with me?"

Abby sat there for a moment, completely surprised. "Why would I do either?"

Summer-Ann came toward her, but stopped at the other side of the table. "You shouldn't, I guess," she said sincerely. "But please consider it. I was so wrong to hurt you and Chase that way. I was wrong for a lot of things."

"And what brought on this change of heart?"

Summer-Ann looked down at the floor, and when she raised her head, her green eyes were wet with tears.

Not the pretty tears Abby had seen before, but real tears that streaked her makeup and made her eyes look swollen and bloodshot. Despite the gorgeous dress, Summer-Ann actually looked plain.

"To be honest," she said, her voice quavering, "at first, I didn't realize the horrible thing I'd done. Well, I did, but I still thought I did it for the right reasons. Then after you left the party at the Leavitts', I looked around at the other people there. All I saw was anger and scorn and pity. But even then, I didn't think I'd done anything wrong. I thought they would eventually see that I just did what I had to. That once Chase forgave me, and we were together, they would see that I was in the right."

"And has Chase forgiven you?" Abby asked curiously.

Summer-Ann shook her head and a tear rolled down her cheek and landed on the green material of her dress. A dark spot appeared.

She swiped at her cheek. "Then the other day, I picked up Willy from school. He wouldn't even look at me. I questioned him and questioned him about what had him so upset, and finally he shouted, 'You!'" A sob escaped her, and it took her several seconds to gather herself and continue. "Some of the kids that were at the Leavitts' told him what I had done, and what I said about Chase. Willy couldn't understand why I would hurt Chase that way. And why I would hurt you."

Her voice hitched, and she stopped again to wipe her eyes. "And I suddenly saw what I looked like in Willy's eyes. And I don't ever—" Her voice hitched again, and she stated more firmly, "I don't ever want to look like that to him again."

Abby could feel the woman's pain. She could see Summer-Ann's sincerity and her shame. She sat there for a moment, then nodded. "I'll go."

Summer-Ann actually sagged with relief. "Thank you," she whispered.

Ellie came to the table. Excitement brightened her blue eyes. "Well, we'd better get you two ready. You have a party to go to."

And like a chubby, adorable fairy godmother, Ellie herded them upstairs to work a bit of magic.

Chase was fairly certain that the past members of the Millbrook Inn's elite literary society were doing more than turning over in their graves. They were probably spinning like tops.

The decoration committee had done quite a job, including crepe paper wrapped around and tacked to every object in the room. Foil stars hung from the beautiful molded ceilings and blue Christmas lights bordered the walls. But his favorite ornamentations were the blown-up graduation pictures of all the class of 1988 alumni that lined walls like mug shots.

He wandered over and half-heartedly regarded them.

When he reached Abby's, he stood there and stared at the forgotten girl who was now so familiar to him.

The photograph had been taken in her backyard. He recognized her grandmother's magnificent peonies in the background. Her hair was down, instead of in the tight bun she'd worn in school. Her huge glasses hid half her face, but he could still see the touch of sadness in her eyes.

She wasn't homely at all. She was actually quite cute. Why hadn't anyone noticed? He stared at the picture for a long time, then finally moved on.

"Well, at least they are so enlarged you can't tell if it's acne or just grainy," Mason said from beside him.

Chase turned to his friend. "They're scary."

Mason nodded.

They stopped perusing the poster-sized pictures and watched the crowd. The room was already crowded, and the disc jockey had begun to play songs from the '80s.

"It's like a high school dance that ended up in the Twilight Zone," Mason stated.

Chase nodded.

"I need a drink."

Chase nodded again and followed him to the bar.

Once in line, they ran into Paul Cormier and Chad Moore, who chatted with Chase as though the scene at Tommy's house had never happened.

Chase was thankful and began to feel a bit more relaxed. In fact, he was slowly realizing that people weren't going to mention his dyslexia.

He and Mason got drinks and returned to the dance floor, which was littered with clusters of people standing around talking.

They joined a group with Tommy and Becky and Billy Norris.

"Billy," Chase greeted his old friend with a quick embrace. "How are you?"

"Doin' good. Just tellin' Tommy here that I bought a new boat. Really sweet little rig."

Chase smiled, but he was only half listening. His gaze was back on the picture of Abby. Was she with Nelson again? Was she happy back in Boston? Was she thinking of him?

"Well, hell," Mason said, shaking his head, an amazed look on his face. "Now that is something I never expected to see."

Everyone followed Mason's stare. Summer-Ann Bouffard walked into the party with Abby Stepp beside her.

"Well, I'll be jiggered," Tommy exclaimed.

That was putting it lightly.

Chase stared as the two women searched the crowd. Then he couldn't see anything but Abby. He half believed that he was imagining her as she started toward him. She looked so damned beautiful in a red dress that showed her bare shoulders and swirled around her ankles. He fought to take in a breath.

"Hi," she said to him like she was as breathless as he felt.

"Hi." Damn, he wanted to touch her.

She turned and greeted the others warmly. Her warmth was met in kind.

"Can we talk?" she asked him.

"Yes." He led her over to the corner of the room, near the DJ. The synthesized sounds of Flock of Seagulls reverberated around them. It took all his strength to remove his hand from the small of her back. He wanted to touch her, to kiss her, to make sure she was real.

"Why on earth were you with Summer-Ann?" He knew those shouldn't be his first words, but curiosity got the better of him.

"She came to me to apologize for the hurtful things she's done. And I decided to forgive her."

He gaped at her. "Why?"

"I guess I learned to be forgiving from this guy I know. He forgives easily, and I think that makes him quite amazing."

He was thrilled at her words, but he couldn't truly believe she was here for him, not after the way he had run off.

"Did you come back for the reunion?" he asked, trying to sound conversational.

She frowned, then an amused smile curved her lips. She had such amazing lips.

"No, I'm here because I'm living in Millbrook now," she said slowly. "And I also came back to see if this guy I am madly in love with has stopped acting like a fool."

"Has he?"

"The jury's still out."

"I'm sorry."

"You should be."

Not the reply he expected. "I shouldn't have run off."

"No, you shouldn't have."

She was going to make him work for this. As well she should.

"I didn't—" He hesitated, trying to find the words that wouldn't make him sound too pathetic. "I didn't want you to feel sorry for me." He sounded pathetic.

She didn't seem to notice. She touched his cheek. Her fingers felt like a brush of heaven. "I didn't. I felt proud. Proud of the wild, defensive boy who overcame huge obstacles to become the strong, intelligent man before me. So you have a learning disorder. I can't cook."

"Not quite the same. You could learn to cook."

"And according to Ellie, you have learned to read."

"Barely." His voice was laced with self-derision.

Abby touched his arm. He could feel her heat through his sleeve. "Barely is more than you could before. But even if you never learn to read another word, I wouldn't care." She moved her hand up to caress his cheek. "I have loved you since we had study hall together in ninth grade, and I'll probably just end up loving you forever."

Her words humbled him. He caught her hand, bringing it to his lips. "I should have trusted you."

She nodded, her cheeks flushed, her eyes heavy-lidded as she stared at his mouth. "I expect that you will from now on."

"Yes, I will," he said, leaning closer to her. "I promise."

"And you won't run away?"

"No. Never. At least not without you." He leaned toward her more, his lips hovering over hers. "I love you so much, Abby Stepp."

"Then I forgive you." She closed the small space between them, pressing her lips to his. She tasted wonderful. He caught her against him, and they were oblivious to the mass of people around them, lost in each other.

When they finally parted, he whispered, "You forgive too easily."

"Yeah," she agreed. "I learned that from the wisest person I know."

Epilogue

Abby plunked the cheesy, plastic, gilded crown onto Chase's head and lounged back on the bed to admire him.

He stood at the foot of the bed wearing nothing but the crown and a smile. He looked very regal indeed.

"You know, I'm starting to think these crowns are becoming fetish items for you," he said, although he didn't sound like he found the idea too objectionable. "I might have to return them to Mandy Blanchard and tell her to find a new king and queen."

She grinned and pushed a matching one onto her head. "No, she worked hard on these. Besides, you're definitely my only fetish."

"Good," he murmured, as he crawled onto the bed, his crown adorably askew.

He pulled her against him and they lay entwined in each other's arms, enjoying the closeness and the warmth.

Chase lazily brushed his hands over her hip, and she languidly twirled a lock of hair that curled over his ear.

He roused slightly. "I think we should wear these at our wedding."

"Definitely," Abby agreed. Chase had surprised her with a beautiful diamond ring on Christmas Eve, and she had readily accepted his proposal.

She had been living with him from the night of the

reunion on. Abby still couldn't believe that someone as amazing as Chase Jordan was in love with her. But she got the feeling he felt the same way about her.

Life in Millbrook was turning out to be a wonderful experience filled with friends and happiness and love. The whole town had accepted Chase's learning disability as though everyone had known all along. And Chase had learned to not be ashamed of something he couldn't control. He still worked with Ellie on learning to read. And Abby suspected that because he wasn't so ashamed, he found learning easier. But Abby didn't care one way or the other. Chase was and always would be perfect to her.

Chase, being the easy forgiver he was, offered Summer-Ann her job back as his office manager. She declined, telling him she was actually happier as a hair stylist, but Abby was glad the animosity was gone.

They had picked a wedding date at the end of September. It was the soonest they could get a church and a reception area big enough for all their loved ones. But Abby liked the idea of marrying when the leaves were changing and the scent of wood smoke filled the air. She had always dreaded fall, as it marked the beginning of school. Now her old dread seemed so silly.

She squirmed a little as Chase's lazy caress became more purposeful, sliding from her hip up her side and back again, each sweep coming closer to the underside of her breast.

Finally his hand found her breast, toying with the puckered nipple. She wiggled closer.

He rolled her onto her back and rose up to capture the eager nipple with his lips. She closed her eyes and let her head fall back. The crown slipped down over her nose.

Chase stopped, took the crown off her head and placed it on the nightstand. His followed.

"Those might be a bit dangerous for what I have in

mind," he told her with a sexy grin. Then he returned his attention back to her breasts. She caressed his strong shoulders and reveled in his touch. But before she slipped into mindless oblivion, she glanced at the crowns. One rested on the other, and the titles they bore glinted in the low lamplight. Both read MOST LIKELY TO SUCCEED.

Who would believe that both the class nerd and the class bad boy could win that title? But Abby had no doubt that together she and Chase would do exactly that.

Please turn the page for a preview of Ellie Stepp's story
WANTING WHAT YOU GET
by Kathy Love.

A Zebra release in November 2004.

He lifted a hand to knock, but when his weight shifted, the old wooden floor creaked.

Without looking up, Ellie said, "Do you remember if we ordered one or two copies of the new Jane Blackwood novel?"

Mason hesitated, then pushed open the door. "I don't recall."

Ellie's head snapped up. "Oh," she uttered, her lips formed a cute little *o*, and her cheeks grew pink. "I thought you were Prescott."

Mason smiled. "I figured. Sorry to disappoint."

"No," Ellie shook her head, "you didn't." She looked uncomfortable.

He stepped further into her cramped office and closed the door behind him.

When he turned back, Ellie looked even more ill at ease. He could hardly blame her. After all, here stood the letch who'd bargained sex for his political backing, between her and her only escape route.

He shifted away from the door, but the move only made it seem as if he was looming over her.

She stared up at him with large, wary eyes.

He cleared his throat and tried to think of how to start. "About last night—"

"I accept," Ellie announced, the words bursting from her, startling him. Her eyes widened even more, as if her declaration had surprised her too.

"I'm sorry?"

"I . . ." She fidgeted with the edge of the catalog she'd been reading. "I considered your—proposal last night. And I accept," she said firmly.

Mason's reaction was instantaneous. Desire ripped through him. Images of laying her across her desk and making love to her right there flashed through his mind in vivid detail.

But in the next second, guilt gripped his chest with such force he could barely breathe. He couldn't simply have sex with her and walk away. Could he?

"That is," she said quietly, "if the offer still stands." Her face colored a deeper pink that matched the rosy color of her sweater. Her cornflower blue eyes were filled with such apprehensiveness that he felt like an even bigger cad than he already did.

"About that proposal," he started, knowing he had to withdraw it. Even though he longed to continue the arrangement and take her to his bed.

Ellie looked down at the catalog, running a small finger along the edge of the pages.

He lost his train of thought for a moment, entranced by the unintentionally seductive gesture.

"It was," he said more determinedly, "a mistake."

Ellie's head shot up, worry furrowing her brow.

"But I'll be glad to back you against Winslow without any—compensation."

Her eyes had darkened to the color of stormy seas, and they seemed to well up. With relief, no doubt.

She looked down at her desk. "Thank you," she murmured so quietly he had to lean forward to hear her.

"Don't thank me," he said grimly. "I want to help."

She nodded, still not making eye contact with him.

He studied her bowed head for a moment. Deciding the best thing to do was leave the poor woman alone, he said, "I'll be in touch once I've found out where Winslow stands with the community."

She nodded again, and the movement caused a tear to roll down her cheek and splatter on the catalog. The wetness seeped into the paper, leaving a dark splotch.

Mason immediately admonished himself as the world's biggest jerk. "Ellie, I am sorry about last night." The words sounded so inadequate, but he couldn't think of anything better.

She shook her head, but refused to look at him. "It's okay. No apology necessary."

A derisive laugh escaped him. "I owe you far more than an apology."

She lifted her head, and her tear-filled eyes ate at his conscience.

"You shouldn't have to apologize for realizing you made a mistake."

Mason frowned. To him, that seemed to be the exact time a person should apologize.

"How you feel is how you feel. Or in this case, how you don't feel." She gave him a tremulous smile.

His frown deepened. What? She was speaking far too cryptically for his hungover brain. "I'm not sure I follow you," he finally admitted.

"I'm . . . I'm just saying," she struggled for the right words. "I'm not surprised you decided that it was a bad bargain."

"It was a terrible bargain," he agreed.

Ellie winced. Another tear tumbled down her cheek. "Right." She wiped her eyes, the gesture resolute. She took in a deep breath. "Thank you again for your help."

Mason was confused by her sudden dismissal. He thought she would be thankful he wasn't following through with the arrangement. Instead, she seemed hurt.

Suddenly, the truth hit him. Ellie *wanted* a one-night stand with him. She had accepted his vulgar offer not for the library, but for herself.

Well, damn, this was an outcome he hadn't considered. An odd sense of smugness and overwhelming rush of desire came over him.

Of course, her wish to be with him didn't change the fact that she was a completely unsuitable woman to have a fling with. But he wasn't going to let her believe that he didn't want her.

Because he did. Damn, he did.

"You think I decided to end this deal because I don't want you? Because I don't want to sleep with you? Well, that's crap."

She looked embarrassed. "Please, Mason, don't do this. You don't have to."

"I'm not telling you this to make you feel better. And I'm certainly not telling you this to make myself feel better. Because frankly, it's going to be hell, knowing that I could have you. But I won't. I'm telling you this, because it's the truth. Hell, last night's kiss should have showed you how much I want you."

"I . . ." She blushed a deep scarlet. "I want you, too." The words were no more than a whisper, said so honestly and with such conviction that he felt overcome by them. By her.

"But I can't do this." It nearly killed him to deny her and himself.

The wariness returned to her eyes.

He moved around the desk so he could touch her, even though he knew he should stay away. Far, far away. His hands caught her upper arms. "Ellie, you aren't the kind of woman who has an affair. And I can't offer you anything more."

She gazed up at him and, again, he was struck by the

openness and sincerity in her eyes. "I want whatever you can offer."

He stared at her for a moment, and then despite his better judgment, or maybe judgment played no roll at all, he pulled her up from her chair and kissed her.